Alix Christie is an author, journalist and letterpress printer. She apprenticed to two master printers and owns and operates a 1910 Chandler & Price letterpress. A dual citizen of the United States and Canada, Alix holds a Master of Fine Arts degree from St Mary's College of California and lives in London with her husband and two children. GUTENBERG'S APPRENTICE is her first novel.

Praise for GUTENBERG'S APPRENTICE:

'A sophisticated and moving story of the creation of the Gutenberg Bible, seen through the eyes of Peter Schoeffer, a scribe working closely with the man whose presses will destroy his art. Christie provides a powerful portrait of the intense, irascible and egotistical Gutenberg, but her novel's real strength lies in its depiction of Schoeffer, drawn unwillingly into the struggle to build a new technology, yet eventually becoming its most committed advocate'

Sunday Times

'One thinks of Donna Tartt's obsessive accounts of furniture restoration at the heart of Theo Decker's story in *The Goldfinch*, or even Philip Roth's lovingly twisted empathy with glove maker Swede Levov in *American Pastoral*. Such novels of craft and specialisation take a writerly delight in the most intricate details of a particular trade while spinning rich prose out of its mysterious threads. Christie's novel is a worthy tribute to the technological revolution it reimagines, as well as a haunting elegy to the culture of print'

ihington Post

'A bravura debt

iews

D1144065

'An inspiring tale of ambition, camaraderie, betrayal and cultural transformation... Wonderful'   *Booklist*

'If ever there were a historical novel with up-to-the-minute resonance, this is it... Brilliantly observed detail. Her characters are engaging, the world as beautifully crafted as one of Gutenberg's hot-metal letters, and the themes more relevant now than ever... Richly imagined'   Naomi Alderman

'Alix Christie's debut is intensely observed, so much that I felt in the dark rooms of history with the people labouring over the metal and words to bring us print, but also labouring over their own lives and love and survival'   Susan Straight

'Vividly portrayed'   *Choice* magazine

Gutenberg's Apprentice

ALIX CHRISTIE

headline
review

Copyright © 2014 Alix Christie

The right of Alix Christie to be identified as the Author of
the Work has been asserted by her in accordance with the
Copyright, Designs and Patents Act 1988.

First published in Great Britain in 2014
by HEADLINE REVIEW
An imprint of HEADLINE PUBLISHING GROUP

First published in paperback in 2015
by HEADLINE REVIEW

1

Apart from any use permitted under UK copyright law, this
publication may only be reproduced, stored, or transmitted, in
any form, or by any means, with prior permission in writing of
the publishers or, in the case of reprographic production, in
accordance with the terms of licences issued by the
Copyright Licensing Agency.

All characters – other than the obvious historical figures – in this
publication are fictitious and any resemblance to real persons,
living or dead, is purely coincidental.

Cataloguing in Publication Data is available from the British Library

ISBN 978 1 4722 2015 8

Typeset by Palimpsest Book Production Ltd, Falkirk, Stirlingshire

Printed and bound in Great Britain by Clays Ltd, St Ives plc

Headline's policy is to use papers that are natural, renewable and recyclable
products and made from wood grown in well-managed forests and other
controlled sources. The logging and manufacturing processes are expected
to conform to the environmental regulations of the country of origin.

HEADLINE PUBLISHING GROUP
An Hachette UK Company
Carmelite House
50 Victoria Embankment
London EC4Y 0DZ

www.headline.co.uk
www.hachette.co.uk

In memoriam
Lester Lloyd
James Robertson
Master printers

For there is nothing hid, which shall not be made manifest: neither was it made secret, but that it may come abroad.

— THE GOSPEL ACCORDING TO MARK, 4:22

In the annals of innovation, new ideas are only part of the equation. Execution is just as important.

— WALTER ISAACSON, *Steve Jobs: A Biography*

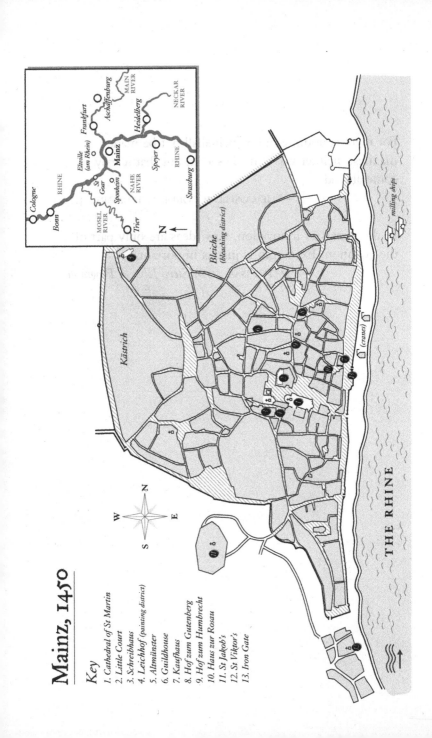

Mainz, 1450

Key

1. Cathedral of St Martin
2. Little Court
3. Schreibhaus
4. Leichhof (painting district)
5. Altmünster
6. Guildhouse
7. Kaufhaus
8. Hof zum Gutenberg
9. Hof zum Humbrecht
10. Haus zur Rosau
11. St Jakob's
12. St Viktor's
13. Iron Gate

Bleiche
(bleaching district)

Kästrich

(cranes)

milling ships

THE RHINE

Inset map

Cologne

Bonn

RHINE

MOSEL RIVER

Trier

St Goar

Eltville
(am Rhein)

Frankfurt

Sponheim

NAHE RIVER

Mainz

Aschaffenburg

MAIN RIVER

Heidelberg

NECKAR RIVER

Speyer

RHINE

Strasburg

N

SPONHEIM ABBEY, GERMANY

September 1485

Many years afterwards, when Abbot Trithemius first asked him to recall the true beginnings of the glorious art of printing, Peter Schoeffer refused. The story was too private, he informed the abbot, and not really his.

'Exactly so. No man invents alone! Creation is the Lord's own province.' The monk, with a wide smile, was pitching towards his guest. 'It follows that the man who made this miracle was touched by God.'

He's young – too young to be the abbot of this hilltop cloister, master of a vaulted study lined with books whose brass clasps shimmer in the golden autumn light. Nor does Peter Schoeffer like the glint of satisfaction in his eyes. Although he knows why it is there: Trithemius has netted him at last, has drawn the celebrated printer up to his own abbey after many tries.

'I plan to write it all,' the abbot says, and lifts an arm to circumscribe the library, the thick stone keep, the Rhineland down below. 'A chronicle of all that has transpired here in this blessed time. None of more import, surely, than this great invention in which you, sir, played a part.'

He uses me to make his reputation, Peter thinks. Is this how chronicles are made, the story told to those who'd make their name by those whom time and fate have unaccountably left standing?

On his way into the abbey he and the abbot wove through courtyards past the chapel, to the open cloister walk where even now the monks sit writing, backs bent, desks positioned to receive the slanting harvest sun. How long it's been, Peter remarked, surprised, since he has seen a group of Benedictine brothers in such busy, scratching rows. Once every cloister of the great monastic orders had scriptoria where God's Word flowed from hand to parchment, but hardly any now survive.

The abbot did not even break his stride. 'They curse me for it,' he said with a tight smile, 'and protest that the printing press should spare them this hard drudgery.'

Peter has brought books from his own press to give to Sponheim, mainly standard works of liturgy and law. His thoughts have started turning to the prayers the monks will say in thanks when his soul nears its time. Trithemius receives these printed volumes greedily, though his own shelves are filled with handwork of the scribes. He strokes their leather bindings, and fixes Peter once again with his light, intense eyes.

'You are the only one who knows the truth, now that both Johanns have been called home to God.'

Johann Gutenberg, he means, and Johann Fust.

Peter Schoeffer's mind is clear, his fingers as strong as they have ever been. He's over sixty now, a father to four sons, and the wealthy founder of the greatest printing house in all of Germany. A lean, tall man, he wears a close-cropped silver beard on his narrow, sober face.

'The truth.' He smiles.

Much has been said in the decades since, but almost none of it is true. They've practically canonized the man who found this wondrous art. How Gutenberg would laugh if he could see them from above . . . or else below. The final disposition of the master's soul is far from certain.

'They say he died in penury, abandoned and betrayed.' The abbot's voice turns hard.

Well Peter Schoeffer knows the charge: that it was he and

Fust, his foster father, who wrenched the Bible workshop from the master and robbed him of his whole life's work. For years he's borne the slander of this heinous accusation.

'It is a lie.' His voice is clipped. 'He died a member of Archbishop Adolf's court, highly praised and well attended.'

'While your own firm went on and prospered.'

'Success, dear brother, is no crime.' He gives the monk a piercing look. 'Betrayals there were, certainly – but not how people think.'

'Then there's a tale to tell, indeed.'

The abbot moves towards the window, where he stays a moment lost in – or feigning – thought. His plain black habit hangs on his large frame like fabric on a birdcage.

'We have a duty, don't you think?' Trithemius looks back. 'A duty to the past, and to the future?'

Though more than thirty years have passed, Peter is loath to blacken the master's name. Deep down, he still must love the madman, Gutenberg, that burning, brutal genius who tore down as much as he created – who took the credit, always, regardless of whether it was due. He conceived the craft and forged the metal letters before anybody else, this none could reasonably deny. But without Peter and his father, that great Bible would never have been made.

'Think of the ark of history.' The abbot tries a different tack. 'Does not the great vault of *historia* contain all past and present and the whole created world? Is not each word, each action that we take, therefore a part, however small, of the vast architecture of God's plan?'

Trithemius has a domed forehead and unblinking eyes. He's confident, wellborn, without a doubt – and the same age that Peter was when it began, with that same burning drive. Peter searches in the corners of the memory palace in his mind. God's vault is vaster, and by far: he's always pictured it a nave that fills the sky.

He once believed that what they did would lift them higher, ever higher – he sensed the godliness that flows throughout Creation brush them. Until it cracked, and their whole workshop filled with anger and recriminations. With each succeeding year Peter has seen the world become unhinged, cacophonous, the very earth stunned by the pounding of machines. And he's begun to wonder if God did not unleash some darker force with that great shining net of words.

He's never wanted to expose the master, not out loud. He's prayed for years to find forgiveness in his heart. But deep inside he still blames Gutenberg for how it all came crashing down. He scratches at his beard. Trithemius is right. Posterity should know the truth; the world should know the role he and Fust played.

The abbot sits and reaches for a reed.

A tool – that's how the master saw him at the end. Yet which among them is not the Master Craftsman's tool? Peter feels a sudden lightness, like a bubble rising through a molten mass. He'll tell it as he can. With modesty, he prays: God knows he's struggled all his life against the sin of pride.

'It may take many visits,' he says, rising in his turn and looking out on the fading orchard, the mottled auburn hills that step down to the valley far below.

Who can say if what they made will prove a force for good or ill? God alone can know. To pretend otherwise is to presume to know His mind. Yet isn't that just what they did in those few heady years, inflamed by ardor, hubris, youth? Imagined that the three of them with their own newfound art could rise as high?

'*Historia*.' He nods. 'All right. Perhaps you'll find a way, where I have not, to spy the meaning that the Lord inscribed.'

GENESIS

GENESIS

Chapter 1

MAINZ, GERMANY

September 1450

'I was twenty-five the year my father called me home.' So it began. The letter was delivered to the workshop on the rue des Écrivains, where he sat copying some proofs of Aristotle. It did not state the reason why. His father just reached out his merchant's hand and plucked Peter up, as if he were a number to be transferred from one column to the other in his fat brown ledger. From Paris, back to Mainz: Peter felt the sting of it the whole three days it took to cross the flat French plain and sweep home down the Rhine.

Stepping on the market boat at Strassburg, he tried to calm his mind – just wipe it clean, the way he'd scrape and chalk a parchment. He'd learned this discipline from monks some years before: to steady first his breath, his pulse, and then his fingers and his eyes, to join the text he copied and his nib in one taut line. At least it was a blessing to escape that stinking, jolting coach. He gripped the railing, filled his lungs, and faced downstream.

The ship was weighted low with cargo; passengers who had no railing clung to staves nailed to the central hold. They were mere specks upon the river rushing towards the sea. The vessel pitched and rolled, and he could feel the shiver of that mighty force beneath his feet. The river seemed to fling him backwards, down, with every bend that hauled him closer to his home.

When he was young, he'd thought the Rhine ships looked like ladies' slippers: flat and low along the prow, then rising aft to curl like some outlandish petal at the captain's back. He'd been a boy the last time he saw these shores. Yet he returned now as a man – a man of letters, a *clericus*, a scribe. He bore the tools of his profession in a pouch slung like a quiver at his side: the sealed horn of ink, his quills and reeds, his bone and chalk and chamois.

The valley of the Rhine peeled off to either side in banks of green and gold, and farther up outcroppings rose, perched high above the river like so many gnomes. An ancient peaty smell mingled sickeningly with the pomades and the late-September sweat of bodies crammed together at the rail. All he knew was that the matter was urgent. His father would not have called him back to celebrate the birth of his new son, although a child this late in life was wondrous news. Nor was he likely to have picked Peter a wife. First get yourself established, Johann Fust had always said, and then you'll have your choice of brides. The only clue lay in a postscript in his looping hand: *I've met a most amazing man.*

The Seine had smelled of chalk and stone, a sharp and thrilling city striving. The Rhine was wider, darker, rooted in the forest and the field. Peter breathed in its odour, the odour he had known most of his life. They were not far from Gernsheim now, where he'd been born and raised and tended sheep. Where he'd been orphaned, and then saved. Fleetingly he saw the farm, and Father Paul. He never would forget the old priest's palsied paw, and then his own small fist, tracing out his letters in fulfilment of his mother's dying wish. He looked down at that very hand clamped now upon the railing – that hand that was the master of a dozen scripts. It was a perfect tool: with it he stood, at the Sorbonne, right at the apex of the world.

And what a world it was! Even decades later he could taste

the feeling of that year of Jubilee. The Holy Roman Empire pulsed like a rich man with a fever, fearful yet exalted at the prospect of the light. All Christendom hung in the balance, waiting. There was a new pope on Saint Peter's throne, and some strange new spirit rising. The schism of three popes had been laid to rest; the cardinals had bowed at last to the authority of Rome. The new Italian pontiff, Nicholas V, had vowed to sweep the vile world clean. He'd called his Jubilee to bring the faithful back to penitence, and undo years of plunder, ruled by greed.

That new wind was sweeping through the markets and the lecture halls, the streets and seats of learning from Bologna up to Paris. It licked around the stools where new men laboured at their quills, copying the texts that fed the best minds in the western world. That wind had swept in masses of new students, lifted by prosperity and trade, all avid for their chance; it threw the scribes together in long ranks, writing madly to keep up with the demand. He'd felt the force of it up his own arm, lifting his eyes to heights he'd never dreamed, for he was one of these new men, these scholar-scribes.

And then the wind stalled, stopped short by the thick brown band of the Rhine. Peter watched the other trading boats, as thick as krill upon the water. Merchants, moneylenders, bureaucrats, and priests, all servants of Mammon as much as of God. He knew for certain that the winds of change were dead upon these shores when in the afternoon their boat put in to Speyer. He hung back when the passengers leapt off; he'd spied some merchants friendly with his father he would have to greet if he were seen. Instead he hung about the pilings, watching as the docker swung the crane dug deep into the bank.

He'd brought only what little he could carry, including a new manuscript of Cicero he had just started when the summons came. The rest he'd left behind in Paris as a kind of charm. His father could not mean he had to stay in Mainz.

Not after all that Peter had achieved: his rapid rise through the ranks, his luck at being chosen not a month before to represent the workshop to the rector of the university. He wrote these extra books at night, to earn the coins for things his father's stipend did not cover and he'd rather not reveal. The manuscript, and ten blank sets of pages, he had packed inside a barrel from the family trading firm. Cicero, *On Moral Duties*. Oh, the parallel was rich: the great man's lectures to his son. It floated with him now, lashed to the others in the hold, the vellum snug inside its curly nest of shavings.

At least, that's where he had last seen it stowed. Until, with shock, he saw his small brown cask tossed up and lashed onto the massive hook that swung the goods to shore. He leapt and shouted, waved his arms. The docker hauled on the rope. The barrel bore the mark of Mainz, he grunted. And no goods could transit in or out of Mainz these past three weeks, since the archbishop slapped the city with an unholy ban.

'What ban?' His father's friends were at his back then, breathing sourly. 'Leave it,' Widder hissed, 'or you will never see it back.' The barrel branded 'Brothers Fust' sailed slowly through the sky. 'Don't get much news, I guess, up there in Paris?' An elbow dug into his side. Excommunication was Archbishop Dietrich's favourite means of brandishing his fist; he would shut a city in his diocese for weeks and sometimes months if local councils tried to cut into his power or his revenues.

The captain blew his whistle and the passengers all piled back on, propelling Peter forwards on that rank and jostling tide. He was wedged in, hauled back, no better than a shipping cask. Three years he'd been away, by God, and not a bloody thing had changed.

As they gained speed, he prayed that he might soon escape this spent and feuding place. He bent his body with the current as the river coiled itself past Gernsheim, looped three times like some gigantic spring, then shot the boat that bore him up the few remaining miles.

The city looked the same. Not battered in the least, though he had heard enough in transit to conclude that Mainz was in extremis. She still stood proud upon the bank, an island girded by a high white wall, tipped red and blue as if by an illuminator's brush. The ship moved slowly past the vineyards of the abbeys that encroached upon her southern door like fattened bishops. Across the river to the right, a smaller, muddy mouth drained from the Hessian plain. The cathedral city of the archbishopric of Mainz sat just astride the confluence of Rhine and Main.

The foreshore that late afternoon seemed drained of life. Out of instinct Peter raised his eyes to check the colour of the sky. The Iron Gate would soon be shut. The day's last stream of men and carts was toiling up the rocks, and he scrambled to join in, feet sinking into brackish sand. Up close the mighty wall was flaking, puckered at the massive hinges like a toothless hag. Beneath the arch he kissed his palm and touched it to the city seal. A dogleg left and right, and he was on the square they called the Brand, and home.

It was strangely quiet as he stood there, tensing and untensing his long hands. Drays waiting for unloading stood before the Kaufhaus, the huge customs hall. Horses stamped, the starlings wheeled, yet over everything there hung a pall. His eyes went to the jerking clock hands on the tallest spire, the red cathedral of St Martin's. He waited until they stood in a straight line. They clicked, the mechanism cracking sharply in the silence. No bells. In all those forty churches, he could hear no bells. The archbishop's ban was just another sharp reminder of who really held the reins, his father's friends had said. The work-ingmen had won the city council and tried to halt the years of plunder by the ruling Elder clans. But when the council would not pay the interest that those clans demanded on the sweetheart deals they'd engineered, the old guard simply called in Archbishop Dietrich's fist. It was the same old litany of greed, the grappling for power in this backwater that history had left behind. Peter turned and struck across the square towards the Haus zur Rosau.

His father's house was not the grandest of all the timbered merchant homes that ringed the Brand. Yet it was imposing, like the man himself: broad and solid with an unexpected grace inside. Its floors were of blue slate, its yellow walls warmed by new tapestries from France and Flanders – though in the heat of this late summer these were rolled away, the window gaps all hung with gauze.

His foster father had the big man's way of crushing those he loved against the ample shelf that was his stomach. And then he held Peter at arm's length. 'At last.' He smiled.

'You knew full well which boat I would be on.'

'Yet still I watched for every one.' Johann Fust had eyes as blue as Mary's vestments in a face that with the years and success had reddened and filled. One eye winked.

'Then you'll have noticed I come empty-handed.' Peter rolled his eyes.

'They stopped you then? At Speyer?'

'You might have warned me.'

His father squeezed his shoulder. 'Nothing that a shilling in a palm won't fix. What matters is that you're home.' Fust turned as Grede stepped out into the hall. His father's wife looked wan, but on her lips still played the wry smile she had always worn. 'Wonder of wonders.' She turned her cheek to his. 'I'd given up all hope you'd see your brother before he could hold a stylus.'

'I left the Palace of the Louvre in some despair.' He grinned and bowed, raking the floor with one limp hand. 'To grace ye people in your humble homes.'

She laughed. And yet his father's bright young bride – his second, and a kind of sister to Peter – appeared exhausted: as if, having survived once more the terror of the childbirth bed, she had at last left youth behind. She had not looked this way when she bore Christina five years before.

They went on to the big front room and stopped before a cradle. Fust took the bundle in his arms. 'We call him Henchin. Little Hans,' he said with unmasked pride. The baby yawned, its face scrunched up like an old wizened apple. Its eyes flew open, blue as those that gazed in wonderment down on them. Peter put a finger to the tiny fist, and bent to kiss the tiny head. He'd never had a sister or a brother who shared his own blood; his mother died in bearing him. He'd been saved, adopted into this fine house, by her first cousin, Fust's first wife. Gently he unwound the little clinging fingers. He'd grown to manhood in these walls. But this in no way meant he held a claim against this little red-faced chap – only because of his late arrival had Peter been welcomed years before into this house.

All through the meal that followed Peter watched his father, hoping for some sign. Grede had put out beeswax candles and her prized Venetian glass. The cook had made roast lamb, potatoes, chard, some fowl baked in a pie. They'd wash it down with Rheingau from St Jakob's vines. Peter had brought gifts: a calfskin workbook for Tina, five by now and as primped and blond as any cherub, and a baby's beechwood game of catch-a-bob. The servants filed in silently as Fust stood, leafing with a frown through a worn pocket Bible. 'A reading from Saint Matthew,' he said finally, and cleared his throat. 'Whose birth we honour in these days.'

Peter caught Grede's eye. Since when did Fust say blessings at the table? *The ban,* she mouthed back, nostrils flaring. Dietrich backed his own class, naturally; the lower orders might pretend to rule, but they would have to fall in line. There'd be no sacraments until the upstart council had backed down. The archbishop's word was law: none of his priests would say a mass or take confession; the newly born were unbaptized and the dying were deprived of their last rites, consigned forever to the agony of limbo. Grede's face was dark with anger.

You have heard that it hath been said, 'An eye for an eye, and a tooth for a tooth.' But I say to you not to resist evil: but if one strike thee on thy right cheek, turn to him also the other; And if a man will contend with thee in judgement, and take away thy coat, let go thy cloak also unto him.

Fust looked up and fixed his elder son with shining eyes.

You have heard that it hath been said, 'Thou shalt love your neighbour, and hate thine enemy.' But I say to you, Love your enemies: do good to them that hate you: and pray for them that persecute and calumniate you: That you may be the children of your Father who is in heaven, who maketh his sun to rise upon the good, and bad, and raineth upon the just and the unjust.

The assembled foreheads flickered in the candlelight. Fust bowed his large and white-fringed head. Had he chosen that passage just for him? Peter wondered. It wouldn't be the first time. He tried and failed to catch Fust's gaze. What message did his father mean to send? Acceptance of injustice, and the stilling of one's own desires? Impatience flooded him as he stood waiting, willing Fust to make the meaning of this journey clear.

'Though we may chafe, let's not forget the wisdom of the scriptures.' Fust signalled for the wine. 'Nor, on this joyous day when Peter has returned, dwell overmuch on persecution. The fathers of the church were far more persecuted in their time.'

He smiled and raised his goblet to toast Peter. And Peter, chilled, raised his. How should he not? He owed Fust everything. He could not see into the merchant's heart, yet he could guess what Fust saw every time he looked at Peter: the boy he'd raised, the life he'd forged, the skills and travels he'd unstintingly bestowed. The life of mud and dung from which he'd raised the grubby offspring of his first wife's cousin. A line appeared in Peter's mind, as fresh as if old Cicero had penned it just that instant: *There is no more essential duty than returning kindness.*

Words of guidance, penned in deep antiquity and carried forwards through the long, dark centuries by Christian scribes.

'The feast of Saint Matthew is auspicious for all business ventures.' Fust's teeth were gleaming in the torchlight. Peter waited, long legs stretched out from the willow chair. The heat of the day had left the air of the courtyard warm and scented by the rose, and from the lane beyond he smelled the tang of fruit, the thick hot earthiness of livestock. He heard the call of owls, the intermittent roar out of the gaming house – those old, familiar sounds.

'What do you mean?' he asked, when Fust did not continue.

'Just that I have a proposition.' His father sat upright.

Which I may not refuse. 'And this is why you called me back.'

'We have a chance to shape the future.' Fust leaned forwards, peering at him in the dusk. 'You and I together, I mean.'

'I shape the future now,' said Peter, straightening.

'Not quite like this.'

'I haven't had a chance to write to tell you' – Peter spoke as though he hadn't heard – 'that I've been asked to join the rector's office at the university.'

'Ah,' said Fust.

'Imagine how the trade could benefit,' his son went on. 'I'll see them first, whichever titles he selects. We'll know exactly what the market will demand.'

The last time Fust passed through Paris, he'd asked his son to act as scout: to scour the stalls where books were sold across from Notre Dame, to keep his ears pricked and so learn the titles that the firm might sell to buyers east of the Rhine. Peter, meanwhile, toured him through the scribal workshop, one of dozens serving that great university. He showed him all the stacks of sections – written out by hand, then lent to students who would write out their own copies – hundreds of them, not only by the Greeks and Romans but the greatest scholars of the day: Duns Scotus, Bernard of Clairvaux, Thomas Aquinas. Those ink-stained scribes were like a mighty army, Fust had marvelled, ranks of angels on the move.

'You said you envied me, when you last came to Paris.'

'That's true.' His father pulled the flesh beneath his chin. 'But that was all before I met this man.'

'This "most amazing man".' Peter made no attempt to disguise his scorn.

'Look first.' His father reached into his lap, brought out a set of folded sheets, and laid them on the table. 'Just look. And then I think you'll understand.'

The quire – five folded, nested sheets – was of parchment of middling quality. Part of a schoolbook, judging by its short, square shape. Peter recognized at once the Latin grammar of Donatus: he had written out those declensions a thousand times. A common, tawdry work; he looked up, horrified.

'Feel,' his father said, and flipped the booklet to its last, blank page. He lifted Peter's finger, rubbed it lightly on the empty space.

He felt a stippling, a kind of roughness on the hide. As if the parchment maker had not scraped the skin entirely smooth. He rubbed two fingers, three, and all at once they sensed a strange, sharp symmetry. He flipped the page back to its written side. His blood jumped then, his palms grew damp. The textura lettering was squat and ugly, yet every string of letters was unnervingly even, all across the line. Each of those lines ended with an utter, chilling harmony, at precisely the same distance from the edge. What hand could write a line that straight, and end exactly underneath the one above? What human hand could possibly achieve a thing so strange? He felt his heart squeeze and his soul flood with an overwhelming dread.

'You see now. Why I had to call you back.' Fust's voice was high.

'What work is this? What hand did this?'

'No hand.' His father took his fingertip again. 'Feel how it sinks? The way the ink lies not on top, but in a hollow in the skin?'

Peter closed his eyes to sense it more precisely. It was as Fust had said. The parchment yielded in some way: it was not smooth beneath the ink, as when he wrote it with his pen. 'Whose work is this?' he said again.

Fust's heavy face was shining. 'This man they call Gutenberg has found a way to make the letters out of metal. He lays the ink upon each one, then stamps them in the page.'

Peter raised it to his eyes. So close that he could see the faint depression, a slope so slight as to be almost imperceptible: from the surface to the gully of each stroke. The space in which the angels – or the devil, surely – danced upon a pin. He could not speak at first, the shock was so extreme.

'I was approached by a man who knew I dealt in books.' His father mopped his brow, as if relieved to share this thing at last. 'Gutenberg sought an investor, I was told. I went to see him, and he showed me this.' The man wouldn't show him more, though, he told Peter, nor divulge how it was done. For his part, he'd been mystified, he added: he had never heard of any Elder family having anything to do with books. He'd thought that man's whole clan content with running half the abbeys and the Mint, and weaving gold from wholesale cloth they sold beneath St Martin's eaves.

'I thought, like you,' he said as he pressed Peter's hand, 'that it was just another of those wretched grammars. But then this Gutenberg said he made it with a new technique. *Ars impressoria*, he calls it. To think he's been at work at this, in secret, just a lane or two away . . .

'You know the house.' Peter heard the words dimly through the roaring in his brain. 'The Hof zum Gutenberg, on Cobblers' Lane.'

'I have a trade,' he said thickly and flung the sheets back on the table.

But Fust by then was standing, pacing, giving not the slightest indication he had heard. 'It's not the evenness – that's just one part of it!' His voice was high; his cheeks were flushed. He had a canny and familiar look on his trader's face – yet also a strange expression Peter didn't think he'd ever seen. A kind of ravishment, an exaltation. Fust turned and fired a question. 'It would take you how long – four days, five? – to copy this?'

'Two days. At most.' Peter was fast, and young, and proud.

'In those two days, this Gutenberg can make, by "printing", as he calls it, half a dozen copies, each one perfectly alike.' Fust came around the table and reached for Peter's wrist. 'Without the need to wear your fingers to the bone.'

His son was pinned, immobile. Fust loomed above him, blocking out the bright stars in the sky.

'Imagine it! My God, you have to see what this will mean. We can make ten times, twenty times as many copies of a book – in the same time and at the same cost.' His father's hands were flailing in the air. 'A book like this – or even longer ones. It's limitless.' The look of wonder was replaced by triumph. He dropped a hand on Peter's shoulder and shook him hard. 'The moment I saw it, I was certain. This is the miracle the Lord has been preparing for us all along.'

'A blasphemy, more like, or just some shoddy trick.' Peter shook Fust's hand off, reached back for the printed sheets. In truth that booklet was a soulless, lousy thing. The letters were as rough as those cheap woodcarvings that the Dutchmen hawked; the lines were blotchy and the edges slopped with ink.

Fust darkened. Then he straightened, and wiped a hand across his face. 'But you must see. It is no accident that brought you here. Each step that brought you to this house, each book we've seen and sold, or that you yourself have written. What were they all, if not a preparation? What is our purpose here, if not for you to learn this blessed art?'

'Blessed?' Peter jerked his hand; the pamphlet dropped. He stood and pushed the chair away. 'This is no art. Who is the scribe here, you or I?' He shook his head. 'I am a master of this art, as you well know. I have a trade, a life.'

'You've had your wander years.' His father's voice was curt. 'They've gone on long enough. I need you here.' His feet were planted and his look severe.

'You'd keep me here?' It came out as a bleat.

'I shouldn't even have to ask.'

Peter felt his face flame up. And still he twisted, scrabbling for a handhold. 'I never heard of any Elder lifting up a tool. What proof have you that this man Gutenberg has even made this in the way you say?'

The thing could easily have been a carved wood plate, as crude as any made to crank out images of saints and the few letters of their names.

'I am told that a goldsmith does the carving and the casting of the metal shapes.'

'A smith.' The very word was leaden. Fust had tried once already to make a smith of him, a goldsmith like his uncle Jakob, and their father before that – and when that didn't take, a merchant or a lawyer. But Peter had found a trade all his own and had excelled. Must Fust now snatch it all away?

His father had lent this man vast sums. Now he would lend

him his own son. Not his only begotten, though, Peter thought, the anger surging. He was no longer that.

'Do it,' his father said. 'For me.'

Peter heard the words of Jesus, on that dreadful eve. *Do this, in memory of me.*

'It is a shock, I know.' Fust's voice was gruff. 'But at least try to see. This is the change for which I've prayed.'

A man would leave a legacy, Peter heard him say. The feeling that his sojourn on this earth was not for naught. The words, however well meant, rose and circled like a noose around his throat.

'Will you not let me choose?' he whispered, already knowing.

Fust held his eyes for a long moment. 'I think that God has long since chosen for us both.'

The Hof zum Gutenberg backed onto the Cobblers' Lane and looked out on its parish church, St Christopher's, atop a knoll that banked down steeply towards the river. The place was featureless and grim; Peter looked in vain for any grace on its grey facade. There were three granite steps, a massive door, a knocker. His father wore a tunic made of red velour. Too fine, his son thought, standing in his shadow, waiting for Fust's arm to rise, the iron ring to lift and drop. Peter stood immobile in his plain dark breeches and his one good shirt, still reeking from the journey. Just as he'd stood as a boy of ten, when sent to Fust: the sudden, piercing memory returned. That awkward, silent lad, bathed carefully and dressed, put on the market cart to Mainz – clad in what to those grand folk must have seemed like rags. How frightened he had been, how stiff in his desire to please lest he be put back on the cart and sent away.

The man beyond this door was an Elder – a patrician of the highest rank and undoubtedly haughty. Fust dressed to show that though a merchant, he was just as rich. A strange alliance, when Mainz was riven between the old clans and the rising trading class. This Gutenberg was one of those who held the city ransom, thanks to Dietrich's iron fist: a member of the old elite that ran the courts, the commerce, and the churches – and most of all sucked income from the loans that bled the city dry.

'A leech, then,' Peter had observed, as he tried to worm out information over breakfast.

'More of a pragmatist, I think.' Fust shrugged and cracked his hard-cooked egg. 'I hear he's viewed with some suspicion by his peers.' The man had only recently returned to Mainz; he'd spent some thirty years in Strassburg. Which did explain, to some extent, why no one knew just what to make of him. He'd put out a story that he was making trinkets for the pilgrim trade in hopes of keeping prying eyes away.

The merchant dropped the knocker several times, then started pounding. With every fruitless blow his neck grew redder. He cursed beneath his breath and was about to turn when finally they heard a grinding sound. A bolt was wrenched, the door burst outwards, and the two of them sprang back. In the entry stood the master of the house, unlikely as it was for any scion of an Elder clan to answer his own front door. Yet judging from the clothes, it had to be: he wore a belted linen tunic and shoes with silver buckles, though there was grime on both his leggings and his rolled-up sleeves.

'Herr Fust.' A sharp, planed face, dark probing eyes that did not look entirely pleased. 'I might have known it would be you.'

'I would have sent you word – but my impatience was too great.'

Gutenberg just grunted and looked out behind them, peering with suspicion up and down the lane. He waved them in beneath one arm. 'Patience is for fools and saints.' He slid the heavy bolt and turned to face them. Strangely for a man of his high caste, he wore a long, dark twisted beard.

'This is the son I spoke of.' Fust nudged Peter forwards.

A ripple underneath the skin pulled the man's lips into a grimace. 'I don't see much resemblance.' His eyes raked Peter. 'He has a name, this gifted scribe?'

'Peter Schoeffer. Sir.' He bowed his head. Already he knew how it would go. He'd been apprenticed twice before, the lowest of the low.

'I'd offer you a drink – but where the devil is Lorenz?' The master of the house looked around testily. 'I'm in the thick of it, I can't—' He broke off then and smacked his forehead with his hand. 'Forgive me,' he said, giving Fust a rueful smile. 'Of course – I quite forgot that you might call. It's second nature now, to keep stray eyeballs out.'

Yet they were hardly strays. If Peter understood it right, his father was this madman's financier.

'I thought it time that Peter saw your new technique,' his father said.

Instantly, the man's sharp face was inches from his own. Up close his eyes weren't black, as they had first appeared, but brown and flecked with topaz. His hair was wild and bristling to his shoulders, and his beard cascaded from his chin down his whole chest, glinting here and there like twists of wire.

'You'll swear to keep it secret first. Upon your life.' The breath that sprayed on Peter's face was rank.

'I swear,' he muttered, and at that, this Johann Gensfleisch, known as Gutenberg, spun quickly and began to lope down a dim hall. They followed through a door and out into a courtyard where, half blinded, Peter saw the dark shape turn once more and bark, 'Your life!' before it yanked the heavy stable door.

Heat and noise hit them first. A searing darkness, stoked by fire, a throbbing clatter: battering of mallets on metal, the duller thud of wood on wood. As Peter's eyes adjusted he could see that just three men caused all this din. A red-haired giant stood beside a weird contraption made of wood; in the far corner two other men were silhouettes before the orange glow of a hot forge.

'*Impressoria.*' The master of the place stretched out his arm. 'Printing. Though the word alone does not begin to do it justice.' Inside his workshop his face had come alive with a fierce pride. 'It's more a system like a watercourse, a clock – a series of precise and interlocking parts.' His right arm scooped the whole thing towards him. 'I had to devise each bloody part – each tool, each instrument, each wretched motion of each lousy hand – and make the whole thing mesh.'

He led them towards the fire, into a smoke so foul and so astringent that he tossed them cloths to cover up their mouths and noses. 'Hans and Keffer make the metal.' Four reddened eyes surveyed them above filthy scarves. The master turned to Peter, eyes like those of some demented barber-surgeon. 'I hope to hell that you can smelt.'

God, no. The hissing of the coals and acrid fumes had plunged him instantly back in that filthy corner of his uncle's shop where he had sweated and endured. Alongside any number of poor grunts, his cousin and a clown named Keffer, too – if this staring swaddled face was he, and not some brother or cousin. The bloodshot eyes gave off no clue.

'All Fusts were raised up at the forge,' Fust slid in before Peter could respond.

Gutenberg gave a brusque nod. 'We cast the letters in reverse until we've got enough to set 'em into lines.' He jerked his wild head towards his financier. 'You see now why I started small.'

From there they lined the letters into pages, covered them with ink, and gave them to the pressman, he went on. The ginger giant promptly straightened when the master strode towards him. 'You need a mountain bear like Konrad here to heave the bar.' This bar was a long handle jutting from a wooden platform that looked strangely like the presses they erected in the vineyards for the harvest. Peter walked around it, studying its parts. There was a long and narrow tabletop the size of a small coffin; over this a kind of wooden gallows rose. Through its topmost bar was threaded not a noose but a huge wooden screw, from which was dangling, just above the tabletop, a massive wooden block.

'My press,' said Gutenberg. He stood there for an instant, fiddling with his beard, watching their eyes. The man called Konrad slathered a black paste onto a block of metal that on closer view was seen to be a half a dozen lines of letters, bound securely with a length of twine. He laid a sheet of paper over these, and then a light wood frame containing a stretched length of vellum. He grunted as he shoved the whole tray underneath the dangling block. Fust winked, and Peter finally exhaled. He'd been holding his breath since he'd first stepped into that pit.

Konrad grabbed the lever and yanked it full across the press. This action dropped the heavy weight onto the tray. There was a thud, and then a crashing, grinding sound; Peter felt the impact in his bowels. The process was repeated in reverse; the master spat into his hands and wiped them clean, then took the paper as the pressman peeled it from the letters. He frowned, mouth working; Peter peered over his shoulder as he turned. The text was clearly crooked. 'Blind buggers,' Gutenberg muttered as he strode towards the workbench by the forge. Peter and Fust, forgotten, trailed behind. Despite himself, the scribe felt a stir of interest.

Amid a mess of crucibles and cupels on the bench stood a wooden box, and next to this a row of long brass letter punches. These were the same as those used by bookbinders to press letters into leather spines. Square-cast metal hunks were scattered randomly around.

'We use a mould.' Gutenberg stalked past the table. 'An idiot could do it. Show them, Hans.' He went on towards the window and left them waiting for the older man. The smith plucked up a piece of metal, held it out to Peter between burned, misshapen nails. He was a wizened thing, all bent and brown. 'I hear you know some'at of scripts,' he said, his eyes so hooded they were hardly more than slits. Peter nodded as he took it, weighed its heft: as thick as his own index finger, and roughly half as long. It bore the letter *a*, protruding in relief upon its tip, and had been cast out of some dense silver metal. He jiggled it and frowned.

'We cast 'em in the box.' The old smith gestured at the flat, hinged casket. A basic mould, like those that Peter'd seen in Uncle Jakob's shop – filled with fine sand that held an object's shape for a brief time. Jewellers used them to make brooches, ring heads, and seals that later they would fix to pins or bands. And now they used them to make letters out of metal.

Peter went around the bench and saw more letters – dozens, scores, all dully gleaming. A pile of *a*'s and *u*'s and *m*'s, each one identical. He blanched and crossed his arms to hide his hands, afraid that they might tremble. He felt a dizziness, as if the ground had dropped away. Noise battered at his ears: he heard the furnace roar, the crude press crash, as if to rend in two the very fabric of the world.

Gutenberg was standing in the mottled light of a small, dirty window, holding up the freshly printed sheet. Fust prodded Peter, and they gingerly approached. The man was frowning, fingers twisting at his lower lip. Though weak, the sun's rays lit up every smear and imperfection. 'Blind me,' he repeated, shaking his strange, hoary head, scowling as the two of them approached.

Suddenly there was a gleam in his dark eyes. 'You.' His head jerked. 'You there, young scribe.' A thin, cruel smile flickered. 'Let's see what you advise.'

Peter saw the smiths exchange a sidelong look. He took the paper sheet. The ink gave off a sweetish smell; he felt the strange raised welts the press had left on its reverse. He took a breath, willed his hands still, and held it up to focus on the printed lines.

Which should he say – the truth or polite falsehood? He felt his father shifting at his side. He dipped the paper slightly, looked the bastard in the eyes. 'Not bad. The letterforms are strong. Though I would say a bit too rounded.' He was a master scribe – he would not hide. 'A thinner form, with finer spurs, might be more pleasing.'

'Not bad!' The master's laugh was caustic. He looked with hard, forced mirth around the room. 'We forge these bloody letters in a metal he has never seen, and all that he can say is it's not bad!' When those dark eyes returned to Peter's face, he felt his neck hairs raise.

'What else then, boy?'

'I did not come here to find fault.'

'Why not? If it's your trade?'

All guilds put trainees on the spot. The goldsmiths made up coins as false as any the dishonest man might pass. The jewellers gave them gemstones made of paste that shattered underneath their knives. Peter glanced at Fust; his father gave the barest nod. Warily he raised the sheet again. He let his eyes unfix, groping with his inner vision for the larger, more aesthetic shape. The whole displayed a lumpiness, a lack of grace.

'The ink is pale in parts, too dark in others.'

'Exactly right.' The master snatched it back. 'It is a Calvary, God knows, to file and plane each bugger so it stands at the same height.'

He'd passed. Peter felt a little stab of pride – then horror. For from the workbench he could hear the loudest silence. He cast a smile, apologetic, towards the smiths. Too late: they both looked sour. Keffer – it was Heinrich Keffer, after all, all grown up now and burly – scratched his yellow beard and raised one eyebrow. The old one, Hans, was scowling. Peter's stomach turned. He looked back at their master, staring at the sheet still, mouth drawn down. What kind of man was this – what kind of master? – who treated his own men no better than a pair of senseless tools?

His father's voice came low in Peter's ear. 'I'd be obliged if you would come. We've still some business to discuss.' And so they left the shed and trooped into a little room in the main house that Peter took to be the master's study. The hearth was piled with ashes from the winter past; heaps of paper on the table had been shoved aside to make room for plates. The room was chill, the furnishings unvarnished and crude.

'You see how I have spent it all,' their host said, waving carelessly about. Indeed, the home hardly seemed to be one of means. Yet they ate well and drank a quantity of Spätburgunder. Perhaps what lacked was just a woman's touch, Peter thought with a little nod to Grede. There seemed to be no wife nor kin: Frau Beildeck, wife of the manservant, was as rough and chapped as any fishwife.

'I was rich once.' Their host was more expansive once he'd downed a jug or two. 'But as you see, I spent it all – and more I've begged from here and there these thirty years.' He turned amused, sharp eyes on Peter. 'I'd plundered all my kin before your father came – some more than once – to carry on this work.'

'It is an honour,' Fust said, 'to be sure.' He took a square of linen from his vest and blotted at his lips. The only question in his mind, he said, was which book they should print first.

'I'm sure the scribe has some idea.' The master's tone, though dry, was far less cutting than before. He drained his cup and slapped it down. 'The training fee is ten guilders every annum.'

Johann Fust – smoothly, oh so smoothly – smiled. If he was startled, he did not let on. He only chuckled. 'You wouldn't ask for payment now, Herr Gensfleisch? Not after everything I've lent?'

'Gutenberg. I go by Gutenberg.' The printer glowered, started speaking once or twice, thought better of it. Finally it burst out. 'You moneymen! You're all alike. There's nothing you won't trade or give a price. Yet if a poor man tries to sell his skill, you baulk.' He spread his hands in a queer parody of supplication. 'You seem to think a man should give up his life's work for nothing.'

'Eight hundred guilders are not nothing.'

Peter struggled to control his shock. Eight hundred guilders! Holy Christ. The sum was staggering, enormous even for a man of Fust's ambitions. Enough to buy eight houses or several farms. He felt the blood drain from his face.

'I don't have time to waste in holding hands.'

'Those hands are worth more than you think.'

Peter watched those two face off across the battered table, moving not a muscle as they tossed his life between them. He should have stood and walked away. But he could not; his duty bound him hand and foot.

'You've not advanced the whole.' The printer's voice was querulous. 'I need the rest for metal and equipment.'

'You'll get it when the contract's drawn, as soon as I can raise it all myself.' For all his wealth, Fust didn't have that kind of ready gold. He financed major outlays from the Lombard or some Jews in Frankfurt. 'In counterpart,' his father said, 'you'll train my son, and pledge the instruments you make as guarantee.'

'I don't impart my knowledge on the cheap.'

'It is my wish that Peter learn this art.'

Gutenberg looked sharply at Peter, then returned his deep-set gaze to Fust. 'I already said the whole thing's much too tight.'

'The Latin grammar will sell well. And once we've picked the book to print you'll find and charge apprentices, as many as you please.'

The silence hung like something breathing in the room. It pressed against the cobwebbed rafters, slithered down the blank grey walls. Peter stifled a cry for his old life – for feathers flashing, all the whirling on the place de la Sorbonne. Was this why God had raised him up? So He could fling him back into the muck from whence he'd come? He clenched his fists to stop the pricking in his eyes.

'One thing.' Gutenberg had risen. 'If there must be a contract, I will have your pledge.' His eyes bored into each in turn. 'Everything I teach remains within these walls.' He scowled and threw his sharp, impatient gaze about the room; when he reached out and seized a crucifix that hung above a desk, they understood. Peter laid his hands on it and swore to tell no man the art and manner of the work; he pledged his honour in the eyes of God.

It felt exactly as if he'd been inducted, blindfolded, into some black and cabbalistic brotherhood.

Chapter 2

~~~

MAINZ

September — October 1450

Thus began his apprenticeship.

The day he started, he rose before dawn. His feet propelled him out and up and down the silent lanes of Mainz, shrunk now to just six thousand souls – less of a proud free city than a crumbling town.

When he'd first come here, Mainz glittered. Peter still remembered how the dukes of Katzenelnbogen raced their sledges, banners flying, through the icy streets around the market square. Golden Mainz, they used to call her, a city with more gold- and silversmiths than any other in the empire. But then the workers dared to claim a piece of all that wealth, and the ruling class cried foul.

More than once, and over many generations, the guildsmen had risen up in desperation, but were always beaten back. This time they'd won the council fair and square, and so the punishment exceeded all the times before. Most of the Elder clans had withdrawn to their country homes, his father said, incensed at being told to pay their share of taxes. The work fled with them, starving all the local craftsmen – but this was not the worst, to Fust. Archbishop Dietrich's ban also throttled the river trade, cutting off the long-distance merchants. Mainz was besieged not from without but from within; she was a stunted place, sealed from the world.

A candle flickered lonely in the sacristy of the cathedral as Peter passed. The ban had muzzled all St Martin's bells and chained its iron grille. The market square was darkened at its edges by prone bodies that he took at first for rags. Along the lane before the house of the Franciscans, he was forced to pull his cloak up to his nose. The wine the friars poured just puddled afterwards as vomit spewed by idle workers seeking comfort in their courtyard. Peter turned his feet away and sought the ramparts, yearning for fresh air. Each of the city's gates – the Iron, Wood, and Fish, the others doubtless too— was posted with a man from the archbishop's guard. They eyed him coldly as he hurried past. The little stair was crumbling; the wall was in sore need of repair. Once there had been a dozen constables patrolling in rotation, shoring up the city's main defence.

A streak of yellow like ripe flax began to tip the eastern hills. He stood chest-high against the battlement, surveyed the river and the farther bank, the faint trace of the road that led to Frankfurt. A snail's track from this distance, it was deadly nonetheless: infested with the desperate and thieving, men who did not pause to ask your name before they emptied out your innards. Even when they could set out, the merchants moved in guarded convoys. They'd heard about, or seen themselves, the Dutchman who'd refused to pay, whose hands and head were staked out at the junction, one leg set towards Trier, the other one towards Worms.

Behind Peter to the west were roads that led to Luxembourg and Burgundy and France – but these too were now barred. The whole archdiocese was shut to any man of Mainz until the city scraped up the interest for the Elders and their bankers. The facts of the dispute were plain and brutal. For centuries the ruling class had run the city like their private bank. They'd lent the council sums they then repaid themselves at crushing rates of interest. These bonds they then bequeathed to their own spawn, in perpetuity. Thus was the city fated to insolvency, like half of the free cities in the Reich. Each time the treasury was bare, Archbishop Dietrich would step in, prop up that rotting edifice, enact some other tax that only workingmen and merchants had to bear. But not this time – the riffraff claimed to rule. So cry away, the Elders sneered; there's no one else to blame. The council was to pay the debt, or else dissolve. Dietrich proposed to pay the loans if Mainz would hand him back the reins. His message was plain: stay in your place.

A wedge of starlings flashed above the muddy bank below, empty now of ships that once had jostled in a floating herd. How hollow the world seemed without the hoarse cries of the boatmen and the creaking of the cranes. A solitary man picked his slow way along the shore, and Peter pictured the lone figures stealing in at night, those priests that Grede had told him of from distant parishes who'd bless an infant, say a hurried prayer, or even ferry off a corpse for Christian burial for those few families with sufficient gold. The devil take the archbishop, Peter thought fiercely. Every citizen of Mainz was trapped, including him. He turned and started down.

How he had scoffed at them – his father and his uncle, with their impotence and fury. His uncle, Jakob, most of all: the *Brudermeister* of the goldsmiths' guild, who in Peter's absence had been voted to the city council. How could a man waste his whole life in futile stewing? Better to carve out a life of the mind far from this dried-up husk. Fury rose and strangled Peter anew, to find himself once more a hostage to their endless wrangling.

The feud in Mainz was ancient, and perhaps eternal: between the man who makes things – *homo faber* – and the man who trades what others make to his advantage. Mankind was greedy, grasping, Peter thought: it went straight back to Cain and Abel. In the archdiocese of Mainz, this conflict had destroyed the peace for all their lives.

That first day the old smith thrust an apron and a glove at him, both stiff as armour plate. 'I made the fire. You'll make it from now on.' Hans Dünne looked skeptically at Peter's slender wrists. 'Let's hope to God you can.'

'Fust swears he took the teat right at the fire.' Gutenberg came towards them, lacing his own apron. 'Though I would wager it has been a while.'

'It isn't something you forget,' said Peter.

'I'll be the judge of that. Let's see those hands.' The master took each by the wrist and turned them. Peter's right hand had a callus on each fingertip, the middle finger a thick rusty oval. His palms, though, were as pink as baby Henchin's cheeks.

'Sweet Jesus.' Gutenberg looked up, lips coy. 'The last time I saw skin this soft—' He rolled his eyes. The old smith sniggered; Konrad, the big redhead, laughed and lumbered towards the press. Peter glanced at Keffer and caught his eye. By dint of twitches and squints, the journeyman conveyed the message that this master was as rabid as he seemed. With butcher's skill, the man probed forcefully at the thick joints of Peter's thumbs, then dropped them without warning. 'You'd better know right now. I haven't got much use for fancy hands.'

Keffer was the only one to show the slightest friendliness. He made a point of shaking Peter's hand as they were suiting up to face the flames. Thank God, he seemed to hold no grudge for what the scribe had said the day before.

'The last face I had thought to see,' the goldsmith said and grinned. Back at Jakob's shop he'd been a frisky lad without the slightest whisper of ambition. Half the time they'd played at divination with the drops of lead that landed in the water pot. Now he was huge, surmounted by a yellow beard and curls, his neck and shoulders thick and muscled as an ox.

'And me.'

'I thought you'd up and gone.'

'Not far enough to slip the Fusts.'

There was a flicker of surprise in Keffer's light blue eyes. 'At least you saw the world,' he said, and pulled the scarf above his lips and nose.

'And you have made the grade.' The journeyman just nodded and handed Peter his own scarf. It must have been six years since they had toiled together. Strange, that after his four years apprenticing Keffer had done his wander years right here, and not gone out to seek his fortune. But maybe he had found a girl. He'd always been quite the magnet, with those honey-coloured curls.

Their master stood apart, bent over something at his desk. 'Best watch your back,' said Keffer underneath his breath. Peter nodded, warmed; he could do worse for allies. The journeyman was just sweeping the jumbled letters from the workbench on a tray and moving it to the side to make a space for casting when Gutenberg whirled suddenly, a metal letter in his hand.

'Look at this shit.' He moved towards them with alarming speed. 'You know it, damn you, Hans. What smell has shit?'

'It stinks, just like your mouth.' The old gnome wagged his head.

The master's laugh was a hard bark. 'Damn right. Now move your sad bones over here.' Hans gave a loud sigh, peeling off his gloves with exaggerated care. The master waited, eyes hooded, revolving the hunk of metal between his fingers.

When Hans arrived, he thrust it in their faces. Each man could see that it had buckled under pressure: the shank was twisted and the base had splayed. 'Unadulterated, stinking shit.

How can any smith call sludge like this a metal? No bloody wonder it won't print.'

He stood there for a moment, almost daring them.

Hans took the twisted hunk and held it right up to his eyes. 'I'll be damned.'

'Not soon enough.' Gutenberg looked balefully around at his small crew. Keffer shifted nervously. 'What in God's name did you put into it?' The master thrust his mug right up to Keffer's.

'Lead, tin, and copper,' Keffer answered without flinching.

'Body of God,' the master muttered. 'Weeks and weeks, and this is all you have to show for it.' He thrust his lips out, pulling at them; his eyes went inwards as he stood there thinking. Hans scratched his flaking pate; the others waited.

'Saint Jude, grant me patience,' Gutenberg said at last disgustedly, and raked his hair back with his hand. Impassively, he dropped his arm and coolly, in one long, unbroken motion, swept the heavy tray of letters to the ground. Keffer leapt back, wincing, a hair too slow to dodge the mass of lead. 'Try again. I don't care how you do it, do it right.' Gutenberg curled his tall, spare body towards the older smith. 'Don't make me do it all myself, by damn.'

Hans, absorbed in the examination of the damaged letter, grunted without looking up. 'Just let me think.'

The master bared his teeth and stalked away, flinging instructions. The new boy was to smelt. Keffer was to wipe that goddamned smirk off. Hans would scare up some more tin. Konrad better teach that press of his to kiss the letters and not crush them.

Hans put the spoon and basin, pennyweight, and cupel into Peter's hands. Up close, he wasn't quite as ancient as he seemed. The leathered folds and burnished pate were just the residue of an eternity spent screwing up his face against the flames. A madman and a midget, yoked bizarrely, Peter thought. He took the vessels and started slowly towards the forge.

'It's not a blessed sacrament.' Gutenberg's voice came wheeling at his back. 'You'll move your tail here, boy, or you'll feel my hand.'

Under the law, the master was his father from the moment Peter entered his employ. In loco parentis: as apprentice, he belonged now to this madman, just as surely as if he'd been born his child. Unless a master beat a poor apprentice senseless, used him sorely, or punished him without due cause, no soul on God's green earth – not guild, not church, not even his own kin – could intervene.

The man whom Peter served marked out his territory like a wolf: lifting his leg, baring his fangs, establishing who led the pack. There was a canine aspect to him, with his thin lifted lips, the glowing points of amber in his eyes. Keffer told him later the whole episode had been intended to impress on Peter his low place. Gutenberg had spent the day before grousing about the merchant's son who had been forced on him. Bad enough to have to beg – he had to take the grocer's spawn as well. He was the kind of man who could not abide being reminded that he depended on another soul in the whole world than his own, anointed self.

The work those first few months was brutal, mindless, and dull, designed to crush the spirit or to breed a craving to rise up and find some other, lower soul to crush. Peter swept and scoured, lit fires that choked the throat and stung the eyes. He rose before dawn to clear the piles of ash; he lay and lit and banked the day's new fire. And then he weighed the ores and ground them down. When he was finished with these tasks, the master found him others just as rote and stupid: sieving sand to mix with water to a paste inside the mould, cutting heaps of sheepskin into squares that they would use for printing off that Latin grammar.

His thoughts revolved around a single word: escape. There had to be a way – more devious, perhaps, than he would normally have entertained. He did not feel he had a choice: he could not simply take his writing pouch and announce that he was going. His father would feel bound to cut him off and cast him out – pursue him, even, for a breach of contract. The only hope lay in some other work that might release him from this stinking Hades.

Grede told him he should pray for patience. She knocked lightly on his door one night that first week when the household was asleep, saying she had seen his light beneath the door. 'You do not rest,' she whispered. How could he? he responded. She sat upon the narrow bed, put her candle down, and frowned.

'What I don't understand is why he has to drag me into it. An idiot could work that forge.'

She gave a quick shake of her head. 'He needs you. He depends on you.' She watched him as he paced, creaking the floorboards, and put a warning finger to her lips. He stopped; they listened for an instant, but all was silent. 'He trusts you, Peter.'

'He said that in Paris too.' Not even half a year had passed since Johann Fust decreed that Peter ought to represent him there.

'Things change.' She gave a little shrug. How satisfied she was to take what life dished out. He had always thought that there was more – had been lulled into believing he was destined for some higher calling.

'I could have made him proud.' He saw himself deciding with the rector which new books were worthy of the work of copying. Composing one himself perhaps – a work of scholarship. 'Now I'm to throw away my life.'

'A life you'd not have had, except for him.' Grede looked at him, her dark head cocked. 'As nor would I.'

She too had been raised above the grinding labour of a working life. She was a furrier's daughter, quick and fine of shape, whom Fust, then newly widowed, spied and made his second wife. Peter still remembered those first awkward months six years before, this girl his age appearing in his life. They'd circled warily, at first, but found with time that they were much alike.

'So we are to be forever grateful?' Peter sneered.

'He said he'd only do this, with this man, if he was sure he had someone there he could trust. He's gone too much, he needs somebody on the spot. There's too much hanging on it.' She looked at him with the frank, clear gaze he'd come to know in all those times that Fust was on the road – Peter writing when the day was done, Grede always stitching, laughing, telling stories by the fire. 'He needs a surety, a pair of trusted eyes.'

So Peter was not simply drudge, he realized, but spy.

That master worked them fourteen hours a day each cursed day of every week. Sweating, stoking, crushing, pouring. They did not even get a pause to celebrate the Sabbath; despite a host of meetings between clergymen and council, Archbishop Dietrich's ban remained in place. The one brute fact was work, and then dead sleep, as if the pope himself colluded with this Master Gutenberg.

They cast no letters for the whole first month. Instead they smelted, wreathed in noxious smokes, to try to find a metal alloy that would hold. They stooped around the forge like witches, eyes red-rimmed, hands black, their faces draped in clotted veils. Peter ground the ores to powders and shoved them deep into the coals. Lead, tin, bismuth, iron, copper: it was his job to win the molten metal from the roaring fire, turn the dull earth into a shiny, deadly fluid. The master then would reach a claw, take out some drops to mix inside a beaker; he'd growl amounts that Peter noted on a parchment. The tests went on, each mixture entered in the scribe's firm hand. *Two of this,* the master muttered. *Four of that.* Gutenberg would swirl the stinking streams together, lips drawn up, dashing the sweat from his long nose. *Throw that slop out. Another drop. Ah yes, perhaps.* He'd glance up, grimace, hand the beaker off to Hans.

Hans poured it in the casting box and counted up to ten, then Keffer drew the cast letter from the mould. They craned to see. Sometimes the alloy hardened before it even left the beaker, other times it did not harden fast enough. The hollows in the mould might fill right up, but then the metal would disintegrate or snap when Keffer tried to draw it out. Each time the master scowled and pulled at his lip, and sat back down.

For all this time he took no notice of his new apprentice, standing silently at his right hand. It seemed to Peter that he had no eyes for any living man. He would mutter to himself, or raise his head and snarl. *By the blood of the saints. Cannot a runt among you fix a spoon?* He did not eat unless Frau Beildeck brought the dishes to the workbench; he bent so low above the molten metal that great gobs of it adhered, then hardened, in his beard. It seemed to Peter that he sucked up every breath of air in that hot room.

The others laughed at Peter when he washed his hands before the midday meal. They laughed louder when he dried them off and worked some tallow into his chapped skin. Both Hans and Konrad had come from Strassburg with the master and spoke mainly to each other in their strange Alsatian twang. Foreigners, said Keffer, glad to find a friendly face. The journeyman was nimble with his fingers, always drawing with a lump of coal: blank faces with breasts, a nest of thatch. What luscious lips he could show Peter, he'd wink and whisper, if they ever could get sprung. Peter whispered back that you could pay in Paris with silk stockings if you liked. He was no prude, for all the years he'd had to hold his lust in check on monastery stools. Another reason, as if any more were needed, to get free. He couldn't take his pleasure here the way he had in Paris, unwatched and anonymous. He felt his cock stir at the thought of all those satin entries, the dim red lamps, the damp, inviting archways of the street of Saint-Denis.

Fust stopped by once in mid-October, in between his autumn journeys, to check that things were 'well in hand'. Choice words, his son thought darkly: 'in hand' was what he was, his very essence. The master barely looked up at his partner, simply waved a splattered arm. 'Godspeed on your work,' he let fly. 'I'll take the same for mine.'

It was not God's speed, no – the very opposite. September and October passed; the daylight hours began to wane. Yet strangely they could feel a force drag the shop forwards, silver drop by silver drop. There was a movement there, excruciatingly slow, yet inexorable— though where it led them, none could say.

And then one evening a change came.

The master raised his head, eyes bright, as if he'd caught a scent. He rubbed his eyes. 'Yes,' he said. 'Yes, yes.' The batch they'd made the day before had hardened just as soon as it was poured into the mould. This next batch they completed replicated that result. The letters sliding from the mould were crisp and hard; Konrad had run the first lot twenty times beneath the heavy press, and not a single one looked the worse for wear.

'By God, I think that's it.' Gutenberg turned to Hans and smacked him on the arm. 'You look like hell, you know.' He thrust his chin towards Peter and pointed towards the ladle. 'If we can get it right again, at scale, we'll drink tonight!' He drew his bushy brows together, chanting it like some old alchemist:

'Two tin, four lead. Then just a quarter of antimony – to stiffen your sad pricks.' He smiled – a brief, exhausted flash. Hans and Keffer laughed.

Peter went to fetch the requisite amounts. The powdered ores were piled beside each other on a slate that Konrad had erected in a corner by the forge. 'Not just a beaker, either,' Gutenberg hollered. 'I want a bucket of the stuff.' He fake-punched Hans again. 'And put some speed in, will you? I have got a wicked thirst.'

Peter hurried. He scooped and hurried, smelted and hurried. It was this hurry that wrecked everything, he thought as he dashed the sweat away. The pressure of racing to accomplish things without the wit to see if they were any good. He held his two hands steady as he poured and mixed the molten streams, longing for the slow and careful scoring of the pages, the focused trimming of his quill. The time to settle and to think. In half an hour he'd mixed a bucketful and carried it back to the bench. There, he thought, setting it down. The bastard ought to be content.

Gutenberg dipped in the ladle and splashed a test out on the stone. He pried the metal off and put it to his teeth, bit, and spat. 'Good Christ,' he croaked, and thrust his tongue out, flecked with greyish crumbs. 'What crap is this?' His face contorted as his hand flew out and knocked the basin over. A searing pain tore Peter's hand; he screamed and flung it wildly to throw off the scalding ore that poured across it. Hans grabbed the flailing silvered glove and swiftly plunged it into the cooling bucket that stood ready by the forge. Peter was jerked along, twisting on his knees, aware of nothing but the ringing pain. The old smith held his whole arm under water, his own hands rapid as they shucked the now-cold metal from the puckered, raging skin.

'Crap,' the master thundered on, as if he had not seen. 'Tin, for the love of Christ,' he bellowed. 'Not iron, imbecile.'

Peter twisted up to look at him. His whole being burned
with hate as much as pain. 'Then label them, for God's sake.'
He pulled himself up with a monumental effort, lifting with
his right arm the full bucket that contained his throbbing hand.
At least it was his left.

'You watch your mouth.' The master plainly did not care
that he was hurt. Hans stepped between them and said, 'Buzz
off, Henne, if you want your metal.' Gutenberg stopped, grum-
bling; he snorted once and shook his head. If Hans could only
bottle that; Peter nearly laughed despite the pain. How did he
have the right to call him Henne, and even better, shut his trap?
He looked at the old smith with new respect. 'That tallow that
you have,' growled Hans, and Peter gestured with his free hand
towards his things hung on the peg.

He was sent home, hand salved and wrapped in a clean rag.
Where they had found it, Peter never knew; most likely Keffer
tore it from his shirt. Hans pushed him brusquely towards the
door and grunted when he stammered out his thanks. 'Serves
you damn right. Come down a notch or two now, fancy hands?'
As Peter left he saw the pressman, Konrad, coming down the
stairs: they'd all be forced into the smelting he had failed to
do.

The little chimney clock struck nine as he slipped into the
Haus zur Rosau. With stealth he climbed up to his room. His
father was away, and he could not bear to speak to Grede.
Awkwardly he pulled the tinderbox to him, held it underneath
the elbow of his bandaged hand, and struck the flint. The flame
was weak; his image flickered in the glass that Grede had hung
above the basin. Peter stared a long time at his blackened face.
He saw a ghastly, staring beast, eyes white against the grime
that caked its skin. He poured an icy stream with his right hand
and watched as the dipping of his hand, the wiping of his cheeks,
turned the water from clear to black. His eyes were coals now,

in that brutal whiteness. Which was he then, a man or beast? This wasn't even work that in the end brought forth some lovely thing. A brooch, a chalice, or a gleaming monstrance could at least lift a soul above the flames. He might as well have left the farm and gone straight to the Saxon mines.

Peter dried his right hand and pulled the candle towards the parchment he had left upon the table. His Cicero had been returned without a scratch – as if to prove once more his father's power. The calfskin bore a few dark swirls of pasture life, the residue of loam or blood or sinew. He pinned it with the elbow of his bandaged hand, moving the pumice in a growing circle with his right until the colour was more even. He set the stone aside and blew, brushed off the few remaining grains. The sheet was ready now, smooth and unblemished.

He heard the voice of his first real writing master nearly every time he drew the ruling lines. Brother Anselm, at St Peter's on the hill in Erfurt: *Your hand is but His tool.* Peter flexed that tool and grasped the ruling bone. *The parchment that we write on is pure conscience, on which all good works are noted.* He struggled, with his damaged hand, to smooth the sheet. *The ruler that we use to draw the lines for writing is God's will.* He laid his ruler flat and with his bone scored a sharp line, then dipped his quill: *The ink with which we write is pure humility, the desk on which we write the calming of our hearts.*

He breathed, and wrote, and in the writing felt it enter him: the stillness at the centre of all things. The stillness and the soaring freedom of the Word. Not only God's, but all the wisdom He imparted to those willing to receive it. When Peter was but shepherd's son, he'd dreamed one day he'd be a priest – transfixed as he'd been then by all the beauty and the mystery of trees and fields. At university he took all four lower orders of theology; the Benedictines beseeched him to remain and take his vows.

But he had known – or merely prayed – that God had traced for him some other path. He knew it still, and more acutely, faced with this new devil. The candle guttered in a draft, and Peter paused. *What is your meaning here, O Lord?*

Père Lamasse had counselled him not even one full year ago, when Peter confessed that he desired to leave the library at the abbey of Saint-Victor in Paris. Much as he loved the worship of the monks, he felt a pull towards the swirling, pulsing world outside. The abbot touched his head and said the Lord had portioned out to each his own appointed task. This was the goal of our life's journey: to listen and to wait, and when it came, to heed the call.

Peter sat there, feeling every heartbeat in the scorched flesh of his hand. God knew he was no priest. And if one thing was clear to him, he was no smith – and never would be.

Chapter 3

MAINZ

October — November 1450

His father returned just before All Soul's Day. Grede's bustling – the hanging of the tapestries, the laying of the fires – let the household know that he was due. Peter's hand was nearly healed. His stepmother had used the age-old remedies of women from the land: a comfrey poultice mixed with feverfew to leach the heat. The scars were hard to see unless you knew to look.

Fust had been gone a month by then. Grede said he might still try to squeeze in one more trip before the snows. He'd managed to evade the bishop's ban; somehow he'd found a way to buy and sell. Peter did not ask how lucky or how foolish that might be. As he went to find Fust at the customs hall, he had more pressing matters on his mind.

The Kaufhaus had been magic to him once. Many times he had been sent by Fust's first wife into its lofty, aromatic vault – had woven, senses stunned, among its sacks and bales to fetch the man he'd learned to think of and address as Father. It was a temple too, Fust always said – not to the Lord, but to the trade that made His world go round. Teak and tusks and barrels of Madeira; carded wool and coal; oils and spice and Rhineland wine; nuts and ores and semi-precious stones. How Peter as a boy had breathed in all those swirling scents: of skins and wood sap, tang of sweat and citrus, flavours of the distant lands from whence these goods arrived.

From the knoll outside the Hof zum Gutenberg he could see its cornice lifting up above the blue slate rooftops, surmounted by a lordly frieze of statues hewn from red Mainz sandstone: the seven prince electors – three archbishops and four worldly lords – of the Reich. Their own archbishop, Dietrich, held the centre, gazing down on them with massive, sightless eyes.

The more substantial merchants kept their offices up on the gallery that ringed the trading floor. The hall was quiet, just a few high wagons left unhitched inside the portal. Peter threaded past the shrouded stalls and climbed the worn stone stairs towards the office marked 'Fust Brothers'. A scribe had lettered it in gold some years before, each word inside a shield that hung from a brown *fustis*, the knotted branch that was the emblem of their house. Peter heard men's voices, recognized his uncle's, knocked and pushed the door.

'Peter!' Fust rose, smiling broadly. 'You must have second sight. I only just arrived.' Indeed, he was dressed as plainly as a tinker, leggings and dun jacket splashed with mud, a filthy robe tossed on a chair. He'd have tucked whatever coin or weapon he carried right against his skin. Jakob twisted in his seat and raised a hand, a thinner version of his older brother. 'Aha,' he said. 'The prodigal returns.'

Peter forced a smile. 'That was the youngest one of three, I thought.' He reached to shake his hand.

They hadn't seen each other for an age. Jakob had lost weight: his cheeks were sharp, his slicked-back hair gone silver-grey. Small wonder, since he sat upon the council now. His tunic bore the six-spoked wheel of Mainz, picked out in ruby thread upon his breast, a mark of rank to add to the thick ring he wore as leader of the goldsmiths' guild on his right hand.

'I was just telling Jakob how relieved I am to be back home.' Fust shook his neck as if to throw off the accumulated weight and reached into a cupboard for the brandy.

'As if home is any respite,' Jakob said. His eyes were blue, like Johann's, only milkier and paler, winter ice.

'Trouble?' Peter asked.

Fust shrugged. 'The usual. Thieves and thugs and spies.' He poured three glasses from a crystal flask. Down on the trading floor, the goods he'd brought were being counted and taxed. Where had he been this time, what had he brought? More knotted balls of linens, lace from Ghent, the products of Parisian looms? If he had headed west, perhaps. Around the turning of the century, his grandfather had dealt in powders of all kinds: saltpetre for the men at arms, metals for the smiths, salts and roots for chemists. Johann in his turn had branched out more widely, adding semi-precious stones and manuscripts and other luxuries; he'd built an empire based on the vanity and envy of the minor nobles east of the Rhine. The German counts and margraves had little to compare with the bright baubles of their cousins on the thrones of Burgundy and Savoy, England, Scotland, and France.

'You should have seen the Neckar surging.' Fust grinned and tossed his liquor back. 'We damn near lost the load.' How pleased he seemed.

'Heidelberg, then,' Peter said. He'd never seen the castle of the Dukes of Palatine, perched famously above that river gorge.

'Less risky overland. Though who knows for how long.' Fust frowned, with meaning, towards his brother.

'We're doing all we can.' Jakob pulled his cloak up tighter. There were negotiations between Mainz and the archbishop – if one could call them that. The situation was the same as it had always been: who could be blamed, and who would pay. Rebstock and Weinberg had been seized, his uncle told his father. Outside of Höchst, along the road towards Frankfurt. By whose order? Fust asked. The archdiocese. The merchants had got off with just a fine, and nothing worse – if Mainzers had been seized by Frankfurt, they'd still be rotting in its jail.

'That's why I took the woods.' Fust stroked his chin. 'Wrecked the axles, had to pay off half the foresters.' The brothers sucked their teeth and shook their heads – like children, Peter thought, or pawns grabbed up at any point along the board. You seize me; I'll seize you: it was a pointless game. He waited for Jakob to shut up and leave. But this was not to be.

His uncle turned cool eyes towards him. 'I hear you're smelting after all.'

Peter glanced at Fust, who gave a little nod. 'You hear well,' he answered, keeping his voice even. The crew in that hot hell was barred from setting foot outside; they couldn't even slake their thirst or lust among the taverns or the brothels. But somehow Jakob knew.

'We have a certain . . . dispensation, I suppose you'd call it,' said his father, 'with the guild.'

'For now,' said Jakob.

'I'm not much better than a fire-boy.' Peter kept his face towards Jakob. Let Fust hear what he had to say this way.

'It is an honest calling,' his uncle answered.

'That isn't what I mean.' Their eyes locked; Peter saw that he had never really been forgiven. It was Jakob who had taught him how to smelt and carve – Peter and his own son Jakob the younger, and Keffer, all those half-formed boys who'd been apprenticed at his forge – though since becoming *Brudermeister* Jakob rarely dirtied his own hands. He was the truest son of Mainz, rooted in the Rhineland soil; he would defend her tooth and nail. He'd never understood how anyone could just pick up and go. To him departure was repudiation: he'd seen his nephew leave not once but twice, his own son taking up the stool the foster boy had shunned.

'I told your father, and I will tell you too,' Jakob said. 'This . . . "workshop"' – his voice curdled – 'is outside the rules. The man's an Elder, and no doubt a snake. I plan to keep the closest eye upon it.'

Peter caught his father's fleeting irritated look. 'Why don't you let me watch my business,' Fust said, 'and you watch yours.'

'The one destroys the other, that's the point.' Jakob drained his glass and stood. How fitting, Peter thought, that he'd ascended to the post of city treasurer. His first act had been cancellation of the Elders' interest payments. 'They either fund the city like the rest of us and pay their tax, or they can bloody well decamp.' He turned to Peter, one hand on the doorknob. 'If I were you, I'd watch my back.'

His footsteps faded on the great stone stair. Fust snorted, slicked his hair back. 'He always saw the black before the white.' He gave his son a look. 'Though there is money to be made, while they are at each other's throats.'

Roll in the barrel, he said next; Peter fetched it through the small, arched door.

'Something for you.' Fust grabbed a chisel from the rack. He popped the wooden lid and started drawing out the volumes he'd procured. Tomes of canon law, the decretals of Boniface and Gregory, some copies of the cruder sort of romance. And then a packet wrapped in suede: an unbound group of folded sheets, perhaps three quires. He handed it to Peter, who opened it. A calendar of saints filled the left page, in red and black; the right was blank, awaiting a fine painting. 'For Duchess Mechtild,' said his father. A lovely copy of the Hours of the Blessed Virgin Mary.

Peter's body tightened. The lines of the textura hand were a rich brown, exquisite, written with a seamless grace – almost certainly the work of a Carthusian scribe. *Textura* meant 'woven': the monks had always said the scribe wove his own spirit into God's.

'What use is this to fire-boys?' Peter's voice was harsh.

Fust blanched; he genuinely looked surprised. 'I thought you might advise me in the painting.'

'As I had thought my life was mine.' Peter pushed the packet back across the desk.

Fust leaned both palms against the wood and stood there looking at him a long while. At last he sat down heavily. 'You have not grasped the whole of it.'

'I grasp enough.'

Fust frowned. 'You disappoint me, Peter. You, of all people, not to see what this will be.'

'I see a crude and ugly copy of the best that men can do. There's not a lord alive who'll touch a book this madman makes, you know it.'

'Not yet.' His father's nostrils flared. 'Not yet – but give it time. You can't imagine it, perhaps, but I can. Books everywhere, and costing less than manuscripts – in quantities that simply stun the mind. Imagine how the world would look if anyone could buy one!' His eyes fell on the book of hours. 'I can't live just off these. I sell the things, I ought to know.' He raised his eyes to Peter's own. 'In ten years, twenty, who will pay a prince's fortune for such things? The gentry are not all as rich as that. It's finished. I am sorry, but it's true. Once we have found the secret to the letters, there will be no need for scribes.'

'And everything of beauty is destroyed.' Peter rose. 'Everything that matters, in the praise of God – or learning – trampled. Do not forget, I know a thing about this business too.'

His father nodded. 'Of course. You must defend your interest. Your hands, your trade, I understand. It changes nothing,

though. It's over. The life of scribes, the value in your hands
– you may as well accept it now.'

'I beg to differ.'

'Beg all you like.' Fust's eyes went steely. 'It will not change
the truth – or your own duty.'

His duty, then. It was his duty to trail Fust, like a hound,
beyond St Martin's to the square they called the Leichhof, where
the painters and the binders had their workshops. Peter's duty,
to feign courtesy at meeting this Klaus Pinzler, to marvel at his
altarpieces and his scenes of noble revels painted on wood and
glass. His duty, to wait as the fellow scraped and bowed and
Peter gave a nod to show his brush would do. His duty and his
torture to sit beside the men as they agreed the contract, and
to greet the wife and daughter as they sidled in and grinned.
He watched his father ooze that bonhomie that greased the
salesman's path in life, and told himself that he would take the
other way. He was Fust's son, but not his slave. He stood as
soon as it was seemly and made his excuses. The family rose
as well; the daughter moved to open the low door. He noticed
that her fingertips were blue, tipped still with the bright paint
of some Madonna. He had a sudden, fleeting urge to wrap his
hands around the slender throat; how like a beast a cornered
man becomes. The hands he hid inside his cloak were hardened
– almost deadened now. He would not stoop to show his father
how that master had scarred him. The girl looked after him,
pale, almond-eyed, without a trace of interest or pity. The last
thing that he saw before he turned were three small blue-tipped
fingers, disappearing as she slammed the door.

Chapter 4

~~~

SPONHEIM ABBEY

September 1485

'**M**y doubts were more than justified.'

The abbot, busy writing, startles at the printer's dry, sardonic tone. 'What do you mean?' Trithemius lifts his head, and then his nib, his left hand cupped beneath.

'You know yourself,' says Peter Schoeffer, 'how little was achieved.'

The world is flooded now with crude words crudely wrought, an overwhelming glut of pages pouring from the scores of presses springing up like mushrooms after rain. Churning out their smut and prophecy, the rantings of the anarchists and antichrists – the scholars of the classics are in uproar at how printing has defiled the book.

'Not all is worthless, surely,' the young monk protests.

Peter turns his face away. 'Not all, but much,' he says.

He feared it from the moment he set foot in that foul workshop – that this art hailed as sacred would instead prove a dark art. How glorious it might have been! How tawdry it was now, a vehicle for man's base lust for fame and greed. The printer watches with a certain pity as the abbot tries to hide his shock. This is not the proud recounting that Trithemius expected.

'You would go back, then, to the days of scribes?' The abbot bends towards him, his face intent. 'My monks here copy scripture for six hours a day, when they are not at chapel or at work. I'm still convinced it is the only way to truly learn the sacred texts, and practise pious discipline and self-denial.

'Communion with the Word of God, engraved indelibly on heart and mind – this is what I tell them.' His eyes are wide. 'The press, for all its magic, has removed that vital link.'

'Nor did it bring the liberation that it promised.' Peter holds his eyes a moment, and then smiles. 'Still, no one has yet found a way to put a genie back into a bottle.'

All these years later, Mainz is more a vassal than before. The products of her presses are all censored and the workers' rights curtailed. The dream was gone: that with those metal letters they might lift up man from bigotry and want and greed, and raise him page by page towards heaven's peace and plenty.

'The press is used for lucre now, and that I lay at Gutenberg's own feet.'

'How so?'

'He was the first to turn the art to commerce. He cheapened it; he would print anything so long as someone paid him.'

'Anything?' The abbot gives him a strange look.

'Pamphlets, screeds, decrees, whatever raised a fee.'

'And you do not?' Trithemius controls his voice, but Peter hears the edge.

'All are corrupted.' He hears himself too then: the weary, jaded voice of one who'd hoped for more. 'I no less than all the rest.'

He should have stayed a scribe, he sometimes thinks; at least that way he would not feel this disappointed. He has his printing works, two of his four sons who have followed him as printers; he has made hundreds of fine books. He's richer, more upstanding, than the master ever was. But part of him still mourns that touch, the feeling of such closeness to the Lord's creation. At night sometimes, he'll reach for his old pouch of quills, and stroke the skin of God's lamb with the feather of His fowl, praying for some sign.

Chapter 5

MAINZ

November 1450

Peter was enslaved by duty, and it chafed. If Fust would not release him, he might spend his life in filth and smoke, his spirit shrivelling like twigs thrown on the fire. His only hope was to secure a new position that would both set him free and allow his father to save face. He'd thought first that Jakob might help: there wasn't anyone who loathed the Elders more, and Gutenberg was nothing if not an arrogant, abusive Elder. But then Peter saw himself, cap in hand, grovelling before his uncle for some kind of clerkship. Mainz is bankrupt, dunce, Jakob would say. What scraps remain should go to those who pulled their weight. Not that Peter aimed to stay in Mainz; the place was heavy with the venom of that internecine war. For the first time in his life, he thought of purposefully failing – of doing work so foul and tortuously slow that Gutenberg would have to cut him loose. He could not bring himself to do it. He had his pride, and pride did have its uses: mixed well with bitterness, it hardened in the backbone. There had to be someone he knew, some former teacher or a fellow who could get him a scribe's post inside a chancellery, with luck a distant bishop's or a duke's.

His suit was buried in a chest beneath the bed: a short dark cloak, a cap pierced by a raven's plume, a high-collared long white shirt and leggings, and the chamois pouch in which he kept his writing tools. As he unfolded them, he could feel that inky world receding. It seemed a dream, his old Parisian life. Who did she flirt with now, Céline with her russet curls? What did his former fellows say about his sudden disappearance as they gossiped in the morning at their lecterns?

He pulled his old skin on and slipped out after dark one evening from the Haus zur Rosau. The moon was low on the horizon, and the lanes that led to the cathedral were black tunnels, houses clawing towards each other overhead. The market square split open in a sudden pool of light. There was a mist about: November had its foot wedged in the door. Soon it would be the feast day of Saint Martin, the city's patron saint. What chance was there they'd act the play this year upon the broad cathedral stair? Jakob would scream bloody murder if they tried. The people would not stand for such hypocrisy, he'd rail: the rich man tearing off his cloak and rending it in two to share with some poor lad dressed up to play the beggar.

Peter's destination was the Schreibhaus at the corner of the painters' district – the Writing House, belonging to the monks who dwelt outside the city wall at St Viktor's. In those days the scriptoria were in full flower all across the empire; in Mainz the finest books were written at the Charterhouse of the Carthusians or at the hilltop monastery of the Augustines of St Viktor's. The order's house inside the wall had served for decades as their city school, and hostel for the lay scribes that they sometimes hired. In recent years he'd heard that it had turned into a meeting house for clergy of all kinds, although some scribes still worked in a back room.

He'd never set foot in the place before. It was a fetid den, his uncle said, where Archbishop Dietrich's priests and abbots schemed – as much despised by guildsmen as the Elders' tavern at the Tiergarten. The higher-ranking canons of the different orders stopped there when they passed through Mainz, en route from Rome or Aschaffenburg, the Hessian city where Dietrich had his court. Most of them also held high posts in the archbishop's vast administration or the pope's, along with parishes they scarcely ever darkened. The Schreibhaus had become a trading hall, except that they no longer bartered manuscripts, wine, and wheat, but pulpits, favours, sinecures, and prebends.

The place was dim and stank of rancid food and wine. For an instant Peter mistook all those shrouded forms for sheep: fat woollen humps of black and brown, all lowing underneath dark rafters. Then the room resolved into the black of Benedictines and Augustinians, the brown of Franciscan friars, here and there a white Cistercian lamb. Off to the right, the priests of the cathedral chapter sat like folded exclamations, sharp and black, a band of white at every throat. Peter walked with purpose towards a half door at the back. A silver heller bought a cup out of a monastery cask. He turned, surveyed the room, and wished that he could stopper up his nose. Otherworldly scents mixed with the sweat wrung from the fabric of those unwashed robes: the chalk of cloisters, the bite of oak gall, the aftertaste of thin communion wine.

The faces were all known to him – in the way that any face, in a place as small as Mainz, was known. They didn't change: the jowls just spread, the noses grew redder and more bulbous. Elders all, patricians from the city or the minor nobles from the land: the clergy was made up of second sons from wealthy families, stashed and suckled by the Mother Church for life. It was amusing to him how their eyes slid over him and then went back to their own business. He had been gone for long enough for his own face to change. He was a stranger, with a stranger's anonymity, which brought both freedom and a certain risk.

He feigned a spark of recognition and advanced across the

room. He did not know what he would do if he fetched up empty-handed at the far wall. He wove around the brothers at their stools and tables, said a prayer when he was spared: a glance, a sandy head in a dark cowl, a low familiar drawl.

'Petrus Opilionus! Do I see right?' The puffy face of Petrus Heilant cracked in a wide smile.

'Your eyes are fine.' Peter could not help but smile as broadly in return, so sweet was it to hear his Latin name. 'Peter Shepherd,' Peter Schoeffer had been called.

Heilant stood and embraced him, then looked him over with heavy-lidded eyes. He wore the black St Viktor's robe and stood just to Peter's shoulder, as short and stocky as a well-fed goat. 'Good Lord, it's been an age.' There was a laugh on his full lips. 'Where have you got yourself to? Look at you, a proper scribe.'

Two acolytes were sitting at his table wearing white probationary shifts. 'Eberhard, Lubertus,' Heilant said. 'An old schoolmate, Peter Schoeffer, pen divine.'

'You seem to be the one who's blessed,' Peter whispered in his ear. 'I can't believe you took your vows.'

Heilant shrugged and smiled; there'd always been a cunning spark hid well beneath that puffy, hibernating look. 'I work, I write.' He flipped the rope ends girdling his full waist. 'In penitence and patience, waiting for the Lord's reward.' He tilted his fair head and smirked: 'And once a week, I'm paid to take confession from the sisters.'

'At St Viktor's?'

'The Altmünster.' His old friend winked. 'A little something on the side, to keep myself in drink.'

'I always knew that you'd go far.' Peter laughed, swung his cloak onto the chair, and raised his cup to toast his luck. If any man could get him out of Mainz, that man was Petrus Heilant. He'd never seen much point in aiming low. His name alone explained it: Petrus Heilant von Erbach had been born to wealth, and born to climb. The level of his scholarship was average, and as scribe he had a slapdash style, but he had never shown the slightest doubt that he would rise. He hailed from lands along the river Main, just like his distant kinsman, Archbishop Dietrich, Schenk von Erbach.

They fell to reminiscing, probing the whereabouts of others they had studied with. The pimpled youths sat silent for a while, then started making mewling noises: curfew, prior, the long hike. Heilant rolled his eyes as they retreated. 'At their age we'd have nursed a drink for hours in hopes of picking up some useful gossip.'

'You, maybe.' Peter laughed.

'You always did think you could make it without dirtying your hands.' Heilant smiled archly.

Lies, all lies, thought Peter Schoeffer. Everything had always come from Fust. He felt, and pushed away, a little needling of guilt inside. 'In youth,' he quoted with a bitter laugh, 'I saw as through a glass, but darkly.'

'The truth is, you have to make your own way in this world.' Heilant screwed his eyes up, looked intently at the tables at the far end of the room.

'Amen,' said Peter.

'It's all in who you know.' A little gleam – ambition, and alertness – glimmered in those sleepy yet dissembling eyes. Heilant cocked his head and pitched his voice low. 'See those two priests? That's Volprecht Desch. And Greifenklau.' He singled out the two in habits of the Mainz cathedral. 'And back behind that screen' – a heavy hanging, cutting off an alcove – 'the men you really need to know: Quelder, Konneke, von Isenberg. A clerk for Rosenberg.'

The names meant nothing to him, except for the last. 'Hermann Rosenberg?' he asked, and Heilant nodded. The vicar general of the Mainz archdiocese, personal confessor to

Archbishop Dietrich himself: they'd seen him years ago, offi-
ciating at some function at the university.

'This is the place, then,' Peter said softly.

It seemed a stroke of the most unimaginable luck, to be
connected with so consummate a climber. The names that
Heilant whispered with such awe were not just canon regulars
at St Viktor's, but men who also held the leading posts in the
archdiocese, each with its tidy income every annum. A deacon
or a cantor might wear two hats, even three: clerk to the archbishop, envoy to some noble, priest to several parishes, officiant
in any of the city's forty churches. The clergy were all Elders,
and the Elders were the clergy; one hand ceaselessly washed
the other. That trafficking might once have made Peter sick,
but he relished all those contacts now.

'You'd know, then,' Peter said, keeping his voice low, 'if any
of those chancelleries require a scribe.'

Heilant cocked his head, eyes bright. 'I wondered why you
graced us with your presence after all this time.'

'You knew I was in Mainz?'

'I know a lot of things.' His schoolmate smiled.

'I need your help. My father dragged me back – you knew I
was in Paris, too?' Heilant nodded. 'I was about to join the rector's
staff at the Sorbonne.' Peter did not fake the grimace. 'He's forced
me into some harebrained scheme to crank out books.'

'Crank out?'

'I can't say more.'

Heilant's eyes went wicked, and he licked his lips. 'With
wood? I've seen that tripe.' He flicked his plump right hand.
'Carpenters,' he scoffed. 'The stuff they chisel isn't any better
than the junk that Lauber and his ilk churn out.'

'Just as I see it. They seem to think they can replace real scribes.'
Peter bent close. 'I hoped that I might find a post where skills like
ours are better valued. But no one – I mean no one – is to know.'

'Where? Here in Mainz?' A little hardness entered Heilant's voice. Swiftly Peter answered no. It would not do to step on Heilant's turf.

'Away from here. That's all I care about.' He pushed away the thought of Fust and Grede, of Jakob or the children.

'That's good. This place is just too backwards for belief.' Heilant ran a hand across his face. 'I'll see who I can show you to. Perhaps sneak you in to chapter mass.'

'Mass?' Peter said, surprised.

'You don't imagine we would go without it, just because some peasants think that they're in charge?' Heilant's smile was barbed. 'The ban will soon be lifted anyhow. They'll take His Grace's offer and say please and thank you as he rams it down their throats – and all of it in time for Advent.'

'You sound as if you know.' Peter looked at Heilant's rosy face, the cheeks of one who in his later years would tend to floridness and fat; he scanned the room and took in all those larded monks, and saw as if in shadow all the townsfolk, saying their own prayers in their frigid houses. A feeling of revulsion rose.

'It's just a question of the price.' Heilant gave a careless shrug. 'If they can't pay, they'll have to take the terms their bankers – and their betters – dictate.'

Somehow Hans had talked the master into freeing them a few hours every Sabbath afternoon. They were as thick as thieves, that master and his foreman; even Konrad, the big pressman, did not have the right to talk to Gutenberg as the old smith did. Peter spent the cold grey afternoons inside his father's house, writing out his Cicero to pass the hours.

Grede tucked her feet beneath her as they sat before the fire, and said it felt just like old times. 'One of us, at least, is glad to have you home,' she said.

He made a face and kept on writing. 'Come, read to me,'

Grede said, patting the seat beside her. 'From Proverbs, please.'

He wiped his pen, blew on his sheet. Reading was as good as anything; at least that way he didn't have to speak. 'You ought to learn to read,' he said. 'You could.'

'I leave that to Tina.' Grede's eyes were calm. They swivelled to the whirring mantel clock. 'She'll be down shortly.'

She'd roped him into teaching Tina's chubby hands to form her letters in a tray of wax. No child of mine, Grede said, will grow in darkness as I have. How Peter had always admired her: the way she steered that older, slightly pompous husband with the gentlest of touches, her calm persistence covering the steel beneath. He felt a twinge at hiding so much from her now. Once they had been so close, conspirators in youth and their own unexpected freedom. They'd kicked their shoes off, eaten with their fingers, thrown snowballs at each other when her husband was away. Like brother and sister they had always been, determined to make life obey.

'For just a while, but then I must be off.'

'Not on the Sabbath? Shame.' Grede raised one dark, arched eyebrow.

'I only meant to take a walk.' His tone was sharper than intended. He took the small handwritten Bible from the shelf. When he sat down, he felt her eyes reproach him.

'What should I say?' His voice was querulous, but he was powerless to change it – powerless, in fact, in every way. 'Everything I do here is at someone else's pleasure.'

'I wouldn't have asked a favour then, if I had known.'

'I should have thought that it was obvious.' He flipped the pages, lifted up the crimson band of silk.

Grede frowned and, shaking her head, restrained him with a hand. 'Stop fighting everything and place your trust in God.'

'How long? Tell me. You must know – if he shares more with you than just his bed.'

He regretted it the instant it was out. She flushed and drew back.

'How you have changed,' she said.

How could he not have, once he'd tasted freedom and felt his destiny begin to beat inside? Could none of them see this? He felt it in him, greatness – he had practised all his life, done everything they'd asked of him. In his mind's eye the archdiocese of Mainz rolled out across the valleys either side of the great Rhine. He saw the tiny, jewelled cloisters in their swales, the columned porticoes of law courts, chancelleries, where talents such as his might finally be recognized.

'How long?' he repeated.

'He has not spoken to you?'

His head jerked up. 'Of what?'

She looked into the fire. 'He'd like to see you stay. And settle down.'

'Settle. You mean marry. Say it.'

'Marry, then.' Her lips compressed. 'For heaven's sake, what did you think? That you could lark about your whole life long?' *Your wander years are done.*

Grede picked her needlework up again and shifted slightly, turned her body half away. 'I wonder sometimes what goes on inside your mind.'

'I'd rather die.'

She rolled her eyes. 'I'm sure that can be arranged.'

'Which of those horse-faced hags does Father have in mind?' He slapped the Bible shut. 'Kumoff's? With her breath like shit? Sadler's? Kraemer's, maybe, for her sacks of fat?' His voice was cold and low and hard. 'No – Windecke's, now there's a match: mute, or maybe just too stupid to pronounce a word.'

Grede sat looking up at him, a glinting needle pinched between her lips. Her face was grim. 'You do yourself no favours, Peter, with your pride.' *Remember where we come from*, said her

Alix Christie

look. 'You think that you can see the path ahead, but it's not ours to chart.'

Gutenberg kept their small crew concealed as much as he was able. By day they slaved; by night he bought their silence with his wine. That first autumn he ordained that they would spend their evenings at his fire, to keep their mouths out of the alehouse. He had Lorenz roll in a cask and left them to their own devices. Gutenberg himself went off before they'd even finished wiping down the press from printing all those cursed grammars. The master had the luck, said Keffer darkly, to drink among his peers at their own tavern. Peter wondered how he knew this, though the fact itself was not in doubt: the master drank, prodigiously – the proof was in his morning breath.

Peter set himself to writing every evening in a corner of the master's study in hopes of penning his own transit out. He'd need some samples while he waited for a word from Heilant. He did not mind the work; it was a graceful way to keep himself from Fust's house and Grede's eyes. The only irritation was the way that Hans regarded him when he pulled out his quills. The old smith might have salved his damaged hand, but was no warmer in his manner. Doubtless they thought him cheeky, Peter thought as he unfolded his clean parchments and installed himself at Gutenberg's own desk. He didn't care.

The others huddled together, playing tablemen or carving; Keffer piped from time to time upon a flute. Peter rolled his shoulders and shook out his arms; he bent and emptied out his mind. Across the page he wrote line by line – across and back and then across again, the way a farmer ploughs a field. It gave him some small consolation to see that he remembered all the hands that he had learned. He pushed the thought of Fust into the furthest corner of his mind. He would not tell a soul until his bag was packed – he'd leave, and never look behind. It grieved him, but he saw no other route.

When Peter looked up once, he found the old smith watching him, a strange look in his narrowed eyes. Hans pulled a wooden pick out of his mouth and said, 'So you don't play, eh, fancy hands?'

Peter said he didn't think he'd be much contest.

'My point exactly.' Hans put the gummy splinter back and winked at Konrad. 'We got to squeeze it out whichever way we can.'

'Pay them no mind,' said Keffer, looking up from his own scraps of parchment. When he didn't have his flute, he drew. The delicacy of his sketches and his music was surprising, given the thick power of his hands. He had a little ash-wood flute and a larger one that he had cast in brass to gain the rank of journeyman. It was well wrought, as were the tablemen that Konrad carved: strange gnomes, fantastic horses, each detailed and grotesque. Hans too would sometimes etch on sheets of metal, little engravings that were just for fun.

In truth it was not that unpleasant, bolted in there with the cold wind battering outside. They wet their whistles with the master's wine, and hummed and played and scratched. Keffer's pen was ribald. Cackling, he would bring over his drawings: bulbous tits that squeezed a massive cock; a finger or a fist that vanished in a hairy slit. Hans and Konrad bickered gently through an endless game, to judge from that same grubby pile of coins they just kept shifting back and forth.

For several days the talk had turned to wondering about the project that the master had in mind. Gutenberg had gone away for a few days and left them printing under Hans. But that grammar was small fry, Hans averred – a practice run, before whatever better book the master planned.

'Don't care what it is, just so we're moving.' Konrad used his knife to shave a curl from the oak table. 'I'm sick of waiting on you clods.'

'Careful what you wish for,' Hans said knowingly. 'I'd lay good money it is big.'

'Or else a schoolbook he can pop at half a shilling,' Keffer put in.

Konrad nodded. 'The main thing is, it should be quick.'

Peter lifted up his head to hear them better, catching as he did a sour look from Hans. 'Why don't you save your breath and ask the scribe,' the old smith scoffed.

As one they looked at Peter.

'As if I had a clue.'

Keffer scratched his yellow beard. 'You must have some idea.'

Greek and Roman titles whistled through his head. Aristotle and Aquinas, Virgil, Euclid, sprang to mind. But they were miles away from markets for such learned works.

'Just pray it's short.' Konrad began paring his nails.

'A psalter, maybe, or a history. Neither is that long.' Peter weighed the buyers up and down the Rhine: mainly nobles, merchants, Elders, and the church.

'Nah.' Hans hoiked a gob of spit into the fire. 'I warrant he's got something bigger on his mind.' He turned back towards the scribe, eyes narrowed. 'A sacred work, perhaps.'

'It's just a guess.'

'You wouldn't know?'

'I wish I did.'

It struck Peter that Hans must have downed a jarful, by the way his eyes were rolling in their sockets.

'You scribble all damn night. Don't tell me you don't know what for.'

'It's just my practice, to keep my hand.'

'Your precious bloody hand.'

'Now, Hans.' Konrad lifted his, a great big slab of meat, and shook it at the smith.

'"Now, Hans".' The old smith spat again; his voice cranked

higher. 'Don't Hans me, man.' His eyes were shot with red. 'I'm sick of it, I tell you. Pussy here thinks he's the bloody saviour.'

'Cool it.' Keffer reached to grab him, but Hans jerked to his feet, then clutched the table with both hands to keep from falling. 'I'm sick of it, I say.' Hans's voice was thicker, slurring. 'Fancy hands has prolly gone already, drawn some pretty new type for the master, little shit.'

'Shut it.' Konrad grabbed Hans by the belt and sat him roughly down, then smacked him smartly on top of his thick skull. When Hans kept cursing, Konrad stood and flung his blade into the wood with a loud *thwock*, the steel inches from the old smith's hand. Hans flinched and held his tongue.

'Forget it,' Keffer offered. 'He's just drunk.'

Even so, it irked Peter. He crossed the room and loomed above the little leathered man. 'It's just my trade. The craft I learned.'

'Like you had to learn a craft. Pretty little merchant's boy like you.' Hans tried to hoot but succeeded only at a phlegmy cough.

Peter looked at each of them in turn: Hans bald and slumped, Konrad worrying at his blade, Keffer poking at the fire. The story of his goddamned life – mongrel, bastard, orphan, he had heard them all. Labels, like the tags that designated trades, or ranks, or ores. He scowled and rolled the sleeve up his left arm. The scar from shearing he had borne since he was five snaked from his wrist up to his elbow.

'Peter Schoeffer, born at Gernsheim. Not a Fust. The sheep were kept inside, so you could say, I guess, that I was born in a stable.'

'Now he plays the Christ child,' Hans said snidely. Konrad laughed, though, and something in the room shifted.

'You shut your gob,' Konrad said again to Hans, and pulled his knife out of the table. He smiled and surveyed the full length of that white scar. 'That's mighty nice. It might look better, though – more balanced, if you get my meaning – if I could carve you something matching on the right.'

They got on better after that. Hans never admitted that he'd been out of line, but he thawed bit by bit throughout the Advent-tide. The more the world outside iced over, the more the mood inside the workshop warmed. It helped that Gutenberg had gone away again; it also helped that Hans, for all his bluster, was a man who honoured work. He knew that the new apprentice had not once voiced a complaint through all those hellish weeks of smelting.

A few days after Peter bared his forearm, Hans pulled him aside and said that he was sick of pouring molten metal into that damned casting box. He much preferred to smelt and mix the metal, and to leave the blinding part to someone else. He nudged Peter towards the casting table. 'Fancy hands make you the man.'

It was a change – and in the absence of a sign from Petrus Heilant, Peter craved change of any kind.

He listened and watched closely as Hans demonstrated how to cast a piece of metal type. First he lifted off the top of the wooden casting box to show a row of trays filled with damp sand. Hans pressed a letter punch into the sand, and then another: first the long ascending stroke, and then a rounded shorter one, to make the hollows for a letter *h*. He did this in each tiny square and then closed the lid, divided into narrow chimneys just above each tray. He took a ladle, dipped it in the pot of molten metal, and poured some into each shaft. When they were full, he waited, counting up to five, and then opened up the box and pulled the hardened letters out. 'Still need some filing,' he said, tossing each one on a pile. He handed Peter the two punches. 'An idiot could do it,' he said, grinning.

Hans had never cared to know his state of mind or heart and

did not seem to do so now. He simply watched, his leathered eyelids half obscuring his keen eyes – then reached, correcting: straightening Peter's elbow, sliding his hand a fraction farther down the punch. His words were few and focused on the task: 'Not so deep.' 'Put a little power there.' He taught Peter how to hold the punch at one precise, specific angle, how to ease the top on without disturbing one small grain of sand. He skimmed the skin that formed upon the metal, with a flick of his wrist showed how to pour the molten trickle in.

The chunks of metal with a letter on their tip were no prettier than they had been before, but for the first time Peter understood – in the plain act of moulding and of making – that what they did was utterly astonishing. No one before had ever made small letters out of metal: it was the unexpected combination – the marrying of metalwork to writing – that had birthed a thing that no man on God's green earth had seen before.

The master's insight had been simple: take a binder's tool and make a mould. But he had seen that he could never make a punch for every single different letter of the scribal hand. So he had broken each one down into its elemental strokes: the straight descending line, the round form of the *n*, the *o*. Thus armed with a bare score of symbols, they could build each letter of the alphabet by layering each stroke in the damp sand.

It was a Calvary, as Gutenberg had said. But something in the blinding focus of it worked an alchemy in Peter nonetheless. His mind was stilled, the bitter chatter overwhelmed by the necessity of steadying his breath. Each stroke had to be placed at the same precise depth, or else the letters would come out uneven. Each tiny slip required him to start over, smoothing out the sand. He screwed his eyes in concentration, hearing nothing, seeing nothing but the motion of his hands. He shut the box and tipped the ladle – and in so doing, tipped and emptied out the roiling in his soul.

Chapter 6

MAINZ

Early December 1450

The fact that Gutenberg could come and go as freely as he did was a clear proof of his high rank. He did not seem to worry that he'd be seized abroad as a debtor citizen of Mainz, as the merchants and guildsmen feared. Fust for his part paid dearly at each junction, his silver greasing countless palms to move his wagons out along the smaller, less-watched roads. If someone knew just where the master went, that someone would be Hans – but Hans, with a swift shake of his head, said only that he'd gone out prospecting. Which book the workshop cranked out next made little difference to Peter. Let Gutenberg and Fust decide; by then he would be off, once more a scribe for hire.

As it happened, the project was decided for them. The second week of Advent Lorenz arrived in haste, his old face pasty white, and thrust a letter at the master. Gutenberg set down the file he held, wiped his hands on his smeared apron, and examined the folded packet, which was heavy with official wax and seals.

'My appointment to His Majesty the King, no doubt,' he cracked and broke it open. They watched him read, the weather moving in swift bands across his face: first clouded mist, then squall, then sudden clearing as he dropped his hand and stared a moment, far away. His eyes met Hans's. 'Rosenberg,' was all he said; the foreman nodded. 'I am to dance attendance up at Eltville. Somehow they've heard . . . or got their mitts on one of the first copies.' He spun, surveyed the rest of their poor crew; his eyes were knives that moved across each man.

'They' – the archbishop, plainly, and Hermann Rosenberg, his vicar general *in spiritualibus*. The vicar could not have heard from Heilant, surely – nothing Peter divulged could possibly have led to this. Nonetheless his hands were slick as he turned his face away and pressed the thin punch in the sand.

After Gutenberg had gone striding off, intent on making inquiries, the rest of them put down their tools and made a silent circle around Hans.

'What?' He scowled. 'It's not as if he tells me either.'

Even so, Hans did allow that the letter might have come from Gutenberg's own business with the higher clergy; he'd been to see them more than once. Why, back in Strassburg he was friendly with the bishop, and of course his godfather had been Archbishop Dietrich's close adviser years ago – though he was dead now, rest his soul. As for the rest, who knew what Rosenberg had seen or heard – you lot had best get back to work.

It took another day before the master's plan emerged. He would take Peter, though God knew he'd never thought he'd need the cover of a scribe. He wasn't sure exactly what the vicar general knew – how much or little of his new technique – but they would carry on as if they made what Gutenberg and Fust pretended. Knock out some pilgrim mirrors, he told Konrad and Hans – and as for you, boy, write me out a canticle or two to take to Dietrich in his country castle on the Rhine.

'Which ones?' asked Peter warily, uneasy at this turn.

'Whichever ones would go into a psalter for a pope,' the master snapped.

He must have looked astounded. Gutenberg just shook his head, his tufted eyebrows raised. 'You do, I plan.' He cocked his chin at Hans. 'I'll take a printed sheet from the Donatus too, and five new mirrors if you've still got those blasted stamps.'

Hans laughed. 'Don't throw away a thing, now do I?' he said, and moved towards some shelves along the back. He reappeared with several dusty objects that on close inspection proved to be dies cast from some hard metal. These were used to stamp out mirrors for the pilgrims: shiny convex badges that, held up from far away, could capture holy rays that emanated from cherished relics like the finger bones of saints or shards of martyrs' crosses. Or so the credulous believed.

The master scratched his face. They had a day to crank these things out; best not to keep the high and mighty waiting. He grinned as if delighted with himself. What was he playing at? Peter wondered. What did he have in mind, with one small printed sheet, a pilgrim mirror, and a page of written psalms?

His whole life Peter had never seen Archbishop Dietrich from any but the greatest distance. The prince elector was a jewel-encrusted mitre at the far end of St Martin's nave, a golden blob that led some grand procession. So it was with a certain thrill that he found himself about to float into that august presence on the morning boat to Eltville-on-the-Rhine.

His father had not taken the news lightly. Suspicion pleated his broad face when he discovered that his partner – and his son – would bow and scrape before the archbishop. He bent his head and whispered urgently to Gutenberg, back turned so none could hear. It was not hard for Peter to divine his main concern. Too many people knew about the press – and worse, the very ones who knew were those who considered every man in Mainz their tool. Fust looked at Peter with acerbity and commanded him to be his ears and eyes. His son nodded, wadding up the pleasure that had opened in his heart. How lucky that he bore the name of Schoeffer and not Fust – for Dietrich surely knew the names of those on the city council who opposed him. How lucky, and how right, that Peter should be chosen and not Fust; he'd been a fool to think his father might be proud. For after all, his son would stand where Fust, for all his gold, could never dream of standing: face-to-face with the highest priest in the whole Reich, second only to the king that Dietrich, as last prince elector, chose with his deciding vote.

Peter's feet had not even grazed the timbers of a boat since his return. The siren of the river whispered as he rose before first light and made his way down to the baths. The winter air was crystalline, though snow had yet to fall. He heard the bells of cloisters on the land, and up above him scudding clouds were sweeping up the stars. Each gate he passed showed a brief flash of dark grey water, teasing him with longing for the ride. He paid the maid who drew the bath a silver penny, twice the normal rate, and told her he'd take comfrey oil to match the greenness of her eyes.

He soaked and thanked the Lord that only crazy fools like him would think to bathe in utter dark. No other soul intruded on his calm, embroidered with the call of doves and the first footfalls in the lanes, until the maiden reappeared and lightly brushed her fingers at his neck. 'A silver day,' she said, and Peter stiffened slightly, felt her hands begin to rub the tension from his arms and shoulders. An angel sent down to speed him on his way. He closed his eyes and gave himself up to the sweetness of her touch, like fishes nibbling at his limbs. He had to fight not to cry out, as she stroked harder, found and met his hardness in the silken water, moved and moved beneath the waves. The world went white, and it was long before he opened up his eyes. Froth lay upon the cooling water, and the green-eyed maiden was long gone.

The passengers stood waiting while the boat manoeuvred to the wharf before the Wood Gate. Gutenberg had dug a splendid suit out of some mouldy chest: a triple-layered grey beret that dropped half to his shoulders and breeches of the same dark grey, with slits that showed brief flashes of maroon. He laughed when Peter bowed and mimed his awe.

'Oh yes.' The master showed his teeth. 'We must put on a show.' He swept onto the boat, handed off his cloak, and strode up to the captain, who he seemed to know. A yeasty, fruity smell rose up from hops and oats and wine stored in the hold. They went up to the prow, the Rhine stretched out invitingly before them, a pewter band beneath the cold grey winter sky. The railing was at their chests, the wind full in their faces. If he but let her, Peter thought, the river would convey him to the sea, which he had never seen. One day he'd take it there, he told himself, quite giddy with release.

They both leaned forwards as the boat pushed off, arms draped across the rail. The master smiled, his long beard spangled with the spray. 'I've half a mind to just keep going and not stop until we reach the Dutchmen.'

His mood was strange. He seemed both coiled within himself and yet elated. Guardedly his young apprentice watched and tried to judge how much he dared to ask. The archbishop's castle was beyond the bend at Wiesbaden. Peter pictured the vast river winding, saw it as a shining snake across the land, as God himself must see it from on high. 'How long a ride?' he asked, the answer tossed back by the wind: 'About two hours.' Gutenberg gripped harder at the railing as the boat began to toss, and Peter couldn't help but notice a large golden ring he'd never worn before. The master caught his glance.

'I am a wanderer, like all my kin,' he said, and held it up.

The Gensfleisch family seal was that of a lone figure like a humpbacked beggar with a walking stick. It wore a pointy cap and held aloft a cup for alms, and underneath the cape, a lump that might have been a basket.

'Saint Christopher?' asked Peter.

Gutenberg gave a queer smile. 'Perhaps. I've always thought it apt. Not the traveller, so much as some poor fool who spends his life in begging.' He pulled his collar up then. 'I should like to have that cape.'

When Peter fetched his wrap for him, he muttered, 'Thank you,' much to his apprentice's surprise. This gave Peter courage to inquire who they might meet and what he should know about their business there.

Gutenberg regarded him with his deep, gold-flecked eyes. 'A man who thinks he runs the world.' He expelled a little mirthful spurt. 'For what that's worth.'

Peter waited – he was a master now in the fine art of waiting. Gutenberg looked swiftly right and left, and then he bent, as if imparting some great secret. 'You have to think of Dietrich as a *mappa mundi*: all the world below, and at the top his fat round head.' His eyes were wicked. 'The rest of them append-ages to exercise his will. His right arm is his soldier, the knight Erlenbach. His left is Rosenberg, the vicar general, who tends what's left of his black soul.' His teeth glinted as he grinned. The legs were chancellor and chief clerk, he went on, warming to his little game. Beneath these all the countless earls and margraves clinging to his heels. But this was nothing to the terra incognita spreading out from his vast bulk – the forces that he alternately schemed against or plotted with or fought tooth and nail: the other German dukes, princes, and arch-bishops, and above all, the pope in Rome.

'You know him well,' said Peter with a little smile.

'I used to go there fairly often long ago.' Gutenberg turned back downstream, his face in profile sharply chiselled, with that long, aristocratic nose.

The Martinsburg, when it came into view, looked almost dainty through the screen of trees. As they came closer, Peter saw that it was fortified, its tower twice as tall and broad as Mainz's Iron Gate. Atop its turrets fluttered Dietrich's arms: the six-spoked wheel of Mainz and then the house of Erbach, two white stars, one red. The fortress could not be approached directly from the river, ringed as it was by sharply pointed stones. They slipped instead into a side canal and disembarked onto a jetty like a tongue extended from the wall. 'Keep your mouth shut,' the master hissed as they were led inside. 'Just kiss his hand and then fall back.'

Peter had expected gold and jewels – pomp, excess. Such was the picture of this monster in the mind's eye of the city's guilds. He was astonished instead to find the great man in his morning dress, all pink from bathing, wearing only a black robe, his scarlet collar nearly hidden by his neck and jowls. He sat on a golden chair, that much was true, flanked by a man-at-arms and a priest in dark red robes. A silver tray of fruit lay at his right, beside a kneeling knave whose sole employ appeared to be advancing bits of food towards his mouth.

'How kind to take the time to see us, dear Johann.' Languidly Archbishop Dietrich lifted up a fleshy hand. His eyes were heavy like a tortoise's.

'Your Grace.' The master bent his knee and kissed the rings upon that hand. Then it was Peter's turn; he heard the master say, 'Peter Schoeffer, lord, a *clericus* of Gernsheim and of Mainz, a scribe in my employ.'

Peter backed away. 'Warm greetings, Father,' Gutenberg was saying to the priest who must be Rosenberg: black brows beneath a bright white fringe that circled his black skullcap, penetrating, deep-set eyes. The knight, a hard, thin elder warrior

all in leather, looked right through them both; to the side sat
a secretary with a writing tray. The archdiocese had scores of
scribes, but none so high as this, thought Peter with a spurt of
hope. Two velvet stools appeared behind them, and they sat.

Even afterwards he barely could describe the room, so closely
did he bend his ears to hear. He vaguely saw that it was large
and paned with squares of painted glass on doors that gave out
on a garden. What other decoration there might be, he did not
see. They had been turned and twisted through the tower
hallways to arrive in this bright chamber. Now as they waited
Dietrich dipped his fingers in a silver salver, dried them on a
linen towel, and, leaning forwards, placed them on his knees.

'Your metalwork, I see, does not extend to razors.' His own
chin was white and smooth, a promontory jutting from a sagging
sea of skin. His blue eyes opened, huge and oddly vacant.

Gutenberg sighed loudly. 'My lord, you know I'm an old
sinner. The razor, I confess, is the least of my faults.'

Dietrich's cheek twitched. 'You do consort with trouble-
makers, it appears.'

Raising both his hands, the master supplicated brilliantly.
'Forgive me, Grace, if you can understand. I'm quite unable to
find craftsmen from the noble classes.'

Dietrich had a pair of full and drooping lips that parted only
slightly when he slipped a morsel in, or when, as now, he truly
smiled. 'Indeed. Yet we have need of smiths' – his eyes lapped
briefly over Peter – 'as well as scribes.'

The humour snuffed out then, just like a candle, from
Dietrich's eyes. 'You have a way with craftsmen, it would seem.'
He turned towards Rosenberg. The vicar general bowed and
pulled a volume from his sleeve.

'It's said that you made this,' the vicar said, black eyes upon
the master's face as he began to turn the leaves.

The master rose, stretched out a hand. 'I might have known

I could not keep so marvellous a thing from you,' he said, inclining himself slightly towards Dietrich. It was a mime he played, thought Peter – Lord let him play it well. He felt an unaccustomed pressure on his shoulders, seated on that stool below the dais, his head right at the level of the henchman's hilt.

'It is some trick with wood, they say,' said Rosenberg, and Peter felt his chest seize.

'Wood!' The master laughed. 'I leave the whittling to lesser men. No sir, it is not wood.'

'But still – some trick, not with the hand?' Rosenberg was frowning, holding out that grammar towards the master as if it had the clap.

Gutenberg took it and raised it up. He squared his shoulders and turned to the archbishop. 'A new invention, by your leave. A great technique born in the golden city of the Mainz archdiocese.' He held the grammar up as if it were a chalice until the archbishop reached out his hand.

'With this technique, Your Grace, I can make many copies of a book, each one identical.' Dietrich took the little volume and laid it open on his knees. 'This is a grammar – as you see.'

Gutenberg glanced at Peter and mouthed silently, *The leaf.* Peter dug into his pouch and produced the Donatus page. 'If I might approach?' the master asked, and Dietrich nodded.

Gutenberg stepped on the dais, raised the printed leaf, and laid it next to the same page, bound now into a book. 'As you can see, there is not a single difference you'll detect – and most of all no slips or errors, as we encounter all too frequently from scribes.'

Dietrich peered; his pale and bulging eyes moved slowly back and forth. 'So it would seem.' His face remained impassive, but Peter thought he saw a look of shock, or at the very least surprise, in those veiled eyes. The archbishop beckoned Rosenberg, and Gutenberg resumed his seat.

They sat on tenterhooks as those two whispered, Rosenberg intent, explaining something. The consultation seemed to stretch from minutes into hours, or maybe it was just the slowing down of time in that long moment in which Peter understood. They all knew – every one of them – while he and the whole crew had been locked down. The master had kept shooting off his mouth, while they'd been sworn to silence. Gutenberg sat there with his head high, and Peter felt a blaze of fury on behalf of Fust. His father had a fortune riding on this secret, which apparently was not as secret as he thought. Doubtless Gutenberg had waved the little book at half the Elder clans in Mainz in search of funds, Peter thought, before he'd seduced Fust.

Finally the master started fidgeting. He did not like to wait. His mouth worked until he said beneath his breath, 'The psalm.' In the rustling that ensued as Peter drew it out, the archbishop and his vicar both looked up.

'I hoped' – the master smiled, a little sheepishly, and stood, the psalm secreted in his hands behind his back – 'that with my new technique I might be of some service to you too.'

He spread the double sheet on which the scribe had written out the canticles of Moses and Isaiah, in sharp black letters with two blazing gold and red initials. 'It seems to me,' he smiled, 'the pope would be well pleased with this technique. A little gift made in this way in your archdiocese – a fine pontifical in gauge of your respect and love, and by the way, a nice distraction from the tithe.'

Dietrich opened his pink mouth and smiled. 'You never cease to surprise me, Johann.'

'I learned my lessons well.' As all men knew, the pope required a tenth part tithe from every diocese to fund his Jubilee. The rumour was that Dietrich refused, along with the archbishops of Cologne and Trier.

'And for the love I bore your godfather' – the archbishop said – 'I might agree.' He waved at Rosenberg to take the sheet. 'But there's another task we must consider first.'

The master tensed and waited.

'You've heard perhaps that there are new monks at St Jakob's.' Dietrich sat back, tenting his white hands. 'There is a push among the Benedictines for reform.' There was no movement in the room beyond the scratching of the scribe as they all waited for him to make his meaning clear. 'Reform, of course, is something everyone supports.' He smiled blandly. 'And so we ought to do our best to help this new congregation.' He signalled Rosenberg to carry on.

'His Grace has authorized a revised missal, which some among the Benedictines feel essential,' the vicar started. 'A new and standard text based on a strict interpretation of the Rule, replacing all the variations that have sown disorder.' Shrewdly Rosenberg looked down at Gutenberg. 'It seems to us that this – technique – falls like a gift, for if it makes a single text identical in every copy, then each one is entirely free from error.'

The master licked his lips. He stood a moment, stunned, it seemed to Peter. What whirred in the mechanics of his mind? Dietrich leaned his great black bulk towards them.

'A missal,' said the master, pulling at his beard.

'This tool of yours could be – extremely useful,' said the vicar. 'So long as it does not . . .' His voice trailed off.

'So long as we are all assured it does God's work.' Archbishop Dietrich smiled, pretending that he waited. There was no possibility, of course, that his desire would be denied.

'The Word of God, Your Grace.' The master dipped his head. 'You do me a great honour.' The words were obsequious, though underneath it Peter knew that he was calculating madly.

'One thing, though, I must beg, Your Grace.' Gutenberg looked briefly left and right, as if to fix his words into the minds of both the soldier and the priest. 'I must insist on secrecy. I cannot work without it – for if word of this gets out, it is stolen from me in a moment.'

Dietrich nodded, bobbing that huge face, made large as if to counterbalance the great mitre of his office. 'It will be so.' He turned to Rosenberg. 'You need not keep these things.' The vicar bowed, and handed book and sheet back to the printer.

'You will need money, I suppose,' said the archbishop.

'Always,' said the master. They exchanged a smile.

Dietrich turned then to his knave and raised the jewel-handled knife. The boy lifted up a pear – a pear, and in December! An instant later the archbishop raised his eyes, as if surprised to find them both still there.

'Go with God,' he said, and lifted up the knife in a slow, lofty gesture. Peter recognized it with a shudder. It was the same dismissive gesture that he used when lifting up his shepherd's crosier on the rare occasions that he deigned to visit Mainz.

They exited the castle warren through some gardens and an iron gate that opened to the little town of Eltville-on-the-Rhine. Gutenberg stalked swiftly, his closed face not betraying what he thought. Nor did he say a word to Peter that whole day about the thing that had transpired. The scribe was mute, an appendage, a slave the master put back in its place when it had served its purpose. Yet all the while the shock of it was lodged inside him, blocking any other thought. The Word of God reduced to that crude, soulless type – the handbook of the Mass, this precious volume filled with sermon and with song, stamped like some tawdry trinket onto hide. A grammar was one thing – a holy book a sacrilege, a horror in God's eyes.

Mammon ruled, Peter thought darkly. This day as every day, Johann Gutenberg had business to transact. The man had fingers in all kinds of pies; they saw his niece, his nephew, and a pastor. He'd spent some early years in Eltville, it was clear – most likely every time the Elder clans decamped from Mainz, refusing to submit to taxes from the guilds.

The sun was sinking when the boat to bear them back arrived. Despite libations at each visit, Peter was not warmed. They climbed on, and the master joined the captain in his shelter at the aft. Peter huddled on a bench up front. Spent horses were unhitched, and fresh ones tethered to the long, stout lines that ran between the towpath and the ship. The vessel struggled hard against the current as the dray team strained, the horses' heads bowed nearly to the ground, before it heaved and started back the long, slow haul upstream.

Chapter 7

MAINZ

Mid-December 1450

Reform was a prayer that bounced across the Holy Roman Empire and the rest of Christendom that year, a hope that something in the world might change. True Christians yearned for a return to a purer, more ascetic faith, and change had been agreed on at the conclave of the cardinals four years before in Basel. The world was wormwood, pocked with greed, and none plundered more than those who had been called to serve the church. The pope himself, in ordering his Jubilee, decreed that the abuses had to stop, and lent his weight to many projects of reform among the Benedictines and the Augustinians as well as within his own house, the hierarchy of the Holy See.

It was a pious hope indeed. Peter knew it from the instant that he saw the archbishop's knowing smile, his bland assurance that he endorsed reform. The only reform Dietrich wanted was the restoration of the abbeys' wealth, for every monastery in the archdiocese was in his jurisdiction. For decades noble families had run them as their private fiefs and stripped them nearly clean, but this would henceforth cease – to honour God, return the monks to upright lives, the monasteries to their former economic strength, and thus increase the archbishop's own receipts.

This missal for St Jakob's was a marvellous commission, Gutenberg assured his partner, then his crew – the centrepiece of a great push among the Benedictines of the Bursfeld congregation for reform. He had no doubts, and through a night of talking convinced Fust as well that this was just the book they had been waiting to produce. Fust did not like the prospect of the clergy in command of that whole printing works he underwrote, despite his own faith and his uncles' high positions in the city's churches. But Gutenberg was a master of manipulation, Peter thought, observing as the two of them discussed it out of earshot of the crew. The master was quite able to convince them all to lift and drink directly from that poisoned chalice.

For poisoned it most surely was. The handbook of the Mass was hellishly complex, even for the most accomplished scribe. It ran two hundred pages and was written in two, if not three, contrasting scripts: one for the priest's words; a larger letter for the Gospel readings; and in finer books a third hand for the lyrics of the Psalms.

The partners called the crew together two days after their return from Eltville. Gutenberg was quite unrecognizable: his hair was trimmed, as was his beard; he seemed to overflow with cheer. Beside him Fust stood, chest thrust out, his cheeks and chin smooth-shaved, convinced no doubt by the sheer money to be made. Who did he take himself for? Peter asked himself. It was a strange inversion, to be sure: patrician Elder wearing whiskers, common merchant fresh of face.

The master's hands held something at his back. 'I hear there was a bet.' He pulled a volume out and grinned. 'It's neither long nor short, but just the thing.'

They craned to see the first page of the *liber ordinarius*, the handbook of the Holy Roman rite. 'The first of many, let us pray.' Fust smiled and glanced at Peter.

'They'll go like fishcakes at the fair.' Gutenberg looked around at the four men. Hans plucked his throat; Konrad stretched a hand out, gauging the proportions of the page. Keffer pursed his lips and looked at Peter. A little flame inside the new apprentice flickered and went out.

'Two hundred pages, worth their weight in gold,' said Gutenberg.

Every priest in every parish, every abbot in his chapel, every soul of wealth and standing, had to have the handbook to the Mass. This edition would be newly drafted by the prior of St Jakob's, to be used by all the monasteries of the Bursfeld congregation, he explained. But nothing said their workshop had to limit it to that.

With curving yellowed nails he started ticking off prospective buyers: seventy for Bursfeld in the dioceses of Mainz and Bamberg; forty, fifty more for churches in the cities, who'd strong-arm the wealthy of their parish to endow their pulpits with a copy. Nor was the Latin rite restricted to the Rhineland, nor to Germany and Austria and Bohemia, comprising their own Holy Roman Empire. Peter grasped at once their overarching goal: one single, uniform edition, which could be sold in every kingdom from the Narrow Sea of England to the Middle Sea that laps the Holy Land. Hundreds, thousands, of them, priced to undercut the products of the scribes.

'God's given us the means to multiply His Word!' Gutenberg was fairly dancing with delight. 'At last His own benighted clergy, too, have seen.'

Fust had a bottle in his hand; he twisted at the cork until it popped.

The pressure gave then, too, in Peter's head: he heard the platens of a hundred presses crashing, books churned out as hot and rough as bolts bashed out by blacksmiths. Big volumes too, not puny little grammars: vast quantities of brutish, ugly, soulless tomes.

He scrutinized Fust's face: his blue eyes shone, his cheeks were glowing. Did he feel no compunction about selling out that beauty, all the praise and grace that God invested in their hands? He glanced at Konrad, who had lately started muttering that he would like to push on home. Keffer would be glad, he guessed, of extra work. Hans – well, Hans was as loyal as a hound. Which left just Peter Schoeffer to spit in the soup.

'There is a reason books like these are done by scribes.' He reached and took it out of Konrad's hands. 'You need at least two separate scripts, at least two sizes.'

Gutenberg's glass stopped, half raised. 'Really.' He cocked an eyebrow, looked around, and drawled it mockingly. 'I'm much obliged. I guess then Brack is short of scribes.'

'Heinrich Brack,' Fust put in, looking hard at Peter. 'The prior of St Jakob's.'

'And author of our text.' The master wheeled, gave Hans a jovial whack. 'His Grace is more than pleased. You should have heard old Rosenberg!' He cackled. '"Such a means to make a perfect text, and in his Lordship's diocese!"' He mimed a high falsetto.

'I guess he didn't look that closely at the type then,' Peter said grimly. He saw again that cheap Donatus, open on Archbishop Dietrich's knee.

'I guess he did.' The master's back was up; his eyes were glinting.

'With due respect.' Peter glanced apologetically at Hans. 'This letter will not do.'

'Says who?' The master's face was twisted.

'It is too coarse.' Peter spoke as pleasantly as he was able. 'Too heavy, and too square.'

'You, of course, could do much better.'

'That's not my meaning.'

'Although . . .' Fust's voice broke in, meditative and slightly probing. 'It might not be a bad idea. It might just—'

Peter, stunned, could only gape.

'A finer letter, as he says, might well improve it.' Fust fished out his spectacles and reached to scan the written missal.

'A whole new face – that takes six months – to draw and cut and cast?' The master barked a laugh. 'God's body, man. It's madness.'

Fust stroked his chin, and held his ground. 'Even so. It's worth a try.'

Konrad looked at Peter and traced a blade across his neck; Hans thrust his lips out, sighing. The master turned his back and walked a moment up and down, one hand inside his vest, the other torturing his beard. 'Two hands and in two sizes,' he muttered blackly, spun, and then returned. He brought his face so close that Peter saw the tiny red threads in his eyes. 'You're not the only one who's ever seen a missal, Master Scribe.'

'Let it be on my head,' said Fust in a loud voice. Unspoken, his real meaning: it is my money, sir, and I decide.

'So be it, then. The purse prevails. But let me warn you.' Gutenberg recoiled from him, still holding Peter in the tight grip of his eyes. 'The thing had better blind me with its brilliance.'

What kind of man was this? What kind of stunted and inhuman being, to whom Peter had been yoked? For all the years he worked with him, he tried to understand. The truth was that he never really knew. Peter came as close as anyone: he'd seen the master's childlike wonder and delight, and then the darkness that erupted, demons lurking just beneath the surface every time. He was a man who made the weather. He was as changeable and dramatic as the Rhineland sky: sunny and expansive at one moment, black and pelting hail the next.

It seemed to Peter then that each of them contained his separate humour. Gutenberg was choleric, all fire and passion.

Fust was sanguine, full of appetite. The Roman doctor Galen would have classified Peter himself as phlegmatic, as cool as air or water. The colours of their humours thus were black and red and white. But most of all it was the black of choler that prevailed.

That afternoon they were allowed to venture out. Hans had wangled it, somehow. If Gutenberg had had his way, they would have started on that missal then and there. Instead the master shut himself up in his study, and the crew received a sharp and sunny winter afternoon. They ambled to the Iron Market at the river's edge, where Konrad made a beeline for the locks. He needed something small, to fit a chest.

The Mainzers, when they saw them, eyed them with suspicion. The story had circulated that these strangers made some trinkets for the pilgrim trade, which almost certainly would cut into business. Peter's uncle had made clear that the goldsmiths' guild would tolerate this cockeyed workshop just so far. Peter wondered how long Fust and Gutenberg could keep up this pretence. At least the priests and scribes of Mainz were far too fine to venture down along the docks – but just in case, he kept his cap pulled down.

The market overflowed with every metal object men could fashion, laid out on cloth or spilled from baskets: buckles and rings and hooks, tin plates and pans and candlesticks, brass salvers shaped like fish. The locks were sent from Nuremberg, whose smiths were known for their precision and their patience. Konrad fingered every shape and size on offer. None could touch the Nurembergers for a lock, or cogs or wheels and balanced shafts that ran the vital works of scales and clocks. He demonstrated how the tumbler dropped to lift the barrel. 'As tough to crack as Keffer's balls.' The pressman laughed. The big smith grinned to hear his name. 'In point of fact.' He elbowed Peter, jerked his head towards the public baths.

'Another time,' Peter said, and pushed him playfully away. His head was ringing still with this fresh madness.

'You then,' Keffer said, and Konrad nodded, paying for and pocketing his lock. Hans made a face as they made off. 'One thing on his mind, that lad,' he said, watching as they shouldered through the crowd.

Hans and Peter moved on southward on the empty towpath. The city had been cut off for four whole months. The market boats had drastically reduced their traffic, waiting for the haul downriver in Cologne, then linking in a long towline that only stopped to switch the teams in Mainz. The wind was all that now alighted in that excommunicated place; Peter walked against it, the folly of the morning turning in his mind. Hans plodded at his side; he'd never broach the topic. They crossed the frozen rill that cut the city from the quays of Selenhofen, where a huge new ship was being built. Workers swarmed its frame. Peter's eyes rose above the busy scene and picked out the long row of roofs that was the Charterhouse, stretched like the beads of a great rosary along the bank. Inside each small peaked cell a monk sat writing, with his quire of parchment and his scripture and his quills.

'They're mad.' It burst out of him. 'Right off their heads, to think that we can do this.'

'Damn right.' Hans laughed. 'Else none of us would be here.'

'Ten thousand letters, Hans. It can't be done, not stroke by stroke.'

'You should have kept your trap shut, then.' Hans scanned the vacant shore, then squatted down and plucked a piece of reed. 'Eight months, I reckon, give or take.'

'Monstrous.' Peter looked downriver, far away.

'You, a man of doubt?'

'Completely.' He dropped his cloak and sat.

Hans was fishing in his teeth with the thin reed. His eyes held Peter's, weighing. 'But we can't use the one we've got.'

'I didn't mean—'

Hans flapped his hand. 'He doesn't give a damn how it is done, so long as it gets done.'

'He'll kill us all.'

'Well, I'm still standing,' Hans said, and stood, spat out the chewed stalk. He held a hand out and hauled Peter up.

'He doesn't have a clue.'

'That's where you're wrong.' Hans scratched his grizzled beard and looked across the river towards the distant fields. 'He knows damn well. He isn't going to get another chance.' He pursed his lips. 'He'll have to throw it in, if it don't work this time. And that would fair near kill him.'

'There's nothing that could kill that man.'

'You'd be surprised. We're not as young as we once were.' Hans pulled his cloak up higher on his neck. With his bare pate, his ring of hair, he might have been a barefoot friar. They walked on, came up to a rope that cordoned off the boat works.

'Quite a monster.' Hans whistled. 'Windows out of glass.'

Though raw and keeled onto its side, the ship recalled to Peter Mainz as she had been. The hull was that of any Overlander, lifting high above the water, flat of keel to skim the river's shifting sandbars. When it was sent downstream for painting, it would bear the Katzenelnbogen coat of arms – and quantities of tax-free fish and salt and wine the council had allowed, to sway the duke in their dispute with the archbishop.

'You people like 'em big,' Hans went on. 'Burgundy's not half so grand.'

Peter looked at him, surprised. 'The Katzenelnbogens hold the toll,' he answered. 'Downriver at Saint Goar.'

'Thieves. They'd melt the gilding off their fathers' coffins.'

Peter laughed. 'You've worked for nobles, then?'

'My old man's shop hung on the Strassburg bishop's orders.' Hans looked slyly at him. 'I've seen my share, believe me too, with Henne.' He screwed his eyes up. 'Nasty brutes, the lot. Always grinding at the prices, pitting brother against brother in the guild.' It was a speech, for Hans.

'I heard the master was a member there.'

Hans grinned. 'He couldn't carve to save his life. But he was damn sure tickled to be asked.' Hans turned, and as he did, whacked Peter on the back. 'If it makes you any gladder, he's as rude to all them high-and-mighties as he is to you.'

They walked back across the stream that cut the fishing village from the city proper. They'd almost reached the lower Rackgate when they heard the bell: a deep, commanding boom. The tower of St Martin's. Peter had not heard or felt that sound in years. The rumble of it tolled his very bones. Before they'd crossed the span and made their way inside, another bell rang, higher by an octave, and then a third: St Stephan's, St Quintin's. The voices of the churches opened one by one and swelled into a giddy chorus.

They made their way along the streets, filled suddenly with people rushing out. Strangers fell on strangers, hugging, laughing; Peter felt his own throat fill. The ban was lifted – there could be no doubt. The clamour of the bells drowned out all other sound. As Heilant had predicted, peace in time for Christmastide: Dietrich had released his fist. The crowd surged blindly, bearing them like sticks towards the marketplace and the cathedral. St Martin's doors were now flung wide. But at what price? Peter had the time to wonder, as the tide tossed them like dazed survivors at the Golden Mallet – where for once they entered undetected, raised their mugs, and drank to golden Mainz among their fellows.

Chapter 8

MAINZ

January — May 1451

He'd worked the calculus of duty in his head. Peter owed an alphabet of lead, no more. What they would do with this new letter mattered little to him as he pictured the great chancelleries in which he'd find a place. There was no further talk from Fust of marriage contracts; Peter guessed his father knew that he might bolt if pushed. Gutenberg meanwhile procured a missal book that he dismembered, fanning out the pages on his desk. Sacks of ore appeared, a bale of paper half as tall as Hans. Konrad hammered a new casting box, and Peter took a spot beneath the window frame and started tracing.

For all that he despised this art as crude, it was not in his nature to draw badly. The paper that he used was of pure linen, free of imperfections, to avoid the slightest wobble in the lines that he would transfer onto metal punches. The alphabet he planned must be as fine as any he had drawn, to sing the psalms and say the words of the apostles. He traced and retraced each line, swash, and spur, and spaced the letters widely on the large white sheet. Each time the bell struck one more hour he rose and stretched his arms and thawed his fingers at the forge. Hans, peering over his right shoulder, bellyached that all those fine

connecting lines would drive them blind. The master and his
father hovered too, until Peter brusquely said he couldn't concen-
trate with them both breathing down his neck.

It took him three full weeks to draw the letters to his satisfaction. He made them larger, blacker, tighter than the letters
of the grammar: written closely, they resembled a thick mat of
woven thorns. He could not do it any faster. He understood
by then that every single one would be the progenitor of all
the hundreds, even thousands, they would cast precisely in its
image. He drew full letters in two sizes, majuscules and minus-
cules, ligatures, abbreviations; each size required two hundred
different hunks of type. Hans and Keffer looked like cattle
stunned before the kill when they considered how long it would
take to carve and cast those alphabets.

'I'll pray for you,' said Peter with a little smile, touching one
stiff finger to the cap he wore to keep the hair out of his eyes.
When he was done, he left the finished sheets for Gutenberg
in a clean pile.

He didn't want to care, and yet he did. He came in the next
day both wary and expectant. The master was already sitting at
his desk.

'I might have known you'd bankrupt us,' he started. The
flame lit only half his face; he wore a pair of lenses on the bridge
of his long nose. 'You'd have us slave a year, I guess, to cut
these?' The words were as caustic as ever, yet there was something different in his tone. He lifted up one sheet and scrutinized
it, and turned to Peter standing there. Gutenberg's apprentice
saw the flicker of a smile. 'It's strong, though. Black. And still
with a slight feeling of the hand.'

'It is compressed, compared to many.'

'So then it saves on parchment.' The master grinned and
handed all the pages back.

Hans showed Peter how to forge the brass in rods they

clipped and hammered to a square-tipped shaft. They made hundreds of these golden wands, which they then carved. Peter watched the old smith hunker at the bench, the shaft clamped in a vice, a little square of paper with the first of all those letters in his hand. Hans let a drop of flax oil fall onto the paper, watched it go translucent as the ink began to shine, then flipped it. The letter was as perfectly reversed as if they viewed it in a mirror. He laid the letter on the metal tip and rubbed it softly with his finger: the inky shape lay on the brass now in reverse, and ready to be carved.

The goldsmith fingered through his chisels for a tiny blade no thicker than an awl. 'Pray for us,' he said, with a bare smile, and screwed a glass into his eye. It was an old, familiar sight: the craftsman bent, absorbed, his eyes and fingers joined in one exacting act, the world shrunk to a space no larger than his touch and breath.

When it was Peter's turn to try, he stretched his neck and arms and emptied out his mind. He grasped the chisel – like the quill, it was a pure extension of his hand. The metal peeled like shavings of cold butter from his blade. He tapped, and watched it flake, moved down a hair and tapped again and blew the shining shards away. Hans said that metal had a grain, like wood; you had to learn to know the way it gave. The letter was the simplest stroke, an *l*. Peter tapped and flaked and blew. Deeper, Hans said. Straighter. There. An hour, then two. And then the slanted cap atop the stroke, the angled basin of its heel. Hans handed him a brush, an even smaller awl. Peter felt a stinging in his eyes; he wiped the sweat off, bent back down.

Scribes often noted in the edges of their manuscripts the ways they suffered in the handiwork of God. A sharp complaint, secreted in a margin: *Thin ink, may night fall soon. I've finished now. For Christ's sake, bring me drink.* Writing caved the ribs and torqued the back and fogged the eyes. Once in Saint-Victor's library in Paris Peter had discovered a whole string of notes from the same scribe: *This parchment is certainly hairy*, he had carped, *this lamp gives a bad light*. And yet until he bent for hours above that shaft of metal, Peter never really understood his closing thought: *Just as the sailor yearns for port, the writer longs for the last line.*

At last he straightened, stretched his aching neck, and reached the finished punch towards Hans. The smith turned towards a candle, held the tip above the flame, rotating it until the whole was covered in a film of soot. 'Smoke proof,' he grunted, pressing it onto the paper. And then they saw where it was wrong, where right; they placed the punch back in the vice, and sliced minutely at it one more time.

The work of the apprentice is the taming of all impulse: in place of pride, humility; impatience mastered, then subdued. It took Peter back to his first weeks at the scriptorium, where Anselm started by removing feathers, vellum, leather pouches, ornament of every kind. He stripped the pupils down to one thin reed, a lump of lampblack, one plain sheet. To learn the silencing of will, of the murky self: to strip their bodies and their minds to the essential. Apprenticeship, he said, was patience, and a deep, abiding faith: again, again, and yet again, until the hand was firm, the soul scoured clean. For only then would they be purely Adam's flesh, a conduit, a channel.

Hans told him that he had 'the feel'. The way that he touched Peter's elbow, took his proofs out to the light, and traced his horny nails around each contour was a sign of his regard. He grumbled out of habit when the 'scribbler' wasn't satisfied. 'Feinschmeckery,' he'd mutter. Fussbudgetry. Yet Peter noticed how he started taking just that bit more care at his own carving, holding his own work to that same 'fancy' standard.

As fast as they were finished with each punch, the others took them to make moulds and started casting: not just Keffer and Konrad but the master as well. Through that dark Lenten season Gutenberg too rolled up his sleeves. It wasn't, Peter thought, that he was suddenly awash with fellow feeling. The truth was that the man could not sit still.

It weighed on Peter, nonetheless, the fact that the master hadn't even had the grace to compliment his draftsmanship. He said as much to Hans. The goldsmith looked into a middle distance. 'Never had to,' he answered with a crooked smile. 'Everybody comes to him regardless – like bees to nectar, trout to flies.' Gutenberg in Strassburg: those had been the times! Everybody wanted something from him, and he pulled them to him with his tinkering, his strange ideas, just like iron filings. Important people seemed to think he had the next big thing secreted in his sleeve. They damn near threw their money at him: there was a bishop's nephew and a paper miller, some patricians with large holdings, paying court. His first machine convinced them: a wheel for polishing that he had dreamed up to smooth those pilgrim's stones. They backed him handsomely when first he fit those stones into the frames that Hans had stamped to make the bloody mirrors.

'We had a good ride there, by God. We didn't hide away like here.' The master was admitted everywhere: not just into the noble houses but the craftsmen's lodges. He'd been respected and praised, much more than in the city of his birth. He didn't give a rat's ass for the Mainzers' clannishness, their snobbishness.

Which did make you wonder, Peter said, why he'd come back.

'Inheritance. This house.' Hans looked balefully at the bleak, soot-streaked walls of their confinement. 'His mother left it to him and to his late brother, Friele.' Besides, those foaming Armagnacs had Strassburg in their sights – it was a panic, Hans said, knowing that the mercenary army was a day or two away after having raped and pillaged half Alsace. The master paid his share to buttress the defences, but he didn't wait around. 'We hot-footed it, believe you me.' The old smith grinned. 'To him this house in Mainz was providence.'

Lent came late that year, halfway through March. It was a lucky thing, for otherwise the Main would have been frozen and the merchants forced to travel overland to Frankfurt for Lenten Fair. Fust sailed away, but Gutenberg remained, although they knew the Elders claimed the payments on their bonds two times a year, at autumn and at Lenten Fair. He must have sent a proxy, Peter thought, as he went to the Schreibhaus to see Petrus Heilant. The Elders still collected interest on the loans they'd made to Frankfurt, Speyer, Worms – though only half on every guilder that Mainz owed. This was the deal that Dietrich had exacted in exchange for lifting off the ban: he'd bailed the city out in part – and in return had kept immunity from tax.

The staleness of the air inside the clergy's meeting house disgusted Peter more and more. Or maybe it was just the act of begging that disturbed him every time he stooped to enter the low portal. Heilant was blandly reassuring that a break would come in time, but precious little seemed to come from this. In the depths of that cold penitential season, Peter felt the hope begin to leach out of his bones.

He told himself each letter punch was one more link he broke in the thick chain that anchored him to Mainz. He'd add one to the pile; another shattered link would drop. He'd asked for his own workshop key so he could work at night. If he could pick the pace up, he might finish by midsummer and be off.

One evening a few weeks after Easter he was working late, taking advantage of the light. Spring had come at last, and with it the sweet lengthening of days. The men had gone upstairs, the master back across the courtyard. Gutenberg appeared to find it unremarkable that Peter chose to work on his own time. He must have thought that his apprentice drove himself the way he did – or so his brief, distracted nods conveyed.

Peter lit two candles to chase any shadow from the metal in the vice. He lost himself in concentration. Some time later – one hour, two – he heard a door close, quick steps, then the workshop door heave open. The light had gone, he saw as he looked up. The master crossed towards the workbench and started rummaging among the tools. He took a blade and then came over to where Peter laboured.

'Night work.' He snorted. 'The guild would stop it, if they ever got their nose in.'

Peter nodded, looked back down.

'It isn't any of their bloody business.' The master's face was waxy in the dimness; he held a book clamped underneath one elbow.

'No.' Peter looked back up, surprised. Gutenberg had been a guildsman, ex officio; Hans had said so.

'Time and tide waiteth not.' The master stood there, lost in thought. And then he shook himself and lifted a finished punch that lay at Peter's elbow. 'What, six weeks? Thereabouts?'

The end at last was in their sight. Again Peter nodded.

'Ligatures tomorrow, then,' said Gutenberg, half to himself.

The main alphabets were done; the master had ordered Konrad to build trays to hold the letters, certain pockets made larger for the characters they'd need in great abundance. There was a rigour to that logic even Peter could admire. There were no rules when Gutenberg set out: he'd cobbled everything from what he knew of smithy, weavery, scriptorium. He'd had them knock together slanted racks to hold those letter cases, wooden trays to hold the finished lines and pages. It was the brilliance of that mind to see a thing – a person too – in pieces, Peter thought. Efficiency and speed, he always said: no step or motion should be wasted.

'Brack will have the text to set in a few days.' The master set the punch back down and fingered his long beard.

Peter stretched his aching hands. 'He knows how you will do it?'

'More or less.' The smile was sly.

'You must know him then, to trust him.'

'I know them all, to my everlasting sorrow.' Gutenberg smiled cagily. 'Far better, luckily, than they know me.'

'I understood that you had studied, too, in Erfurt.'

'An age ago.' He shrugged. 'Half the city did; the other half just wanted to be priests.'

Peter allowed himself a smile. 'I found the same among the scribes.'

'All angling for the teat.' Gutenberg made a face. 'Though there are some worth heeding.' He pulled out the book he was holding. 'This one knows ten times more of metal than the guild.'

Peter looked down at the curling hide.

'I thought you ought to read it.'

The inside leaves were soft as suede, and spattered from long use.

'*On Divers Arts.* By Theophilus. You only need book three.' Gutenberg leaned over him and started flipping through the pages. 'Everything I know I got from Hans – and this.'

Chapter heads flashed past: Workshop. Forge. Bellows. Chisels. Punches. Chalice-making. Soldering. Repoussé. Refining Copper, Silver, Brass. Strange lessons for a scribe. Peter murmured his thanks.

'I'll need it back.' The master turned. 'But you can copy out the pages for yourself.'

By Pentecost they'd cast enough of the new letters to begin to fit them into words. Afterwards it seemed to Peter that the timing was remarkable. The day before, the parishes had celebrated the arrival of the Holy Ghost, that rushing wind that swept on Christ's disciples, searing all their foreheads with bright flame. It would be blasphemy to think that what seized the scribe that day was any way akin. And yet, and yet . . . at twenty-five, he did feel grazed – by a brief spark, the most fleeting of breezes.

They'd had only their smoke proofs until then; they did not know how well the types would really print. It was the master who suggested that Peter take the new black ink and choose the lines to set and pull as a first proof. This ink was also Gutenberg's invention: darker than the plant-based ink used by scribes. He boiled linseed oil to varnish, added lampblack and a pinch of carbonate of lead. This made a sticky, tarlike paste that could be slathered on the letters and then smoothed to an even film.

It startled Peter, hearing the master say that he was owed the honour of composing those first lines. But then Gutenberg did understand paternity – the pride of bringing forth a thing entirely new. Peter tipped his cap to him by setting words from Theophilus, Benedictine craftsman:

Therefore, act now, prudent man, . . . by whose labour and zeal so many burnt offerings are being shown to God. Henceforth be fired with greater ingenuity: with all the striving of your mind hasten to complete whatever is still lacking in the house of the Lord.

Keffer showed him how to tie the lines into a block he called a *forme* and slide the whole thing on a tray. Peter carried the full slab aloft as though it were an offering, and set it gingerly upon the bed of Konrad's press. He took the leather balls that they had dubbed 'dog's tongues' in either fist and smeared each with the inky paste, then rolled them on the stone to spread the ink that he applied onto the type with care.

There was a fair amount of joshing as he laid a dampened paper on the glistening lines. It took a man, not a monk, a bull and not a saint, that sort of thing. 'Then lend a hand,' he said. One blond giant and one red put beefy mitts upon the bed and helped him push it underneath the hanging platen.

The lever he would pull alone. It almost was past Peter's strength, but in that instant he was lifted up in every sense that he could name. His feet came part-way off the floor, and the blood rushed to his neck as he heard first the weight drop, then a grinding sound as it made contact with the letters.

'Fiat imprimere!' the master cried, and they hauled back the bed. Peter opened up the wooden frame. Carefully he peeled off the sheet, as the others stepped back to a respectful distance.

A power surged out of those words, a strength that even Peter had not pictured. The ink was as black as heaven's vault, the letters sharp and gripping. They wove into a trellis just as Pliny said all lines must do, to hold the meaning of the text like wires among the vines. The Word is as a fruit, he thought; the vineyard of the text is thickly twined. He stared, transfixed. In their austerity and density, the letters made a page of extraordinary beauty. His letters – his! – the very lines he'd drawn and carved, now lay proudly, blackly, making words upon the page. He felt his insides quicken with the thrill of it – and then a kind of falling.

Gutenberg was fairly hopping just behind him. Peter felt his energy and eagerness, and from the corner of his eye he saw him reaching. Peter held the page out to him, his fingers grazing the deep bite the words had taken in it.

'By God!' The master's face was open, softened, every trace of sharpness gone. 'A scribe, my eye! A bloody carving genius, more like! From here on out you sculpt my types.'

That was the moment it all changed. Peter saw it clearly at the time. There are in every life some moments that stand out, as if embossed – moments when a man can sense the hand of God. That day, for the first time, the scribe asked – first in shock, then gradually with disbelief, and bashful, dread-filled pride – if what His servant Peter did there, in the Hof zum Gutenberg, might be in fact what He intended.

This was the spark, the breeze, that entered him – the understanding, too, that all the ways he knew were coming to an end. None of the arts he'd learned could remain unchanged. None of the ways of his fathers and their fathers, the familiar rhythms of their lives, would be the same. The genie was released from the bottle. *Ars impressoria*, known ever after as the *ars divin*. Peter watched the master take the sheet and hand it off to Hans, and heard his triumphant words: 'Fetch Fust.'

His fellows – Hans and Keffer and Konrad, bound now in wonder and in pride – were clustered close together with the master, staring down. Gutenberg looked up and smiled. 'By the will of the most Holy Father, we have been delivered,' he said, with a look no less amazed than that of his whole crew.

'Amen,' said Hans, and, turning towards the young apprentice, raised his hands and clapped.

Chapter 9

MAINZ

June — September 1451

Peter's father did not hide his satisfaction with the script, and by extension with the hand that moved his own dreams that much closer. The name days of his sons fell close together in late June – Johannes, John the Baptist, and then the feast day of Saint Peter. Little Hans, at one, could only gum his polished tusk, but Peter could read easily the message in the rosewood box Fust gave him. It had compartments lined in silk the exact length of quills. He had been hasty and too commandeering, Fust conceded as he placed it into Peter's hands. These metal types are born of writing: there will never be a time when hands are not our first, most sacred tools.

The knotted *fustus* of their house was inlaid on the top in repoussé of silver from the family shop. 'The race is not to the swift,' Peter answered, bowing. He had been hasty too. There were many ways to spread the light of learning, after all. Then there was peace and reconciliation and feasting in the Haus zur Rosau.

Almost a year had burned away since he'd been summoned back from Paris. In the workshop all the type was done, the preparations for the printing of the missal made. The text they were to set, however, had not yet arrived. The prior of St Jakob's begged their patience and their faith. July passed in stupefying heat, but still his text did not appear. The crew made grammars to bring in coin and pass the time. The master started sending Lorenz to the monastery on the hill to fetch the first few pages, but every time the servant brought back the same answer.

'Patience!' Gutenberg would snort. 'A vice and not a virtue in my book.'

On 6 August, the Feast of the Transfiguration, Peter caught a glimpse of Petrus Heilant, his old classmate, at the portal of St Martin's. He had not heard from him for quite some time, but neither had Peter sought him out. The farmers and the monks and sisters from the cloisters on the land had all arrived in carts and long processions, draining through the gates towards the market square. The feast was new, reminding all the faithful that they shared in Christ's divinity as it had been revealed upon the Mount. More like a chance to make another grab at the collection plate, his uncle Jakob had observed. The monks of St Viktor's stood sweating in the unforgiving sun. Heilant looked quite ill, all pink and twitching in his thick black habit. Peter caught his eye; the monk held up his hands and mimed them empty. It hit Peter then with certainty: whatever post there was to pluck, Heilant sure as Satan would have snatched it first. Peter smiled and turned away, humbled yet relieved by his own slipshod calculation.

And in the shop they kept on printing those sad grammars, cursing as the heat intensified. The parchment curled before they got it near the press; the ink just melted to a slop that left the letters thin and blotched. Konrad by then had gone back home to Strassburg, leaving Hans bereft. Ruppel, the new man who ran the press, was taciturn, which did not help. Keffer muttered curses when the master ordered them to work at odd, inhuman hours to beat the heat: before the dawn and through the night, eyes gritty and their weary bones begging for their beds.

All through August Gutenberg just stalked, twisting at that sorry rope he called a beard. If in the spring he had been civil, even friendly, now the crew were just as stupid as they'd been before: cock-ups and dogsbodies, laggards, useless whelps. The prior didn't fare much better. 'Light a fire beneath your bloody habit,' he would mutter as he reviewed the sketches and the calculations for the missal Peter had prepared.

His apprentice reckoned they'd spent more than half Fust's gold already. Four or five hundred guilders had gone out on paper, vellum, lampblack, resin, ores and wood and candles, not to mention food and housing for the men. Everything stood ready for St Jakob's missal: a hundred sets of royal sheets were trimmed, the letters made. The harvest moon rose and waxed and waned, but still they had received no text to set. Fust and Gutenberg vanished into the master's study with the ledger, emerging after sounds of argument with mouths turned down. 'Another month,' said Gutenberg; 'Not a day more,' growled Fust.

Out in the city there were signs of the great mustering to come. Mainz was next to be instructed in the pope's great mission of reform. His special envoy, Nicholas of Cusa, known as Cardinal Cusanus, had called a diocesan meeting to explain the edicts that the cardinals had passed in Basel. Even in the Hof zum Gutenberg they heard the rustle of the clergy coming. They swooped in like winged beetles, brown and black, the leaders of the seventeen thousand priests in the archdiocese – from Freiburg in the west to Thuringia and Franken in the east and south as far as Baden. At least the visit might shake loose the text from Prior Brack, Fust said. Gutenberg thought just the same: he seized a pen and wrote a note and sent Lorenz back up the hill. For hours he waited on his stool, his eyebrows twitching like a cat parked at a wainscot.

When his servant finally brought the monk's reply, the master seized the scroll and cracked the seal. His face alone destroyed all hope. He stormed away without a word; it fell to Fust to extract and then to share the truth.

Archbishop Dietrich had indeed endorsed the prior's version of the *liber ordinarius*. That draft in fact was long since done. But – here the *but* – apparently there was a second and competing text; there was dissension in the ranks over the prior's vision of reform. His Grace, the Cardinal, Cusanus, quite naturally would have to choose.

Fust looked hard across the crew towards his son. His rigid face spoke volumes. He'd trusted Gutenberg – they all had, to a man. For months the master had assured them that the text was coming; not once had the inventor shown the slightest doubt. 'Our missal,' he had even called it. And now they stood there, pants down, holding out their hands, as Dietrich covered his backside. Gutenberg himself had left the room.

Fust saddled up and left the first week of October, more to stop him ranting, Peter knew, than out of any appetite for sales. Eight hundred guilders he had riding on this missal, nearly all of it tied up in heaps of type and stacks of vellum. Peter meanwhile racked his brain. There had to be some way to move the project on. It came to him one morning as he stared up towards St Jakob's from the rampart wall. They'd have to set some of the missal text in their new type, to give the monks – perhaps Cusanus, too – a taste, he told the master. Just beg a page or two, that's all, and let them see how fine this thing will be. Gutenberg at first did not respond. His mood was fouler then than even Hans had seen it – until a few days later, when abruptly he told Peter to grab cloak and hat and climb the hill with him to see this Prior Brack.

The way to St Jakob's lay directly south. But they were forced to leave the city by crabbed routes around the markets and great houses. The master strode so quickly that Peter lost sight of him a time or two among the jostling passers-by and carts. He would have lost him utterly, had Gutenberg not stood a head above the rest, and worn a bright red fur-trimmed cap. He slowed as they came out behind St Martin's to the painting workshops and the street began to flow more broadly towards the gate. Some paces on, the hatters seized upon him, crying 'Fine sir! A muskrat, or an otter, that's a better top to wear in such a season!' He laughed and dodged and doffed his own. Peter pulled his stole up tight. They passed beneath the gate and crossed a stream that chattered blithely in the cold. They were the only ones that afternoon that went not into Mainz, but out.

Ahead and to the left the hayfields shimmered in a rime of frost, stitched into blackened rows. The sky was banded in more hues of grey than all their trays of metals. The highway bore away into the mist and split: one tongue licked left down to the river, another straight ahead, the right-hand fork up towards St Jakob's. Geese splashed along the inlet. But save for this, there reigned a stillness so complete that it erased all haste from Peter's soul. The master must have felt the same; he took a great breath in and turned and smiled.

They felt as much as saw the Jakobsberg, looming up above them just outside the city wall. The monastery on that sudden rise reared up so high and close that on a clear day all the monks might hail the deacon of St Stephan's in the city on the other side. Peter never had been up to the Benedictines' keep. Yet he knew like any son of Mainz that to the people of the city it had ever been a threat. The townsfolk rose each generation in revolt against the wealthy abbots and the Elders, burning and destroying in resentment and despair. And just as often did those heavy, jewelled hands swing, biting, back. The bloodshed soaked the marrow of each family, guildsman or patrician, poor or rich.

Gutenberg surveyed the vine-crabbed slope down to the trench cut just beneath the city wall. 'They'll never dig it deep enough. Nor lack for fools on either side.' He straightened, making for the fork and the steep uphill climb. 'You know who had it dug?' He glanced at Peter, a sly look in his eyes. 'My granddad's granddad – Wirich was his name. Common workingman of Mainz – you'd think at least the guilds would give me that.' He gave his barking laugh. 'My mother's blood flowed down from his – and cost me entry to the Mint. They drove the ingrate out, of course – although I left of my own free will.'

These grapevines once had been the abbey's, he went on as they toiled upwards. His ancestor had led the city charge that torched them all – St Jakob, St Albans, St Viktor – clawing back those vineyards for the city. An empty victory, of course, for Mainz had been required to pay the restitution. 'They pay it still,' he said, and shook his head.

They stopped and stood to catch their breaths before a ramp that led to a great gate. Peter looked across and down, astounded; he'd never seen the city from this high. Everything was tiny: the threadlike rigging of the ships, the toylike wagons, and the people, tiny specks on lanes like veins.

'No wonder that they see us all as pawns.' He didn't realize, at first, that he had murmured this aloud.

The master stretched out one arm towards the hillock near the river's edge. 'Though on my father's side, a cousin ran the school at St Viktor's.' He raised one eyebrow. 'I guess that makes us brothers of a kind.' It surprised Peter, Gutenberg recalling his apprentice's brief tenure in that order. The master flashed a grin. 'I count on that good brotherhood to pray for my black soul when it is time.'

He cinched his belt and squared his cloak. He stood erect,

pitched forwards on his toes, as if he steered a moving boat. And for the first time Peter saw him, really saw him: the way he straddled those two warring worlds, beholden to no group – no clan, no guild, no class, nor, in God's truth, to any other man. He stood outside, alone, a solitary soul.

They were expected. The gate swung open with a shudder, and they stepped inside. Peter had expected something grand, but when they entered that wide courtyard he stopped short, amazed.

The monastery was an empty shell, a propped-up and half-built facade. The building right before them was the only one intact; off to the left the abbey church, which should have been its jewel, was only half constructed. It spanned the hilltop like the long stroke of a U, joining to the central building. Its walls were newish, tall, with space for windows, but the nave stood open to the sky. Beneath his breath the master said, 'It used to look much worse.' Across the courtyard there were stables, storerooms, a granary that in that season overflowed with hops; a well, a muddy pool, and several wagons. And that was it: no rows of barrel-chested peasants, not a single fatted friar, no sense of busy, serene plenty. The Benedictine abbey of St Jakob's, it was clear, had fallen on hard times.

The prior received them in the sacristy – at least the office seemed to serve that function. There were holy vessels, vestments on a shelf. A case of books, as well, in that large room, which looked out on the river from the second floor. Heinrich Brack was older than Peter had imagined: tall and stooped, with hair like iron filings and great pouches underneath his small, dark eyes. He made a jangling as he rose and clamped a hand on his hip to still the ring of keys.

'Dear friend.' He clasped the master's hand. 'I thank the Lord to see you well.'

'My health, sir, lies I think more in your hands.'

Peter caught the faintest ghost of a smile. The master introduced him as his scribe. The prior offered wine.

'One of my greater victories,' Brack said, his hands held deep within his great black habit. 'I managed to hold on to most of the harvest this year.'

Brack had come to Mainz from Bursfeld: that was all Peter knew. The reforming wing had sent him to root out monks who siphoned off donations to the common good, restore the common life, the strict ascetic rule. St Jakob's abbot, one von Bubenheim, did not appear to have survived the purge. Yet even so it did not look as if Heinrich Brack had made much progress. Peter's heart had sunk as soon as he set eyes upon the prior's shelves. He'd pictured more and finer books, codices blind-stamped and stacked in gracious rows, the way they'd been at Saint-Victor. These were dog-eared, though, and scattered in haphazard piles. The prior saw him looking, and he smiled.

'There's not much here, alas, to tempt a scribe. Though I have done my best to supplement the manuscripts I found.' A novice tiptoed in and poured the wine. 'I had to call for many more,' the prior said, 'to help me with my work.'

'Ah yes,' the master said. 'Your work.'

Brack wiped his cheeks with both his hands, as if to rid them of a weariness. He left them folded just beneath his nose. 'It has not gone as I foresaw.' In his eyes, a flash of anger, swiftly mastered. 'The cardinal is much beseeched.'

'How soon will he decide?'

Brack sighed. 'I wish that I could tell you.' He rose and paced. His habit swung around him as he walked; his voice was thin and hard. 'The truth is, many lack the stomach for a real reform.' The master waited, crouched upon the edge of his hard chair. 'My text is written, and it was approved. Or so I was led to believe.'

'Our Peter here is anxious to begin,' said Gutenberg. 'We

hoped you'd part with a few pages – something to convince them, made with our new script.'

Brack looked sharply at the brother who stood sentry, made a sign. Without a word the novice turned and left, pulling tight the door.

'There's nothing that would please me more. But it would not be . . . politic for excerpts to appear just now.'

'My shop is hardly public.' The master's voice was tight. 'And no one can imagine how it looks until they see with their own eyes.'

Had Rosenberg told Brack exactly how the master planned to make those books? Had he not guessed, at least, that he would not just send the text to monks for copying, as he had always done before? Peter did not know. Gutenberg had given him permission, though, to set a sample – the Our Father – in their new, amazing type. He bent to take it from his pouch, but Prior Brack restrained him with a lifted hand.

'The moment will come. It must. There is no question that we will prevail.' His voice was soft, but had a cutting edge. 'There is no room for failure. Reform is all that can save the church now from herself.' He looked at both of them, his dark eyes sober. 'The voices of dissent grow ever louder, and with cause. Cusanus is quite mindful.'

On one side, Peter thought, the fattened forces of the status quo, chief among them Archbishop Dietrich – and on the other, the gathering momentum for reform led by Cusanus, Pope Nicholas V's avenging angel.

'Why, then?' Gutenberg pitched forwards. 'Why can't he just approve it?'

Slowly Brack sat down. 'You know as well as I do, Meister, our keen interest in your technique.' So he did know, thought Peter. The master straightened, lifted by a sense of pride and purpose. Peter felt a stirring in his heart of hope, faint but unmistakable. This Brack, this Cardinal Cusanus: in the whole world they could not ask for greater champions. There was no match more perfect, suddenly the young scribe saw: the Divine Office of the Mass, rewritten for a cleansed and reborn church, sown wider through this miracle of printing that God in His great wisdom had bestowed on Mainz.

'That is good news,' the master drily said. 'Even better would be the order to proceed.'

'What I say cannot go past these walls.' The prior waited for their nods. 'There are, as I said, some difficulties. The archbishop has approved my text. But it requires adoption by the Bursfeld conference.' He pursed his lips. 'Not all my brethren apparently concur. A faction has proposed a rival text, which hardly merits to be called reformed.'

Gutenberg did not move a muscle. 'When,' he said, 'will they decide?'

The prior's eyes were on the farthest wall. 'The great battles are eternal,' he murmured, as if speaking to some unseen congregation. 'And all foretold. Did not God send His own son to sweep the moneylenders from the Temple?' He sighed then, and returned to them. 'You know the church. Everything takes time. Experts must be consulted, opinions issued, reports made. Then there is opportunity for rebuttal.'

'I know the ways of the Holy See.' There was a glitter in the master's eye. 'To my misfortune.'

'I have every faith I will prevail. But I can see too that for you this delay is not desirable.'

There was a long and awkward silence. Gutenberg was folded deep into himself. Brack, too, lapsed back into his own thoughts. There seemed no point, and yet – Peter reached and pulled the proof out of his bag. He smoothed the lines he'd sketched and he and Hans had carved and cast and proofed.

Brack lifted it, and held it to the light. 'Fantastic,' he murmured, eyebrows lifted into sharp, dark arches.

'Keep it,' said the master as they rose to go. 'For all the good that it will do me.'

'Not desirable! Witless cowl.' They were barely out the gate before his dam gave way. '*Not desirable!* Bloody monks. Mooning away in their crumbling halls.' He went on in this vein, wrapped moodily in his cloak, loosing a string of invective that subsided only slowly as they wound their way back down.

The sun was sinking behind them, above the abbey's shell. The dying rays bathed their backs and the hillside and the river in a reddish glow. Peter saw his master age right there before him: saw his skin slacken, his keen eyes grow rusty and dull. It might have been no more than a trick of the light, but still it moved him. He begged him not to waste his mind with worry.

'It is not I who waste my mind, but those too blind to see.' Gutenberg's voice was low and bitter.

'Have faith. We will prevail.'

'Faith! I've had this faith my whole life long. You see where it has brought me.' Gutenberg looked back up at the Jakobsberg. 'Tight-mouthed scribbler never even breathed a word.'

Peter put a hand out on his shoulder and tried to make things light. 'What else did you expect from a monk?'

'Vow of bloody silence.' The master growled it, but at least he laughed.

They came to a turning where orchards rose off to the right and the road to the city turned the other way. Without warning the master scrambled up the bank among the trees. 'Rest for the wicked,' he said, and made as if to sit. He stumbled; Peter took his arm and loosed his cloak for him to sit on. Gutenberg batted it away. 'Dirt is good enough for me.'

Peter felt he saw a man, then, stripped to his very essence: his gift, his greatness, offered in full knowledge of its value, and rebuffed. Johann Gutenberg stared out across the valley of the Rhine, his face drawn, seeing nothing.

'It's but a moment's setback,' Peter said. 'Your partner won't give up so easily.'

'I've had many partners, and just as many setbacks.' He gave Peter a queer, almost pitying smile. 'I wouldn't stand here begging, would I, had I ever met with great success?'

'I thought that was your meaning. When you spoke of the Holy See.'

The master's eyes went back across the river. 'They burned me once before with those damn mirrors.' Peter nodded. 'We sank a fortune in that pilgrimage to Aachen. Once every seven years.' Gutenberg ran a hand across his face. 'But Rome, it seems, can only count to three.' He looked back at Peter. 'We made thousands of the things. Then they postponed it – due to plague, they claimed. I got out with a lawsuit and my shirt; I guess the others sold the rest. Only through the grace of God was I not ruined.'

The mass movements of pilgrims, like the great Crusades, ebbed and flowed on some vast tide – as if their destinies were charted by caprice as much as by all-knowing God. And yet, thought Peter, there had been design. Had not that failure served to turn the master to this new, more fruitful work?

'It was then you started on your letters.'

'Though that, too, was a fair disaster at the start.'

Peter had thought so often of that single question – of the one, transforming moment in the master's life – in the long hours spent carving at his stool. He'd never have a better chance. 'What impulse was it,' he asked quietly, 'that steered your hand?'

The master's hand rose absently; he pulled his lips between his finger and his thumb. 'I was a young man,' he said finally.

'Not so different from you. Thrown out of my own city, forced to find my way.' His eyes closed briefly, and he said: 'It came to me while I was walking in the orchard at St Arbogast's. I was obsessed, you see, with the idea of making the many from the one.'

His eyes flew open. 'Did He not say: "Be fruitful and multiply"?' His smile was slightly wistful. 'I was walking in the garden, thinking about Eden. I dreamed those years of making things that could be endlessly repeated: over and over the same. I was barred by my mother's blood from striking coins as a Companion of the Mint – yet still I must have heard those mallets striking in my mind.

'I knew then that was how I'd make my mark.' He looked keenly at Peter, who nodded, trying not to break the spell. Never had the master spoken so freely or so personally to him. 'There was the matter of money too. I had barely a pot to piss in, for all my rank.' His smile was wry, and more in keeping with his customary self.

He leaned towards Peter and dropped his voice, though there was no one near for leagues around. 'After the mirrors I knew it would have to be something every soul would need. Nothing precious – just something necessary, and reasonably cheap. I thought of all manner of things – prayers stamped in tin, hand-bells ringed in verses. Ask Hans. We spent hours spinning every idiotic fancy. But all depended somehow on the church – and that, in my mood then, was sheer anathema.' He raised an eyebrow, added drily: 'Would I had kept to that belief.

'That's when I hit on the Donatus. I kept asking myself: What did we all have to have, or do? What needs has any man, besides those needs we share with beasts? And then I knew: he has to read. All lettered men had learned that text. I saw it clearly, in an instant: I would make that grammar, in the thousands, for the masses.'

Peter felt a twinge of disappointment. What had he hoped? That God himself had touched his hand? In truth, he had.

'The Lord works in strange ways.' Gutenberg was staring at him. 'I've known for decades that my life would never be like other men's.' In those dark and kindling eyes Peter saw an unaccustomed depth of human feeling and compassion. 'And yet it is a burden too – this strange compulsion. As I think you know.'

He continued to regard Peter steadily, as if he saw in him some thing that Peter could not see himself. He felt a heat suffuse his cheeks. That was the moment that the master chose to go. He gathered himself; for once he let his apprentice help him to his feet.

'When you get to my age, Peter,' he said as they turned towards Mainz, 'you do begin to wonder. If it really is a gift from God – and not a curse sent up from hell.'

Chapter 10

MAINZ

October — December 1451

It augured well that Cardinal Cusanus rode into Mainz upon a donkey. At least the master said so. The great reformer entered every city on his journey just as Christ had done, on a humble ass, dressed in a plain red habit: the symbolism was not lost upon the waiting crowd. The workshop crew lay down their tools and went to watch. A human crush received the delegation, three souls deep, with shining faces and waving arms. The cardinal had come, to free them from corruption and venality, tossing his blessings not in Latin but in their native tongue. For Nicholas of Cusa, born plain Nikolaus von Kues, was one of theirs: a Rhinelander, stern and upright.

The clergy stood in dark and splendid rows along the cloisters of Archbishop Dietrich's Little Court, fur-collared, hung with crimson stoles, the autumn sunlight winking from their jewels. Peter spied Petrus Heilant jammed among the canon regulars of St Viktor's. There was a grim set to the scribe's slack jowls and to the jaws of all his fellows, at the thought that they might lose all they had managed to obtain. Well then, thought Peter, smiling to himself: let the bloodletting start.

It all came down to money, as Jakob and Johann Fust always

said. More trade was done inside the church than at the Frankfurt fair. How loudly all those clergymen proclaimed their poverty, his father said, bitterly complaining of extortion at the hands of Rome. Fust's uncles, in their pulpits, screeched in that same choir. And yet the working folk knew otherwise: the world was eaten from within, the abbeys stripped by noble monks and nuns who clawed the riches to themselves, the city clergy fat and bold, resisting tithes to Rome, then issuing indulgences and pocketing the proceeds. Nicolas the Fifth had sent his envoy to root out that rot and curb their greed.

Archbishop Dietrich had not deigned to show his face. It sickened Peter. How few of them were humble and devoted to the Word. He searched among the crowd for Prior Brack, but could not see him. The Benedictine seemed an ascetic man, unmoved by worldly pomp and power. Scoured by that same dry wind that had cleansed Saint Benedict, the founder of their order, whom God a thousand years before had ordered to preserve His Word. It was this same wind Peter felt, with growing strength, guiding his hand. He watched the bright red beam of Cardinal Cusanus move with purpose through the throng and knew there'd never be a place for him among those grasping prelates, in their cloisters and their chancelleries, estranged from God's true flock.

The people stretched their arms and clamoured. Gutenberg turned towards him, raised his hands, and mimed a prayer. Deliver us, approve the book – and while you're at it, sweep the stables clean. Only later did they realize that in the sweeping and the breaking that Cusanus undertook, the minor battle of St Jakob's missal was the last thing on his mind.

Three weeks remained until the formal meeting of the synod. The cardinal took residence at Guldenshaff's, around the corner from the workshop, passing his days down at the Charterhouse in writing and in meditation. Peter found it an exquisite torture knowing that he breathed that self-same air and walked those self-same streets: as great a star as Germany had given to the world, a common man who'd risen to the pope's right hand.

Cusanus was a scholar, though a boatwright's son from Kues on the Mosel. He saw the Lord's hand in all matters, large and small: the movements of the stars, the workings of the earth, even the properties of elements, including metals. Peter found himself rereading all his writings. Cusanus preached each man's capacity to feel God's touch, regardless of his birth, his wealth, even his creed. Man was himself a pilgrim mirror, catching and reflecting back the rays of God's own essence. He could not know, of course, his own Creator, as an owl could never look into the sun. Yet he alone received the gift to fashion his own world with mind and hand – and with that gift he might approach that divine spark through small creations of his own.

Peter knew this spark – he'd felt it in the making of his metal letters. But such ideas angered the established clergy, convinced that they were God's exclusive representatives on earth.

Most mornings through those long, excruciating weeks he waited, poised in the small doorway that gave out onto the Cobbler's Lane, hoping for a glimpse of that tall crimson figure dashing past. Of all the men who walked the earth, it seemed to Peter, Nicholas Cusanus would perceive their letters for the miracle they were. Cusanus laid great stress on learning, and predicted ever-swelling shelves of books – as if he knew what God had granted Gutenberg. Peter kept a printed sheet of the Our Father rolled up in a pocket, praying for a sign that he should show it. But no sign came: he could not break his vow of silence.

They all felt great relief when finally the synod started. Master Gutenberg attended daily, as if going to some cheap entertainment. Each evening he regaled them with the scene. Dietrich in his golden robes 'like Pharaoh' had appeared at last, surrounded by his staff; across from him 'your cardinal,' the master cracked at Peter, 'encircled by his band of crows.' The archbishop was livid from the start, but he couldn't let it show. King Friedrich, 'that Hapsburg whelp that Dietrich put upon the throne', had ordered the archbishop to Ferrara for his coronation as the kaiser in that very week. But Dietrich wasn't leaving the archbishopric of Mainz, not while that upstart cardinal swept through with sharpened knife. The master laughed again. The proclamation of the orders for reform took up the whole first day, and chilled and darkened the archbishop's people like a sudden, brutal downpour.

The master kept his finger on the pulse of it, and on the margins tried to wheedle those of rank to speed the cardinal's decision on their missal. The rest of that long meeting, though, was much too tiresome for words. There was haggling over tithes and taxes, who got which commission or the naming rights for vacant parishes, a grim and bloody battle over who could issue letters of indulgence. Cusanus took this latter deadly seriously, and accused the bishops of a tawdry traffic in redemption that besmirched the pope. A letter of indulgence was a sacred grant made by His Holiness, and its integrity must be respected. He calumnied them as well for trafficking in relics, and for promulgating more new holy days that only meant more offerings in their own salvers. Only when the session dealt with blood and women did things liven up, the master said, grinning. There'd be no rites around some sainted smear that just as easily could be a gutted goat – 'or even, God forbid, the mess of Eve.

'You ought to see the way they clutch themselves, those monks, to hear their concubinage condemned,' he added, chortling. 'It seems they take their members for their vows, and go so far as to propitiate them in their abbeys!'

And then as loudly as it started, it was over. The clergy beat

their great black wings and raised the dust with their departure
– just like the merchants at the Frankfurt fair, leaving nothing
but their rubbish and soiled sheets. By then it was December.
Cardinal Cusanus left their city on the seventh day of that last
month in the year of our Lord 1451, bound for parleys between
England, France and Luxembourg – the matter of the missal of
St Jakob's clearly unimportant in those state affairs.

The days were at their darkest of the year. Johann Fust wore
that same darkness on his brow. They had been commissioned
to produce a book that clearly would not be forthcoming.
Everything he had invested was tied up in useless piles of paper,
wood, and metal. Halfway through the month, he called
Gutenberg and Peter to decide what they should do.

Fust's back was to the fire. His arms were crossed and his
head hung heavy to one side. Gutenberg sat slumped on the
wood settle, face in shadow, with Peter between them at the
battered table. The type was made. The crew was trained. They
were like actors in a passion play, just waiting for the tarp to
rise. For a very long time there was no sound beyond the
popping of the flames. Down the street at the great houses,
merriments abounded: madrigals and jugglers and feasts. Yet in
the Hof zum Gutenberg all was sombre and still.

The master stirred first, speaking as if continuing a conversation begun some time before. 'But to proceed would be folly.'

'As it was folly to trust a text that was not final.'

Johann Fust breathed heavily and settled in a chair.
Disappointment etched the corners of his mouth. He had
believed – had relied heavily – on the judgement of Johann
Gutenberg. 'Is there no way,' he asked, 'to gauge Cusanus's
interest?'

'His interest is the same as ours. At least, I thought our work
could serve his ends.'

Gutenberg sat caved in, hardly moving. To Peter he looked

just as he had looked up on the mount below the Jakobsberg, a man who turned in ever-tighter circles, proffering a gift that others spurned. The master roused himself and started speaking bitterly. 'Apparently he's influenced by Hagen.' Fust frowned. 'The leader of their bloody congregation. They think that Prior Brack has gone too far.'

'You never said a word about another version.' The tone of Fust's voice was accusing.

'How in the hell was I to know?' The master scowled, and curled more deeply in himself.

'Cusanus will support that text, then, and not ours.'

'No doubt.'

They lapsed back into silence.

'No point in trying to print the other, I suppose,' said Fust.

'Forget the cursed missal.' The master's growl was almost animal.

If Brack's text wasn't chosen, Peter thought, the monks would never know how they had planned to make it. Those who prevailed would copy out the winning text by hand, as they had done for centuries before. And in the Hof zum Gutenberg the three of them would still be sitting looking at each other as they sat here now – the money sunk into ten thousand hunks of lead for which they had no use, no project.

'Is there not . . .' Fust broke off and raised his eyes towards the heavens. 'Did the cardinal not say he wanted something else? A psalter, maybe, or a breviary?'

Gutenberg looked up then too, as if the answer were inscribed in the thick beams. The Bursfeld Benedictines had petitioned Rome for years for the permission to enact reforms. He'd told the whole crew so when he'd proposed that missal, months before.

'The standard texts,' he said. 'To wipe out variation, incorrect interpretation.'

'There must be something else, then, we can standardize.'

The fire sputtered as they strained their minds.

'They're meant to unify all practices,' the master said.

'Each mired in some arcane dispute.'

The master sighed and nodded. He hauled himself up to his feet and leaned against the chimney, staring into the fire. 'It has to be something they can't claim. Like the Donatus. Something in the domain of the public, not the church.'

Fust stroked his chin. The walls pulled in, and it seemed hotter as they bent their minds in thought – as if they stoked them, as a furnace sucks the air in to intensify the flames. 'Something over which no church or prince can exercise control.' Peter's father spoke in a low and meditative voice. 'What else did he tell them to review?'

Johann Fust asked it; Johann Gutenberg replied.

'The Holy Gospels.'

They stared at one another in shocked silence.

'Each abbot was to do his best to get a copy of the Holy Book, as free from error as the hand of man can make it.'

And still they only looked at one another. Gutenberg for once was shorn of words.

'It would not just be used by those two dioceses,' his father said.

'But the whole Latin world.' The master closed his mouth and folded his long hands beneath his nose. 'A massive market.'

'The Bible,' Fust echoed, thunderstruck. A flock of hopes and fears went spinning through each heart.

The master's eyes had kindled into blazing light. 'Undoubtedly they think they own it. But it springs from a higher source.'

Amazement filled them then – and yet at the same time an utter calm. Peter rose, his mouth half open. He could feel, quite instantly, the way it fell upon them like a blessing – so purely, in so straight and bright a beam, that each could only cross himself, and bow his head and offer up his thanks to God.

In principio creavit Deus caelum et terram.

These were the words that brought a new world into being.

Peter set them flush against a nothingness; hard against a non-existent margin he arranged them, floating like the world itself in the great void.

In the beginning God created heaven, and earth.

If the pope, the cardinal, the prior, could not give Gutenberg a text to print, then they would choose and print their own.

This, then, was their true beginning: bitter winter, creeping blue-toed to the ashes, blowing heat out of the humped-up coals. Peter set those first words purely for himself, in the frozen heart of the year when the reaper stalks, culling the weak and sick.

He hung them like a lodestar just above the forge, to remind them of the spark that springs from the Creator, running kindling down the ages straight to us. He set that sentence flush against His boundless grace and inked it with the black of space. And then he pressed its darkened lips on skin and hung it just above his eyes, and knew that this, too, was a kind of genesis.

EXODUS

EXODUS

Chapter 1

CALCULATION

February 1452

T he picture Peter carries in his head is that of Moses, dark hair streaming as he parts the waters, urging on the tribes. Gutenberg resembled him remarkably that hopeful spring. The master stood apart, his arms outstretched, scooping towards them every kind of good this monumental Bible would require. Peter had to laugh at the way he windmilled his long arms, directing the whole stream into the chute that fed the workshop. 'You look just like an abbot at his busy hive.'

'You could do worse than watch Cistercians.' Gutenberg pulled at his beard and smiled.

There was no question of remaining in the Hof zum Gutenberg. They grasped the magnitude this time. Conservatively reckoning, the Bible ran a thousand pages, if not more – five times as long as their aborted missal, forty times the size of the Donatus. That Fust and Gutenberg even entertained the thought revealed how much their backs were to the wall.

They were inspired, enraptured certainly – convinced of their invincibility, thought Peter afterwards. This was pure Gutenberg, of course. But on the other hand they didn't have much choice. The Bible was the only book they could hope to sell in quantity that did not need approval from the church, so long as they adhered to the accepted version. Yet from the start it was a risk in every way – not least the certainty that Dietrich would look askance at laymen operating outside his control. If any of the clergy were to learn of it, they had no doubt Dietrich would swoop in and shut them down.

Their crew then numbered only four – Peter, Hans, Keffer, and Ruppel – and yet the premises the partners looked at were all cavernous and freezing: a granary, more stables, sculleries, the ground floor of a house in town. They settled on the last, a massive dwelling girded by a thick high wall a street away along the Cobblers' Lane. The press would have to stay behind: it was impossible, the master said, to take it all apart and lug it piece by piece along the street. There was no darkness deep enough to trust, no way to stop prying ears and eyes.

'Once burned, twice shy.' He winked at Hans. 'The last time I was fool enough to let my tools out of my sight, we came much closer than a Christian should to robbing graves.' Peter glanced up, amazed. What darkness did he hide? The apprentice tucked that scrap away and vowed to worm it out of Hans.

They left the wood press standing where it was and moved the rest one moonless night across the churchyard of St Christopher's, through a gate left almost imperceptibly ajar. The master's pastor, clearly, was informed. From that black chink between two walls it was no more than a cat's spring across the street that climbed to St Quintin's, into a gloomy courtyard, then to the low door of the Hof zum Humbrecht, its upper stories disappearing in the blackness of the night.

Four steps dropped to the battered earth of a ground floor. Joists the width and girth of a small horse held up the cobwebbed rafters stretching deep into the subfloor of the house. The clay gave off a smell of roots and piss and rats. Chest by bench by bucket, tray by case, they hauled the workshop in. They didn't smuggle only casting boxes, inks and ores and heavy crates of metal type. They had a giant bellows, too, rigged to a treadle, which any fool would know was meant to fan a forge.

Hans and Keffer fit the forge pipe in the chimney stones; Peter and big Ruppel set two casting stations up, and pried the shutters open to scour out the stench. The place was huge and had a space for every need: the longer, narrow halls for drying; the cavern with the forge where they would cast and run the press; a separate room where they could sit and put their letters into lines. The shapes below were echoes of the rooms in which the men would live just overhead. The master sent for Konrad, back in Strassburg, to build a new press; he would not hire some local cretin who might blab. While waiting they removed the walls that separated room from room in that dim underworld. When it was done, no corner remained safe from his keen eyes, the ceiling held by a stripped forest of dark beams. 'The key is speed,' the master said, 'efficiency, by God. No wasted step or motion.' It seemed to Peter as he watched him pacing, barking orders left and right, that Gutenberg saw everything from a great height, his raptor eyes pinned to the slightest movement on the ground.

He sent across the city, then the river and the forests and the mountains, for materials. Paper from a mill in Piedmont, vellum out of Swabia, to supplement the stack they had. Ruppel went with him to the Wood Gate to inspect the hardwoods: maple and beech for benches, cases, tables. He commanded coal and candles, ores and oxides. He was a muleteer, he cracked, a blooming drover. Whipcracker, jack of all trades: polisher of stones, mixer of metal, deviser of devices, maker of machines.

Peter pitched in with his hammer like the rest. Gone was the little brownish lump from writing on his middle finger and the trace of burn on his left hand. He built the letter cases at a slant, then hefted his own letters, thick and heavy as old bones, and laid them in each wooden pocket. Each evening he would stand a moment looking at this massive thing take shape. The naked beams, the half-wrought shop, loomed like the outlines of strange buildings to his eye: half memory-palace, half the vision of God's City that Saint Augustine described.

The partners worked together in those months as they had never done before, and never would again. In the cave of Peter's recollection he and Gutenberg and Fust are figures by a constant fire, stooped and sketching, talking and gesticulating at all hours. What had been left of Fust's eight hundred guilders quickly disappeared into the workshop's maw; they would need more, much more. They'd make at least a hundred copies of the book; whatever they could get as a deposit from each buyer would bring something in, but even so they wouldn't see real revenue for several years. They came to a new business understanding, based not on faith but more on risk and its reward – and most of all on cunning. Neither partner harboured much illusion after all that wasted time; each knew precisely where the other stood. It was the firmest ground on which to strike a deal, Fust told his son: either both would win together, or else both would lose.

A new contract was drawn up, witnessed by the pastor of St Christopher's, one Heinrich Günther. It did not nullify their first deal of two years before, but simply altered its conditions. Johann Gutenberg still brought the know-how; Johann Fust still brought the gold, and held the workshop as collateral. Except that now new capital was to be raised, a second round, to get this fledgling business off the ground.

Peter's father too invoked the old adage: once burned, twice shy. Why should he bear all of the risk while Gutenberg reaped the reward? No longer would he simply play the part of banker. He took an equal share in this, their common and uncommon venture. Fust pledged eight hundred guilders more, and they agreed to split, after expenses, the profits that accrued from what they called, a bit obscurely, to foil spies, *das Werk der Bücher*. The work of the books.

They'd rented the Hof zum Humbrecht from a goldsmith who had moved to Frankfurt. But he still had relations, looping strands of kin all over Mainz. The city was a web of eyes and ears, not just the metalworkers but the butchers, bakers, saddlers, and sawyers, and the keepers of the taverns serving members of those four-and-thirty guilds. Prayer alone would not keep their secret safe.

It was the third time in the master's life he'd had to hide the work he did behind a smokescreen. In Strassburg he had hid away in an outlying farm, and he had done the same in 1448, when he returned to Mainz. Nobody even guessed for months that he was back, so well dug in was he among the fields by St Viktor's. But this time it was different, he said. They had to hide there in plain sight.

He brought the metal dies out to where Peter and his father stood, surveying the new press. 'You'd better tell the guild,' he said to Fust, 'that your new forge is set on making mirrors.' He wiped the stamps with a clean rag and glanced at Hans and grinned.

'Mirrors,' Fust said, slow to comprehend.

'Pilgrim mirrors. Hundreds of them, thousands.'

These were to cover up the purpose of the lead and tin, the bismuth and antimony, that entered through the cellar door. The Humbrechthof was flanked on one side by a shoemaker whose shingle hung just at the angle of the Quintinstrasse and the Cobblers' Lane, and on the other by a house whose sole inhabitant was one old man whose relatives just waited for his death to pounce. For all the time they laboured there, the printers came and went like rats along the alley behind the row of houses that ended in a cul-de-sac not fifty paces from the market square.

'The tinsmiths will cry foul,' said Peter.

'Not if you have a word with your upstanding brother.' Gutenberg looked hard at Fust. The merchant pursed his lips, eyes flicking back and forth between his partner and the dies.

'Two guilds,' he said. 'The smiths and then the gold- and silversmiths, both wanting dues.'

The master raised his outspread hands, as if to ask if they had any choice. He looked acerbically at Fust. 'You know as well as I that even silence has a price.'

To that almighty Book each man brought his specific knowledge, which he tipped into creation's forge. If Gutenberg could grasp and shape the larger whole, then Peter and his father brought more focused skills. Which mines were best for tin and lead, and at what price, which farm the cleanest linseed, which buyers might take paper, and which vellum: all this Fust could provide. Which version of the text to use, which form and shape upon the page: to Peter's great amazement, Gutenberg deferred to his own expertise in this. And it was that confidence, that unexpected faith in his own skill, that finally brought him back into himself. This was Peter's place, his path: to hold these alabaster sheets once more between his hands and make of them a meaning.

The Bible had to be a lectern book, of course: large enough for monks to read in the refectory, yet still austere and within any abbot's means. Reform meant modesty in every way. For buyers they were counting on those abbeys in the Bursfeld congregation, seventy at least. To start, though, they required a model they could copy. The master snorted at the tattered pocket Bible the Franciscans used that Peter had brought back from Paris. Nor was he impressed by Fust's more ornate books of hours. They had to get their mitts, he said, on one of proper size. To Fust's look of horror he responded with a barking laugh, 'No, not to buy! I mean to steal one with my eyes.'

Instantly the volumes at St Jakob's sprang to Peter's mind. 'Brack has the testaments,' he said.

The master tapped his finger at his forehead. 'As well announce our business by the crier.'

One might have thought it easy to put hands on a monumental Bible in a place like Mainz. She did not lack for churches or chapels. Yet in those days the only full texts of the Bible were in cloisters, not on pulpits. Here and there a parish had received one as a gift, but these were locked up in their sacristies. Fust's uncles were both ranking clergy at St Stephan's; he would pretend some bookish errand. Peter meanwhile would approach the priest at St Quintin's. Before two days were out, though, Gutenberg had beaten both of them. He sauntered in with a huge parcel underneath one arm: the parish Bible of St Christopher's, as fat and bulbous as a little dog. 'I've got the deacon, too, to help correct the pages.'

Fust blanched. 'Nobody else.'

'It can't be helped.'

There was a moment when their eyes locked and the air between them crackled. Then all three bent above that hard brown leather mound.

The master placed a horny thumbnail on a ruby line that marked the ending of one chapter. 'A hundred, hundred and twenty,' he said, his look sombre. 'A job enough to print the black.'

They debated for some time how to produce it. Fust said the buyers should receive the plain black printed sheets directly from the press, folded and collected into quires. They then could have them decorated as they pleased, as they would do with any product of the scribes. They'd hire someone to write the running titles on each page, and pen *incipits* and *explicits* and the other ruby lines that marked the sections of the text. In his experience, a duke preferred a different kind of painting to a merchant to an abbot; each would hire a painter to illuminate the margins, and a binder who would sew and then encase the quires.

'You think of dukes?' the master asked.

Fust smiled. 'Why not?' He paused then, looked at Gutenberg through narrowed eyes. 'Everything depends upon the quality – and price.'

Gutenberg exhaled. His right hand rose, raked back his hair. 'A bloody monster,' he said softly. 'Twelve hundred pages, at the least – a hundred thousand pulls upon the bar.'

'If it can sell for less . . .' Fust did not finish.

Balefully, the printer stared down at that hidebound creature. 'We'll have to go like hell,' he said, 'or else this beast will have the best of us.'

He taught Peter in that second winter that the art of making was the art of movement. In his relentless mind, all things were reduced to their pure motion. By his ripe age, he'd say, one ought to hope he'd learned a thing or two. The business of any business is stripping away – the cleaner and simpler the better, he would mutter, standing over Peter's shoulder, watching as he carved and cast. Set your tools for every prospect and prepare: then clean the track and go like Satan's hounds. 'The men are not the vital thing – although I know it's harsh.'

Though it seemed madness at the time, the master ordered them to add more characters to those they had already made. Scores more: in total they would need nearly 300 different letterforms. Each combination they could possibly conceive, five kinds of *a*, a half dozen *u*'s, exactly like those variations used by scribes. It had to look exactly like a Bible written out by hand, Fust said, or they would have no prayer of buyers. This way, as well, they'd have the letter that they needed at their fingertips each time. And then they'd have to cast scores more of every character, so they could set up three full pages at a time; each Bible page was twice the size of any missal.

To help them set them into lines, the master dreamed up little trays of wood for them to hold in their left palms, while their right fingers roamed the typecase to search out the letter. He had them switch from sand to clay inside the casting box, once he had seen how many letters they would need. Though clay too held for just one casting, it was far faster to prepare than sand.

They set the start of Saint Jerome's prologue to the Bible in that dark, tight face that Peter had designed for their aborted missal. They laid it out in double columns in the strict proportions of the golden section: five thumbs across, eight down. The type made forty lines in two black towers down the page, with room between for vines, the curling tails of great initials. Gutenberg and Fust were more than pleased.

Then Peter did the reckoning. The first page they had set had taken fifteen hours.

'Thus can we judge,' the master said, 'the weeks and months—'

'—and years—'

'—ahead.'

Quailing, Peter counted it once more. Sixty-six quires this Holy Book would make, approximately fourteen hundred pages.

'A quire a fortnight,' said the master, twisting at his beard.

Fust was more gimlet-eyed. 'More like a quire each moon.'

Twelve quires a year were five years and a half. *Dear Lord. Protect us, in Thy wisdom; keep us from all harm.*

Grede came once to the new workshop to 'inspect all this commotion,' as she put it. It must have been late winter; Peter remembers her in furs. Her husband guided her around the letter cases, one hand planted firmly at her back. She brought to mind an otter, with the sleekness of her muskrat cape, her winter cap of fox. She moved as smoothly too, her fingers roving over parchment, pigments, pots of varnishes and resins. The men were struck entirely dumb. The master barely touched her outstretched hand, as if it burned. He made an awkward bow, retreated stiffly to his elevated table. Peter laughed inside, to see the way a woman could reduce their swagger to the rictus of such smiles.

She marvelled at each piece of joinery, the punches and the letters that cascaded from the casting box. 'Ingenious,' she murmured, staring fascinated at the press. She walked around it, eyeing it from every side. Konrad had built it sturdier this time, with tapered handles on the weighty carriage to preserve the pressman's hands. It looked a little like a palanquin, she said, or else a bier. 'Praise God, pray not,' Fust said and crossed himself. Death writhed beneath the gates and crept inside the city that whole year. In early Lent the plague had reappeared in livid spots and rattling coughs among the farmers first, then striking indiscriminately, highborn or low, not caring if its victims pushed a cart or rode a carriage. Veils covered the few faces on the streets; they shrank in doorways every time a stretcher passed, borne to the hospice of the Holy Ghost, returning laden with another corpse bound for the Kästrich graveyard. If fear of Gutenberg did not suffice to hold the men inside the shop at night, the stench and groans and terror of contagion did.

Grede ran her hands across the stacks of hides; she flicked and tested both the sizing and the weight of the new vellum. Even married, she was still a furrier's daughter. For years she'd mended tears in manuscripts that Fust procured with tiny stitches to erase the blemishes. Now she raised one skin up to the light and *tsk*ed. The master watched, lips twitching, as she turned to Peter. 'They ought to tan the man who did this. Another rubbing, don't you think?' Behind her Peter saw the master frown and turn away. Gutenberg could never take a criticism from a man, much less a woman. Yet Grede was right. The calfskin could have used another pass.

No sooner had she gathered up her skirts and left than Keffer gave a hoot. 'A young and juicy wife has brother Fust!'

'Retract your tongue, you clod.' Hans flung a hand towards the forge and screwed the magnifier back into his eye. The big smith was still grinning as he strolled away.

'Frau Fust, might I remind you, is a lady.' Gutenberg moved like a panther when he had a mind to. 'As such we'll have no leering and no lust – and by the saints, no bloody contact.' He looked at Peter then, thin lips drawn in a jaundiced smile. 'Except for Peter, the poor sod. He hasn't got the choice.'

Hans rolled his eyes but did not comment.

'You never had a mother, sir?' said Peter, smiling.

'We all slopped out of Eve. You know the good that brought.'

'Humanity, perhaps?' He said it teasingly.

Gutenberg gave a loud snort. 'Woman!' he said. '"More bitter than death, who is the hunter's snare". Ecclesiastes.'

'"Strength and beauty are her clothing, and she shall laugh in the latter day".' Peter crossed his arms. 'Proverbs.'

On even Ruppel's stony face he caught a faint trace of amusement.

'Eve, Pandora, Magdalene. Go read your Greeks and scripture.' The master's face was puckered as if he'd eaten something sour. 'You mark my words, young man: a woman will destroy the best a man can be.'

He turned and walked, chin up, towards his desk. Peter watched that haughty, ramrod back. What had poor woman done, to be so calumnied? Strange way he had of showing Christian love. Peter thought of Grede, and Fust's first wife, Elisabeth, and Céline who sold her father's paintings by the Seine – each just as quick of hand and eye as any man. The early guilds were filled with women – weavers, painters, carvers, even. Everywhere – from Bruges to Louvain, Venice, Paris. What had she done, to man and more particularly to Gutenberg, to make her such an object of his hate? Peter glanced at Hans. Another mystery that one day, after several pints, he would extract from the old man.

Chapter 2

~~

COMPOSITION

March — April 1452

It was dark when Peter stepped into the workshop every morning, dark each evening when he left. He wondered sometimes if the day had ever even been. While Keffer and the master cast, he and Hans practised setting type. Each typecase was a slanted wooden labyrinth he had to look at first to find the letter he required. But bit by bit the lay of those three hundred pockets graved their places in his mind. The pages they were using as their manuscript were clipped onto a stand before his eyes. He and Hans would sound the letters as they groped, and Peter's heart was glad at that low mumbling hum that he had missed from the scriptorium.

There was an art to it, he found to his surprise; it was not rote, as he had once believed. His right hand held each option in its grasp, as with his pen. He chose which of the different forms to use, which ligature to shorten or expand a word. Each line required a certain spacing to achieve a perfect weight: he'd set some lines, then have them proofed, then move a space, exchange a letterform, and proof and look again. It troubled him, at first, to think that in this way he might achieve a perfect line. Was man not flawed, by definition? And who was Peter to imagine they might reach for more? And yet the lines, when he composed them, were magnificently balanced. This, too, in his own mind, a proof of God's intention, and the holy mission they fulfilled.

Above all he found unexpected joy in working hand in hand among those craftsmen. He'd never worked that way before: for all that scribes worked side by side, their lines were singularly theirs. But in the Humbrechthof, he found himself a link in a much larger chain. He'd carry his full tray to the composing stone, and hold the lines as Keffer tied the *forme*. Then Keffer in his turn would heft it towards Ruppel at the press; they'd ink it, pull the proof, and pass it back to Peter. They did not banter much; there was no need. There was a pleasure and a rhythm in the work itself that took the place of words.

It struck him only afterwards that this was Gutenberg's most lasting gift. The man had faith – and fire and ruthless expectation – that they would bring to it the best they had. This faith was harsh, demanding, unrelenting, and it pushed them far beyond themselves. He worked beside them much of that first year, no better and no worse, their work implicitly a piece with his own brilliance. If afterwards they were appalled at how he viewed them, there was a kind of fairness in that cold assessment: all men were equal before Gutenberg, and God.

Peter did not know then just how precious were those weeks and months. It felt as though they tossed a rope ahead and hauled the whole thing sweating forwards. Sometimes he fancied he could see the very operation in the smoulder of the master's eyes: fixed on some distant spot, Gutenberg would cast his thought out far before him, straining towards the spot where it would land. For once Peter dared to hope that his own stubborn striving too might finally be recognized – not mocked, as it so often had been in his life.

That hope was answered suddenly one day in early May. He

was sitting, staring at the shape of those two columns on the page. He thought he knew the skills he had, his limits – when to his amazement he was gifted with a vision that exceeded, and by far, his own mind's reach.

The frayed edge of both those right-hand margins had disturbed him from the start. They were uneven: some lines ended short and others were too long, and broken by a hyphen. A sloppy, ragged edge was the result. He was staring, irritated, at it when suddenly he saw: in one swift stroke the hand of God just pushed the birdlike scratches of the punctuation to the right, leaving a crisp and perfect margin. Peter saw how easy it would be. A miracle, indeed – of pure mechanics.

Excitedly he went to Ruppel. Build me a wider type-stick, man, he said, an *m*'s width broader than our column. Ruppel scratched his head, but did it. Peter set a dozen lines in something like a frenzy, lining each precisely up to end at the same spot. When necessary he dropped a hyphen or a stop into the extra space beyond the margin. He took the tray back to the press and waited for the inking and the grinding and the proof. And then he knew.

It was perfect. Absolutely perfect: more exquisite than the dream of any scribe. The block was sharp, perfectly squared: the punctuation floated softly in the margin, brushing like the lashes of a bashful bride.

Until that day, his father had just seen the press as a much faster set of hands. The master, for his part, was driven by a vision of that never-ending replication, making many from the one. That evening, when he showed them both, they grasped that this was much, much more.

'No scribe can rival this, for evenness and strength,' said Peter.

Gutenberg was staring fascinated at the page. 'I guess the geese will be relieved,' he cracked, 'to keep their quills.'

Fust placed the printed sheet beside a manuscript he'd recently commissioned. 'What need for *clerici*, indeed.' Their letter was much darker than the written words; the text block was much sharper, more defined. Peter's father pursed his lips, then dropped his finger on one red-inked line. 'Why can't we do the red as well, then? And put the rubricator out of work?'

Peter looked at Gutenberg. By then they had a way of speaking without words. Two craftsmen, silently assessing a technique: *If the lines are movable, changeable.* Gutenberg was nodding, dark eyes ratcheting between the printed and the written sheets. *If we can add, subtract, the elements at will.* He put a hand upon the merchant's shoulder as his mouth began to widen in a grin. 'By God. Why not?'

'If you can put a line in, you can take it out,' said Peter slowly. 'We could print it later with a different ink.'

He pictured it, the miracle of all those lines that scribes would letter in bright red to mark a difference from the text: *Here starts the book of Job; Here ends the prologue of the Four Evangelists.* Those lines just lifted out – removed, invisibly, so that they wouldn't print in black. And then – he tried to see how it would work – each line dropped back, alone, a solitary thing that they would somehow ink in red.

'Just run it by itself.' The master looked with glinting eyes at his apprentice. 'A second pass on the same sheet.' He grinned and shook his hoary head. 'You're seeing now the way I see.'

A startled laugh burst out of Fust. 'We can remove the hand of man!' His eyes were wide. 'Replace the hand of man!'

Gutenberg looked up towards a point on the dark beams. 'The symmetries of metal, now of space.' His smile was wide. 'The Lord alone knows where it will end.'

By Easter half the type was fashioned, and they'd made good progress in the cutting of the skins. One evening not long after,

Fust asked his son to see him once the household had retired. His father stood outside in the small courtyard, drinking in the breath of spring. His mood was ebullient: his merchant's sap rose every year with the greening of the buds and the thawing of the Alpen passes. Peter took the cup he offered and asked where he was headed first.

'To Basel, I should think.' For silks and dyes brought through the Bosphorus from the Levant.

'Don't worry overmuch about the shop,' said Peter. 'In point of fact' – he tipped his cup – 'I owe you an apology. It's everything you ever said. Forgive me for not seeing it before.'

Fust touched his goblet to his son's. 'For which I'm more than glad.' He settled back. For a long moment he just looked at Peter, blue eyes gleaming.

'And so . . .' he said, a half smile on his lips, 'we come to the next step.'

The man was nothing if not logical. The sanguine man lived by the things that he could touch and count. The job was found; next came the bride. He'd be remiss as his adoptive father, Fust said, not to broker Peter an outstanding match.

'For some poor scribbler?' Peter kept it light. 'For that is all I look like now.'

'We've got the time.' Fust clasped his hands across his girth. 'A year, or eighteen months – then we can safely let this news disperse.'

The Elder houses all would flock then, he was sure. He mentioned names of daughter this and daughter that: Fürstenburg and Gelthus, Echenzeller. Dowries, yes, but more than that, a place at all the highest tables.

'And once you thought that I should be a priest.' Peter ribbed him gently. Time was, he would have bridled at his father's heavy hand, but in between had come this Book, and with it now, an even deeper trust that God would clear his path.

'A waste, to join the clergy.' Fust cocked his head, appraising him. 'When you think how far you'll rise with these skills.'

Ah, yes. How Fust desired, had always yearned, to rise. It was the curse of all those born too low, yet still endowed with brains to chafe against their chains. Fust had a list, his son had long believed, of all that Peter, as the eldest, should achieve. As big a business as his father's, and as fine a house, the honour Fust himself had gained as a Companion of the Mint, a member of the *Münzerhausgenossenschaft*. The man had all of this. What more must Peter do, to raise him even higher? Already Fust had risen, in some ways, higher than his own patrician partner.

Peter wondered how much Gutenberg resented being barred from that old club where his forefathers had sat, minting coins and guaranteeing all the weights and measures. Things were much looser now than in his youth: the proof was that they had admitted Fust.

'In any case, I'd mull it over,' Fust said, pouring more wine.

Peter and Fust did not look alike, nor even think alike, his foster son reflected as he brought the wine to his lips. Yet how much had he given him, this solid, balding, kindly man. Peter had to honour this, no matter how his new awareness burned inside. A simple truth, but one that pounded hard within him. The scribe had made his mark: he was essential now. The workshop could not run without him. Fust and Gutenberg both knew it, too. No other man could carve those letters as he did, nor set them into graceful lines. It was remarkable, the lightness that this brought. How marvellous to be so needed, and how freeing.

Chapter 3

ALCHEMY

April — May 1452

There was no end then to the roaring of the forge. The ores went into it in shovels and came out transformed. In cataracts the molten metal poured into the iron pots and mixed, and in thin streams sought out their moulds. How long? they asked themselves, bent sweating from dawn to dusk. For every score of letters that came gleaming from the casting box, another hour went by in planing and in filing until they stood at the same height. When would they have enough? Peter asked the master, but the man just waved his hand.

'Keep on,' he said, and Peter thought of Pharaoh hardening his heart. Each plague the Lord sent down to free His chosen people from Pharaoh's grip just tightened it, so stubborn was that slave master. *Deliver us, O Lord*, he prayed, stiff fingers guiding every punch into the clay. *Bring us into the good and spacious land, the land that floweth with milk and honey.*

His father returned and went on swiftly westward towards Bourges and after that to Paris. Somebody had to raise the gold they poured into that forge. The Duke of Burgundy by then had moved his court to Flanders, but there were markets still for pigments and for precious stones across the Loire and

Île-de-France. The family saw his three big wagons off, the merchant perched up on the dashboard with his driver holding the long reins. Little Hans was like an eel on Peter's shoulders, writhing as his elder brother gripped his legs. The boy was blue-eyed, golden, like his father; Peter dared to hope his father's dreams no longer rested solely on the firstborn foster child. He and Grede and Tina watched the dust of their departure from the wall above the Martin's Gate. The wagons disappeared in a great cloud along the thin brown line that ran between the abbeys, heading south and turning westward only after they had passed the line of hills. Behind the watchers, on the hill inside the city wall, white shards of Roman ruins poked out of the loam – just like the teeth of giants, Peter teased. Little Hans and Tina looked alarmed. He thought of this again a few days later as he took the long way from the workshop to the Guildhall – how the fallen of the past remain, their traces a reminder that all peoples perish.

His uncle Jakob had requested that he stop to see him, on some business, Peter had assumed. He climbed into the clear air high above the Kästrich, breathing deeply to expel the poisons from the forge. He walked along the wall and dropped at last onto the lane above the livestock market, looking at the city spread beneath him, sparkling like the waters of the Rhine.

The day was warm and bright; the double towers of the Altmünster were to his left, above their green fields sliced by a bright stream; below and to his right stood the red sandstone bulk of the cathedral. To either side poked up a score of spires, and just before him, in a cascade of blue slate, spread out the warren of the Jewish quarter. He plunged directly down a narrow lane. The Guildhall was two houses joined and tucked away among the heathen, as was only right: as hidden and remote from Elder power – Mint, cathedral, the archbishop's court – as it was possible to be.

Peter dodged the hawkers clutching at him, crying out their wares, and turned into the Betzelstrasse and the hall called Mompasilier. The name was bastardized, a Rhinish hash of *monplaisir*. French for 'my pleasure': tavern, haven – coven even, some might say – for members of the city's guilds. Peter had never liked the way they looked at him in there. He never had belonged – it struck him as he put his hand on the claw that served as doorknob. Not to a single guild, not even really to this city, until now. Until he hewed to Gutenberg, he'd hewed his whole life long just to himself and God.

His uncle had one corner of a private room reserved for *Brudermeisters* of the guilds. He raised a hand and waved Peter towards his table. Ale was drawn, delivered in two foaming tankards. Thirstily, Peter raised his: the brewers always sent their best to Mompasilier.

'I thought you might have heard about this order for indulgences.' His uncle was not one to waste his breath. As soon as Peter sat, his ice-cool eyes had raked his face and hands.

'No, sir.'

'Two thousand more, I am informed.' Jakob leaned towards him. 'To pump the people even drier.' His fingers tightened on his beer stein. The city council frowned on the proliferation of these letters of indulgence. The letters in themselves were not the problem; all faithful people had the right to speed their way from purgatory if they could. But now the clergy seemed to crank them out at every chance, and this pumped more scarce guilders out of Mainz. Peter shook his head: he hadn't heard.

His uncle held his hands so that the light would catch the massive seal on his guildmaster's ring, it seemed to Peter, striking fear into the hearts of those whose lives were governed by those two crossed hammers.

'Your man Cusanus has requested them for Frankfurt.'

Jakob's eyes went left and right to verify that no one heard. 'You're not . . . involved, by chance . . . in making them, in that excuse that Gensfleisch calls a workshop?'

'I don't know what you mean. We're making mirrors.'

'Come now.' Jakob smiled. 'He could produce a thousand chits with all that metal, I am sure.'

How like the man to pounce before his father's trail was even cold. Of course Jakob did know; they paid his guild their dues. Then Peter started, as the meaning of his uncle's words sank in. He had not thought of it before – the prospect of their art abused, its glory twisted to the traffic of the church.

How had it not occurred to him? He had thought only that the clergy would abhor the very notion of some trumped-up yokels printing off God's Word. He hadn't even seen that it was just as likely that Archbishop Dietrich would perceive their press as a new way to serve his economic interests. For metal letters could be used in any order, set and printed to decree whatever new insanity either side in that sad war desired. Peter leaned towards Jakob. 'No one else knows. Outside of you – and Biermann.'

The mention of the tinsmiths' leader irked his uncle; in the hierarchy of the trades, the goldsmiths had no truck with common smiths. It did not matter. Peter cast his mind back to that visit he and Gutenberg had made to Eltville-on-the-Rhine. The master claimed that Rosenberg, Archbishop Dietrich himself, had long since put the press out of their minds. But Peter wouldn't be so sure.

'I wouldn't put it past the cheat,' said Jakob, meaning Gutenberg.

'The answer's no.' Peter sat back and raised his mug. 'We've work enough to do.'

'Work's fine, when it is done within the rules.'

Peter did not answer.

'I told Johann; I'll say the same to you. If he's protected by the guild, he will abide by the guild rules.'

'That's a matter for my father and my master.'

'Your *master*.' Jakob's face contorted. 'The only thing he's mastered is the art of fleecing Mainz. The man's a snake, I say.'

'It's not my business,' Peter said again. 'It is a matter for your brother.'

'He doesn't listen. Never did.' A thin white line rimmed Jakob's nostrils. 'They suck you dry, then have the gall to blame you for the mess they've made. This so-called *master* is the same. I don't suppose he told you how he held the treasurer of Mainz for ransom? Had him tossed into the Strassburg jail, some years ago – to squeeze out payment on his cursed bonds?'

This Peter easily could see; it was entirely Gutenberg. It was as much as he could do to keep his face straight. He turned the conversation back. 'Is it the Jubilee indulgence, then?' he asked.

His uncle nodded. His face was drawn, the lines as sharp and deep as those made by a master carver. 'And all the while the city is left dangling. They made us pay a hundred yearly just to lift the ban, but still they drag their feet. The debt with Speyer isn't even cleared.' His voice was bitter.

Peter pictured Erlenbach, the bishop's fist, sheathed in his metal-studded leather as he rode through the archdiocese. They said he missed the bloody warfare of crusading, and was glad to get a taste of fighting when he could. 'But this indulgence isn't Dietrich's,' he objected. 'It's the pope's.'

'Which in the way of things will trickle down until the poorest of them pay. Dietrich is an expert at extorting his one-quarter of one-tenth.

'And then' – his uncle looked with some ferocity at Peter – 'there is to be another tithe. They're squeezing, hard, from Rome all the way down, to pay for all those pilgrims.' He sighed then, and his features softened slightly. 'They squeeze us from all sides.'

'Our workshop has no part in it.' Peter spoke as calmly as he could. 'No part at all.' And yet the fear had sprung to life inside. They must not get their hands on it, he thought.

'They cannot know.' He uttered it before he knew it. Guiltily he glanced around, conscious he had spoken much too loudly. The other guildsmen were still hunkered drinking, their heads down. 'If Dietrich gets his hands on this, we all are finished.'

Their press was more than blessed – it was pure gold. He'd been so taken by its beauty he had missed this fact: whoever held that press held total power. They might as well mint coins with it, if they could use it to print letters of indulgence to be sold. It was a thing of monumental value, to the free city that was Mainz – and to Dietrich, ever itching to revoke their hard-won freedom. Gutenberg and Fust had surely seen this value, down the road.

'You see it, don't you?' Peter whispered. His uncle sat back, looking at him strangely: thoughtfully, and with a glint of new respect.

'His people know,' Peter went softly on: 'there was a meeting once, about a missal.' His uncle nodded.

'We pray that it is long forgotten, but who knows?'

'They don't forget,' his uncle said.

'If they should hear even a whisper . . .' Peter shook his head. 'He'll have it seized, no doubt – and use it in whatever way he pleases.'

That evening Peter made his way with purpose to the Schreibhaus. His only access to the clergy was his old mate Petrus Heilant, scribe and snoop. He found him warming the same stool, his eyes as ever roving that full room.

'We haven't seen you in a while,' the canon of St Viktor's said, his regard shrewd.

Peter cocked an eyebrow. 'Nor have I heard much news from you.'

'In times like this,' the scribe said lightly, 'they clamp on to their posts like leeches.'

Peter gave him a world-weary smile and sat. 'I figured so.' He shook his head. 'So I've been left to drafting contracts, credit letters, now and then a bit of law.'

'That's bitter, truly.' Even as he spoke, the scribe's eyes swivelled back to track the traffic to and fro.

'Though . . .' Peter made a show of hesitating slightly, 'I did hear there might be *confessionalia* about.'

Heilant paused in his scanning. 'You're well informed.'

'Whatever I can do to scrape a fare back down the Rhine.'

Primly Heilant pursed his lips. 'I wouldn't count on it. There's no love lost right now between His Grace and the pope.'

'Meaning?'

Archly, Heilant smiled. His eyes probed Peter. If he struggled over whether to divulge a thing he shouldn't, the struggle was both brief and futile. He dropped his voice. 'The Jubilee indulgence is as good as dead. They're even planning to refuse the pope's new tithe.'

'Enough of pumping dry the Holy Roman Empire of the German nation,' Peter whispered; Heilant nodded. At least, thought Peter, Dietrich's thoughts were not on Mainz. 'A little stand-off then, between His Grace and Nicholas the Fifth,' he said.

The look was withering. 'His only aim is to extort us.'

The words could have been Jakob's. Peter laughed. He stayed and drank a while, to cover up his tracks, but learned no more.

As fate would have it, entering the square as Peter left the Schreibhaus was Klaus Pinzler, altar painter, illustrator to the book trade. How now, the fellow said, we rarely see you up this way. Come share a drop of cherry wine. Refusal would be taken as a slight, Peter knew – not just by Pinzler but by Fust, who treated all his furnishers as equals, the better to extract his terms. The cherry trees that lined the Leichhof and marched up along the stream to form a good-sized orchard were in frothy bloom. The blue door of the painter's workshop brought his daughter with her blue-tipped fingers to his mind, but only Pinzler and his wife were there. 'A pity Anna's out,' the woman said and laid out cheese and bread, a hunk of sausage. Her keen eyes assessed the weave of Peter's tunic, his green cloak; he saw great swags of cloth suspended from the rafters. As she counted up his threads and weight and worth, he toasted to the speedy restoration of the gentry's appetite for painted panels, banners, saddle silks, and cloaks.

Klaus Pinzler probed with some acuity the state of Fust's affairs. 'Things will go ill for us,' he said, 'if there is war between Archbishop Dietrich and the Palatine.' He pulled his short dark beard and frowned; his buyers were restricted to the nobles in the local countryside. 'Not so your father, though.'

Fust's books and baubles flew across and past that ragged patchwork on the Rhine, the independent duchies poking up in Dietrich's quilt: the seats of Wertheim, Falkenstein and Nassau, Katzenelnbogen. 'He thinks that it will calm,' said Peter, 'if for no other reason than that the princes are too poor to war.' Or we might hope, he added, smiling, that Dietrich will direct his anger at the pope and keep the tithe to spend on fripperies in Mainz. If they but knew what Peter knew, he thought. The feeling lifted him with secret pride.

He was about to take his cloak up when the daughter of the house appeared. He had not seen her that whole intervening year, except for glimpses at the market. A slender, solemn thing she was, not more than seventeen. She entered from the street and stopped, looked sharply at her parents, dropped a half curtsy.

'Anna,' said her mother. 'You remember Master Schoeffer.'

'Good evening,' she said simply as she started moving towards the stair.

'You got it?' Pinzler asked. He shrugged his shoulders Peter's way, as if to say his daughter might learn better manners.

'Of course.'

'We had run out of paste,' Pinzler explained.

'I've always wondered how you mix your paints.'

'Anna will show you,' said her father. 'If she would be so kind.'

She flipped her braid as if to say, *Whatever you require*.

The table in the upstairs loft was covered by a jumble of small shells and vials, towards which the painter's daughter flapped a small, thin hand. 'Forgive the mess,' she said.

His eyes roved over brushes and vibrant powders: cerulean and forest green and crimson, lapis lazuli. He glanced at her pale hands and said, 'I liked them blue.'

'I *do* wash, now and then.' Anna Pinzler rolled her dark almond eyes.

There was a little vial of dried red beetles Peter knew; he had himself used these to make the ruby ink for rubrication. He bent and inhaled the bitter, earthy notes of gum and wax and oil. He felt a sudden urge to sit and open up his pouch, unwrap his vitriol and lumps of gall – though they sat unused now in his own room. The girl was taking out a packet from a pocket in her smock. Instantly he smelled it.

'Fishy,' he said, and then blushed scarlet.

She looked at him as if he were entirely mad. An innocent, a virgin, then. Inside the wrapping she pulled open lay a dried, translucent membrane. 'The lining of the sturgeon's breast,' she said. Peter must have looked perplexed. 'Part of his lungs,

I guess.' She stroked the pearly sheet. 'Which when he dies, gives us the matter we dissolve to fix our pigments.' She frowned, a pretty little scowl. 'It has to soak in lime and vinegar an age.'

He thought he'd never seen a girl so self-possessed. She bent, dark-haired and elfin, and started naming things. 'Malachite, azurite, minium, chalk. Auripigmentium.' A warning finger: 'Never let the metals near the mouth.' A row of drying plants swung by her casement window. 'Blue woad and indigo tinctoria, crozophora for the mauve.' She gestured at a row of vials, a mortar and its pestle. 'Amber, hempseed, linseed. Tears of Arabic.' She lifted up the little waxy balls. 'And then the Kermes bugs, poor souls.' She peered into the jar. 'I never like to think of how they get them.' Or else the way they die, he thought, but did not say: the females only blazed that red when pregnant with new life.

'I use them too,' he said, 'sometimes.'

Then as abruptly as she started, she was done. 'That's all there is.'

He looked around: a window and a mirror and a narrow bed. 'Oh, I don't know. There's also quite good light.'

He caught a flash of little pearly teeth. 'It's better in the orchard.'

'Perhaps you'll show me then, sometime.' The words were stupid, but he watched with pleasure as they brushed a rosy wash across her cheeks. He felt himself stir in response, and clattered down the stairs to seize his cloak and cover up the hunger that arose. He did not look to see if she had followed, but slipped out, his blood pounding, picturing those pale, delicate fingers in his mouth.

Chapter 4

———

BROTHERHOOD

June 1452

Theft was the fear: theft of an idea that, unmoored from its true genesis inside one mind, might readily be snatched, passed on, proclaimed by an impostor as his own. The law protected property, but not the private precincts of a bold, inventive mind.

The master knew this more than most. Had he not come back from a trip to Holland the preceding year, muttering about a book he'd seen with images and words printed from wooden blocks? A man with half his wits might see how easily those lines of wooden letters could be sawed apart. Had he not sworn them all to secrecy and double-locked the shop and the men with it, every night and morning? Had he not hidden all his life – as he hid now behind this subterfuge, installing every evening the fake moulds for making mirrors in plain view?

The threat emerged in earnest early in the summer when Fust returned to say he'd heard about a man in Avignon who taught a secret art involving alphabets of steel. 'You haven't shown it anywhere?' he asked his partner sharply. The master's face had darkened at his words, but he answered just as curtly. 'I keep my affairs secret, as you know.' He glanced at Hans, his thin lips working. 'But spies are everywhere. I've had them try to steal from me before.'

They could not be too careful. Pray to Saint Benedict, or Paul or Peter, to all fourteen Holy Helpers, I don't care, the master said. Just pray for some protection: the workshop was ringed round with thieves, and they'd not even printed the first sheet.

'My point precisely.' Fust said it like a banker. 'How much longer until you get started printing?'

'Three weeks – or four.'

And then, thought Peter – months and months – and years, more years – until they'd printed all one hundred and twenty copies of those scores of quires. They'd need a host of angels, he thought, sick at heart – the whole host of the archangels with their bright enfolding wings – to keep this secret under guard.

'What about Rosenberg?' He pushed it grimly out. 'He's seen our printing, too.' The master's head jerked up.

'And quite forgotten it,' snapped Gutenberg.

Fust looked between them. 'What gives you that assurance?'

'There's a new order for indulgences,' said Peter, turning to his father, 'which might well jog his memory.'

The master shot his apprentice a sour look. 'Leave them to me.'

Fust wiped his forehead with one arm. 'If only we were sure of silence.' He looked out through the grime that streaked the upstairs window. 'But how – how do you buy the silence of six thousand souls?'

Instantly, the thought arrived. 'The guilds,' said Peter.

Both men looked at him with incredulity. The vision had passed swiftly, but Peter had no doubt of what he'd seen: his uncle, twisting that great golden seal.

'It's in their interest, surely.' His heart was racing as he worked it out. 'It's in all our interest – the whole city's – that it not fall into Dietrich's hands.'

'Insanity.' The master's lips drew back. 'I wouldn't trust a Mainz guild any further than I spit.'

'You were a member of a guild yourself, I thought.'

'Another place. Another life. The guildsmen here are poison—'

'—no more than are the Elder clans,' Fust cut across him, folding both his arms. They stood that way a moment, facing off.

'It seems to me,' said Peter, stepping in between them for the first time, although not the last, 'that to the council this might seem a step towards freedom. Not now' – he held a hand up to thwart Gutenberg from speaking – 'but when we're done. The press might help them too, then – I don't know, to mint some gold, shake off that yoke.'

'This press is mine.' Gutenberg pulled himself to his full, imposing height.

'Not only.' Fust stood planted, balancing as he always had between the working class from whence he'd sprung and the upper classes he now served.

'You think some yokels can protect us?' Gutenberg laughed harshly.

Fust kept his head. 'What other shield would you suggest? None of your friends, or relatives, Johann – not any member of the clergy.'

'I've got it well in hand, I said. I have his ear, and I can work him like a piece of putty if I have to.' The look he shot at Peter was pure venom.

'It takes one whisper, only one.' Fust pursed his lips. 'You cannot guarantee that none will leak, not over all this time.'

'So you would drag it through each tavern.'

'That isn't how it works.' Fust drew himself up too then,

every bit as proud. 'I know these guilds. I know the leaders, every one. If they're convinced it's in their interest, they will take our dues and keep the secret sealed.'

Gutenberg looked first at Peter, then at Fust, and knew he was defeated. 'I bow then to your great superiority,' he said, and turned and vanished down the stairs.

It wasn't that the master loathed the guildsmen, Hans said when he learned of the new plan. It was more that he had never feared the nobles or the clergy. Why, back in Strassburg, he'd had them eating from his hands. The parties at his farmhouse were a legend. He rigged a way to make a liquor out of every plant that grew about the place. He had the gold, you see – and then that roaring, blazing mouth.

'Mainz gold,' said Peter, not without admiration.

'He even held your treasurer for ransom once.' Hans grinned.

'I heard.'

'The stories I could tell you,' said the smith, and laughed, his brown face creasing in a thousand folds. Peter should have asked him then about those cryptic comments that the master made about the business he had there. But something else was on the young man's mind.

'Stories about women?' he prompted.

'You heard no word from me.' Hans held him with a beady eye. Peter nodded. Well, said Hans, it happened long ago, before his time. 'The way I heard it, he was once engaged.'

'Poor wench.'

Hans laughed. 'The lady thought so, anyway – and when Henne refused, she sued him for breach of promise.' That much he knew for sure. That, and her name: Anna of the Iron Door. The master won the suit, but had to pay the court a fine, to compensate for the extremity and foulness of his mouth. Hans shook his head and grinned. 'He said he didn't care who knew it, it was God's own truth: he wished to hell her iron door had rusted shut.'

And Peter wished for just the opposite when he took Anna Pinzler walking in the fields. She was a slip of girl, a clean-limbed filly – yet possessed of such a keenness that it took his breath away. He bent his energies to capturing her bright and concentrated gaze, threw off without a backwards look his monkish habits.

It seemed to him his youth returned, slipping with ease inside the man he had become. They dashed among the crumbling dirt clods of those summer lanes and barefoot through the copses, picking cherries; lay panting on their backs, picking out the pictures in the fleet and shifting clouds. The first time that he kissed her, Anna closed her eyes and stood on tiptoe under-neath a tree. He held her narrow face between his palms and watched the sun and shadow play across its smooth, sweet planes. Her eyes flew open. 'What?' A sylph, a woodland nymph, is what you are, he almost said. Instead he took her in his arms. He did not care from whence she came or who her father was. The world was shifting and the old rules breaking down. His own father, after all, had married down in choosing Grede. Down, up, in any case were monstrous fictions – each one of them was equal, in the Book they made – this Book that one day all would reach with hungry hands to grasp.

His Anna's eyes were dark, yet brilliant in their shining, and her painter's hands both delicate and strong. She brought chalk and charcoal and a little sketchbook everywhere; she was a maker as he was. What most delighted him, though, was the way she saw. Despite her stillness, her containment, she could be touched quite instantly by beauty and transformed. It might be a sudden blazing of the flax, gone yellow overnight to gird the city in a sunburst. Or else a tiny thing, a drop of dew that swelled with rainbows on a leaf. Her painter's eye saw harmony in every shifting contrast. She'd take his hand and point, and marvel at God's artistry. She'd turn to him and say she guessed he did the same with his own hand and quill. He found that he could not naysay her. It was a gift, he said, that God had given him: a scribe he was, and always would be. He longed to tell her how that grace had put his hand now to this new, uplifting service. But he was bound as ever by his vow. He'd teach her then, he said instead, to wrest the magic of the meaning from the letters that he used. It was not Anna's fault that she'd been born a girl, and poor, and never learned to read.

Somehow Grede guessed: it was that women's mystery, their strange alertness to the unseen world. There was a new lightness to his step perhaps, or else she marked his Sunday absences. However she had learned, she bent her wiles to teasing out the secret of which maiden might have caught his eye. He'd scouted out the Elder girls, both she and Fust assumed. No harm there, said his father, just so long as you are sure to quench your ardour at the baths. Take Echenzeller's Hannah, he would say, or even better, Molsberg's Judith. Peter laughed, and left them guessing. He was too happy then to gird himself yet for the battle that would surely come.

He never knew just how it was arranged – which guilds were brought into the secret, and what sureties they gave. The only thing he knew for sure was that from then on Gutenberg and Fust paid guild dues to a dozen brotherhoods.

Jakob must have taken some delight in writing out the notice. He might have handled it the way his brother had, with subtlety. But then he would have had to pass up that rich chance to taunt a member of an Elder clan.

They knew the notice had been served by the loud kicks they heard among the stools that lined the drying hall. Gutenberg stalked in among them with a sheet unfolded in his hand, and threw it down among the crucibles and cupels.

'So much for bloody freedom.' He swung his grizzled mane around, a baleful look in his gold eyes. 'We're all inducted now.

'You're all to scratch out your full name, and year of birth, if you sad bastards even know it.' His eyes on Peter were remote and cold.

Peter laid his punch down and came to sign his name.

The master smelled of beer and smouldering resentment. He licked his lips and bent his head close; his eyes and mouth were foul. 'From here on out you keep your tongue inside your head,' he hissed, 'or I will nail it there myself.'

Chapter 5

SPONHEIM ABBEY

Winter 1485

'It was his arrogance – his hubris and his arrogance that wrecked it all.' Peter Schoeffer stands and takes a turn about the room.

Trithemius is rubbing at the closed domes of his eyes. '"Therefore he set over them masters of the works, to afflict them with burdens".' Wanly he smiles and quotes the book of Exodus.

Peter's throat is tight. It is surprising – and disturbing, to discover rage still lodged against his ribcage after all this time.

'The man could never bear to share – or to be challenged.' He shakes his head. 'He thought of all of it as his, from start to finish.'

'It's not surprising, considering it was his whole life's work,' the monk observes.

Peter snorts. 'Try working for a man like that. He thought of no one else – he thought of nothing but the glory he deserved.'

It was the way that Gutenberg could open up his heart, then snap it shut that hurt the most, he thinks.

Trithemius is nodding. 'How hard is too hard? That is what I often wonder.' He smooths a hand across his close-shaved scalp, a strange expression on his face. 'Ruthlessness does serve its purpose.' He adds, after a pause: 'My monks hate me, to speak truthfully. But they are lazy, stubborn, gluttonous – they are a blot, I think, on the whole order. One must be hard, sometimes, push far beyond our human weakness to fulfil God's will.'

Peter turns it over in his mind. He too has been a hard man – a hard master – in his workshop. It's years now, yet he knows it must be true. He was as jealous as the master to keep safe the secrets of the art. But he never rode roughshod over friend and foe alike, the way the master had.

'How do you know if it's His will you're serving – and not simply your own pride?' He sees all three of them in his mind's eye, each doing his own part. 'If we are truly touched by Him, what need is there to shout it from the rooftops?'

Johann Gutenberg felt himself anointed, chosen, just as Peter did. But this was not enough. He had to rub their noses in it, claim it all – make sure that he was seen and praised, acknowledged by the world.

Chapter 6

JOHANNESFIRE

Feast of John the Baptist [*24 June* 1452]

On Midsummer's Day they laid the fire out in a flattened field behind the waters of the Bleiche. The air was too dry to risk the need-fire closer to the houses. The council had considered banning any bonfire altogether, until the livestock handlers howled. There was a need, that year as every year, to purge all sickness from the herds. There could not be relief, for man or beast, without Johannisfeuer.

Who did not feel renewed, indeed, by flames that burned the dross away? The summer bonfires of Peter's childhood still were close inside his heart. 'Higher, higher!' voices always chanted, children crying 'Two ells, three!' and leaping and laughing to feel the hellfire licking at their feet and know the harvest would be just as high. Each year he'd watched the women gather the St-John's-wort on the bright and shadeless stroke of noon; how he had marvelled, as a child, to see them rub those yellow stars that gave off bright red drops of Christ's own blood.

The master let them put away their tools before the sun had started sinking in the sky. Not out of any kindness, or to free them for the celebration, though. Peter saw him make his way towards the quay and the Frankfurt market boat. Of course – for it was the feast of John the Baptist, the twenty-fourth of June, the day that payments on the Elders' bonds were made. The only heavy hearts were on the councils of free cities that were forced to pay. Each rich man had his little sack of gold, each workingman a copper heller for his purse, which wife or daughter lined with orchid root to keep the luck from draining out.

Peter told Hans and Ruppel they should find a high spot on the hill to view the spectacle of bonfires burning on each distant slope, each village and each peak along the Rhine. It seemed to him that God above must love that sight, for all its heathen roots: the pinpoints strung along the river like a gleaming rope of fire. By the way that Keffer brushed his yellow beard, they knew that he would court that night – as Peter would himself this year. He'd asked Anna to come watch the fire with him on the hill of the Altmünster. It happened that the year was one in seven, so the pilgrims from the east had come by oxen train and mule to board in Mainz the ships that would carry them to Aachen. They camped outside the cloister walls, and reverenced the relic on its altar, a sweat cloth used by some early Christian martyr. It seemed to Peter quite a fitting place to stand and watch, for goldsmiths, most particularly, were cautioned to keep distance from the solstice flames – and he did count himself, by now, among their number. Their patron saint, Eligius, warned Christians quite expressly to beware the dancing and the chants, the heathen burning of the herbs for luck, as superstition if not worse.

Anna's mother was a dyer and a weaver; for that reason Anna knew the Bleiche well, and gave him as a meeting point the dyers' hut. She'd paid a boy to send her note; when it arrived, he tried to open it in private, but Ruppel saw it and sang out.

'Sweets for Saint Peter, eh?' He grinned and wiped his hands upon an inky rag.

'You know a setter does it with great feeling in the fingertips.' Keffer winked.

'I hate to think what pressmen do,' Peter laughed in answer, conjuring some strapping, well-built lass. 'Each to his own, I say, and may we all come back half sober.'

He dressed with care in fresh fawn leggings, belted on a blue-green tunic. He did not wish to make himself too fine, yet as he prepared his body for her eyes, he felt that any less would be too little. Smoke was curling from the chimney as he neared the hut; the order had not yet gone out to douse the city's fires. His heart pressed hard against his ribs, which seemed to spring and open like a lock when he first saw her waiting with a basket on her arm. She took his outstretched hand and put it to her cheek, then gave it back. He asked her what she hoped to gather in her basket, and she looked out from those dark almond eyes and laughed.

'What would you like me to collect?' she asked.

'My fingers, and my toes, my hair, my eyes, my clothes.' He made to peel each thing away in naming it, and cast each part inside her woven bowl.

'Ah, that would never do,' she said. 'For I would have you whole.'

She showed him in. He understood that she was showing, too, the women gathered there that all was seemly and correct. Her mother smiled, and straightened from her stirring at the tub. She could not greet him properly; she flapped her blood-red hands. It shocked him, just a little – all those women with their skirts hiked up, above that boiling tub of madder root, their aprons stained as if with gore. They dyed the linen there in shades of coral, brick, and rose, and dried it on the posts along the brook. The boiling room was hot and close, like a confinement, he supposed. They fled at last to cooler air and sweeping vistas from the hill.

There was a little bridge that led them up across the fields and to the wilder bushes just below the Altmünster. Anna would not go beyond the hedges to the holy ground until she'd gathered up the herbs she'd need that evening. He nodded, dumbly, said he'd be her willing slave. Here we can find the comfrey and the elderberry bush, she said. He held her basket as she plucked and did not try to hide how much the watching of her slender, bending body pleased his eyes.

'But you can pick as well,' she said after some time. 'Why should the woman do all the work?' He laughed at that, and called her rebel, and she flashed her eyes.

'I think such hands as yours are used to labour.' She took one, turning up his palm. He felt her trace the lines with every tingling fibre. 'Such hands, on such a gentleman.' She laughed and shook her head. For they were rough, of course, and shiny with hard wear.

'The wonder is they have not lost their feeling.' He squirmed inside, recalling Keffer's jest.

'Why should they? When they do the same, with God's Word, every day?'

He wanted then to kneel before her and bury face and arms and heart. Yet when he raised his eyes he saw upon her face a strange, contorted look. It pierced him, how she seemed, all turned within herself. He did not know then how to read her.

'These hands,' he said, and raised her palm to place it praying to his own, 'are simply tools. For gathering or painting, making letters, it is much the same.'

'You know that it's not so.' She bit her lip and shook her head.

He thought he understood then her reluctance, her shrinking.

'What makes you think this hand is different?' he asked.

'You know as well as I,' she said, and looked severe.

'I do not, truly.'

She shook her dark and shining head; he saw the struggle on her lips. 'It has – much finer things in store,' she said at last, her hand still captive in his own.

'And that's the matter.' Unequivocally, he knew it. 'That's why you turn and look away. Because of who my father is?'

She took an elderberry from her basket, crushing it between her fingers. Pale green juice ran down her skin. 'I am a painter's daughter. You, a *clericus*.' She looked him gravely in the face. 'I do not think your father has a bride like me in mind.'

'My father's dead these fifteen years.'

But she was not convinced.

He told her then that Johann Fust could not refuse. How could he possibly, when he himself had chosen Grede? A craftsman's daughter, and a binder, with strong hands like hers, though not so elegant and fine.

'You do not jest?' She cocked her head, a little ember glowing in her eyes.

He laced her arms around his neck and laid his forehead down to hers. 'Here in the sight of God, I swear to you. No other woman holds the keys to this poor kingdom.'

In the shimmer in her eyes he saw as much of heaven as a man can pray for in this life, the darkness stirring with a flame that burned him to her, soldered him forever to her frame. They pressed together, scorched, their eagerness and hunger naked as the white curve of her neck. Only with the greatest effort did they step apart and, bodies bursting, gasp the sweetness of the evening. Never had he felt such torment, yet such peace.

'Shhh,' she said, as he began to speak. She put a finger to his lips, and he could not prevent himself from seizing it, and sucking it, and pulling her back to his hips. She groaned, and they were only saved by a great sound, of men and women cheering, and the thud of axe on wood.

'God help me,' he said hoarsely. 'I am but a beast.'

'No beast, but Adam's flesh.' She kissed him, chastely, and began to straighten up her hair.

He wove her a garland of St-John's-wort, for even Peter knew that it was used for strength on a long journey. They embarked that night for somewhere neither one had been before. She took it from his hands and said to add more blossoms, so he did, and then she placed it on her waist and let him fix it there, with kisses up her dress and to the open swelling of her breasts. She reminded him of the tradition as she led him towards the fire. The solstice belt of mugwort is a charm against all sickness, for the leaching of all evil: a pledge they tossed into the fire to guarantee their health. 'They even say' – she smiled – 'that if you hang one in your house, it wards off looks from evil men.'

'Then hang a dozen, when this night is done,' he said as they stepped into the mass of dark and dancing bodies in the bonfire's glow. He saw her parents there, her brothers, painters, tanners, weavers, bakers, coopers, saddlers: men and women lined and hard from scraping, beating, shaping, forming. Hans, too, Ruppel, Keffer, those last two with girls, drawn like himself to that communion with their fellows. He thought he saw his uncle, then his cousin, in the flashing of the fire; he saw them, then he lost them in the dance, which wove and leapt around with screams and shouts – and all that while, as he could hear the reeds and flutes beneath his skin, as if the music rose from his own soul, he thought not of God or devil but of Anna, only Anna, with her fire-kissed skin all flushed with love. He knew himself at last to be a child of earth and heaven, body fused to spirit in the sight of God and man, when as the solstice flames died down they looked at one another and agreed, without a word, and ran, and sprang across the embers and came down in one another's arms. *If this be sin*, he thought, and tore the belt from round her waist and cast it in the flames and heard the crowd roar praise. They stood there, panting, joined before the world.

Chapter 7

IMPRESSORIUM

Tuesday after Saint Augustine [*30 August* 1452]

The days of the saints are lettered in red. It has always seemed to Peter Schoeffer that this day should be remembered the same way.

The morning they began the printing on the Bible, the crew came round the press in the cool darkness before dawn. The master stood before that oaken frame, his hair pulled back, his eyes uplifted as if at an altar. 'May God Almighty bless this work,' he boomed and raised his arm.

Peter held his breath through that first pull, ears waiting for the telltale metal bite, the little grunt that Ruppel always made at the last tug. Then everyone stepped back as Keffer hauled the whole works out and peeled the printed sheet away. Gutenberg and Fust each took a corner of the sheet and bent their heads, one dark, one fair, and surveyed it closely. Peter never would forget the look of triumph they exchanged.

'Fiat imprimere!' his father cried this time.

The crew all hooted. The press began to crash as the two pressmen found a rhythm. The others should have gone back to their stools in the composing room, but none of them could tear themselves away.

Peter fell in love with the whole motion: of the great sheet lifting and then settling; the hard and painful kiss; the sweet, slight sucking sound of linen peeling from the metal. The master's ink was as black as the night before Creation, blacker than the oak gall ever was. Peter held it to his eyes and marvelled. Never had lines ended in such symmetry; never had the world seen such a thing.

The city just outside their door receded utterly. They were aware only of the chain of being, one man handing the sheet on to the next: the boy who reached it to the inker to the pressman who returned the printed sheet back to the master, his beard tucked into his shirt. Like a living creature they were now, a new and many-headed thing.

And then the glow wore off, as it must always. Yet even at the time Peter knew those days were incandescent, without rival. There was a bursting in him – a heady sense of strength, that wondrous feeling of pure rightness that does shine in every life for some brief time.

It fell to Peter to set the first five books of the Old Testament, the Pentateuch of Moses. Hans didn't care which lines he set, so long as he could do them sitting down. His back had started aching.

'How old are you, then?' Peter asked. Hans scratched his pate and reckoned. 'Fifty, maybe,' he said, shrugging. 'Sigismund was on the throne.'

They'd work in parallel, the master said: Peter would start on Genesis, Hans on the book of Judges. The text they took from pages torn from that small scribal Paris Bible. The man who'd written it used every trick to shorten the words so he could cram in more. It strained Peter's mind sometimes to grasp which word was meant by which abbreviation – and he'd been trained. For Hans it was a horror, plainly. 'Ex-audio, ex-animo, ex-bloody amino,' he'd mutter, lips protruding with the effort. Peter felt for his old friend. But how to help him, without seeming that he flaunted his own skill? He started turning now and then to him, and asking what he thought some word might be. Hans would grunt, and spit into the can he kept below his feet for just that purpose. How in the devil should he know, if it was gibberish to fancy hands? So Peter wrote a list out of the words that were most common, and their usual abbreviations, made a show of looking at it, asking Hans to scan his lines. Thus did they find a way to choose, together, phrasings of felicity, and lines neither too loose nor tight.

They set it *seriatum*, page by page. Peter had never read the scriptures in this way, from first word of each chapter to the last, *historia* unspooling in his hands. He was amazed that he should be the one to put these words on this skin and paper. They shaped it physically, he and Gutenberg and Hans: they made the Word incarnate. Peter would pause sometimes and gaze on his wizened friend as they sat hunched above their letter cases, and ask the Lord how such a task had fallen to such two unlikely men.

If copying a manuscript was prayer, then this was shouting out the psalms from every rooftop. It grew in him with every passing day, this feeling of abashedness and wonder. *Why hast Thou, Lord, put such a gift in these poor hands?*

It could not be for beauty's sake alone, or even just to multiply His teachings. It seemed to Peter that God had sent His Word, as He'd once sent His son, to cleanse their corrupt and misguided world. Was this not the clear message of the Gospel according to John? *In principio erat verbum*: in the beginning was the Word – a Word they flung out now, a boundless net of shining letters, cast out by that great fisher among men.

And when he asked just why this miracle had come to Mainz, the answer came back just as clearly. This gift had been bestowed upon the city of Saint Martin, who tore his cloak in two to clothe a beggar. It was intended, then, for all mankind: the humble just as surely as the rich.

The testaments, of course, are full of trials. From the moment in the Garden that temptation raised its serpent's head, God set his creature tests to prove his faith. So was it too inside the Humbrechthof as soon as they embarked. Within a week, the problems started.

The sheets were so large and unwieldy that they flapped and slipped. They'd miss a pin, and lodge lopsided when the frame was lowered on the *forme*. Ruppel, sweating, nearly lost his hand the first time he tried to straighten one that went half-cocked, only springing back just in time. Gutenberg stood over him, haranguing, cursing at each wasted sheet, threatening to dock his pay. He scooped up the wasted sheets, counting and recounting them, his face a frightful sight. A half a dozen, creeping Christ, a bloody fortune. He was seething as he called a halt. 'Nail half a dozen extra pins on to that blasted cross.' Ruppel obliged, and the paper slipped much less, although the printing went more slowly for it. Each night the master gathered up those sheets that had been fouled and sourly counted them before he locked them up. Thank God the ones they lost were mostly paper, and not hide; the first time that the pressman and his beater lost a sheet of vellum, the master came up and tore it out of Keffer's grip and rolled it in a bat that he used to whack him. Then it was laid to rest like a dead thing inside the crate of wasted sheets.

Nor did his glossy, sticky ink hold its shape in that furnace of late summer. With each advancing hour it melted to a slop that either beaded on the letters or just dribbled down their sides. Though Gutenberg reduced the oil and sent for drying agents, still it slopped. So then they'd have to work by cool of night, he said, and cursed the cost of extra candles.

And even so the pages dried and shrank before they had a chance to print the other side; they'd have to dampen the sheets again, but gingerly, and pray they held their shape. Of course the printed sheets could not be laid atop each other, out of fear of the ink smearing. Peter still remembers how young Wiegand staggered, arms held stiffly out, toes seeking out the ladder to the drying line. The drying pages hung above their heads, and swayed and rustled when the master thundered past: a flock of great white gulls that hectored them from overhead, with sharp, black markings on their sides.

Gutenberg was a blur in constant motion, darting back and forth from forge to press, back to the master book upon his desk, prodding, poking, pulling at his lips and beard. He was the only one who moved; the rest of them were chained to their respective stations. Fust appeared each evening as the crew began their nightly shift, but Master Gutenberg was always there: he never seemed to leave, even to eat or sleep. There was no moment – waking, sleeping, upstairs, down – when they were free of him, his beady eyes, his dark, oppressive presence.

And even so, the thing just crawled. A week passed, then ten days, and all they'd managed to produce was the first three pages of Saint Jerome's prologue. They'd had to print two dozen extra copies of each page, to compensate for wastage. Then it was three weeks, halfway through September. Soon it would be Michaelmas, and they had managed only six pages in a book that ran to nearly fourteen hundred. At this rate, Hans said, chewing at his lip, even if you rounded, it would take them seven years.

Fust's face grew blotched, the master's blacker. Like rabid dogs they watched the crew: the more they watched, the more the ink balls slipped and the paper missed. Peter felt for Ruppel and Keffer; he sensed their fear of slipping and the sickness in their guts. He and Hans were not exempt: woe betide the man who made a setting error, if the master found it printed there. 'F!' he'd bawl, or 'M!' and reach a lightning hand to pluck out the offending letter. Hans or Peter would step out with the replacement, flinching as the reject whistled past. Gutenberg made not the slightest effort to control his temper, flinging, shouting, cursing, punching at the air. Pustules, cretins, misbegotten blackguards, spawn of Satan – he dispensed them all. He'd left no margin for such errors, it appeared – and that, to Peter, was the greatest error of them all.

The book had been designed to save on paper. There were no blanks left for a lavish painting; every line was calculated closely, to squeeze the most from every paper bale. Those bales, of course, were paid for out of Fust's new capital investment, which he had borrowed not just for supplies but for the workers' pay and room and board. It took no special skill to note the waste sheets mounting and the corresponding tightness in the partners' jaws. Vast sums were riding on it, every man among them knew; the master had spent frugally, but freely. No man alive had ever before ordered ten full bales of paper and five thousand calfskins at a single stroke, Peter was quite certain.

He used to wonder what those herdsmen and those paper makers thought. There must have been a glut of veal and calves' legs up in Swabia, he reckoned. Never in their lives had shepherds seen such quantities, such promises of guilders. They had to wonder, and no doubt aloud – though Fust was satisfied, he said, by the discretion of the leader of the butchers' guild. No stranger came to Mainz who was not welcomed in the tavern of some brotherhood, and quietly paid on Fust's account, and told to keep his business to himself.

The ring that circled them was hard to see, but it was there. When the harvest started, they found jugs of the last pressing of the grapes upon the granite stoop. Round loaves of bread were left, and honey, bacon, in a basket someone set up by the alley door. It must have been the second week when Peter noticed that there were sprigs of mugwort tucked around the eaves, a wreath of rosemary hung on the portal to the yard. The men of Mainz kept their lips shut; the women hung their charms to ward off evils; the Lord up in His heaven watched.

A month went by before Fust grimly said they had to find a faster way. The master flapped his hand at Peter the next morning just as soon as he arrived. Gutenberg was seated at his stool, the desk before him littered with odd strips of print. He started speaking before Peter even came in earshot: ' . . . win more lines.' He brandished a poor waste sheet. 'Cram in more words.' Peter saw that he had pasted one more line beneath each crooked column. 'Don't wag your head at me.' The master's eyebrows bristled. 'Just shut your mouth and do it.'

Mutely Peter took the sheet. In the composing room he walked towards the granite stone on which the second page of Genesis lay waiting. They'd printed off the first real page of scripture just the day before. Fury shook his fingers as he opened up the twine and pulled the top line from the second column, moved it to the bottom of the first. Just yesterday he'd felt his heart sing as he set: he'd marvelled as he etched Creation's shape, and laughed to think he'd set a whale, but never seen one. And now this madman planned to mar this perfect symmetry. Jaw clenched, he set the next two lines to fill the foot of that right-hand column. He tied it, carried it to Keffer. 'Blasphemy,' he muttered, neck hairs rising as the master dogged him close behind. 'I never said that you would like it,' Gutenberg growled in response.

He kept on droning even after Peter had joined Hans at their composing stools. They'd save the price of one whole book, he said. If they didn't learn by doing, cutting costs, they'd never even make it to the Psalms. Already they'd spent more than anyone had reckoned. Peter heard the worm turn in his ear: *We've got to beat this beast, or it will get the best of us.*

No sooner had the press begun to punch those one-and-forty lines than Gutenberg was back, like a bad dream. His long nose poked in through the aperture that served as door. 'We can get more. I'm sure of it. We can win more.'

Peter ground his teeth to keep himself from cursing him aloud. 'You will destroy the page. Distort the golden mean.' He shook his head, past caring. 'It will look cramped and cheap as any pocket Bible.' He threw his hand towards those close-jammed written sheets from which they set. The master turned and disappeared.

An hour later Wiegand summoned Peter. 'Master says you have to come upstairs.'

Gutenberg and Fust were at the great oak table, standing and frowning down at two sheets laid out side by side. His father glanced at him, his arms held stiffly at his back. 'You have refused, I hear,' he said, 'to add another line.' His face was grave.

'It will distort it beyond measure.'

Gutenberg spread one stained hand across the text. 'This shape is sacred, then, you say?' Peter curtly nodded. The master dropped his hand and stared off into space. 'There has to be another way.'

He swept his dark eyes first towards Fust, then Peter. 'Mechanics,' he enjoined his right-hand man. 'Think on the mechanics. What other way is there, to gain more space upon the page?'

He spoke in singsong, like a Latin master. Peter frowned, and strained his inner eye. Blurrily at first, and then more firmly, he grasped his meaning.

'Take some away.'

The master waited.

'Take out some space,' said his apprentice. 'Between the lines?'

'That's how I see it, yes.' The grey, lined face began to lift into a smile.

Which is how the crew spent miseries of days and weeks in numbing labour, filing down the letters. The type was cast on shanks they had made slightly larger for their first, aborted missal. Now they could shave off a tiny sliver top and bottom, thus reducing space between the lines. It took three weeks and endless bellyaching from the men. Even Ruppel, with his fists like hams, was made to wield a file. Ingrates, scoffed the master: better fingerless than starved. When they had planed enough to make the page that followed, Peter set it up and Ruppel pulled a proof.

As he set it, he was filled with great foreboding. The text itself told of the fall from grace through greed and pride, and man's expulsion from the Garden. And still man's perfidy went on, and Cain slew Abel. Peter took the printed proof from Ruppel with a sickness in his heart.

And yet – O wonder – when he laid the proof beside its facing page, no difference could be spied. But to his scribal eye, that second page, for all its tale of woe, was even lovelier than the one it lay beside. The text was tighter, blacker, more a forceful mesh than airy vines. Peter stared at it, quite disbelieving. He looked up and met the master's eye. 'How did you know?'

'Ha,' he said. 'Blind faith.' He gave his doggy grin. 'Should cut the paper by a tenth.'

The wells beneath his eyes were dark with filing and fatigue, for he had whittled right beside them. To anyone outside he would have looked demented. Yet there was method in his madness, Peter had to grudgingly admit. He did not entertain despair: he did not even let it enter the same room. The man just kept on ploughing, probing, pushing – almost seemed to relish how the matter twisted and resisted him. He had more patience for raw matter than for men, that much was clear – and even then some things were sacred, others must be shed. Peter learned this from him, for himself, when it came time to print the separate red lines.

Fust could hardly wait to see those printed rubricating lines. It would amaze his buyers, once they understood that they were inked not by a pen but by a press. The carmine ink the master mixed himself: oil of linseed boiled to varnish, mixed with powdered copper, cinnabar, some carbonate of lead. This yielded a glossy orange red. The oil was key; Fust nodded: he had seen that telltale shimmer in the new Dutch paintings at the fair. He trundled off then to the Kaufhaus, humming to himself, while they made up the *forme*.

At first, God smiled. The red lines starting Jerome's prologue printed perfectly. Simple enough: they topped the column. The second red line, though, sat halfway down the facing page. Peter measured, tried to place the thing just right. They proofed it, tinkered, shifted the line up, then right, then left. Each time they peeled the proof sheet off they cursed, and wiggled it some more. Sometimes it overlapped the black, sometimes it stuck out past the margin. It took six tries – six wasted sheets, a quarter of a guilder – to get the damned thing right.

The whole time Gutenberg looked on, silently for once, eyes narrowed into slits. He'd let them fail all by themselves, thought Peter bitterly. Finally he just reset the whole cursed column, then took away the lines they had already printed black. One hundred and thirty-five red lines went through the press that second hellish day, which stretched far in the night.

Fust had come in halfway through, then left; Gutenberg, too, waited to say anything until the run was done. It was past ten when Peter hung up his apron. Wiegand had informed him that the master wanted him upstairs. The boy shot off, no doubt to haul Fust back. Slowly Peter wiped the scarlet from his hands and dragged his body up the treads.

Gutenberg stood at the window, staring out across the lane on to the synagogue. He nodded briefly. 'We'll wait for him,' he said. Peter sat. His stomach growled. At length the master came and sat beside him at the table. 'You tried it every way you could.' His voice was calm and uninflected.

Peter made a motion of disgust. 'Without success.'

'Success is only ever an equation. Time invested, plus materials, equals the true price.'

They heard Fust's tread then on the stairs. Gutenberg looked long at Peter, as if weighing something. When Fust appeared, he started speaking. 'The red must go. Or it will ruin us, or kill us – maybe both.'

Fust's face lost all animation. His eyes went flat, moving between his partner and his son. He strode to where the sheets lay waiting.

'This one looks marvellous.' He riffled lightly through the pile. 'And this. And this.' Again his eyes rose, past the printer's head, searching out his son's.

'Barely half are fine,' the master shortly answered. 'It took two days, and what – ten sheets, fifteen? – of waste.' He too turned, his eyes resting on his lead compositor.

Peter tried to sit up straighter in the chair. His eyeballs ached, his fingers, shoulders. But what hurt most was that he'd failed. He reached and pulled a sheet towards him and tried to shake the blackness that he felt.

'A Calvary,' he said, almost to himself. He looked at Gutenberg, gave a short nod. He could not meet his father's eyes.

'We can't reset each page, nor build another press, just for the red.' The master's voice had softened. Even he knew Fust would feel it as a blow. 'The only sane thing is to drop it.'

Peter felt his father stiffen. He raised his head, saw Fust shake his. 'We had agreed.'

Surely, Fust said, turning now to Gutenberg, it was a matter of more thought, more calculation. 'This was to be the crowning glory.'

'"Who against hope believed in hope,"' the master said in answer. 'I wish it were not so.' He put a hand out to his partner.

But Fust had twisted brusquely towards his son. 'I can't believe that you agree.'

'These lines took sixteen hours alone.' It pained him, but he saw no choice. 'I don't see how – though I regret it.'

Fust looked between them for a long time: from master to apprentice, both alike in filth and weariness.

'It would take half again as long,' the master said. 'There is a rubric every third, fourth page.'

'We knew that from the start.' Fust's mouth was set, his eyes more grey than blue. The look he gave his son was like a boot. 'I thought we planned to make a fine and mighty thing,' he said, and set the page back down. More perfect than the most perfect manuscript it was always meant to be.

Fust faced the two of them with bitter eyes, as if they'd forged some dark, satanic bond against him.

'We have to gain more speed.' Gutenberg leaned towards his partner. Attend, he said: at this rate they took two months for each quire. 'We need another man, it seems to me.'

Fust's mouth twitched. Then he harshly laughed. The sound was forced, unpleasant. 'First you kick me, then you strip me bare.'

Chapter 8

JOURNEYMEN

[3 quires of 65]

December 1452

The Advent season came, and with it the relief and warmth of firesides and candles, of drawing close in the community of Christ. Peter had been courting Anna all that autumn, walking with her while the married men of Mainz slept off their Sunday lunch. He'd toss a pebble at her window, and they'd steal away into the little lanes or walk among the bare boughs of the orchards. As it got colder, they would slip into an empty chapel and warm themselves in some back pew. Quite early on she'd asked if he would read to her; she brought him block books she collected for the pictures. Though these were crude, she listened raptly as he read their message of salvation. In the dimness he sought other verses, psalms that she had learned by heart, and traced her fine cold fingers on the words.

The Christ's mass gift that he might give her sprang to mind this way. He made a little book of stories she would know, lettered in his simplest cursive: the parable of Dives and the beggar; the raising up of Lazarus; the Pater Noster and her favourite psalms. He has this book still, locked in a small chest inside his big new house in Frankfurt. He still can see her shining face and how she clapped her hands in wonder. *The heavens shew forth the glory of God, and the firmament declareth the work of his hands.*

Her gift to him was likewise from her hands. She painted him a portrait of Saint Peter at the gate, with Peter's own brown beard, his narrow, sober face. 'Heresy,' he said, laughing, and brought her fingers to his lips. They met in secret, though of course her parents knew. A few months in, Klaus cornered him and plainly asked him his intention. Marriage, Peter answered, and Klaus frowned and fingered his thick beard. They both knew Fust would not approve without a fight.

Peter watched and waited for a likely moment, but his father's mood was not improved. He was still angry over the lost ruby lines – disgruntled, too, to see how fast his guilders gushed. They paid dues to carpenters and smiths and tanners, butchers, bakers, brewers, although he drew the line at tipping off the painters who worked hand in glove with scribes. He wasn't just some pig to stick and bleed, he growled – although the new man, too, in due course did arrive, another mouth that he must pay and feed and house.

This fellow hailed from Alsace like the others, though Johann Mentelin was not a smith, praise God. Peter was delighted to discover he had been a clerk in Strassburg's bishopric. Nor was he a mere notary: he specialized in gilding letters and had a flowing, calligraphic hand. How in God's name had Gutenberg seduced him? Peter wondered underneath his breath as they all stood to greet him. Hans shook his rippled forehead and just laughed.

The new compositor swore his oath of secrecy on the first page of their Bible. A sum of money passed into the master's hand: the training fee, which Mentelin would pay half at John the Baptist, half at the Solemnity of Mary. His coming raised the level of the talk inside the shop. His Latin was impeccable; he'd studied in Erfurt a few years ahead of Peter. At noon he'd bow his ginger head, recite the readings with his eyes closed from the book stored in his mind. The jokes were ribald, naturally, when the master said where he would start. He'd pick up setting where they broke the book into a second volume: Proverbs, followed by the Canticum Canticorum, the randy, lovesick Song of Songs.

They numbered nine or so that first Yule at Fust's table – the master and apprentices and journeymen, plus the boys they'd dubbed their devils. His father had convened them on the feast of the Three Patriarchs, those Hebrew men of staunch, unyielding faith. The groaning board was meant to mark their first full year of common labour, he declared. Exceptionally, the workingmen had bathed. Their eyes went wide at the long table draped in Flemish lace, the beeswax flames reflected in the silver platters. Pork haunch with cherries, ducks with sage clamped in their yellow bills, heaps of greens and tubers – and that was nothing to the Riesling and the Spätburgunder. Along the sideboard Grede had ranged a deadly chorus of assorted brandies. The master stood and tapped his goblet with a knife and bid them shut their gabbling mouths.

'I give you Johann Fust,' he roared. Already he had had a few. The men began to drum their feet upon the floor. His father smiled and whispered something in Grede's ear, and rose.

'It's been a long year, but a good one,' he began. 'We're making slow but steady progress.' His eyes went all around the table; when they came to Peter, he paused slightly, then moved on.

The master leaned, and cracked: 'We're out of Kings, is what he means, and into Proverbs. Though I am sorry to report that Peter is still wandering the Garden.' The mugs flew up, and Keffer yelled 'Hear! Hear!' Peter stood, and took a little bow, then raised his own.

'To Johann Fust and Johann Gutenberg,' he cried, 'and Tubalcain.' To their blank looks, he grinned. 'The son of Sella, great-great grandson of Cain,' he said, and quoted out of Genesis: '"who was a hammerer and artificer in every work of brass and iron."'

The drumming of the workers' feet drowned out all other sound. 'As custom holds, therefore,' his father called above the din, 'each one will be rewarded.'

Gutenberg began to hand out gifts. The journeymen and apprentices he gave a little paper roll. The young ones and the servants each received a pilgrim mirror. How very like the skinflint, Peter thought, smiling. He skimmed the ribbon off his roll. The square of linen bore a single sentence in the master's sloping hand: 'To be redeemed, with the Lord's aid and grace, against one copy of the *Biblia latina*, created without help of pen or reed by a new and secret art in the golden city of Maguncia, Christ's mass: Anno 1452.'

Gutenberg was grinning like a cat. 'A gauge of our respect and faith.'

The devil. Peter had to laugh.

'Consider it,' the master added, 'payment against wages.'

'The devil.' Peter whispered it this time to Hans. 'To bind us even tighter in the harness.'

'Worth its weight though.' Hans peered closely at his scroll.

The man was diabolical, in truth: offering the fruit when every bough was bare and nowhere near to budding. Sheer evil genius, Peter thought: a paper Bible was worth twice, three times, what any craftsman earned in a whole year. And yet – he looked back at the scrap – how fine, how marvellous. He pictured it upon a lectern in a home where he would bring his bride; he saw it bright with red and running titles, filled with tiny, brilliant scenes, penned and painted by their two laced hands.

The snow was falling in thick clots when they staggered out towards the Christmas market. The tented canvas lifted, orange and glowing, like a galleon on the market square. They ducked inside: the stalls were wedged so tightly that the flakes were trapped and melted overhead, or else died hissing in the flaming torches, sizzling in the chestnut barrels. Keffer grasped Ruppel by the scruff of his thick neck, steering him around the stands of glassware. They wove past wooden toys and crystal candy towards the kegs along the edge. Nearby a hand-cranked organ shrieked; a crone in rags pressed her hard cup in Peter's ribs. He smelled the rankness of her breath and pressed a penny in her hand. The rich were all shut up in their great mansions draped with fir, their candles sketching steeples on the glass.

They found a cauldron filled with hot mulled wine and drank it fast, and downed some more. Mentelin, for all his freckled innocence, had little trouble putting his away. 'What's on the programme then?' Peter bawled in Keffer's ear.

'First gold, then honey!' Keffer's yellow locks were shining, like his eyes. He elbowed Mentelin, half a head shorter, at his side. 'Best show the bishop how it's done.' The gaming house up on the flax market would be full to bursting. Mentelin looked back and forth between the two large workingmen, Ruppel slumped on Keffer's arm. He threw a smile at Peter. 'I guess I'd better keep these two in line.'

Ruppel jerked his head up, sketched a sloppy curve into the air with one limp hand. 'I'll show you lines!' he slurred.

'You coming?' Mentelin asked; Peter shook his head. The night was far too fine, the wine too pleasant in his veins, to jam into some stinking cave.

'Got honey of his own,' Keffer hooted as they dragged the scribe away.

The departing pressmen half collided with two monks who

stood bemused in the thick, pungent throng, and Peter groaned inside. The damage they might wreak tonight could be extreme. He was still laughing as he turned towards Hans, shaking his head, when someone grasped his arm.

'I hardly recognized you,' came a low, unwelcome voice.

Peter forced himself to focus and cursed the drink that fogged his sight.

'They let you out,' he thickly said, 'to spy the seat of sin?' With a forced smile he embraced Petrus Heilant. The scribe looked at him archly and nodded briefly towards Hans. His fellow monk was no one Peter knew.

'The better to combat it,' Heilant answered drily, his right hand lifting to inscribe a cross, ironically, before their eyes. 'Drowning your sorrows, like those roughs who nearly crushed us?' He cocked an eyebrow and glanced back, but the three printers had been swallowed by the crowd. 'Nice friends you have.'

'Once a smith,' said Peter, shrugging. 'Half my uncle's workshop's here tonight.' Heilant looked a trace too long at him, with a smile that Peter didn't like. He dipped his head. 'We'll leave you to your business then, and hope to see you in more . . . salubrious . . . surroundings.'

They moved away, and Peter watched them long enough to see how Heilant glanced back once, his features calculating, before pretending he was gazing past them at the stalls.

'Nosy bugger,' Peter said to Hans.

The smith nodded. 'Don't know why you give that kind the time of day.'

'Know thine enemy,' said Peter, as they edged back towards the stand of wine. They gave their cups back, pocketing their penny caution, and started roaming. Now and then they paused to look more closely at a clock, a hide, a whirligig, a feathered cap. Eventually like homing birds they fetched up at the goldsmiths' stands along the Chapel of the Blessed Virgin. Across the square, the columns of the Mint were dimly lit, but here the smiths had made the huts where they sold goods throughout the year resplendent. The Windeckes' shelves were draped in crimson velvet, piled with jewellery that flashed with semi-precious stones. To either side stood a dour smith, a dagger at his belt. Jakob's shop displayed its silver goblets, copper chafing dishes, candlesticks and sconces on three rising tiers, each carpeted in lamb's wool. Beside this Gottholt's stand was filled with cutlery, then Isenmenger's, iron pots and clasps and tongs.

Hans bent, examining a ring, and Peter asked, 'You ever miss it?'

'Now and again.' He put the ring back. 'But then there's only so much you can do with gold.'

'You'd rather muck about with lead.'

'Wouldn't know what I should buy with it.' Hans shrugged.

'You'll keep your copy then?' The others, Peter guessed, would sell their Bibles just as soon as they were finished. Hans ran his tongue across his teeth and shook his head. 'Don't ride your horse before it's shod.'

'Sound advice,' said Peter.

'Not that Henne ever heeds it.' Hans smiled grimly. 'Always rushing on ahead.' He called the master by a name nobody else would dare to use – knew him more closely, Peter thought, than anyone. A mouse ran down a hallway in his head. Was this what happened, way back when, he slowly asked – that thing he'd said, a while ago – something about a Christian robbing graves?

Hans glanced quickly left and right. He jerked his head, and Peter followed to the market's darker edge. 'You swear,' he said, and Peter nodded. A brief smile lit the smith's creased face. 'A scene, it was. They even hauled me up before the judge.' Then he went serious again. 'It wasn't nothing, though, but greed. He had these partners, see. Two fellows called Andreas – for the mirrors. He already had me carving letters too, one at a time.' Hans rolled his eyes back, as if rolling the whole thing back through his mind. 'Anyway, they paid a heap to get in on the business. Then one of the poor bastards got the fever. You should have seen the master tell Lorenz to run like hell and grab the *formes* and under no condition touch the man.' He grinned. 'He's always had a deathly fear of pox and plague.'

'And came much closer than a Christian should, to robbing graves,' Peter murmured.

'The dead man's brother went after him hammer and tongs. The thieving dog, he tried to grab his brother's piece. Called in the law and witnesses, the lot – for all the good it did him.' Hans shook his head. 'Master won it fair and square, according to the contract.'

'But even so he didn't stick around in Strassburg.'

'We had to save our skins, too, don't forget, from all them Armagnacs.'

They drifted back. As they were passing the last stall, a chalice caught the goldsmith's eye. He picked it up and ran a finger along the square flanged base. 'Too thick,' he said beneath his breath.

'I'm sure that yours was finer.' Hans would have made the rank of master, surely, if he hadn't followed Gutenberg – yet he had been content to stay a journeyman. Hans set the chalice back, looked with disdain upon the rings, some of plain gold, others made of plaited bands.

'We had to do a setting in my day.' He turned away.

These were not *Meisterwerks*, of course, but simple journey-work. In Mainz, like Strassburg, journeymen would have to set a bevelled stone, or craft a silver bowl, at least engrave the inside of a decorated band, to gain the master's rank.

'That I would like to see,' said Peter.

Reflexively, Hans put a hand up to his chest. 'All right,' he said, and started walking swiftly from the market.

'I didn't mean—' said Peter as he caught him up, but Hans just shushed him, trotting out into the lane. The air was colder there; the snow was barely trodden. Hans plunged a hand into his leather jerkin. The little packet he drew out was wrapped in silk; he opened it and held it to his mouth and blew, then polished it upon his sleeve before he handed it to Peter.

By the snip of moon he saw it was a woman's band, in braided gold, set with a large, dark stone. It was too dark to tell the colour. Hans's eyes were on the ring, but by their look he saw instead the hand that ring once graced.

'I made that nineteen years ago.' His voice was low. 'I could have had my own shop, in Speyer or Cologne. I had my eye on a girl in Strassburg, though. Funny, how things go.'

He took the ring back, lifted it to catch the light. Above them there were candles in the narrow windows of the hospice of the Holy Ghost, and the writhing creatures on its gutters cast strange shadows on its stones. Hans shrugged. 'That's how I wound up working for the lunatic, Gutenberg, and made a pile of useless gold.'

'Why useless?' Peter asked.

'We'd planned to buy a farm.' Hans wrapped the ring and tucked it back.

'I'm sorry.'

Hans made a little motion with his head. 'God has long since saved their souls. She died in childbirth, see, her and the baby both.'

Peter put a hand upon his shoulder. 'I'll pray for them.'

'It's just the time of year. It happened at this time of year, that's all.'

Peter thought of saying he had lost his mother, too. But there he stood: alive, full-grown.

They walked slowly back towards the Humbrechthof, past the grocers' guild, decked out in bunting for the blessed birth, the shuttered workshops of the plumbers and the rope makers. The wind came scouring down the river gorge, pushing all the snow clouds to the south. Above them there were patches of deep black and stars. They both looked up but gave no heed to how they trod the snow below. Yet now, years later, as he looks upon them, Peter sees the way their paths diverged. Each went his separate way, to end the feast day in his separate church: Hans to join the master at St Christopher, Peter to the Fusts at St Quintin.

Chapter 9

WILDERNESS

[4.5 quires of 65]

January — February 1453

The task before them was as blank and boundless as the winter fields. In five months they had barely made a dent – less than a tenth of those twelve hundred eighty pages had been set and printed. They trudged half frozen through the days and nights, dulled by the blizzard: the white sheets rose, and fell, and rose again to settle on their drying lines.

Gutenberg sat motionless for hours, perched on his stool. He kept his cloak wrapped tight beneath his chin, his long beard tucked from sight. The strange effect was of a barn owl: all that stirred was his queer mop of hair, rotating as he watched their every move. His head would ratchet, and his body bob in a strange rhythm as he counted. He measured each man's output: lines per hour, the pages through the press each day; the time it took to move a *forme* from stone to press, then back. The time between the printing of one page, and then the setting up to print the next. He had Lorenz bring in a small brass clock that sat there ticking as he eyed it, quill pen scratching, noting every movement of each hand.

A week of this, and he made his pronouncement. Another press would be required. Keffer was to run it, and they'd need two new men to apply the ink, another boy or two. The quantities of type and ink would double. Fust, anxious at the slowness of their pace, had clearly given his consent. The hammers started pounding, and two beaters came to spread the ink, one Götz, from Schlettstadt, then another Hans, from Speyer. Ruppel and Keffer each thus had his own press, with its inker and its devil. Wiegand and two other lads kept the sheets dampened, and when printed, dried and folded. In the composing room, Mentelin sat between Hans and Peter.

The new arrangement helped, at first. They picked the pace up and managed two full pages every day, in a shift that stretched from dawn to well past vespers. But then the pressmen learned the ins and outs and soon could crank the sheets out well before the setters had prepared the next. Those empty hours drove Gutenberg into a rage. A three-gammed gimpy mongrel bitch, he called them, pulling at his hair; he'd have to stagger things, and print the pages in a different way. Keffer would print a recto in the afternoon, Ruppel the next morning do its verso – and then vice versa. The inks he'd trick, so Keffer's, with a bit more lead, would dry in time; the winter chill ensured the pages stayed well damped. That way each press would get half of another run each day; the setters would work longer, to keep both presses well supplied. Dear God, each man thought to himself, and groaned inside, and put his nose back to the grindstone.

Hope waned with the slow waning of their strength. Lent was a week or two away, but it had been a poor year for the grain, and only rarely did Frau Beildeck rustle up some meat or eggs. She tried to keep them going with root mashes and strong beer. Nor was the master's mood improved: by February they had finished just six quires. They weren't paid to idle, he snarled, pacing up and down. If any man got out of step, he was to see him: he'd find him work to do. 'As for you lot,' he bawled towards the composing room, 'I'd whip your buttocks if I didn't need them on the stools.'

Mentelin, as gentle as a choirboy, looked stung. Peter laughed and shot right back, 'You do, and I will fetch the guild.'

Instead, they learned after the fact, he went to Fust and told him that they had to have another pair of setting hands.

Each piece of type by then had gone beneath the press some thirty, forty times. The faces had begun to chip, the edges wear. The first they cast had never been that sharp to start with. There came a day when Hans decreed they had to stop and melt them down, and cast some more. The master was in Strassburg to recruit, and Hans was still the foreman. He kept Mentelin at setting type, to feed one press; the others gladly spent the hours beside the forge. It was remarkable, how lightly they all worked without the master breathing fire. Each man was part, and yet apart, responsible for his own task – just like the scribes who penned the students' books in sections. Peter thought a great deal in those days of that whole world he'd left behind. Anna did not notice any difference in him; it pained him, even as he hid his real life from her. The falsehood roiled within him, as it must have twisted inside Peter, his disciple, on the morning of Christ's death, when three times he denied Him. How practised he was now at lies, thought Peter Schoeffer, tossing on his narrow bed at night.

The peaceful interlude was broken when the master came back unannounced one early February afternoon. Some of the men were seated, stirring; Peter cast with Götz; the boys were grinding ores. All froze the moment he stepped in.

'A pretty picture,' he said, stomping off the snow. 'Though I don't hear two presses going.' He had a youth with him, apparently the latest hire.

'We needed letters.' Hans wiped his hands and went towards him.

'I left you stocked.'

'They were too battered.' Peter stood.

'If I paid you men to think, I'd pay you more.' He cast them his disgusted scowl and went to count the finished piles. 'That's it? Good Christ.' He jerked a thumb towards the youth. 'You'd better learn him quick.' Ruppel knocked the lad a stool and case; Hans and Peter quietly conferred. They'd have to cast the extra letters for this new man after hours, Hans said, or Gutenberg would burst a vein for certain.

Peter looked across the room and saw the way exhaustion dogged the master, too. His face was grey, his skin stretched thin and folded at the turned-down corners of his mouth. It was fatigue so deep it went right to the bone: Peter knew that feeling. He didn't think enough, though, at the time, about those trips Gutenberg made, nor ask himself how they had added to the strain. The man did not divulge whom he had gone to see or what he did – he simply disappeared, then reappeared days later, greyer, sharper, more irate. At the time they chalked it up to their excruciating, crawling progress – and then the ghastly inverse speed with which the costs increased. The master wore the proof upon his face: that long, dark beard, which in six months had turned to pewter, grey mixed in with anthracite and white.

Peter set the dull and droning lists of Exodus: begats and more begats, the endless spawn of Abraham and Isaac. They swam before his eyes, slipping from his turgid fingers. Those generations spooling from their seed did little else but strengthen his desire. For eight months he had courted Anna out of sight; he'd not been back once to the brothel or the baths. When Father Michael spoke that Sunday of right reason, *recta ratio*, it loosened something in his mind. Aquinas said each man possessed this one defining line: the moral compass that should guide his life.

No man could know, until it rose to greet him, which path the Lord had chosen. Nor, with respect, could Fust decide which partner he should have. Peter had been waiting long enough; there'd never be a better time.

He went to see his father in his counting house. At the landing he paused briefly to prepare himself. Up from the great hall of the Kaufhaus came a steady throb of sound. He knocked; his father barked, 'It's open.' His face went instantly from peevishness to something like relief. 'I had expected Koestler, come to sell me short.'

Peter smiled and spread his hands. 'Do I look like a thief?'

His father wiped his face. 'Then sit.'

He did as he was bid, and drew a breath. 'I've made it into Exodus, in time for Lent,' he said. 'And the new lad's working fine.'

'Excellent.' Fust leaned back, hands crossed on his paunch.

'It's well and truly started.'

His father nodded, waiting.

'And so . . . I feel it's time. You'll understand that I am loath to face this thing alone.'

The broad face spread into a knowing smile. 'Ah,' Fust said— and then the words that Peter hoped to hear. 'Indeed. You're right.' He reached into his cupboard for the glass decanter. 'And here I feared you'd come from Gutenberg with some new demand for gold.'

'I've put a little by,' said Peter.

Fust laughed, and pushed the full glass towards him. 'That shouldn't matter, if the dowry's right.'

'It's not the dowry that concerns me.'

'It should.'

He steeled himself. 'I want a partner, not a linen chest.'

Fust stopped, his glass half poured.

'You married whom you chose,' Peter pushed on. 'And not some contract with an Elder clan.'

'I had achieved a certain standing.' Fust's eyes were narrow now. 'I had a certain latitude, from being widowed.'

'Standing.' Peter thought of Grede. He forced himself to keep a level tone. 'A man can fashion his own standing, I would think. You've said yourself the world is changing.'

Fust raised his hands, as if to silence him. 'You do not know the world.' His tone was sharp.

'I know enough to pull my weight.' Peter looked into the blue shards of his eyes. 'And take the woman whom I choose.'

'Who would be—?'

'Anna Pinzler.'

His father's mouth fell in a bitter line. 'You are a fool then, after all.'

A rush of sorrow flooded into him as swiftly as a molten metal, hardening in an instant in his heart. This debt was never-ending, then: no sacrifice of Peter's would suffice. He'd owe and owe until the last day Fust drew breath. So be it.

'You ask for my consent?' His father's voice was hard. 'Or simply tell me that you've ploughed the wench, and so must do your duty?'

Peter might have struck him, had not reason or some ancient prohibition stayed the surge of heat inside. 'Disgusting words,' he said, when he came back to something like himself. His nails bit deeply in his palms. 'I never thought to hear such filth out of your mouth.'

'I'm not the one who will be shamed.' His father heaved his torso up towards him.

'You shame me now.'

'By damn, you're obstinate.'

Peter pushed himself up slowly. Fust was tall and broad; the desk stood in between them. But Peter was no knave, no orphan boy who'd benefit from a hard knock – not any more.

'I will not give you my consent. I did not raise you to throw out your brightest prospects.'

'My prospects?' Peter harshly laughed. 'Mine – or yours? You know they never were for me – but just your own advancement.'

'That's quite enough.'

'Indeed.' He looked at Fust, his face half mottled in his rage. Red marks like posy-rings of pox, he thought. 'And if I left?' One last, sharp thrust. 'Who would you get to make your Bible then?'

'So you resort to threats.'

'I know my worth.'

'You think too highly of yourself.'

'Not one of them can draw or carve as I do, and you know it.'

'No man is indispensable. Not you, not Hans. Not even Gutenberg.'

'And even so you wouldn't like to lose me.'

Fust stared at him as if he were a stranger. 'You've learned from him, I see – just how to bite the hand that feeds you.'

At that his son walked to the door. He glanced once as he put his hand upon the knob, but Fust had turned to look across the trading hall. All Peter saw was his broad back; all that he heard was that incessant roar.

He moved his things to the Humbrechthof that afternoon. There wasn't much to take: his shirts and books and writing pouch. Before he left he sought out Grede to tell her he was going. She had been tucking in the children for their naps; with a finger to his lips, he drew her out into the hall.

'I asked for Anna Pinzler's hand,' he said. 'Your husband has refused.'

She put a hand up to her mouth. 'Dear God.'

He couldn't tell the reason for her shock – the choice of bride, or Fust's reply.

'I'm leaving now.'

She gripped his arm. 'No, Peter, surely—'

'You can reclaim your room. I'll sleep above the shop.'

Her fingers tightened. 'You could have asked me – why did you never think that I might help?' She stared at him, her dark eyes huge.

'He wants an Elder bride or none at all,' he told her brusquely. 'I thought to spare your feelings.'

She stiffened. 'You do not know him as I do.'

'I'm sure that's true.' Peter took her hands in his. 'I'm sorry, Grede.'

'Just let me try—'

He raised her hands and kissed them gently. 'Too late. I should have thought of it before. But now—' He shrugged, and walked away down the long hall.

The workshop was locked tight. But Peter had been trusted once. His father's son enjoyed the privilege of a key. He drew it out and locked himself inside. Keffer was the only man upstairs, curled up asleep on his straw pallet. He cracked an eye when Peter put his satchel down. A grunt, and then he pulled his blanket tighter, rolled back into twitching dreams. The place was freezing, frost on both sides of the thick, waxed windowskins.

Below there was a glowing heart deep in the ashes of the fire. Peter wakened it and fed it and then set to work. In work there was forgetfulness; through all those months and years the need for letters never waned. Each idle moment they would cast some more, and ever more, replacing those the press had worn, making ever-larger piles to feed that ever-growing crew.

Sometime during that snowy afternoon the master put his head in, to complain about the waste of fuel. 'A step ahead,' replied the stony figure at the forge. 'It makes more sense for me to sleep here too.' Gutenberg regarded him, one bushy eyebrow raised. 'At least you don't eat much, the way you look,' he said, and went away. It was, indeed, the gauntest season. Fitting, too, that his expulsion from the house of Fust should fall just on the cusp of Lent – the fasting hunger time.

He filled the space where gratitude and love had been with tin and lead. He did not feel he owed a soul an explanation. Hans knew better than to ask; Mentelin knew nothing of it; Keffer, though goodhearted, was a clown. Gutenberg had doubtless guessed that Peter and his father had had words. But he said nothing, for it suited him, of course, to have the whole crew underneath one roof. As it felt right to Peter too, in that dark time of year, to close himself inside the space where he had always lived, wrapped up in parchment, paper – tied with letters, ink.

He would not lie directly to her face. He could not. Yet even so he lived in fear that Anna – bright and observant as she was – would somehow learn that Fust had refused. It never crossed his mind to throw himself upon her mercy and confess their plight. He knew too well how Pinzler would respond. He'd be compelled, for honour, to withdraw and reject Peter's suit. And so, though he was careful not to lie outright, he breathed deceit: he crept and he dissembled.

He took the Sabbath meal with them from time to time, but not too often, lest they guess he did not dine at home. It steadied him to be at their calm hearth, watching Anna paint and holding up his arms to help her mother wind her yarns. His love worked with a deep intensity, her little tongue poked out as she minutely brushed a scene on a ceramic box: a tiny castle on an emerald hill, its ruby pennants rippling.

If anyone had asked him why he cleaved to her, this quiet slip of a girl – if he had ever been prepared to open up his heart for that inspection – Peter would have said that she was all that stood in those dark days between himself and the abyss. She rooted him, and held him to the earth. He was alone, more clearly, coldly, than at any time before. More so even than when he was orphaned, for an infant does not feel the absence at its back. He had not chosen this, but it was his.

He mimed an ordinary life: Anna never knew that when he left her, he did not return to the Haus zur Rosau, nor did she guess that his Sunday mass was sung no longer in his father's pew, but at the master's in St Christopher's. 'My fondest greeting to your father and your mother,' she would say in parting, as his stomach twisted.

What small allowance he might once have made for Fust's ambition disappeared, corroded by the bile inside. It was his father's fault that Peter had to feign a lightness that he did not feel; but for his veto, Peter might have spared himself – and her – that web of lies.

Klaus Pinzler would not wait much longer for the handshake. The only hope was to present his father with a dowry of the customary size, and pray he'd have to take it or lose face. The *Handschlag* did require a host of witnesses; a minor crowd could be arranged. Peter pictured Jakob's face when he let drop his brother had refused a craftsman's daughter. The Pinzlers had two elder sons as well, who painted manuscripts and doubtless knew his father's clients. Peter felt a bitter exultation at the thought of trapping him at his own game.

The only question was the shape and size of wedding goods the Pinzlers should provide. He thought at first of asking Grede. But he refused to put her in that place, stretched between him and his father. He should have asked her help, and long before; he was a fool. Even so he roughly knew the dowry should be worth a year of a good income, some twenty, thirty guilders. And on the evening that he broached this figure, Anna blanched. He took her face between his palms. What *Mitgift* she could offer was laid piece by piece in a small chest of scented pine beneath the rafters of her room. Sheets and curtains, table linens – serviceable, certainly, but not the finest quality; some pewter dishes, several mirrors, ceramic pitchers painted by a Pinzler hand. Five years' accumulated treasure, more or less.

'There's more where that came from,' he murmured as he kissed the lines of worry from her brow. She kept on glancing down the ladder to her loft. They'd snuck him up to snatch a look; at any moment either parent might appear. They fled into the darkness, running towards the wall, ducking with their hoods pulled close into the foreyard of the Augustinerhof, where townsfolk clustered for the friars' cheap wine and fire. Under cover of the crowd, he told her of his plan. He would build her dowry up himself – buy more fabrics and furnishings, all fine enough for any merchant's house. He had some money put aside; he'd ask his uncle, maybe even Grede. Jakob was the leader of the guild, for pity's sake; he'd cough up cutlery and candlesticks at least. And then, if they were quick, they both could earn a little more. Anna's face lit then with hope. She'd paint a mirror for the duchess, she said, nodding; he could find some work to scribe. They laughed and stole a kiss; like two old hens, he said, scrabbling after fallen groats.

This was how he found himself once more inside the Schreibhaus. He collared Heilant, swallowing his pride. He needed work, he said, a little something he could do at night. The scribe looked at him at first with coolness, then his face broke into a wide smile. 'Perfect.' He clapped his hands. 'Two days ago we lost our best man to the house in Erfurt.' He was in charge of half a dozen scribes, Heilant explained – three from St Viktor's, three hired in from outside – to pen a big new monastery Bible. 'Providence is swift,' he said, his cheeks spreading with genuine delight.

'My father'd have my hide,' said Peter quickly – much too quickly, he thought afterwards, as if he were some wayward child. 'You don't know Johann Fust.'

'Come,' said Petrus Heilant. 'You're years past your majority.'

The blood rose into Peter's cheeks – he felt it, cursed it, as he cursed these lies. And too, the thing was rich – a Bible, God above, another Bible, written out by scribes in Mainz this time.

'I couldn't do it by the piece?' he asked, knowing full well that they would never parcel out such volumes. A tome like this would be a work of years, a dedicated team in a scriptorium.

'You amaze me.' Heilant pulled back slightly, as if Peter foamed about the mouth or showed some other sign of madness. 'Of course not.'

'It's just – I am enslaved,' said Peter, with a smile he hoped was winsome. God knew it was the truth. 'And' – he bent as if to share a confidence – 'the truth is, it's the price of his consent for marriage.' He winked and made a filthy gesture with his index in the ring of his left thumb and finger. 'I'm wed now to the brothers Fust – but let us pray for not much longer.'

It wasn't bad, as fabrications went.

Heilant pursed his lips. 'I am amazed,' was all he said, again. His eyes were veiled. 'You would have given anything to do this, once.'

'Instead I must content myself with an Aquinas or a Virgil.' Peter held up his praying hands. They agreed to a copy of the first part of the *Summa Theologica*. But since the great scholastic was long-winded, Peter would bring back each quire as it was done, and wait for payment. Heilant made a smart remark about his seeming need. 'If you but knew,' said Peter, smiling.

It did amuse him in the next few weeks to watch the way his former schoolmate fawned and flattered as he lay in wait for rising stars. One night he breathed that Peter had just missed Konneke, along with Budenweg, Archbishop Dietrich's private scribe. Peter thought back to that audience, now nearly two full years ago. Was Budenweg the hunched dark figure he had seen, a writing desk upon his lap, at Dietrich's keep? And then it came to him, a blinding bolt, the thing that he had put out of his mind: a mighty gift, a handsome, ornate sheaf – that proposed present for the pope.

The pontifical they'd shown to Dietrich had not come about, as Gutenberg had prophesied. They'd set and printed a few sheets of those four canticles while proofing their new type, long months ago. But then the missal had consumed them, and the pope had promulgated his new tithe. Dietrich then had not been in any mood for gifts, or missals – they had set the thing aside and concentrated on their Bible. Just one of those extra copies, Peter told himself. He could not sell it openly, of course. But in the secrecy in which the guilds had wrapped them, there was no harm in settling a copy on one of those helpful *Brudermeisters,* who could be counted on to prize the prayers in private.

Peter found the pages easily when he returned, tied on a shelf above the master's desk. They'd printed off four sets. What beauties they would be, he thought, embellished by his lover's hand. He hesitated for an instant. These sheets were Gutenberg's, or Fust's. 'Forgive me, Lord,' he whispered, 'as Thou didst forgive my namesake long ago.'

He took one sheaf to show her in their secret pew. When he unrolled the verses, Anna gasped. 'Mary mine,' she said. 'I've never seen . . . its like.' Transfixed, she gazed upon the even blackness of it, ran one finger down the sharpness of the margin. 'You are a saint – I am amazed.' She raised her shining eyes to his. 'To think these hands' – she twined her fingers round his wrist – 'hold this extraordinary gift. To think – they write God's

Word – and will be mine.' She threw her arms around him,
raised her lips.

So full of love, and admiration. So sweet, so trusting. Peter
felt his face begin to burn. How could he lie? What was their
life – what would it be? – if it were founded on a lie? A wave
of shame engulfed him. 'It was not I.' He let the sheet fall as
he peeled her hands away. 'I did not write these lines.'
Confusedly she looked between his fingers and the page.

'I do not understand,' she said. She was so pure, so true –
and he a liar, to her, a liar and a thief. A burning need to purge
this fakery consumed him. 'I should have told you long ago.
But I was bound to silence, and too weak.'

'You're not a scribe?' she faintly said, and tried to free her hands.

'A scribe, yes – but not only. This kind of writing is much
more.' He breathed more freely. 'We all were forced to swear
a vow. But I can stand the secrecy no longer.'

He tugged her to her feet and led her, almost at a run, outside
and down the path along the bishop's Little Court. Across the
marketplace into the Cobblers' Lane, around and through the
back. The lane was empty, just a mangy cat that glared at them,
contempt in its gold eyes. He wondered if the beast could sense
the knocking of his heart as he unlocked the workshop door.
He took her hand and slipped inside.

He tried to see the whole thing with new eyes – her eyes.
The shrouded presses, humpbacked widows draped in black;
the bricks of metal on the workbench like a shining row of
loaves. Beyond these the faint glow of coals kept burning, banked
inside the mighty oven made of brick and stone. He led her
towards the desk beneath the window where he'd sat and carved
the letter punches. That first, totemic scrap of parchment still
hung curling from a nail.

'This is my script,' he said, and took it down and pressed it
in her hands.

'Your script?' Her fingers trembled as she peered in the poor light. He struck a flint and lit a candle. 'Where is your work-bench, and your quills?'

'It's true, I wrote them with a quill – at first.' He raised a finger to her lips, parted now in consternation. 'But these, you'll see, have not been drawn.'

Her eyes flipped back, with dread and fascination, to that solitary line: *In principio creavit Deus caelum et terram.*

'Come,' he said, and drew her into the composing room. He reached into his case, into the majuscules, pulled out a letter *A*. Her mouth fell open as he put it in her hand.

'It is a new, amazing way to write,' he whispered. 'Each letter gets a film of ink, and then we press it on a page.'

She stared dumbstruck down at the chunk of metal. 'This isn't writing.'

'A kind of . . . artificial writing. Come.' He led her towards the hulking presses. Beneath the cloth a *forme* lay waiting, bound in its stiff block. 'See how we tie them all together, into lines—' He ran a finger on the metal, bent to see which page. 'The book of Exodus,' he told her proudly.

Anna stood entirely rigid at his side. When he glanced up, he saw a look of fear, repulsion, in her dark and slanted eyes.

'This isn't writing,' she repeated. 'Nor these books. This is a smithy, do not lie.'

'I do not lie.'

'Not now? When you have lied to me before?'

He reached for her, but she stepped back and put her hands into her cloak.

'I felt the same, when I first saw it,' he said softly – remem-bering how he prayed to Benedict of Nursia, whom God had charged to write His Word. But Anna was just shaking her small head, a look of horror in her eyes.

He crossed the room and picked up a Donatus. 'This was

the first book that we made.' He gestured at the press. 'And that will be the next.'

She blanched. 'You toy with me.'

'I swear it by this scripture.'

'Swear not on something you defile.' She looked wildly around the room, fixed on the little copy of the Bible, broken and dismembered on the master's desk. Her hand flew to her mouth.

'You do not even try to see,' said Peter fiercely.

'I see enough. I see that you deny the very gifts He gave us.'

Silently he begged her. But she was shaking now.

'*He* did this.' Suddenly she whirled and advanced on him. 'He did it, didn't he? They say he is a hard and angry man.' She fingered the slim grammar Peter still held open, looked an instant at it, pushed the thing away.

'We did it, all of us.'

'Then it is truly some dark evil that has overcome you.' Anna crossed herself. And then she looked at him, her dark eyes narrow and her voice high. 'Where are your hands? Your eyes? I thought we shared that touch, at least. Yet now you worship all that's hard and cold and dark.' She shook her head. 'As if the Lord could live inside a hunk of metal.'

'Chalices are metal. And the altar and the figure on the cross.'

'You take yourself for something you are not.'

'It is the path,' he said, 'to which I have been called.' His hands dropped to his sides.

'You truly blaspheme then,' she said. 'And I would leave this pit.'

He raised a hand towards her, empty of words. His breath, his heart, his very being, seized. There was a dreadful silence. Then in that searing gap he heard, far off, the scraping of a door. A distant sound: it entered him and knocked and became known. The door onto the street, then footsteps, unmistakeable and brisk, across the courtyard. Anna's face went pale. 'He'll have my head,' hissed Peter, throwing the cloth back on the press. He took her roughly by the arm and dragged her towards the windows. When there was no mistaking that sharp tread, he thrust the grammar in her hand and turned to face him.

Gutenberg said nothing for a terrifying moment. He did not need to. His baleful eyes raked both their faces. 'Could you not find a barn for fornication?' His voice was hateful. 'Jesus, I should chop it off.' He took two steps and thrust his livid head towards Anna's pale and frightened face. 'And you, my girl, if you so much as breathe a word, I'll have you thrashed.'

She slipped beside and past him, nodding, hurried up the stairs. A flash of her green skirt was all that Peter saw before his arm was gripped as if by death's own bony hand.

'Give me the key.' His breath was vile. 'You are confined from here on out. Thought you were gifted, eh? A special case?' He leered, lips twisted in a grimace. 'You're nothing but a scheming sack of shit. The key, now. Then you get to work.'

What happened next is a white blur. Peter remembers only going to the forge. He sees his hands, carved marble, loading pans of ore into the fire. He pushed them deeply in the flames and thought, as he had not for many months, that it had not been God but Satan who had tempted him and raised him up and thrown him down to die. Injustice twisted in him as he reached his arm in, stirring, leaning in too far. The skin shone and the hairs began to curl. His hopes, too, were no more than flaking, whitened ash. This was not his calling, nor his path. Angrily he pulled the lead cakes from the forge, and in his wretchedness he lashed at them, began to bash his tongs into the cooling metal.

The tongs bit deeply in the molten cakes, leaving clear impressions, deep and sharp as footprints in wet sand.

Peter stared, and stared, and wiped his eyes, and stared some more. He stumbled to the casting bench, groped for a letter punch, a mallet. He held the punch against the still-warm metal, smote it once. It left a deep, sharp hollow of the letter, perfectly reversed. A letter *B*, as in *Beatus*: now a perfect, solid mould. He put his hand upon it, laughed a bit, then wept.

All through that night he worked, cutting squares of metal alloy, some still warm and others in degrees of cooling. He tried them one by one, held fast inside a clamp, testing for the perfect density, resistance to the hammer's blow. By morning he had made a small, square letter mould of cold, hard metal. A mould entirely crisp and fine, a deep impression that would hold its shape through many castings. He did not know it then, but in his wretchedness he'd found that new technique that would transform their work, which printers everywhere would use forever after. A faster way to cast their letters crisp and clean, repeatedly from metal matrices – no longer prisoners of crumbling clay or sand. It was their doing – Master Gutenberg's, and Anna's – although he never told them so.

Chapter 10

SPONHEIM ABBEY

Winter 1485

Trithemius stops Peter there. His voice breaks in, a little squeaky and excited. 'You mean to say that it was you? Not Gutenberg? But *you* who made it work – invented this technique the same as it is used today?' He pitches towards Peter, his quill suspended, pointing like a hound.

'Invention is a big word,' Peter says. A stab at immortality, which Gutenberg had never shied from using. His old apprentice nods. 'But yes.' His voice is calm. 'It's fair to say I did invent a key part of the process.'

He holds two fingers up to show the size of that small letter mould. 'The matrix, which we struck with punches, that's the name we gave it.'

The abbot's head is cocked, his forehead creased. 'Yet we have not heard any of this until now.'

'I did not shout it from the rooftops.' Peter smiles a private smile. He had preferred to show his mastery in every book he made; he'd kept his distance from the man who claimed it all and trapped him in his shadow. 'The world went on, and then he died, and after that I saw no point in making claims.'

The truth had slumbered his whole life, until this abbot in

his cloister called. 'But as you say, posterity deserves to know.' Peter clears his throat. He gives the facts, as clear as he can make them, so that this chronicler will set it all correctly down.

'First Gutenberg devised the art of casting letters, using sand, then clay. But we had come, as I have said, to something of an impasse. By then we'd spent a fortune – four thousand guilders, I would guess – yet made hardly any progress, before I found that faster way of casting letters. Our Bible printing changed completely after that.'

It was Peter's hand that held the mallet. He alone who did it, no one else. And yet he sees now how Gutenberg propelled it, too. He was the kind of man who pushed until things gave, a brute who could extract from them more than they ever thought they had.

That matrix redeemed him, certainly. Peter can still hear the way the master crowed. Oh, he was pleased: he praised him loudly at the time, though not again – not at the end, when it truly counted.

'How did it change things?' Trithemius inquires. He seems deflated in some way: he's gathered back into himself, busy again with ink and quill.

'It was a major step. From this we jumped right to the caster that a man holds in his hand.'

Trithemius just gives him a blank look.

'The apparatus we designed to hold the mould, and cast a single letter at a time. This was the main advance that brought the art up to the stage that it is now.'

They evolved it slowly, over time; he perfected it a few years later with the Frenchman, Jenson. The metal mould itself could just as easily have come from Hans, if Peter had not beaten him to it. None of it sprang to life full-blown. Yet what could a young monk know of the beauty of mechanics? How could a layman understand the many tiny, vital steps of true creation?

Always they said: it was this man, or that man, this great visionary, that genius. Yet invention is a process, unpredictable and long. All Peter knows for certain is that each of them had been essential in some way.

He remembers mainly now how stunned he felt that day. All he could see was Anna's white, revolted face. Nor did his father see the benefit, at first. They could make more type, faster, Fust said: so what? They still couldn't print the pages any faster.

'That had occurred to me as well,' the abbot says.

'Write down that Gutenberg's true genius lay in ordering the work, in breaking down and rearranging all the pieces.' On that Shrove Tuesday, he clapped his hands and spun the whole thing magically around.

'The costs were fixed. The only thing that we could do, he said, was boost the revenue. It struck him almost visibly – that we could easily print more.'

'Ah.' Trithemius makes a note.

That was when they increased the print run. They added five-and-forty copies more, most printed onto vellum. Fust was certain he could sell more lavish copies to the merchants at the northern fairs. What extra cost might be entailed in raw materials paled beside the sums those extra copies would bring in.

'We settled on one hundred and eighty, which – in theory at least – would right the ledger.' The printer shakes his head.

'A lot of sacrificial calves,' the abbot murmurs.

'Indeed.' Peter thinks of Abraham and Isaac. 'One hundred and seventy for every copy.'

They gaze at one another for an instant. Peter sees the green fields of the Rhineland in that spring, the frisky gambolling of calves and lambs. With what excitement they had parted after Easter: Fust against the river swollen with the Alpine melt, to sell in Basel, Austria, Tirol – up to Bavaria, then across the

Thuringian woods back home. He took a quire from each of the first Bible books to show in every city to the merchants and the *Brudermeisters* of the guilds – in every country castle to the princes, dukes and margraves. It was a risky move, but they had little choice. They needed the deposits that those buyers pledged.

Rome was not built in just one day, and neither was that Bible. Each step was key, he thinks: a part of that long chain they forged together with enormous effort. The workshop and the crew, the master and apprentice. He feels the loss then, stirring in a dusty corner where he'd laid it long before.

'The Sunday after that was Invocabit,' he tells the abbot quietly. 'You needn't write that down.'

Trithemius smiles, and lifts his hands – a little raising of his palms that's halfway in between a blessing and a clap.

Invocabit me, et ego exaudium meum.
He shall cry to me, and I shall hear him.

That first Sunday of Lent, in the year of our Lord 1453, Peter had stood once more beneath St Quintin's vaulted nave. Johann Fust had asked him back and Peter had agreed; the painter's daughter in her flight no longer stood between them.

Cry to me. So spoke the Lord unto the Hebrew tribes. *Cry to me, from your wilderness, your weariness: the day of your deliverance is at hand.*

The miracle was the multiplying, Peter thought – then and always. From the one loaf, many; from the two fish, enough to feed a multitude. The mystery of God came in through skin and hand and eyes: take this light, this bread, these words, and cast them wide. It filled the air, the ears, this sound now of the punches striking, platens crashing: ceaseless recreation, over and over, world without end.

NUMBERS

Chapter 1

RETRIBUTION

[18 of 65 quires]

July 1453

They heard the bugles first, resounding in the hills, and then the great bell of St Martin's, striking without cease. A cry went up among the sentries at the Diether Gate. And only then did Gutenberg stand up, alert; the men threw down their tools. The Cobblers' Lane was jammed with men and women clutching at their children, rushing towards the square. Hooves pounded down the lane that led towards the city centre, clattering as they hit the cobbles.

Into their hot and sleepy little city came the horsemen of the Holy See, their cornets sounding, reining in their prancing, foamflecked mounts.

'Christians, awake!' The herald strained, voice hoarse, lifting from his stirrups. 'Be warned! His Holiness Pope Nicholas the Fifth sends dreadful tidings.

'Rome of the East has fallen to the infidel.'

The beggars squatting in the shadows threw their rags over their heads and started wailing. Women screamed; men blanched. And then there was a dreadful silence, punctuated only by the throbbing of the bells. In the crush of people – aproned, sweaty, staring, clutching hammers, brushes, knives – Peter saw his father, wrenched too from the Kaufhaus scales.

'The guns of Satan fired without remorse or cease upon our brethren day and night.' The envoy raised his arm. 'All are slaughtered or enslaved. Our brother Constantine is dead, his city desecrated. The holy church of Saint Sophia has become a mosque.'

Rome of the East, Constantinople, the beacon of the Eastern Christian Church. Destroyed. In every stuttered mind, the prophecy of Daniel: *The End Times come when new Rome falls.*

In stealth the Muslim Turks had struck, attacking in the darkness before dawn. They'd felled her mighty towers, burned and murdered, raped her women, altars, churches. Forty thousand people turned to meat, their corpses bobbing in the Sea of Marmara like melons in the Grand Canal. No siege and sack more terrible, not even those that had befallen Babylon, Jerusalem, or Troy.

'We'll have to fight.' Peter blurted it and turned. Gutenberg seemed not to hear. His eyes were locked on the herald, filled both with horror and a grudging awe.

Mehmet II, the Ottomans' young chieftain, with his lust for blood had caused huge cannons to be forged. They'd pounded at the city wall for weeks, those guns, that force of hell some twenty thousand strong. The largest bombard was as long as your Rhine ships, the envoy said, and gestured towards the waterline. Those few who managed to escape said that the very air was rent with flames.

The master's look was terrible, transparent. Peter read its meaning instantly. How had those heathen Turks forged such a hellish and immense a thing? The wonder froze his mouth and left a flicker twisting in his eyes. What kind of mould, what metal mix, could forge a tube so huge a man could fit inside?

When Gutenberg at last broke off his baleful stare, it was to look up at the great bell tolling in St Martin's steeple.

At length they learned from those who'd fled to Patmos, Crete, and Venice, creeping broken in their caravels across the Middle Sea, of how the Muslims had turned Christian genius to their worst defeat. Hungarians it was, who travelled into Anatolia and cast that monster that the Turks called their Basilic – Christians like themselves, turned to heretics, who forged it for their mortal enemies deep inside a huge clay pit.

God tests them, holds them to the fire. He roars instead of weeps at their stupidity and sins. Why else had Peter, on that very day, been setting up that very passage? He was on the fourth book of Moses, known as Numbers. *This is the number of the children of Israel, of their army divided according to the houses of their kindreds and their troops, six hundred and three thousand five hundred and fifty.* The Lord bid Moses take the tribes and number them and muster them into a mighty army.

Peter turned to Mentelin. The shock in his green eyes was like a mirror of his own. Was this why God had given men these gifts? To put his creatures to a test He knew they'd fail? The sultan's cannon proof that man's techniques could serve the cause of evil just as easily as good?

This happened on the twenty-ninth of May, although the news had only just reached Rome. The tiding reached the pope on the feast day of a local saint: Saint Maximinus of Trier, who once gave succour to Saint Paul, the patriarch of Constantinople. How scripture's web did weave its dreadful meanings.

All were punished. Their sins, their cravenness, their greed, were to be blotted, every sinner swept away. The world was changed. Peter felt it even then, the drop inside the gut, the wrenching as it all began to pivot. What he and Gutenberg and Fust, the workshop, lost that day was not of much account, compared to that terrible bloodbath on the Bosphorus. But still the sultan's strike was the clear cause of all that followed.

'They must be mad!' The master found his voice at last. 'To strike like that!' He punched his fist towards the sky. In the dense crowd a man yelled out, 'Strike back!' Another, then another, until it thickened to a chant: 'Strike back! Strike back!'

'God have mercy!' Gutenberg was shouting. 'Strike them, push them back.'

Mentelin and Peter stood dumbstruck, hearing the great roar of hate. There would be holy war: God save them all.

The master did not monger war, more than the rest. Peter understands that now. Gutenberg just felt, like every Christian soul, profoundly wronged – attacked on his own soil. And yet that blow too struck a gong in him that rang an end to all that had been theretofore. The day they heard of Christendom's defeat, Peter saw a side of Master Gutenberg he'd never seen before: the warrior, with a fey, unseemly lust for battle.

Inside his uncle's house the family sat ashen and speechless. Johann, Grede; his uncle Jakob and his aunt Elisabeth; Peter's cousin Jakob and his thick, slow bride. The children – future, hope – had all been bustled off into back rooms. It was impossible to say what course the kaiser and the pope would take in answer. Fust slid to his knees, and everybody followed. He did not lead, but only mouthed a silent prayer.

Grede raised herself the first and put her feet up on a stool. Her hands she held protectively against her barely swollen belly; she was again with child. A servant came with cool mint drinks and bread and meat. Flies buzzed and buzzed above the untouched food.

There would be meetings, of the city council and the traders and the guilds, in the Rathaus and the Kaufhaus and at

Mompasilier, inside the Little Court, the Schreibhaus, and at Dietrich's central palace at Aschaffenburg – in all the abbeys and the churches of the archdiocese, the empire, all of Christendom, there would be voices raised, debating now.

Friedrich III, first king, now kaiser, burst into tears on learning the appalling news, they heard. They could not count on him to lead: he was a weak-willed man, too lily-livered even to forsake his court in Wiener Neustadt and come to meet his own archbishops in the Reich. This Jakob said; Peter's father nodded. The pope had no control: the city-states of Italy were all at war, as England was with France. They knew too well how all the German dukes and princes warred.

And in that void, who then would rise to their defence? Grimly the merchants and the guildsmen stiffened. The trading routes would close, if they were not already shut: the fleets from Genoa and Venice that ferried silk and spice down through the Bosphorus were commandeered, no doubt, or sunk. There'd be no cloves from Araby, no fabrics from the East, no lapis from the Afghan mines, and certainly no eastern markets for Mainz linen or Mainz wine.

They saw in their minds' eyes the blood-red wave of conquest rolling over Europe's eastern flank: eradicating Cyprus, the Knights Templar in their island fastness, Rhodes; spreading like a stain from Greece across the Balkans into Hungary, lapping at the boot of Italy, menacing Saint Peter's rock in Rome.

'We'll soon be levied,' Jakob said. 'Though where the pope thinks we will find it, I don't know.'

'Not in Aschaffenburg.' Fust grimaced. 'Whatever army Dietrich raises, he'll take out of our hides.'

'*If* he raises an army,' Jakob said.

Peter pictured that huge languid head, its pale blue eyes. He'd never stick out his own neck: already months ago he had refused the pope's call for another tithe.

'He wouldn't dare refuse.' Fust looked genuinely shocked. 'He could not fail to aid the church.'

Bitterly his brother smiled. 'He does not give a damn.'

The smile was one they came to know in the ensuing weeks and months: of mirthless irony, and mockery, and self-defeat.

What good was government? Peter asked himself. What good those lords and masters, if they couldn't at the very least assure the safety of the people in their lands?

'If he refuses, then at least he won't take men and horses.' Grede leaned slightly forwards, turning her white face towards Peter.

'True.' Fust too looked at his son. 'At least for now.' He dipped his fingers in a bowl of water and wiped his forehead. 'But God has acted for a reason. We'll have to act as well, and soon.'

Peter knew by the way Grede looked at him that she wondered if he'd thought of Anna first in those sharp, awful instants on the square. His old friend did her best to read him still. Yet if she'd dared to ask, he would have had to disappoint her. He did not think of Anna then – nor had he, in the months since she had fled, appalled, except from time to time to marvel with a cold, hard mirth at how effectively the will of God was exercised, down to the smallest detail.

This miracle was never his to share.

This Bible was not his, nor Gutenberg's, nor even Fust's – but God's.

In the first days, when, scorched and reeling, he'd reached out to her and tried to make her see, she had refused him. Such was his reward for breaking vows and baring soul and speaking truth. He'd written once again, and still received no answer; he had resolved to write no more.

Grede remonstrated with him, telling him that it was nothing more than a young girl's superstition. It was that unknown, fear-filled world of letters: magic, potent in their strangeness and their power. But Peter saw it otherwise. The weak – corrupted, lacking faith – must all be punished.

Let others quake and mewl. He understood at last the Lord's design. He bowed himself, a tempered thing passed through the fire, a hardened tool at God's command.

The western powers held their breaths throughout the barren weeks and months that followed. Rain did not fall; the crops failed then, as if the Lord had also ordered nature to deprive them of all comfort. Word came of refugees that swarmed the Adriatic ports, emaciated, crawling from the stinking holds. The pestilence crept back with them, oozing up the river valleys, bringing its black marks of death – as if that dark avenging angel too must feed upon the weakened *corpus* of the world.

Who would now willingly recall the nakedness and sense of violation of that time, the strange, unmoored abandon that it bred? The layer that protected them was stripped away. Peter's morning walks were filled with beggars and their speechless offspring, bowls held out, eyes hollow, forced like rats into the city from the desolation of the land. Each morning he saw farmers sprawled in their own vomit, dead to God or devil, stinking of the friars' wine. The churches for their part were never fuller. The faithful rose to gird themselves at the dawn mass, to guarantee an angel at their side throughout the day. Grede, especially, was fearful of the failing of the crops and what it might presage. The news out of the east had come just on the feast day of Saint Margaret, the patron saint of childbirth, although her own time was still some months off.

And Gutenberg became a man possessed, as if he'd been hail fellow and well met before. They had to pick it up, get moving. He cursed the sky, the stars, the sun and moon. Lord only knew how long they had. If he knew more than anyone what Dietrich planned, he did not let them know it. He only took that chart on which they tracked their progress and stared at it unblinkingly, as if it were the Turin shroud.

The quires still left to print stretched to the right like empty squares on a chessboard. The rows marched two by two, stacked one above the other: Peter's work and Hans's, then underneath this, indented by some months, the quires assigned to Mentelin and the new fellow. 'Hopeless,' Gutenberg said, one finger boring on the place they'd reached. Of all those quires, they had not printed even half. He looked at Peter, glittering, but did not see him; Gutenberg looked back, frowning at the lousy chart.

'It is the heat,' said Peter. 'Unless you have some magic way to cool the day.'

The master only raised his eyebrows.

It was then that both those partners started viewing the whole workshop as a monster, Peter thinks – lumbering, insatiable, and slow. Devouring all they tossed into its maw, but for all that not moving one iota faster.

His own invention had done wonders for the text. The printed letters were extremely beautiful and dark, their edges crisp and biting evenly. But the metal matrix had not really helped with speed. Nor was it, frankly, as robust as he had hoped: it held for only thirty castings until the plate began to buckle. He'd shown the master one torqued piece a month before, and said they might try strengthening with copper, but Gutenberg had only snarled. 'With what?' His eyeballs rolled. 'Unless you beg it from your uncle, or your father has a mine up his backside.'

He'd made such remarks before, about how nice it had to be to lay one's hands on ready gold. Once Fust had come back flush from Paris and handed every man a silver coin. The master had just sneered and said, 'And me? And me?'

That late July he tapped his finger on the chart and said, 'Another press, another team of setters. Or we've no prayer of finishing next year.' As if what any of them did would make a difference,

Peter thought. 'And even then,' the master went on, scowling: 'The hounds of war might be unleashed, and buyers all the scarcer.'

He took a blade and lifted all the empty quires beyond the ten they'd been assigned, and placed them underneath in two new rows. There was no council, no debate, for Fust had left in haste for Basel to assess the damage to his Levant trade. Nor did Peter write to tell him. It was no longer his concern. He did not stand between them any more; he floated free now, as he'd hoped, though differently. He was a tool, of this there was no doubt. But it was not this master or this father whom he served.

Peter found it telling that the first wares to be lost were regal dyes – the purple of the popes and kings, crushed out of Adriatic snails. Lost too the medicines: the camphor and the ambergris, the vomit of the whale against the plague. Pepper and salt failed next: who harboured the illusion that their city and their work-shop would remain unscathed? Grede spoke of nothing else each week when Peter came to teach his stepsister Tina. The merchants' wives passed information with the plate that made its way along the pews. The strings of oxen out of Hungary, the convoys filled with oils and olives: none of these set out across the Alps. They said that Ladislaw, the kaiser's nephew, quaked in Hungary, launching frantic calls for reinforcements. The Turks had overrun Salonika and Athens, and now encircled Budapest. As bad for the merchants was the fact that buyers in the West had taken fright, or like the Duke of Burgundy, diverted what they might have spent on goods to weapons for the coming war.

Speed was of the essence, clearly. Thus it was all the more bizarre when Gutenberg produced his two new hires: a pair of brothers out of Eltville, faces smooth as babies' rumps, their fingers white and slender as new shoots. If every other member of the crew had brought some knowledge of writing and engraving, the Bechtermünze brothers at the most had held a silver spoon.

'Nikolaus and Heinrich, meet the crew.' Hans looked them up and down and with his teeth made a low sucking sound. 'Train up, train up,' the master said and turned. It took no imagination to deduce the truth: he'd got a pretty price to take them off their father's hands. Old Bechtermünze surely saw the chance as providential. He was a distant clansman of the master's too – which Elder wasn't, in those looping ties connecting Mainz's thirty wealthy clans? He doubtless saw the workshop as a safer cloister than the abbeys where he might have shelved his youngest sons, before the monks began that cant about reform.

Still, presses are not cheap, nor hands, connected as they are to mouths: four more gullets, with the pressman and the beater, wine and bread and now and then some meat. Fust's face was purple when he learned on his return.

'No warning? Not a blessed word?' He grabbed Peter's elbow after church. 'Is this how I'm repaid?'

'It's not my works.'

'But mine. And that does make it your concern.'

'I did not feel it was my place,' said Peter.

'Your place is where I put you – there, to keep an eye on things, hold up my side.'

Peter smiled. 'I did not know that there were sides.' He stood there, at the portal of the church, a bright late summer's day. 'Do we not pull together?'

'And I buy all the bloody oxen feed,' Fust growled. 'Do not forget who buys these tools and pays the bills, and by the way, your wage.'

The next day their two voices rose in counterpoint to Ruppel's hammer building the new press. In the composing room they eyed their texts, pretending that they didn't hang on every word. They had the room, the master bellowed: hell, they had the space for working, eating, too.

'Who said that you could make decisions for the two of us?'

'As far as I recall, I am the master of this works.'

'Four more mouths to house and feed.'

'What's it to you? So long as your own payment stays the same? The trouble is all mine, as far as I can see. To make it work.'

They stepped into the corridor and into view.

'To make it work.' The words, in Fust's mouth, sounded vulgar. He stopped and raised a finger to his partner's chest. 'No matter how you count it, though, it raises all the costs one-third.'

Sidelong, Peter saw the way they locked their wills: Fust with his belly round and hard, his legs braced far apart, Gutenberg with his beard flowing, pulled to his full height.

'Johann.' The master dropped his voice. 'We have to finish this, and soon. You know it's true.' He took his arm; Fust shook it off. They headed towards the door. 'I saw no other way . . . Besides . . .' They heard the way he tried to smooth that standing fur. 'We're not without resources. We can bring money in as well . . .'

'A charmer, when it suits him.' Hans rolled his old eyes heavenward.

A third pressman was brought in, called Johann Neumeister. Grede's young cousin Wiegand was appointed as his beater. More boys were hired to fold and damp. And so their number – six compositors, two men each for three presses – swelled to twelve. Peter did not think he was the only one to think of the apostles, preparing Gospels for a fallen world. Only later did he look back on that final shape and ask himself which played the part of Thomas, which of Judas? Which ones were steadfast, which deceitful, which of them began to doubt?

Chapter 2

―∾―

APOTHEOSIS

[22 of 65 quires]

August 1453

The master summoned Peter the week they started the New Testament. He recalls it quite precisely – can remember clearly the strange sense of portent, the conviction that it all was willed. The prologue to the Four Evangelists had just come off the press, and in it he saw prophecy. He took a clean proof with him when he locked the shop after the night's long haul, and walked it over to the Hof zum Gutenberg.

'This you must read,' he said, and held out the sheet to Gutenberg.

Jerome's introductions to each Bible book were oddly frank and often out of tune with what was written in the Scriptures. Here Jerome had moaned a bit, and said he feared reprisals, then justified his duty to revise – and, yes, correct – the Holy Book, in words that clearly foretold their own printed Bible.

'"Even the testimonies of the evil-sayers agree that what varies cannot be true." The master read it out. "For if we are to be faithful to the Latin editions, let them answer: to which of them? For there are practically as many editions as there are copies."'

'Excellent,' he said, and gave it back.

'"What varies cannot be true,"' said Peter, smiling, shaking his dark head. 'He knew one day we'd fix the Word, and make it permanent, forever.'

'It is ordained.' Gutenberg half stood and leaned to push the shutters open. A bright new Sabbath streamed into the room.

'Yet still amazing,' Peter said.

'That I will grant.' The master tucked his beard into his shirt. 'To think that such as we might figure in His plan.' His grin was crooked. He poured them each a glass. 'But then again, it isn't ours to ask if we are fit for the task.'

'Indeed.'

'Now more than ever we must fall back on our faith.'

For all the foulness of his mouth, he was a God-revering man. He drank from tin and not from silver; he cared little for the fine things of the world. Peter found himself surveying his disorderly front room, struck for the first time by this fact.

'Frau Beildeck would be horrified,' said Gutenberg and smiled.

'She has her work cut out with us.'

The master nodded, but kept his eyes on Peter just a fraction longer than was comfortable. 'Slaves lashed to their spars.' He lightly snorted. 'Don't think that I don't know it. They'll be just fine – in fact, that's why I called you here.'

Peter's nape hairs lifted instantly. Lately he'd enjoyed the master's high regard – but even so, you never knew just what might issue from that mouth.

Gutenberg leaned towards him, his brown eyes clear and calm and flecked with gold.

'You've learned as much as I had hoped. Not just technique – the men respect you, too.'

A rod of fear swiped through him.

'I've seen the way you treat them – I daresay better than I

do. It seems to me you're ready as you'll ever be to run it day
to day.'

Peter tried to speak, but found his throat was closed.

'Don't look like that!' The hoary face was grinning now.
'You've run it, nearly, these last months. I've seen the way you
keep the copy moving, how you guide them.' He touched Peter
on the arm. 'Don't think I haven't seen as well the way you
watch my every move.'

'No more than you.'

The master laughed and settled back.

'You cannot mean you're going.'

Gutenberg shook his head no.

'But then—'

'I'll keep my eye in here and there. Somebody has to go
ahead, though – sweep the track.'

The master looked at him and, not unkindly, laughed. 'It's
running now with decent speed, correct?' he asked. Peter
nodded.

'There's nothing to it, then. Remember Theophilus. It is a sin
to shirk the gifts that God has given.' Gutenberg seemed not to
grasp the fear that paralysed his journeyman, now elevated to the
master of the shop. 'Come, man. You're fit to go. God knows
I've got no patience for the thousand petty problems of the crew.'

That much was true.

'It is – an honour,' Peter managed to get out.

'We'll see, when we have made it to the finish.'

'Hans—'

'—won't give a damn. He's happy in his corner. You'll be
the foreman now: you'll set the schedule, parcel out the quires.'

'It is an order, then.'

'Indeed.' The master's eyebrows twitched.

To be so elevated. Raised, anointed – set above his fellows.
Peter drew a breath at last. There was a twinge somewhere

beneath his skin, the panicked voice of that young boy: *I am not worthy, Lord.* For just an instant doubt and shame consumed him: that a mere shepherd's son should be so singled out. And then he shook it off.

'I will not let you down.'

'Excellent.'

They bashed their two tin cups.

'The only thing you need is discipline. A hard hand that can drive them.'

He meant to share with him the wisdom of his years. 'God drives us, I would say,' responded Peter.

The master smiled, a trifle ruefully. 'You keep me honest, Peter, that you do.'

'You do not see my less-than-worthy thoughts.'

'I've seen enough.' Gutenberg pitched suddenly towards him. 'No women, that's my only rule.'

Peter did not flinch, although his skin went cold, then hot. 'That's in the past.'

'They'll suck you dry.' The master nodded, sitting back.

He ought to know. Peter smiled and looked him in his beady eye. 'I heard that once there almost was Frau Gutenberg.'

'Deluded wench, to think I'd make a decent husband.' Once more the master snorted. 'She sued me, if you can believe it. Breach of marriage pledge. I won, of course.' His look went far away. 'People make claims, Peter. They'll clutch at you, and try to hold you back.'

'No chance of that,' he answered.

They stood, and Peter reached his hand. But Gutenberg had started shambling round the table like some old demented bear, reaching his arms around him – briefly, awkwardly, as if he did not in the least know how to do it.

Peter left his hand upon one shoulder when the master dropped his and sprang back. 'I owe you——,' he began to say.

'All well and good.' The master's voice was gruff. 'We'll count it up above.'

Hans said he'd seen it coming a mile off. Gutenberg got bored, he said; he started itching for the next thing once the tricky parts were past. Not to take a jot from you, he quickly added: come to think of it, they'd never yet got to the end of anything the man had started. Nor did it seem that any of the other men had dreams of standing in the master's shoes. There wasn't much to gain from it, so far as they could see. It was in many ways a thankless task.

When Peter thinks back on that time, he sees himself alone, a solitary figure like the one upon the master's family seal, bent underneath its burden. Weeks passed without a sign of either partner. The three of them were like the figures on the tower clock: racing past but never touching, never meeting, only pausing when the bells were struck, then off again to trace their lonely circuits.

Thank God he had the crew. Right away Keffer opined they ought to celebrate down at the Mallet. As his first act as foreman, Peter overruled him. Besides, the tavern would be shut when they had finished with their shift at cockcrow, he had claimed. In fact the problem was, the shop was getting porous. The bell of silence that the guilds observed had cracks; as their numbers grew, their secret had become that much more fragile. Recently his cousin Jakob had accosted him, half-crocked in the lane. 'Time's a-wasting,' he had slurred; that shop of theirs had smelted lead enough to line a hundred coffins. God, or else the devil, knew what weapon they were forging, but they'd better get a move on. Mainz could use their help right now.

The crew therefore assembled at the break of day upstairs, to consecrate their newly elevated master.

'To second winds,' said Hans, and started pouring.

'And second halves.' Peter unfurled the chart and pinned it on the wall. Why not enlist them, he had thought, and let them know how far they'd come, how far they all still had to go? The men all looked and found their names, and traced the quires that marched in a long row beside them.

'Second books too, I would wager.' Keffer's feet were on the table as he rubbed his eyes.

'You said that years ago,' said Peter, laughing.

'Still.' The pressman shrugged. 'I'd like to know what he is up to.'

'I'm only glad he didn't hand it off to me,' said Hans, and stepped up spritely on a stool. He rapped his mug to get attention. 'Now,' he said, 'look sharp. I guess I'll have to do the *Brudermeister's* duty.' He nicked his chin at Peter. 'The man's no master till he's baptized, eh?'

He jumped back down, and Keffer, Ruppel, and the rest all stood, except the Bechtermünzes, who looked on, amazed. The table they shoved to one side; then all six rolled the sleeves of their right arms. Hans beckoned Peter to the edge of the ring they formed in the middle of the room.

Each man stretched out his hand and placed it over Hans's, until all six stood linked, their arms connected like the six spokes on the city's wheel.

Keffer reached to fill a cup with his left hand, and placed it on the topmost mitt. They started singing then, and raised their arms as they began to turn, lifting as they turned the tilting, sloshing cup. The great wheel spun as they all shuffled, moving clockwise in the age-old drinking song that ended with the journeyman's or master's bath. When all their arms were well above their ears, the man to be anointed ducked into the circle and looked up, and braced himself for the last bellowed 'To our fellow!' Six arms heaved up the cup and scattered, leaving

Peter, face upturned, eyes closed, legs braced, mouth wide to imbibe the brandy as it plunged.

The tumbler clocked him in the cheek, but he was quick enough to grab it and to slurp what had not spilled. 'Silver sounds much better,' he called, grinning, spinning, showering them with the last drops. The Bechtermünzes were still gaping, ignorant of goldsmiths' ways – until they too were plied with schnapps.

They laughed and guzzled half the day; Peter wondered once if they would pay when it came time to work again that night. But they so rarely got a chance to take their ease or tell bad jokes or tap their toes to Keffer's flute. He owed them that, at least.

Heading towards the outhouse, he crossed paths with Mentelin. The sun was blazing; Peter's head felt hollow. They balanced on a trough and let the heat scorch the fatigue away.

'Salve,' said the gold-scribe, squinting at him and holding out one hand. 'If that is what I ought to say.'

'I never asked for it.' Peter looked beyond him, blinded by the brightness. 'I only thought about the task at hand.'

'I noticed that about you.'

Peter smiled. He was fanatical – perfectionist, he knew. He looked as closely as he could into those green and slitted eyes. 'I have to take it as God's will.'

Mentelin was nodding. 'That's what I told myself when I met Gutenberg.' Something in his tone made Peter ask. 'You don't believe it now?'

'I think the Lord must have a sense of humour' – he scratched his freckled face – 'to put His faith in such a man.'

It hit Peter suddenly: Gutenberg was gone. 'I'll need your help,' he said. 'If we are going to make it.'

Mentelin looked at him levelly. 'I have no doubt.'

'I wish I shared your confidence.'

'"Prepare ye the way of the Lord, make straight in the wilderness the paths of our God,"' the gold-scribe said.

'Isaiah.'

'I set it yesterday.'

'And I'm to drive the coach,' said Peter, standing and stretching as he moved towards the door. And wield the lash, he thought but did not say.

'Perhaps the Book will drive itself,' said Mentelin.

'Perhaps.'

Chapter 3

CRUSADE

[24.5 quires of 65]

September — October 1453

A meagre harvest came. And in the midst of that undoing of the world, Peter Schoeffer led the men. The books at which they laboured were these six: Numbers, Chronicles, Isaiah, Saint Matthew, Joshua, and Ezra. The two partners were dispersed and wandering they knew not where. The workshop was an ark, its stout walls battened as it sailed across the rising waters.

He took the master's desk but not his way, and without question not his title. Peter, they had always called him, and they called him still. Except that now from time to time he heard Johann Mentelin joke softly as he passed, 'There goes the Rock.' And it was true that he was cool, not hot: not warm to the new men, but not explosive and unpredictable as Gutenberg had been. The weight upon his shoulders was as heavy as the mountain-tops of Zion: he alone could see them in the distance, count the miles.

On the last day of September, Archbishop Dietrich formally pronounced the pope's decree. Nicholas V ordered Crusade against the Turk. All Christendom would come together to repel the heathen foe. Inside the workshop Peter fiddled with the setting of the book of Ezra, fixing errors made by Heinrich Bechtermünze. Ezra's verses weren't just prophecies, but answers to the hidden meanings of Creation. He read them with great avidness; it seemed to him their present fate was just as grim as any he had set in Genesis. God had crushed the city of Saint Constantine, as He had rained the brimstone down on Sodom and Gomorrah, and unleashed the Flood. 'I will teach thee whence a wicked heart is,' Ezra said: God teaches through His punishments.

Peter took the finished pages to the storeroom and tucked them under canvas, and then locked the door. The only hope was faith – true faith, like that of Noah, or of Job, he thought, the Word of God the only bulwark in the storm.

The master had cheek, pretending that he handed him a thing that ran without a hitch. As soon as he took over, Peter saw it was a lie. The Bechtermünzes struggled to complete half a page a day; the third press idled. Keffer and Ruppel were accustomed to a lengthy lubricated break while they waited for the ink on their respective pages to be dry enough to print the other side. That staggering would have to go – two able setters for each press meant there should never be a moment when they slacked, except to break for food or water. 'Killjoy,' Keffer muttered with a lowered brow and half a smile, as if to probe how far their camaraderie extended. But Peter remained stone-faced, his eyes unfixed and distant, reviewing those machines, the hands that fed them, and the hands in turn assigned to feed those hands.

'Saint Peter,' they began to call him, mockingly.

Yet Peter did not ask them anything he did not ask himself. He still arrived before dawn's light to start his daily page and did not turn to any business of the shop until those four-and-eighty lines were lying in their tray. He rarely took a break except to wolf down bread that Mentelin blessed each noontime. As darkness came, each day a little sooner, he had the candles lit; he always was the one to snuff them out and climb the last upstairs to bed. He led by his example. The person he had been before – as easy with a smile, a joke, as any other man – was purged. His calling now was vital, holy – terrible, if truth were told.

They hardly knew him, Hans said, some weeks into it. 'For Christ's sake, slow it down.' It was for Christ's sake, Peter answered, smiling strangely, with a distance that his friends had noticed growing. 'Right,' the smith went on, his short legs planted. 'Then you had better listen up.' The pace was crazy – even worse his constant presence, like a ghoul behind them even when they ate or crapped or, God forgive them, tried to catch a wink. Henne had the grace at least to leave them be at night. Hans grabbed him by the shoulder and lightly shook him. 'He's right,' said Mentelin. 'Go home at night, and let the poor men breathe.'

Your father's wife and children would be glad of it, they said. And they were right. It was a hard time, and a frightening one, to be a woman by herself in a fine house. Fust in his letters had already asked Peter more than once to take good care of them, although he'd held back from requesting that he move back to the Haus zur Rosau.

In part Peter kept his distance out of pride – or else his wounded vanity, perhaps. He knew that Grede would always try to pry him open, bring his heart to speech, put right whatever had transpired between him and Anna. Since Grede had learned, he'd seen her now and then in conversation with the painter's daughter at the market stalls. But all of that was past, and ash. The moons had come and gone between, and Peter feared nothing now except the failing of his monumental task.

His old room was unchanged. The children seemed to have grown overnight into grave and wide-eyed things. Tina especially, at eight, no longer let him guide her hand, but shook her curls and made the letters by herself. The Sabbath afternoons with Fust away were just as they had always been. Grede liked, as ever, to be read to while she stitched. She moved more slowly now, somnolent in her pregnancy, although her eyes and tongue were just as sharp. She asked him to read to her from *The Little Flowers of Saint Francis*: fifty or sixty tales, *Floretum* gathered by a Tuscan monk that told how the Franciscans came to be, and of Saint Francis's piety and poverty and all the miracles he'd wrought.

'An interesting choice,' Peter answered with a smile. 'I would not call this a Franciscan house.' She threw a silk pillow at him and said he had no call for carping at her, high and mighty now though he might be. Besides, she liked the stories of the life of Brother Juniper the best, that simple peasant who forever played the fool, abasing himself and rejoicing when the world held him in contempt.

'To be despised and mocked then, here on earth,' said Peter, taking up the little book, 'is to be favoured by our Lord?'

He read the tale to her of how poor Juniper stripped to his underclothes, parading through the city, drawing jeers and rocks and kicks. '"The lower that he sank,"' he read, '"the purer was his own humility."' He looked at Grede and laughed.

'There's nothing wrong with humility, you know,' she said and flashed her eyes.

'I never said there was.'

'Yet you are strange.' She frowned, head tilted, dark eyes sober. 'You keep so much inside.'

She could not see – had still not grasped how he was changed and raised. He looked on her and felt a kind of pity.

'The humble, as you full well know,' she said, 'will be rewarded long before the rich.'

'Then you had best begin distributing these jewels.' He said it calmly.

'You wouldn't be so – cold. If you knew how she pines for you.' Grede put her sewing down and leaned towards him. 'She wrote to you, but you have still not answered – is that true?'

'Truth.' It was a joke. 'I thought it truthful not to lie. My great mistake.' He shrugged. 'I would not do it now.'

She stared at him a moment. Then she looked down and smoothed her skirt and cleared her throat. 'It's not too late.' She leaned towards him, low voice urgent. 'She was afraid; it brings her shame. She sees it now.'

'It is of little consequence.' Peter stood and put the book back on its shelf. 'Though you may tell her, if you like, I wish her well.'

'That's all?' Her face was strangely twisted.

He saw the steeples shining whitely and the soaring towers of God's City sometimes, in his mind.

'Where I must go,' he said, and touched her on the hand, 'I doubt that anyone can follow.'

He was sitting at the table upstairs at the Humbrechthof, reviewing distribution of the quires, when the first man came demanding monies due. Hans came galumphing up, his composing cap in hand. 'I don't know how he knew,' he said, 'but there's a herdsman at the door what claims we owe him twenty guilders.'

The man stood in the lane outside, just at the portal to the courtyard, with a skinny youth beside him. He shifted on his hobnail boots; a bit of straw was caught in his brown beard. 'Don't like to do it, sir,' he said, 'but winter's coming on.' His skin was grooved and brown as an old nut, and Peter felt the range wind scouring till the herder was entirely polished, one with his long staff of yew.

The boy produced a sheet and thrust it towards him.

'How came you here? Who steered you to this house?'

The herder looked at him through narrowed eyes. 'I look for Gutenberg.'

'He lives down the road.'

'This here's his works. He took the hides in here.' The man moved as if to enter; Peter barred the way.

'He isn't here. But I'm empowered to conduct his business.' He took the paper off the boy. 'He owes you then, you say.'

'In consequence of three hundred and fifty skins of six-month calves,' it said, priced at six shillings each. The total, 45 guilder, had been struck out, replaced by 35, a scrawled notation '10 down' in Gutenberg's crabbed hand.

'I see,' he said. Peter looked harder at the man. Why had he come, why was he sent, at this very hour, this very day? 'No date,' said Peter, flicking the receipt with one hard finger.

'This time the year just past.' The face turned one shade darker. 'The whole stock market is my witness.'

Peter too recalled those heaps of skins, close to overwhelming the poor donkeys as they stumbled from the livestock pens. Damn him, he thought. Damn him.

'Why did you not go to his house? He made the terms.' Peter temporized. Gutenberg had left no lockbox, only coins to keep the men in food.

'His man said he was on a journey. As I would fain be too.' The herder's hand went to his belt, where hung a battered sheath.

Hans jerked his head, and they conferred. He could get ten off Lorenz; Henne had a secret jar. As Grede kept her own store for an emergency, thought Peter. He eyed the herder for an instant, recognizing the lean men of his own native farmland.

'Where are you from?' he asked.

'Black Forest way.'

Gutenberg's apprentice, now his foreman, nodded. 'While you're waiting, have a bite.' He left them in the courtyard in Frau Beildeck's care, but not before he locked the workshop and closed up the shutters. 'Hey!' said Keffer. 'Light a candle,' Peter growled.

The bastard, he was thinking. Timed his trip, most likely, to the monthly livestock market. Kept his head down while the drovers and the butchers did their business in four legs with all the traders. *The wily bastard*, he was still intoning deep inside, as he told Grede in all sincerity that Fust would pay the man if he were there.

Both of the partners were due back now any day. Peter paid the herdsman and watched his whittled staff and belted robe receding down the lane. He shook his head and looked up briefly at St Martin's red stone steeple. Who else? The chandler, papermaker, varnish man? He chuckled then and crossed himself and closed the little door cut in the portal. He had been warned.

A few days later, Peter heard from his cousin Jakob that a merchant stopping at the Kaufhaus out of Erfurt had been asking awkward questions on the trading floor. His uncle sent his son to tell him, not a serving boy; Peter understood it was a warning. A year had passed since all the guilds had taken gold for silence, but patience had its limits.

Jakob the younger was a thick man, dark-haired like his mother, not that quick. 'There's them that wager you are casting weapons,' he said. 'They know they're not to talk, but . . .' Up and down went his broad shoulders. 'The point is that your ship is leaky – so my father says.'

The Erfurt merchant had inquired if Fust was in the city, as he'd like to buy a book. They had been saved by a swift wagoneer who said he wasn't – but his brother was Fust's other half. He'd pointed the fellow to Jakob's great fine house, built by their father right across from the cathedral. A lucky thing, Jakob the younger said, though Peter knew it was not simply luck. He wondered only how his uncle answered – if he'd impressed upon the man the need for some discretion, and if so, exactly how. They could not say the thing was secret, not from Dietrich – only whisper meaningfully that this technique was of such value, and so marvellous, that none should hear of it until the Book was done. Then he could brandish it as proudly as he pleased, one of the lucky few to hold one in his hands. That at any rate is how the printer would present the thing, if he were charged with sales – which, God be praised, he wasn't. Why in the devil had his father stopped to show the quires in Erfurt, anyway? It was too close, thought Peter, and too thick with clergymen.

That was the question Gutenberg put sharply to his father too, when in October they both returned home. They rattled in and overlapped just like those tin-plate skaters on the tower clock. Gutenberg was bright-eyed, rested, clean, as if he'd stopped quite close to Mainz the night before, in Eltville or at St Viktor's.

'How much did you get done?' He threw his cloak off, thrusting it at Peter, then kept moving down the hall. Peter looked at Hans, who rolled his rheumy eyes; he tossed the cloak towards a chair, not caring if it fell. The man moved through the workshop room by room, touching things as if to leave his scent in every corner.

'You might have told me I'd have visitors,' Peter told him. First there had been the creditor, and then a nosy merchant. Gutenberg went still, his dark eyes moving between Hans and Peter. 'I'd be obliged next time,' his foreman said, 'if you'd leave more than Lorenz's jar.'

'You're worse than an old woman.' The master waved a hand

peevishly. And then that hand crept up and started worrying the fringes of his beard.

They both jumped to hear Fust's voice a few hours later, greeting someone in the yard. Peter laid aside his composing stick and stood, but Gutenberg was faster, always; he'd already darted to the door. He grasped his partner by the arm and steered him back out into the fall sunlight. Peter watched the way he turned his back, as if the two of them were all that mattered, and the workshop simply ran itself. Silently he followed, pulling shut the door. He was taller than his father, nearly as tall as Gutenberg, and yet more muscled, stronger than the master now. He inserted himself between them.

'You plunder my own household, I have heard,' Fust drily said. 'Ten guilders here, ten guilders there.' He tipped his head in greeting at his son.

'And you shoot off your mouth to merchants.'

'There was a merchant here from Erfurt,' Peter clarified. 'Inquiring after Fust's new Bible.'

His father's lips pulled tight. 'Damnation.'

'I said you'd best take care in how you peddled it,' growled Gutenberg.

'He used the word?' Fust turned to Peter. 'He called it, actually, a Bible?' His eyes were troubled. Peter shrugged. 'I wasn't there. Your "fine new book," or something like it – Jakob knows, he spoke to him.'

'God's beard, Johann,' said Gutenberg. 'We don't need this.'

'Don't tell me what we need.' Now it was Fust who growled, his broad face flat, his eyes reduced to slits. '*You* need to get it finished.' He bent his head and dropped his voice. 'That man from Avignon has disappeared. But not before he trained some others, I am told.' He looked up towards the workshop window. 'You have to speed it up, now, get it moving.'

'What others?' hissed Gutenberg.

'What does it matter? Anybody, damn it, can't you see how little time we have?' Fust's voice rose and a flush began to spread up his thick neck. 'The longer you drag on, the likelier it is that someone else will get there first.' He turned to Peter. 'What is the holdup? Tell me that.'

'There is no holdup,' Peter answered. A man like Fust could never understand the sheer backbreaking labour of it. 'I drive them harder than is human.'

'Unless you want to build another press and hire more hands,' said Gutenberg. He glanced at Peter, just the barest flicker that went back and forth between them: *Lord, these moneymen*. 'Which I don't guess you do. If I were you, Johann, I'd go home and relax.'

'Relax?' Fust's face contorted. 'How should I, when you bleed me dry – with not a blessed thing to show for it? Your bloody needs are endless.'

'We only said that Erfurt is too close,' said Peter.

'You think that I don't know?' His father turned on him. 'I don't see guilders raining from the heavens, though, now do I?'

'It wouldn't cost so much if we weren't forced to pay for all the bleeding widows.' Gutenberg cocked one eyebrow. 'You know I never saw the gain from drawing in the guilds.'

'Water under the bridge,' snapped Fust.

'It can't be run in drips, like piss. We need more, yes – but not like this.'

'You got deposits on a third, or even half.' His father's eyes blazed. 'That isn't piss.'

Ten guilders down on every paper copy, twenty on the vellum; swiftly Peter reckoned. Deposits on a third of the edition came to seven hundred and fifty guilders – if Fust had managed to sell half, they'd banked at least a thousand.

'It goes like shit through a goose. Ink and gullets, coal and candles.' The master lifted up one corner of his mouth. 'You still owe me for this last half year, in fact.'

Fust shook his head and muttered to his son instead: 'Then show me where we are.'

Peter walked him through the shop and showed him their position on the chart. 'Not even halfway,' said his father. His whole body seemed to sag.

'Next time we talk, I want to see your ledgers,' he told his partner as he left.

Sardonically, the master touched a finger to his temple and bowed down.

Chapter 4

BITTER WATER

[31.5 quires of 65]

8 *November* 1453

And yet the Lord giveth, and the Lord taketh away.

His father had departed one last time before the winter, towards the north; the master too was off 'prospecting,' as he called it. The six compositors were seated quietly setting type that wet November afternoon. A paperboy came running down the hall and said there was a dreadful banging. One look at that white face and Peter knew. 'It's Mistress Grede,' the girl gasped. 'Hannah says that you're to fetch the midwife, quick.'

Peter grabbed a boy to send a note. 'Her name's Maria Lambeth, in the lane behind St John the Baptist. You know it?' The dazed boy nodded. Peter scratched some words on two small sheets. 'Then take the other to my aunt, Frau Fust, the *Kaisersberg*. Hurry! Go!'

Hans told him: 'You go, too.'

The terror in his heart erased all sight of the familiar lanes and houses. All Peter saw was that girl's white, white face – and then the housekeeper's, all chalky too, her fist against her mouth.

'What is it?' he demanded as he leapt the stairs.

'She's bleeding, sir.'

The chamber door stood open and the cook was bent above the bed. Grede lay among the bedclothes, skin the same bleached linen white, her eyes glazed wide.

The bed was filled with blood, her body from the hips down wrapped in rags that blotted crimson just as fast as the cook could wind them. Peter raised a hand to shield the sight. Grede reached for it, and he could only clutch her hand the way the terror clutched his heart. Dear God, he prayed. There was so much blood.

'The midwife's coming,' he said. The cook just nodded, lips compressed.

'I don't want to die.' Grede's voice was twisted, trembling, then it dropped, subsiding with her strength. She fell back on the bed.

'Hush, don't say such things.' He stroked her slick white forehead. 'Think of your life. Your strong and healthy babes.'

Her face crumpled, and she turned from him and wept.

'I bathed,' she blurted frantically. 'Oh God, dear God.' Her eyes flew open, hard now, bright as flints. 'What have I done, why does He punish me?' Her hand flew to her mouth.

The cook wrung out a cloth and placed it on her brow, and gave him a swift warning look. Where was the midwife, where his aunt? Oh, Grede. What did he know of women, or of bearing children? The pains she felt were deeper than a man could guess.

'Don't take my child,' she begged the Lord as that bright blood ebbed from her womb. And yet the patron saint withdrew her grace that day. *There shall not be one fruitless nor barren in thy land.* The empty promises of Exodus.

Much later she would say to him that she, and her poor babe, had paid for all the rest of them. Like downy chicks, the first to feel an ill wind's ill effects. It was the hatred and despair, she said, that swirled like noxious fumes across the empire and the city in those days – if not yet through their workshop.

The women came at last, with herbs and boiling water: Lambeth with her surgeon's hands and Aunt Elisabeth. Grede squeezed his hand and let her head fall back onto the pillow. 'Fetch Johann,' she rasped.

He sent a message with the traders' fastest rider, and returned to take up vigil on the stairs. He prayed to God, in humbleness, to save her – to keep her life, and take the child's. As his blood father, in his time – he realized with savage insight – most certainly had done. He bowed his head, beseeching.

What right, what birthright, had a man? What good were his books and tools, the business of his hands? Peter felt his heart cleave as he paced, hearing nothing but the women's murmurs and the clanking of the pans.

It came to him with certainty: the higher they reached towards heaven's stars, the farther their feet lifted from God's earth.

The door swung open finally. The midwife, in a bloody apron, stood a moment to collect herself. She closed her eyes, and opened them, and put a hand out on his arm.

'She'll live,' she said. 'But God has taken back the child.'

He heard his old friend weeping, cries to rend the world, behind the heavy wooden door. He moved to go to her, but when he did, the midwife gripped him all the tighter.

'There's nothing you can do,' she said, 'but leave her to grieve.'

There'd be no public mourning for the unborn babe. Fust held that something few had known should be lamented in the privacy of home. Perhaps he felt too great a show of feeling would diminish him somehow. It was hard to know. All Peter knew was that he'd never heard a woman tear into a man the way Grede did when Fust refused to let her hang the mourning wreaths. She dressed in black from that day on regardless. She knelt for hours at St Quintin's in bleakest penance, bludgeoned by the thought of that small, unbaptized soul alone in limbo. The sorrow spread, unnamed, through the timbers of the Haus zur Rosau.

Men weep behind a mask, as he well knew. That year he watched his father's belt grow slack, what hair remained go purely white. Gone was the paunch, the ready smile, the ornamented jacquards: in their place emerged a stranger, hollow-eyed and sombre, hand lifted to the heavy crucifix he wore now at his neck.

It wasn't just this one cruel loss. It was all of a piece, it seemed to Peter: the drying up of trade, the weight of all that Bible debt, the certainty of holy war. The papal bull was tacked up on St Martin's portal: the pope required all able-bodied men to muster for Crusade. No soul could hope to be exempt; any who hesitated would be jailed and excommunicated.

Yet Fust had taken this news too with apathy – as he took everything in those dark days. He hardly stirred outside the Kaufhaus, and did not even come to check their progress at the shop. Although it stung him, Peter did his best to understand. His father had buried a child and wife before, and bowed before God's will – then God had smiled, and brought him Grede and Tina, little Hans. Why then did this loss, after those others, hold such lethal force?

Old Lothar turned to Peter finally, and said his father barely slept, or ate. 'Reason with him if you would, young master.' He shook his rutted, faithful head. Peter begged his father to remember that the Lord had spared his wife. She would come back; the only balm for certain wounds was time.

'Don't speak to me of grace,' was all Fust answered.

The fear of losing her, of losing all – his business, and his books, the freedom of the open road – had wormed its way into his heart. It was as if everything he'd built, and all he'd reached for, was suddenly fragile and in danger of collapse. Always before there'd been an order and a sense, but now the sultan's hand had throttled his whole livelihood, and God himself had turned His back.

Chapter 5

ILLUMINATION

[34.5 quires of 65]

Late November 1453

Apainter came to Mainz that bleak November, travelling as those roving brush-men did from *Residenz* to monastery, patrician home to ducal hearth. The penning of new manuscripts and painting of their margins still went on, of course. This man, an Austrian, lodged with the painter Pinzler on the Leichhof, Peter heard. Apparently he hoped to get some painting work on the new Bible being written by the monks at St Viktor's.

And in the Humbrechthof they had at last hit the halfway mark. They were not far off now from Psalms, which Gutenberg had chosen as the end of the first volume. The text was far too massive to bind in one book; they'd split it into two. So it was time, thought Peter, going to his father and saying it out loud: time now to think about illumination of the copies Fust had planned.

Right at the start, his father told them he had seen it in a dream. He saw a row of printed pages on a trestle, then a brush – a painter colouring a dozen copies with the selfsame leaves, the same bright birds and flowers. Just as Gutenberg had made the text identical, Fust would hire a painter who would decorate the Bible with identical motifs. A few to start, to see how they would sell – then more, if the new men of means were pleased to buy a book complete and ready-made.

The beauty of illumination, if nothing else, had always worked a certain magic in his father's heart. Peter prayed it might again have this effect. This painter was in competition with the local artists from the Cherry Orchard workshop run by Weydenbach, he said; it was a perfect chance to view the two contrasting styles. Fust, haggard, old now, simply shrugged. He had no interest in the local style. 'Though it is plain enough,' he dully added, 'whom you would have me hire.'

Pinzler's sons, Anna's brothers, worked in that local workshop. Peter saw her jars of unguents and glues, the little curtain to the kitchen and her mother's loom. 'Not necessarily.' He shut the door inside his mind. 'It's up to you.

'Indulge me,' he went on, cajoling. 'Let Klaus arrange a viewing.'

Fust cocked his head. Thinner, he resembled Jakob, with his wary and pugnacious look. 'So long as Gutenberg is not invited.'

Peter looked at him intently. 'I shouldn't think it would be necessary.'

Fust pursed his lips and nodded. It still rankled, the words they'd had, the costs of that third press, the four new workers – but most of all it was the fear, which Peter shared: the sense that everything now dangled by the slimmest thread.

'A little air,' he said, and gently touched Fust's elbow. 'A little brushwork will do wonders.'

Peter sent a note to Pinzler to arrange it. There might be something in it for the painter too, he wrote. What the man might think of him did not disturb his mind. Nine months ago he'd almost been betrothed – now he was not. The Lord of Hosts determined all: no part of it was really in their human hands. The Book just ran and ran into a smoky distance, dragging him behind it, and the crew. A week before, Mentelin had finished the last pages of Isaiah, the Salvation book. Repent, or face destruction, was its cry. Those without faith will not endure. Peter's only mission was the driving and the steering of this pounding team: three presses and six setters, trampling through the sinning, bloodstained world. Making the highway straight, he said inside himself: the highway of the Lord.

The Austrian was slight and weather-bitten, with one squinting eye. Klaus Pinzler clasped Fust's hand and led them to the table, cleared and pushed up to the fire. Markus, Anna's brother, had her nut-brown hair and a look of cautious query in his eyes. Beside him, she stood. Anna. She looked older. How long, one year – two? – since he had come here that first time? How was it he had come again, what was the Lord's intent? All things have their season, Peter thought: *A time to be born and a time to die, a time to plant and a time to pluck up that which is planted.*

'Gracious of you, in such weather.' Klaus gave Fust the cushioned chair.

A little flush described an arc along her neck's left side. Formally, Peter Schoeffer bowed. Markus leaned and spread some quires. 'Depending on the job, we'd vary certain shades,' he said, and fanned some pages from that new handwritten Bible.

Peter had told them only that his father sought a painter for a book. He hoped to keep it just that vague – although he almost slipped, himself, right then and there.

The paper of that written Bible was the very same that they were using in the Humbrechthof. The same cream linen with its wavy chain lines and the ox-head watermark, identical – a pointed shape that looked more like a fox's than an ox's head.

The very same, from the same moulds in the same mill along the river Po: discomfort, then suspicion, needled him inside. Sharply he looked at Markus, who was telling Fust that Archbishop Dietrich had commissioned this new Bible; they'd just finished a new psalter for him, too. Petrus Heilant, Peter thought: he was the scribe who ran this Bible job. What were the chances that the paper handler'd talked – made some remark as he was selling the same batch to both the master and the monk? Peter's skin crawled as he watched the artist's fingers trace the vibrant colours of the borders. The fact of two big clients in the same small place would be remarkable; he made a note to pry it out of Gutenberg.

The job he had in mind, Fust said, was for half a dozen books, each painted more or less the same. He sat and scrutinized the painted margins. Peter watched him breathe the pigment in, his nostrils flaring, body warming to the beauty and the craft. He saw the way his fingers traced the lines. This was beyond all else what Fust, the merchant, had bequeathed to him, he thought: for all that his foster father was a man of commerce, he had been born and raised a craftsman. He did not lack for finer feeling.

That written Bible was a handsome thing: the lettering was fluid, the decoration in the standard Cherry Orchard style of branching bowers filled with buds and birds. Their flowers were orange or red, white-hatched; they used the leaves of the acanthus, indigo or green. The style was graceful, calm, though to his eye – and to his father's and to Anna's, Peter knew – too rote and filled with gold-flecked preening. 'I see now why His Grace approves your work.' Fust gave an enigmatic smile.

Without intending to, Peter glanced at Anna. Her eyes were on him; for an instant he could feel the torrent they unleashed. If they had been alone, he knew she would have scorned that work. With pity – after all, her brothers laboured there. But he had heard her more than once dismiss it as mere shiny surface, just copied from a pattern book. Repetitive, identical – just like those metal letters he had shown her.

All he had offered her. All she had spurned. Peter looked back down.

His mistake had been to think that she was like him – born of this clay, yet able to rise out of it somehow. He felt her eyes still on him, prickling. His face felt taut: he was intensely conscious of that beam of her attention, like a thread across the table, stitching at his skin. Again he glanced up, and the tension broke. She looked away; she could not bear his gaze.

Markus gathered up his sheets. Casually Peter asked how many pages the whole Bible made. Around a thousand, was the answer. He nodded, galled inside – to have to gaze at this, and yet be barred from showing off the wonder of its freshly printed rival.

The Austrian gave a small cough and nudged his papers forwards. They were samples only, he explained; the works of course remained inside the abbeys and the castles he had served. 'You name the thing, I've coloured it,' he said, his mouth a crooked line. 'Choir books, land grants, books of hours, and Bibles too. I heard you had a big one here.'

Fust pursed his lips, then opened the worn sheets. He sat unmoving for a while, staring at a strange and gleaming thicket. This artist's vines were hung with spiky leaves, in shades of silvered green, grey slate. He turned the page, to find the same wild bushiness upon the next sheet, and the next. The man possessed a queer and otherworldly style: Peter had never seen such flowers grow upon this earth as bloomed upon those pages. His large initials used less gilding than the Mainzers'; he formed them out of patterns flecked with dots. Here and there he'd dropped in figures – monkeys, saints – that were more awkward, less successful. The Pinzlers looked on silently, and Peter tasted sourness in the air.

'You must have stumbled into nettles once.' His father clucked his tongue.

The painter kept his sad eyes fastened on the man who might, with luck, become a client. Fust was peering down, evidently charmed by, or at the very least intrigued at, those barbed and writhing lines. 'Nettles, aye.'

'I've tried to paint more true to life.' The painter spread his fingers, long and tapered as an angel's. 'But never seem quite able.'

'You have then, like the others, some pattern that you follow?'

'Just in my mind.'

Fust raised his head and eyed the fellow. 'You were last in Würzburg, am I right?'

'I was.'

'And painted there a Bible.'

'I was one of many hands.'

'Before that?'

'In Bohemia, then Salzburg.'

'I like a man who moves around.'

The Austrian relaxed a bit. 'It is an interesting life.'

'You hear things,' Fust said. 'I would guess,' and tipped his head at Klaus. Their host rose and came back with wine and glasses.

There wasn't much about the tramp, at least, for anyone to fancy. His face was weather-blasted, with a glint of animal alertness in his fully opened eye.

'What news is there, then, from the East?' his father asked.

'The heretics encircle Belgrade.'

'Bad news.' Klaus frowned.

'Shields and banners.' Peter looked at Klaus with sympathy. 'That's all that anyone wants painted now.'

Anna's father drew down his dark brows. 'Chests are what

you need, and altars, windows, if you want to feed a wife and child.' His tone was sharp.

'And to the south?' Fust kept on.

'A man from Graz said I might like to know there was a mountain of old manuscripts on one ship he saw coming into Venice.'

'From Constantinople?'

'Survivors, aye. The Greeks are fleeing.' The Austrian looked up, around. 'Manuscripts of all descriptions, what I heard. They saved some libraries, at least – they say there're books there none of us have seen.'

'What kind of books?' Fust leaned forwards.

'Medicine, geography. Ptolemy and Plato – all of it in Greek.' The painter hitched his shoulders and gave a ghost of a smile.

Fust turned towards Peter; for the first time in long weeks, his eyes began to stir.

The last time anyone had salvaged learning from the East, it had been Cardinal Cusanus. A dozen years before, he'd sailed off to Byzantium, and smuggled treasures from those monasteries that lay crushed now underneath the despot's boot. What other riches had they salvaged in their flight? Things only ancients knew, which few had seen – except in scribbled Latin copied from the Arabs.

'A silver lining,' Fust said thoughtfully, and then fell silent.

After a time Klaus made a sign; there was a scraping as both painters stood and pushed their chairs back. Fust stood and shook their hands. 'The choice is hard,' he said, and tipped his head. Anna stiffly curtseyed, and then they all withdrew. Her waist was just as slim, her hair as long and shining. Peter wondered if she'd brushed it fifty times, as she had done so long ago for him.

Frau Pinzler came and without a word set down three steins of beer. His father didn't notice how tight her lips were, nor how she carefully avoided Peter's eyes.

'It's good to see you back, Johann,' said Klaus.

'This has been – most enlightening.' Indeed, his son thought: a raft of news.

'Share and share alike.' The painter cut the sausage. 'There's precious little now to go around.'

Fust nodded. 'You'll not get lapis now, nor azurite, but what you can from Cornwall.'

'Won't matter if the buyers stay this scarce.' Klaus took a quaff. 'How soon you think you'll need him?' Which 'him' he meant was clear.

Fust glanced at Peter. 'Hard to say,' he said. 'A month or two.'

'By then the Austrian will be long gone.' Klaus smiled, a little lighter now. 'It stands to reason, anyway,' he paused, 'that we look out for ours.' He could not stop himself from glancing at the son he might have had.

He hoped to cut a deal with Markus, plainly: have the painting done right there, and not at Weydenbach's a few doors down. Fust made a noncommittal noise.

'A shame, I mean,' Klaus kept on, 'to spread the benefits too far afield.'

'When you could keep it underneath this roof, you mean.'

'It shouldn't make much difference to your partner.'

Fust's face went hard. 'This has no bearing on that work.'

'You get what's yours, eh? The old sinner gets what's his?' The wink, the tone, were both much too familiar.

'I do not grasp your meaning.'

Klaus licked his lips. 'Just that – he bought a vat of linseed oil last week, for some new project, as he said.' He turned towards Peter. 'I couldn't think what he would do with it – with metal, anyway, if you get my meaning.' He made a little motion with his finger, to show he knew about those pilgrim mirrors. 'Herr Gutenberg was winking and grinning, like he does, you know – like it was something big.'

The sound in Peter's throat was incredulity – a croak he barely managed to conceal as a brief laugh. Fust did not move a muscle; he was a trader after all, extremely skilled in feinting and dissimulation. 'The man is brimming with mad notions,' he said drily.

And then they drank a little more, his father measuring a decent interval until he rose. 'I'm grateful for the hospitality,' he said, and took his cap up from the table, 'and for the news.'

Klaus watched them, brows knit, as they stepped outside. He was still watching as Fust plunged into the swirl of bodies on the Leichhof, weaving with a brusque efficiency along the slick dark streets, his back erect, tight-lipped. Peter had to speed to catch him. The vat of suspect oil, the surging crowd, merged in his mind – became a gleaming canvas by a Flemish master, thick with busy workers and wild dancers and a prancing fool. What new insanity could Gutenberg be planning now?

Fust waited until they had climbed up to his office and shut the door. 'You'll tell me everything.' He stood solid and unmoving.

'I know as much as you.'

His father's eyes were contemptuous. 'Then you are hardly master, are you?' He spun, disgusted, flinging his cloak down. 'What you don't know could fill a cargo ship.'

'I can't control him – no one can,' said Peter quietly.

'More's the pity.' Fust stood moodily, his hands clasped at the back. He turned to Peter and gazed out on the trading floor.

'It must be something for the archbishop,' he said at last, as he turned back, his face bereft of all expression. Loss had left his once-round jowls as slack and sagging as a hound's. 'Erlenbach's in Mainz, you know. Sniffing around.'

Peter's stomach tightened.

'He wouldn't dare,' he said, half to himself – meaning the master, not Erlenbach, Archbishop Dietrich's man-at-arms. His father shook his head; he looked upon him with a mixture of disgust and pity.

'You are a fool to trust him. As was I.'

Perhaps, his son thought. God preserve us, if you're right.

'What is his business? Erlenbach's?'

Fust grimaced. 'Tax, more tax. He's leaning hard on the cathedral chapter.'

Dietrich could not simply wave his hand and squeeze the people dry; he needed the approval of the priests of his cathedral to do that. Was it still possible his people had not learned of Gutenberg's technique? Lord keep them blinded, Peter prayed: just keep them grubbing like blind moles for gold.

'Can Jakob keep him well away?'

'It isn't Jakob who concerns me,' Fust replied.

'It may just be some decoy plan.'

Fust's nostrils whitened. 'A vat of oil.' He stared at Peter, thinking. 'What kind of decoy do you make with that?' He pulled the folds of flesh around his neck, then let them go, hand curling tightly in a fist he weighed against his lips.

'I need to know.' Each word was clipped. 'You will find out, and send me word.' His fist shook lightly, as if weighing dice. 'I couldn't answer for my actions if I had to see the man.'

Gutenberg was there before his foreman the next day. He sprang and turned as Peter entered. It was a shock to find him sitting at the desk Peter had claimed; there was never a soul astir before cockcrow but him and the boy who laid the fire. Peter loved the silence of the early morning, its steadying before the crew converged. But not that winter dawn, when Gutenberg leapt up and strode towards him, waving something in his hand.

Peter had barely slept, his mind engaged in pouring tainted

vats and filling them, repouring then refilling, all the sticky, fitful night. And now came that old reprobate, a curl of glee upon his lips, pushing some pages at him.

'A brilliant morning, I would say.' The master shook the pamphlet eagerly. Take, open, his eyes said, praise me, exclaim!

'A vat of oil.' Peter brushed the sheaf away. '"Some big new project," which we hear about in gossip.'

Gutenberg drew back, then up, the eager look replaced by one of haughtiness. 'I'm saving your damned shirts.' He'd never been a man to quail: he thrust the papers into Peter's hand.

It was a lengthy poem in verse – the kind of tripe you could pick up for pennies on the square. An epic – no, an ode, in close-writ lines that stretched for many pages. *The Sibylline Prophecy.*

'Doggerel,' said Peter.

'A solemn prophecy, in noble verse.' One corner of the master's mouth was lifted. 'The ancient wisdom of the Sibyls.'

'You plan to print this.' Peter looked into that crafty face, those glowing, canine eyes. The man was mad then, after all.

'A certain winner, I would say' – the master's coy look widened to a smile – 'to calm the people at this fearful time.'

He prattled on: the prospects were incredible, the text was tailormade for such a time. It told the story of the coming of a peaceful king, who'd crush the hounds of hell and save believers from eternal flame. 'The monarch's name' – he winked – 'is even Friedrich.'

'They'll lap it up!' The fire had reignited in his eyes. 'We'll get enough to cover all the outlays.'

Peter's pulse was beating in his ears. He could not speak at first. It was a madness even greater than the madman Gutenberg could birth. If Dietrich, in the tumult of reform and war, had pushed the matter of their bookwork from his mind, he only needed a reminder – slight, and made with metal type – for the whole business to flood back.

'You would risk everything,' he hissed. 'Have you no notion what a book like this would do?'

'Save our backsides, fool.' The master's lips were twisted; he lunged to grab the prophecy, but Peter held it tight.

'As well announce our business by the crier,' Peter spat. He hoped to hell the man remembered his own words.

Discovery was death, the end. For months he'd thought of little else: what Rosenberg, and Dietrich – Erlenbach – might do, if they discovered that extensive workshop underneath their noses. It hardly mattered whether they conceived the press as heresy or boon. They might perceive it as a thing that they could seize and use, or else they'd see it as a threat to the scriptoria whose proceeds kept the landed cloisters fat and ripe for skimming. Either was conceivable. Incredibly, Archbishop Dietrich had not yet grasped what this technique could do – for if he had, by now he surely would have swooped.

'The instant you produce another book, they'll fall upon us. Come crashing in, and—'

Gutenberg cut in sharply. 'What will it take for you to understand? The well is dry. The purse is empty. Your father made that more than clear.'

'You cannot threaten the whole Bible just for the thirty, forty guilders it might yield.' The man was arrogant, just lunatic enough to risk it all. Peter bent his force and will against it. 'Nor use this paper – it's a miracle already no one's noticed.' He moved a step towards him. 'He will discover us, for certain.'

'Do not speak of what you do not know.' The master's smile was mocking. 'His Grace is ill. Extremely so. A great misfortune for him – although not for me, nor for the doctor he hauled in at a vast cost from Holland.' He snorted, rolled his eyes. 'You do the job for which you're paid, and leave affairs of state to me.' He held his hand out for the pamphlet.

It took only a moment to scratch out a note and send it to

the Kaufhaus. Some fifteen minutes later, Fust arrived. From the composing room they could not see, but each of them heard clearly.

'I have a rack of bones to pick with you, Johann.'

There was a pause; the master took his time in rising. 'It's good to see you, too, my friend.'

Then they went upstairs, and the compositors bent back to work. Inside a minute they heard voices rising, accusations bouncing off the floorboards. 'Sabotage,' they heard, and 'folly.' And then the master's testy voice: 'For God's sake, let it be, Johann.'

'Finally met his match.' Hans cocked his head and grinned.

Peter thought of Anna, she of the Iron Door. Those brothers back in Strassburg, with their mirrors and their plague. The hapless clerk of Mainz whom Gutenberg had seized some twenty years before. He'd always pushed against the rules – and anybody fool enough to try to block his path.

Fust's face was set when he descended. Peter stepped out, on the pretence of some work he had to place on the composing stone. He understood, as they threw charges, countercharges, at each other on the stairs, that Fust refused, point-blank, to free up any member of 'his' crew for this new work.

That night Fust told his son, as well, that he'd demanded an accounting of the workshop's income and expenses for the past two years. He'd paid the sums he'd pledged; there was no earthly reason they should fall short now. Where had the money gone? He'd like to know. If Gutenberg persisted in this folly, he'd pay himself for any ink and paper that he used. The point was, none of it could interfere, in any wise, with their last push to finish up the Bible.

'He claims,' said Fust, his blue eyes sharp, 'that you'll be done inside six months.'

The man would promise anything.

It was early Advent, a whole lifetime until Easter and midsummer. Each setter still had five or six quires left to do, each one of which might take a month. And over all that time, the workshop would be vulnerable. Peter had to keep them safe, he realized. He had to save their secret somehow.

He too could plan a subterfuge.

He ordered Keffer to produce two hundred pilgrim mirrors, using Hans's old mould. And then he reached up to the master's shelf for those old sample sheets, the canticles he'd set and printed for the pope's pontifical. Within a week or two they would be starting with the printing of the Psalms. It would be easy to print off some extra sheets, as if they truly made that book of papal prayers that Gutenberg had once proposed.

Peter did not tell the master. Nor was Gutenberg around to see the metal poured to make those pilgrim badges. Barred by Fust from using workers from their common shop, he went back to the first press he had made, still standing in his stable. He'd make the bloody prophecy himself, he growled – or find some willing hands to do it. While Keffer poured the mirrors, Peter kept the Bible pages flowing. The stories that those pages told that final winter were of portent and of lamentation: the books of Daniel and of Jeremiah and of Job.

The torments that God poured upon his faithful servant preyed on Peter's mind. Job's suffering and isolation were extraordinary, epic – yet they struck a chord in his own soul. Over and over the phrase recurred to him like an old song – what Job's poor servant said, returning with each tale of woe: 'And I alone have escaped to tell thee.'

Chapter 6

APPARITIONS

[37.5 quires of 65]

December 1453

The books of prophecy began appearing one by one, like random snowflakes through the Adventide. None paid them any notice at the start. Books usually appeared this way, a copy here, a copy there – until the copies started clustering, drifting into noticeable little piles.

The first to wonder in his father's hearing were the traders on the Kaufhaus floor. The wives of Salman and Kumoff had each bought a pamphlet from an urchin near St Martin's. This in itself might have passed unremarked. But what was strange was how alike they were, said Kumoff – like peas in pods – and more than that, the boy had more, and there were others, they had heard, for sale inside the Schreibhaus.

'I told him scribes were just as hard up now as anybody else,' Fust said. Peter reached to take the copy that his father held.

'How many, at what price?' he asked.

'Five shillings each. God knows how many, though. A score? A hundred? More?'

The prophecy made fourteen pages. If Gutenberg had scared

up a whole ream of paper, he could make several hundred, Peter reckoned, using Keffer and Ruppel, pulled after hours to do the work back at the Hof zum Gutenberg. He hadn't had the heart to block them when the men had begged to earn the little extra that the master offered.

'He'd better watch how many he puts out,' Fust said, chewing his lip.

Yet he'd not easily resist temptation – not if he thought that he could dredge up twenty, thirty guilders. 'He might have shown us,' Peter said, and opened the slim poem.

'He didn't dare.'

Small wonder: the thing was nasty and cheap, type badly inked and letters lurching on their feet. Whoever set it had not even tried to justify the lines. He'd used their first poor type, in its last gasp, not for a Latin schoolbook, but *auf Deutsch*: the *v*'s stood in for all those *w*'s no Latin book required.

'A waste of rag.'

'Apparently they're selling.'

Peter tossed it on the desk. 'He'll draw attention to us, far too soon.'

Feet drumming on the stairs stopped up their mouths; there was a sharp knock at the door. As Fust was saying, 'Enter,' Jakob's head appeared. His eyes went right to Peter. 'Well, well,' he said, stepping inside. 'Look what the cat dragged in.'

'And you,' said Peter, rising and reaching out a hand. 'You're looking well.'

'More than I might say of you.' Jakob embraced him, then stepped back, searching his nephew with his eyes. 'You work him to the death, Johann. He's skin and bones.'

'No worse or better than the rest of us.' His brother gestured to a chair.

They all were thinner, harder, Peter thought: not only in the workshop but in all of Mainz, thanks to the sultan and his war.

Jakob did not take the chair. His eyes remained on Peter's face; his hand slipped to a pouch beneath his cloak. 'This better not be why.' He drew a pamphlet out and threw it on the desk, his nostrils flaring when he saw its doppelgänger.

'That's not the reason the guilds shelter you.' He looked at Fust. 'A year.' His face was hard. 'A whole damned year we hold our tongues – for this? I give my word that it will help us, I protect that thieving goat, and this is what I get? Some drivel from a witch?'

Fust wiped one hand across his face. 'Sit,' he said again. His voice was weary.

Bull-like, Jakob swung his head. 'Who made it? You?'

'Gutenberg,' said Johann Fust. 'Though I did warn him.'

'Not at the Humbrechthof,' said Peter, swiftly.

'I don't care where.' Jakob's eyes were like the Alpen ice. 'I owe him nothing – nothing, do you understand? I always said he'd double-cross you, take what he could get and screw us all. I hope to hell you see it now.' He ground the words.

'Six months.' Peter leaned urgently towards him. 'Just six more months, that's all I need. Then we can free the press, and Mainz will get what it is owed.'

Hate distorted Jakob's sunken cheeks. '"What Mainz is owed."' He sneered. 'A pretty promise, presses that can spit out gold. When will we get them, eh? When Erlenbach has dragged them off to Eltville, I suppose?' He brought his fist down on the desk. 'God damn you and your promises, Johann.'

'I gave my word.' Fust's voice was cold. 'I do not break it, Jakob.'

'And yet you let him lead you by the nose.'

Fust said nothing; there was nothing he could say. He faced his brother, the sinews rigid in his neck.

'We can't protect you – won't protect you, if he acts against your interest, and our own.'

They stood there silent for a moment, until Jakob sighed. He pulled his cloak taut and wound it around him like a shroud – at last he sat.

'They'll read it as a call for Crusade,' he said, shaking his head. 'You know as well as I that is the last thing Dietrich wants.' His eyes were sunken, glowing in the shadow of his hood.

'His hounds are here,' he said, eyes swivelling to Peter. 'His spies, too, everywhere.' His smile was bitter. 'The eyes of the archdiocese are trained on Mainz. God only knows what he has promised all his priests to get this tax.'

'So it is done.' Fust sat back heavily.

'And now you lay this in his grasp. There will be nothing, then – no way to restrain that dead hand.'

Der Tote Hand, they called that silent, brutal grasp: the dead hand of the church, exempt from tax on all the property it owned – and yet implacable, invisible, exacting tribute from those under its control. Reaching, always reaching, for some way to suck out their life force.

'You'd better get these on a boat upriver,' said his uncle, 'if you hope to hawk them.'

Peter restrained a sudden urge to bolt and scour the city, gathering the traces of this folly. 'The ship I run' – he smiled – 'is tight, in any case. Secure and battened.' An ark as tough and supple as any cedars out of Lebanon. Levelly he looked at Jakob. 'As for the other . . . who can say?' He shrugged.

Jakob nodded. He looked at Fust. 'I'll do what I can – for you, but no one else.'

Peter went directly towards St Martin's. The day was bright and very cold. Puffs of breath hung in the air; beggars huddled, wound in tatters, on the red cathedral stairs. He scanned their sacking, bodies, bowls, and saw a thin boy at the corner by the archbishop's private chapel, quite clearly freezing, clutching with one paw at a cloak beneath his chin. His other held a sheaf aloft as he called hoarsely, 'Comes the Peace-King! To redeem us and destroy the infidel!'

He was grubby, wiry. God only knew where Gutenberg had found him.

'I'll have one,' Peter muttered, digging in his pocket for the coins. 'How many have you, then?' His eyes went to a satchel at the urchin's feet. The boy just put a hand up to his swaddled ear and shook his head, as if he were stone deaf, and kept on shouting.

Peter turned and started moving quickly at an angle past the Mint, back up and out towards the Cobblers' Lane. He almost ran into the short man in his path, so deep was he in his dark thoughts. He swerved, and looked up into the ruddy face of Petrus Heilant.

'Rushing, always rushing.' Heilant raised a sandy eyebrow. He was covered in a warm grey cloak with bright red piping. 'One might think you had some vital errand.'

'Business waits for no man,' Peter said.

'But surely it must wait for God?' Heilant's cheeks were pink with cold; he wore the close-fitted crimson cap of the cathedral chapter. Plainly he was simple scribe no more.

'I pray to Him along the way.' Still Peter stopped and held his hand out.

'We see too little of you, though.' Heilant's eyes were veiled, ironic. 'I'd almost think you kept your distance.'

Peter faked a smile. 'It looks as if you are the one who's left me in the dust.'

Heilant brightened and touched his cap. 'It suits me, don't you think?'

As well as it ever suited any lustful soul. Peter rolled his eyes and kept his smile on. So Heilant had managed, after all, to creep his way into some well-paid post. One not too high, nor yet abject; he had, like Peter, studied the four lower orders of theology.

'Let me guess.' Playfully, he poked him. 'Not *akolyte* or *ostiar*.' Petrus Heilant would not stoop to altar service, or to ringing of the bells.

'*Lektorat*.' Heilant's voice was clipped.

'Bravo. Of course.' Peter clapped him on the back. The only other option would have been as *exorzist*: far better to read out the lessons than to have to lay one's hands upon some dread-filled soul.

His former schoolmate's eyes roved over him, taking in his threadbare cloak, his ink-stained hands, then froze. He seemed to coil himself up as his hand jabbed towards the pamphlet clutched at Peter's side. 'So you have seen it too,' he breathed. His face was guarded suddenly: if Peter had not known him better, he'd have said that he was scared.

The printer measured out each word. 'I only just now bought it. Why?'

Heilant bent his head close. 'It's more than strange.' His breath was hot in Peter's ear. 'Something queer – ungodly. I've seen three now and' – he was hissing – 'every one is just exactly, I mean exactly – not an altered letter, not an eyeskip – utterly the same.'

He stood rooted, clutching Peter's arm. The look upon his face was clearly fear. It was a look that Peter knew: he'd seen it too on Anna Pinzler's face. If years ago he'd not been told how they were made – and at the very instant that his hand first grazed those printed lines – he would have looked as frightened and amazed.

The scribe's blue eyes were latched onto his face.

'How many are there, do you know?' was all that Peter thought to ask.

Heilant shook his head and reached to tug at it.

'Not here.' The printer cinched it tighter between arm and ribs.

'Then come to me. And we will put them side by side.' Heilant's colour had returned. But there was still repulsion in his eyes. 'It isn't right. I've never seen its like. It was not made by any scribe.'

Soothingly, his hand as steady as a rock, Peter touched his arm. 'We will examine them.' He willed his voice smooth. 'Perhaps the answer is . . . entirely banal. Look at Lauber, he has a writing army now. Perhaps he has a pattern book as well.'

'I pray it's so.' Heilant crossed himself. 'But everything about it leaves a dread upon my soul.'

They parted, Peter promising to come as soon as he was able. He hurried down the lane, passing the Humbrechthof, slowing for an instant to be sure he could hear nothing through its outer wall. Please God, he prayed. His legs strode on past St Quintin's, then to the master's house upon its knoll. He came around to the back door and pounded, his hand coiled tightly in the biting cold.

Lorenz looked startled, dragged from sleep, when finally he opened. The master wasn't there.

Where was he then, God damn him? Peter cursed and spun. Courting favour with the archbishop's men, coaxing coins from merchants, Elders, sousing with whoever paid inside some hole? Scrounging for another piece of tripe that he could spin from lead to gold? Where was he, when it came right down to it, when he was needed? Peter turned back to the workshop, frozen through. The man was gone – had left them, as he always did, to clean up the mess he left behind.

'Let me see it.' Heilant creased one pamphlet open, then the other, to the selfsame page. Peter traced an *a*, then moved his finger to the *a* upon the other page. 'Indeed,' he said. 'Extremely strange.'

There was an unaccustomed bustle in the Schreibhaus common room that night. The back was filled with strangers in a jumble of dark robes; the roads were full these days with delegations, Heilant said. Peter looked up at the counter where the food and drink were served, and saw an orphan pamphlet in plain view.

'Two of a kind,' he whispered into Heilant's ear. 'Let's make a flush, and see.'

He rose and palmed the lonely booklet. There was a tray for coins, a lettered notice in the master's hand. He dropped five shillings in and winced.

'Now then.' He sat down again.

'Look at these lines.' Heilant's voice was low. 'Exactly even, with the breaks in the same place.'

'This one's the same,' said Peter grimly.

'It is some devilry.' The scribe and *lektor*'s eyes were opened wider than he'd ever seen them. 'No hand but Satan's could create such symmetry.' He stared at Peter, thick lids lifted, like a child caught in a lie. 'No human hand could write precisely the same line, a dozen times.'

Peter mimed a thoughtful stroking of his beard, and glanced around the room. 'It seems to me it is some kind of stamp,' he whispered.

'Stamp?' Heilant's full lips opened slightly; a look of merriment, derision, filled those open eyes. 'Come now, be serious.'

'You know, the way Cusanus had them carve the Pater Noster.' Peter made a show of running one flat finger on the page. 'It punches, like those stamps they carve from wood.'

Heilant peered closely at it. 'I see no grain.' He licked his lips and raised his eyes with a bare smile. 'This is not wood. Not quite.' Suddenly, his look was snide. 'You know much more, I think, than you let on.'

'Not wood?' said Peter lightly, as his stomach jolted.

'You play with metal, it's well known. And not just for those mirrors.'

Peter looked him full in his soft, flabby face. Heilant would not be so easily diverted. He dropped his voice and leaned with menace towards the monk. 'You ought not say such things out loud.' He looked around. 'Especially not here.'

The scribe recoiled, but there was enmity in his small eyes. 'If I were you, I'd watch the game you play.'

'No game.' Peter sat back. 'But strictest orders. You'll keep your comments to yourself – or you will answer to His Grace – or Rosenberg.'

For an instant Heilant chewed on this. But he'd not gained his rank without a streak of most self-serving cunning. His smile was acid. 'Then it's a good thing, don't you think, I answer to them both already?'

Each page was tied with twine on the composing stone for him to proof as it arrived. He was teasing out wrong letters with a pick the night he got an answer to that question. It was a few days past Saint Stephen, and that year of woe was nearly at its end. Heilant's threat was unambiguous. But he could turn to neither partner: the only father he could count on was the Father of them all.

He rose and went out to the courtyard, towards the granary, where all the finished quires were stacked. How often of an evening had he come to check on them with Gutenberg, tucking the waxed cloth as a mother tucks her babe. A pain traversed him: he couldn't trust the scheming bastard now, no more than he could hope for help from Fust. His father was a broken dike, his power trickling and dispersed, while Gutenberg was wild and uncontained, a risk to the whole workshop. Now, at least, the scales had fallen from his eyes. Peter had been shown, by each man's carelessness, his weakness, that he alone had been entrusted to complete this work.

He and Fust had managed to prevail, at least, on Gutenberg to box up the remaining prophecies and send them out of

Dietrich's jurisdiction, down the river to Cologne. In the days since, the master had stopped by a few times to check on the workshop. But then, dogfaced, embittered, he had had the grace to leave the crew alone.

The snow fell softly, silently, out of the winter blackness; Peter stood and watched the way it drew the whole dark Humbrechthof beneath its soft white cloak. A few small squares of gold were all that showed, the firelight playing on the paper they had pressed into the windows in vain hope of sealing in the heat. It was past time to shut the heavy wooden shutters. The newly printed sheets would then be shifted to the shed the minute they were dry, Peter thought as he returned in his own tracks across the courtyard. A drumming sound caught his attention far off to the north, but though he waited, he heard nothing more. He entered. All dozen men were busy, half a dozen boys; the clock had just struck five. He stooped to seat himself by Hans. 'Snow all night,' he said. 'Best get the lads to bring more wood.' Hans put down his stick and stretched his fingers and his hands. 'Freeze all them spies too in their beds – that's good.' He gave Peter a keen look.

And yet he spoke too soon: the sound of hoof beats came, now close enough that Peter knew the sound as that low, distant pounding he had heard before. 'Sshhh!' He sprang up, out to the main room, his long arms lifted towards the pressmen. 'Hold off.' He drew a finger at his neck to silence all that grunt and clatter. To a man the crew froze, listening intently, fingers flexing, muscles taut, hearing the hoof beats thudding ever closer. In half a minute they were right outside, a body's breadth from their stout outer wall, trampling the snow to ice along the lane. It was unusual, to say the least, to hear a squad of horsemen in the city just as winter darkness closed the gates.

'Four horsemen,' Hans said, deadpan; Peter rolled his eyes. He bid them wait, went out with Wiegand, hoisting him to spy above the wall. 'Four, aye,' the boy said, sliding down, 'two black, two bay.'

'Which way?'

'St Martin's.'

'What livery?'

'I couldn't see.'

A feeling of tremendous fear swiped through Peter at the very instant they both clearly heard a soft yet rhythmic tapping at the courtyard door. 'Quick,' he said, 'silent, now, close up the shutters.'

He went with slow, cold feet towards the little door cut in the portal. 'Who's there?' he hissed through solid oak.

'Jost, from Fust,' he heard in a low whisper. 'A message, urgently, for Peter Schoeffer.'

As soon as he unlocked the door, a hooded figure slipped inside: his uncle's foreman, Jost, nodding in recognition. 'Erlenbach just rode in, I'm to warn you.' His hood was pulled so tight that Peter barely made out his face. 'They know – that's what he says.' A cloud of mist came from the shadowed lips. 'Put everything away, your uncle says.'

There was no sound now in the lane, no clue as to the way those horses and their soldiers might have gone.

'Just here?' said Peter, 'or—'

The faintest shrug. 'He only sent me here.'

Instantly, he understood. As far as Jakob was concerned, Gutenberg could live or die by his own sword. Peter still could send a warning: the thought was like a bat that darted back and forth as he thanked Jost and dropped the beam across the door. The whole thing was the fool's own fault, he thought. The Bible and the Humbrechthof were all that counted. Let Dietrich seize the prophecy; it serves the master right. Peter might have sent a boy, but in the instant he was given to decide, he hesitated – then left the man to twist on his own rope.

He flew into the workshop, barking orders. Keffer turned as slowly as a man encased in treacle, sluggish, golden: everything moved with a lethargy, a slowing of time's motion. 'Mirrors, now!' said Peter, and the pressman nodded, cranked the bed back out from underneath the platen. He hoisted out the heavy tray of letters. 'To the shed,' said Peter, as he turned to Ruppel and Neumeister.

'You're making a new psalter, for Pope Nicholas,' he told them. '*Formes* out, now, and follow Keffer to the shed. I'll bring you the new pages.' Mentelin and Hans were at his side, the only men who knew, had helped prepare the plan. He did not need to tell them what to do. Mentelin was a red flame as he went past, the sample sheets of canticles, a few new pages of the Psalms, hung like limp curtains from his outstretched arms. He set to fanning some on the three tables, one beside each press, as if they'd only just been printed. Hans brayed back by the forge, and Peter went to help him carry in the trays of type, the pages of the Psalms that they had set and printed in the dread that they'd be needed for this very purpose. Peter felt the blood pound in his throat, fear and defiance coursing through his trunk, his neck, his forearms. Everyone was moving, clipped, efficient, without words, their hands, their faces, all intently focused. Peter felt the fiercest pride. Keffer moved the mirror moulds onto the workbench. Wiegand grabbed the box of mirrors they had cast already, and dealt them out along the bench like playing cards. Two other boys were towing a full pot of molten metal from the forge.

The worst was the huge flock of drying pages, six hundred great sheets, nearly, hanging from their lines. God spare us, Peter whispered, praying that the ink was halfway dried. He called the whole crew hoarsely to come quickly just as soon as they were done, for this, though massive, was not something they could rush. In haste and panic Peter gestured for more barrels, stools – they did not have a dozen ladders. Up swarmed the hands, like tentacles, like harvesters among the vines: each page was lifted, gently, painfully, so slowly that he thought his heart would burst just watching it, his ear trained on the door. Frau Beildeck had come down, astonished at the strange commotion, and he grasped her by her ruddy arm and begged her to ascend again and watch the lane from up above. Another boy was sent to crouch beside the portal in the courtyard, ears pressed tightly to the wood, to sound the first alarm.

Peter left them lifting, laying, jogging finished pages; the boys and men began to stagger off outside, towards the storerooms with those printed piles, one following the other like a trail of ants. Peter was moving like a shuttle through the shop: first to the composing room, removing the torn Bible pages clipped to every setter's stand; then examining minutely all three presses, reaching under one to pull a fallen waste sheet out. Upstairs he unpinned the large chart that tracked their progress, folded it, and took the bundle – dangerous, revealing – of Bible notes and pages out into the cold.

The track between the workshop door and the two storerooms was now wide and trampled. He heard a muffled sound – at least he thought – and tasted acid in his mouth. The men were grave, entirely silent as they filed, except for a slight huffing and the shuffling of their sodden feet. Peter heard again the muffled sound, of feet, perhaps, not hooves, up north again, along the Cobblers' Lane in the direction of the synagogue – or Mombasilier, or even, he thought with a twist of guilt, the Hof zum Gutenberg. Brusquely he seized Ruppel by the arm, and wildly motioned that the tracks must be erased; on his way back to fetch more pages, every man now dragged his feet in an uneven circuit, flattening the pale, untrammelled snow. Their manic loops and jets of breath, their panting open mouths, were an inversion, a perversion, of those jolly Flemish winter scenes.

Then there was noise, and indisputably the chink of mail,

the sound of heavy leather boots approaching. Peter shooed the crew ferociously towards the workshop door. He bent and locked the storehouse, and stood an instant with his head flung back, his face exposed to ice and snow. 'Saint Michael defend us against the rulers of this world of darkness,' he whispered to the cloak of heaven, moving then with such a speed as he had never done before into the shop, looking upon the men – his men, by God – each taking his appointed place, Hans and Mentelin bent with rags behind each man to wipe the melted mush that trailed in from the door.

They had a minute, at the most, before the archbishop's men arrived. Peter looked with shining eyes at all of them: the men poised at the presses and the setters in their places, the drying lines that now hung slack, but for a score of pages Mentelin had draped. He touched his fingers to his lips and raised his hand and made the sign of Christ's cross in the air. A little voice said, 'Sir, they're here,' and then each body tensed, unwittingly, in answer to the pounding of a metal fist upon the courtyard door.

Peter turned and saw the master book, the blank and numbered dummy Bible, on his desk, and swooped upon it as he passed and dropped it, kicking it beneath the desk. The yard when he stepped out looked churned and grimy. He made a sign to open up the double-gated portal. The hinges creaked in protest as the doors swung in slowly, followed closely by six men-at-arms who flattened themselves either side of the wide arch. They stood stiffly to attention, three by three, right hands on hilts, eyes straight ahead, heads cowled in leather, waiting. From the shadow came the dainty clop of high-strung hooves. A lone rider entered, thin, erect, black horse high-stepping, rolling its wide eyes. The face of Erlenbach, crusader, knight of the Teutonic order, glimmered faintly in the white light of the crushed new-fallen snow.

'Bring torches,' Peter told the boys, and stood unmoving in the centre of the courtyard as Archbishop Dietrich's fist approached. Speech failed him for a moment: he was torn between a stiff, reflexive urge to kneel and then cold fury at this violation of his threshold. 'My lord,' he said at last, unflinching as the booted leg in its bright, razored stirrup drew level with his neck. 'You seek a service here in Mainz?'

Free soil, free city, freemen, he intended: he tipped his head both graciously and languidly, to show he felt no deference.

Archbishop Dietrich's *Hofmeister* looked down on him as if he were a grub. His face was skeletal, mere gristle, long of beak and capped with mail, with tufts of white that sprung from ears and neck.

'Search the place,' he said, his visage hard.

'By what right—' said Peter, but the knight was swinging down from the saddle with no more attention than he would have spared a cur. The end of his sheath swung around as he dismounted and struck Peter lightly on the arm.

'Treachery. And blasphemy.' A faint twitch lifted the knight's mouth. He pushed past Peter, tall and slightly stooped, mail faintly jingling beneath his crimson cloak, into the doorway to the workshop where his soldiers had already shouldered through.

The crew looked up, mouths falling open in astonishment, arrayed as if on stage. How they had done this without some direction, each in his own corner, shrinking, freezing, staring with such seeming naturalness, Peter could not say. He planted himself at Erlenbach's left hand and threw his arm out, with contempt, derision. 'What blasphemy, my lord, when as you see, it is your master's work we are engaged in?'

The proud beak tilted, exactly like a bird's; with yellow eyes the man looked at him, head turned slightly to the side. 'My master's work,' he sneered, 'my eye.' He jerked his chin towards his captain, and the men approached the presses and snatched up the sheets. Keffer put up his hands, and Ruppel followed: ashen-faced they watched as two squat, burly fellows reached into the bed of Keffer's press and dragged the *forme* out and began to bash the metal with two cudgels they produced from their thick belts.

'Hey!' said Peter, springing, but the knight was swifter, tougher, and restrained him with the biting grip of his left hand.

'It is the book!' The printer writhed in that hard grasp, no longer feigning his own horror. 'The book that Dietrich asked for, damn you, man.' He twisted free and lunged towards the soldiers with their pile of printed sheets. 'The Psalms, you heathen slugs,' he said, snatching one and spinning, nearly throwing it at Erlenbach. 'The canticles of Solomon and Moses, just as you saw them for yourself, two years ago.' His face was inches from that weathered skull: 'Don't think I don't recall that you were there, with Rosenberg, in Eltville – do not deny you heard Johann Gutenberg offer him this present for the pope.'

The knight looked on him haughtily and smiled. 'A pretty story.' Ruthlessly his eyes swept through the open space of the whole workshop. 'Every piece of paper, parchment,' he barked, the soldiers fanning out, two to the drying hall, two more to the composing room, the first two giving the poor *forme* a final bash before discovering the twine and with an ugly relish pulling on its end to dump the whole tray with a crash onto the floor. A kind of flare went off in Peter, bright and hot, and he moved bodily to block their access to the room in which the heavy frames of letters waited in their cases, six sets of alphabets, set at an angle to six stools.

'You have no right,' he snarled, 'to tear this shop apart.' He hurled the words at Erlenbach. 'You order them to stop. This work is worth ten times their stinking hides.' As if in answer to an order he had not yet even thought, Keffer, Neumeister, and Ruppel moved to block the spaces in between the beams. Like hulking statues, hollow-eyed, broad-shouldered, a living mirror of the Kaufhaus frieze.

The boots sheathed in their jagged metal tips made a strange snicking sound. 'Oh,' said Erlenbach, as he approached; as if amused, he looked them up and down.

'You think that this is yours.' He smiled, a hideous distortion of those bloodless lips. 'From what that tinker Gutenberg said, though, it is his.' His laugh was soundless, a mere scrape; he reached into his belt and drew out a paper, unfolded it, and flung it at him, forcing Peter to bend down and take it from the ground. A waste sheet, from the book of Jeremiah, he saw as he uncreased it. And yet he kept his face entirely blank.

'Nice work,' said Erlenbach, almost pleasantly, 'for liars and for blasphemers.'

Harshly Peter laughed. 'The pope then is the blasphemer on high.' He shook his head, and sneered, and strode towards the desk with what he hoped was utter confidence. 'I take it you have never seen a psalter, or pontifical.' These cretins had a year of Latin, two at most, he thought. He threw the waste sheet down beside the sheets of canticles and psalms.

'Those are not verses.' Erlenbach bored into him with his hunter's eyes.

'Nor are they prophecy – or blasphemy. An introduction, only, words of preface to the book of prayer, written by the saint Jerome.' Impatiently he flicked his hand. 'For God's sake, ask His Grace, or Rosenberg, if you do not believe me.'

A vein throbbed silently in that rigid, sunken face; the old knight looked around. His eyes fell on the pile of pilgrim mirrors. 'Superstitious twaddle,' he said, his lips twisting.

Peter shrugged and gave his coldest, cruellest smile. 'Keep the masses happy – isn't that the way?' The way you bastards rule by crushing, smashing, dulling those who might object with bright new baubles. *Do not the rich oppress you by might?* The words of the apostle James rose up inside, and Peter kept on smiling.

How hateful was their power now, arrayed against the breath of these new men – the stirring of renewal flowing through this workshop, this whole city and their Bible. Has not a poor man the right to heaven? May he too not offer the gift of scripture to his parish, in the hope of speeding his own way? Peter felt his chest swell, heard his voice, implacable and biting.

'You have no business here,' he said. 'I bid you leave us now in peace.'

He lifted one hand; a dozen strong men silently arrived from every corner to surround him. Erlenbach looked out at him from his clay mask, and Peter felt himself exult, and then he saw it: sticking out from underneath the desk, three paces from the knight's shod foot. The master book.

He forced himself to tear away his eyes. But something in his face alerted Erlenbach, who stirred and looked around, sniffing almost, as if he too had sensed that something was amiss.

For terrible long seconds no one moved or spoke. The soldiers came like washerwomen from the drying lines, the full sheets hanging from their arms. Erlenbach moved towards the desk, his right hand sweeping the whole surface clean: of inkpot, quills, a pile of paper scraps, the litter of a half a dozen mirrors. His foot came within inches of the book as he turned, snarling. 'Insolence. You will hear more.'

Obediently, Peter dipped his head. 'I welcome it,' he said. 'His Grace has not yet seen the product of our work.' And from the corner of his eye he watched the heel move, almost grazing the thick sheaf – his breath stopped, his throat closed. He swallowed, then advanced and held his hand out.

The knight just eyed it with contempt and pulled his mesh and leather gloves back on.

'Men die who treat me as a fool.' His tone was thuggish, threatening. 'Gensfleisch will answer for this – if he's not already singing.'

He turned, his long cloak snagging on the corner of the book, then pulling free, swirling above his feet as they receded, followed by the thick tramp of his soldiers, bearing their mean spoils.

The minute they were gone, Peter loped the hundred yards across the Quintinstrasse, through the churchyard to the Hof zum Gutenberg. Lorenz unlocked the door. His eyes were wide, his grey hair flying from his head. 'They've took him off, young master,' he said shakily.

Peter strode down the hall, looked briefly in the master's study, noted how the stools were knocked about. The stacks of papers on the table were all gone; whatever copies of the prophecy the fool had kept there too. The door onto the little courtyard was ajar, a wake churned through the whiteness towards the stable door. He wrenched it open, groped into the alcove for the tinderbox, and struck a light.

The press was stripped of its protective cloth, which they had stamped into the straw. Whatever type had been left standing in its bed was gone. A twist of twine hung from the bar. He turned towards the desks, the master's high one and the table by the window, where he'd cut that type an age before. There'd been a setting case there too, to judge from the now-empty frame they'd left behind. Whatever type the master kept in all those pockets had been seized, along with the large case. Peter wondered for an instant how they'd lashed it, four foot square, onto a horse. God damn him. May God send down His plague on him, the arrogant, self-centred fool.

Wiegand and Lorenz stood behind him, gaping. 'Get everything that isn't nailed. Put any type you find into a sack, and every frame and stick.' The press, exposed, he could not help. To Wiegand he said slowly, carefully: 'Then go to Hans, and have him send as many as he needs to haul it to the Humbrechthof.' The boy nodded. Peter took a final look, and then went out to find the man.

The fool would crack before they'd even heated up the tongs – if force was even needed, any kind of torture. More likely Gutenberg would spill it of his own accord. Peter wished for catgut then, a metal brand – anything to seal that proud, loose mouth.

He paused a moment, undecided. They might have taken him to the archbishop, yet he had heard no haste of hoof beats heading north, towards the river ford that led to Eltville or Aschaffenburg. To Dietrich's residence in Mainz, then: there were cells inside the Little Court, he knew, to hold the miscreants before the court of law, beside those gardens where his peacocks screamed.

The square before St Martin's glowed as if each crystal of the snow was lit up from within. Out of the ragged clouds a strange and diffuse brightness came, from hidden moon and stars. The traders had all shuttered and deserted their locked stalls. Peter headed towards the ghostly pillars of the Little Court. He cursed with renewed vigour as the snow soaked through the flimsy leather of his shoes, and wished belatedly he'd brought his boots – and then his torch and knife. For halfway there he saw a movement in the shadows, a flickering; he stopped and peered across the shifting pools of dark and light. This was no time for fingers, murderous or larcenous, around his throat. He sidled silently into the deeper darkness at the edges cast by the great houses. A figure peeled then from the cloister columns, walking slowly towards him from the gate of Dietrich's palace. Tall and hooded, stalking almost, rustling as its arms swung, punching at the air. Another step, and Peter knew: he heard the muttering beneath the breath, the churning of the consonants, a bitter jumbling like letters clacking to the ground. The bastard's teeth were doubtless ground as well, absent a bone to chew, a body he might lash with that abusive bludgeon in his mouth.

Gutenberg ploughed towards him, head bent, face entirely shrouded by the hood, venting like Vesuvius. Unseeing, wrapped in his own drama; Peter moved out from the shadows in his path. If he had had a dagger he might well have closed his hand around the clean hard purpose of its hilt. Instead he bared his teeth and let the words fall with contempt upon the snow.

'They let you go.'

The head jerked up; the eyes blazed as the hood fell back. His master – once his mentor and his father, in loco parentis – stared right through him, gave a short, hoarse laugh.

'Out of my way,' he said, with such a weight of venom in his voice that Peter for an instant faltered.

'No.' Gathered himself, and stepped a pace towards him. 'Not after this.'

'Don't even dare.' Glittering, entirely foreign to him, furious. The voice was little better than a growl. 'I'm sick to death of interference.' He made a swipe with one long arm, as if to push his foreman from his path.

'Out of my way, I tell you. I will not be stopped.'

He was wild, inhuman. Horned and dangerous, head down, goring all that stood before him. It ended there, in Peter Schoeffer's heart. Regard, the joy he'd mirrored, common cause. He felt his hands drop to his side, those hands he'd raised in some vain gesture of defence. He could not trust him, ever, not to trample everything he held most sacred in this life. Gutenberg just switched his cloak and glowered, passing with a jerk to his left side – the way the sailors on the Rhine since time began had dodged the Lorelei.

Chapter 7

SPONHEIM ABBEY

Winter 1485

'From that point on I knew – he was a danger to the Book.'

'You can't mean that.' Trithemius draws back, his look reproving.

'A liability, of that I had no doubt.'

The dream Peter is spinning ruptures with these words. For hours the abbot has said nothing. From time to time he's bent to scratch a note, attentive as a scribe should be, entirely silent – loath, perhaps to break the flow. Until he flinches, hearing those harsh words.

'This is a weighty charge.'

'He was a risk. I know it sounds . . . ungrateful. But after such a stunt, how in God's name was I – was anyone – to trust him?'

In truth, the master never really trusted Peter or his father, not entirely. He took no man into his confidence; he felt the rules did not apply to him.

For a long moment no one speaks. The room is a suspended bell of wood, outside of which the world is white. They've sat companionably as fall has turned to snow and ice, thinks Peter, each one of his long visits a tick warmer until this.

Trithemius cinches at the cord that girds his habit. 'I am reminded,' he says, in the slightly pompous tone he saves for chapel, 'of what the angel said to Ezra.' He folds his hands into a point beneath his spadelike nose.

'Do you recall? How Uriel asked Ezra who could "Weigh me the weight of the fire, or measure me the blast of the wind, or call me back the day that is past"?'

He drops his hands. 'The answer is that no man can. That is the meaning of the riddle. If we can't even grasp such things, how can we comprehend the ways of the Most High?'

There is a light in him, the light of new conversion. He's only been a monk two years, an abbot even less.

'Thus we can never say how any of our actions fit His plan. Not mine, not yours – not even Gutenberg's.'

Peter's estimation of the fellow rises. He'd thought the abbot driven mainly by ambition, but this steeliness reveals a deeper side. The printer pours himself a glass of the weak red they make on the Mosel.

'Ezra,' he says, meditatively. 'I remember thinking as it went to press that Ezra's howl was like our own. Incomprehension, rage at the destruction of Jerusalem – just as we felt to know the heathen had destroyed Constantinople.' Strange and riddling books they were, that prophet's, filled with visions of apocalypse. The question Ezra posed as painful still as when he'd posed it fifteen centuries before: How, Lord, are we to understand your cruel destruction of your chosen people?

'But I remember thinking, too' – Peter holds the abbot firmly with his eyes – 'that Ezra held the seed as well for understanding the Lord's purpose with our Bible.'

Trithemius lifts one nearly hairless eyebrow. 'Go on.'

'He tells us, does he not, that all this present suffering is just prelude? "For did not the souls of the just in the cellars ask . . . when shall the fruit come of the floor of our reward?"

And the angel answered, "When the number of the seeds in you shall be filled, because he has weighed the world in a balance.'"

Peter waits, expectantly. Surely, if the man is quick, the meaning's clear. And yet the abbot's face does not uncloud.

'The numbers of the just and righteous seeds must swell – to overwhelm that evil.' He leans to drive it home. 'The Word must spread. There was no greater way to swell their ranks, it seemed to me, than by the printing of this Bible.

'And so, it followed, any interference was transgression of God's will.'

Trithemius has told him he has Latin, Greek, and Hebrew; he studied at the university in Heidelberg. He's keen to shake this abbey up and raise again the Benedictine lamp of learning. Yet he is smug as well, a bit too satisfied with his own rise. Peter sees him smile, as if to say *I've got you now*.

'And yet,' – the abbot spreads his hands – 'is it not telling that your former master too spread prophecy? It is a fundamental feature of the Scriptures that what is meant is hidden. The truth is only shown to those disciples that He trusted.' He waits for Peter's nod. 'There is no doubt that it was willed – the printing of it, even your archbishop's efforts to prevent it. For after all, you must admit: you *did* succeed. The Book was made. The Bible, for your master's sins, was never thwarted.'

He settles back, pleased with his argument.

'Success,' says Peter. The word is bitter on his lips.

Was he the only one who saw? The only one who understood what had been lost in the collapse of that first, extraordinary workshop? Anger flares, as bright and hot as years before, to think of all the books that had not been, the masterpieces they would certainly have made, if Gutenberg had not destroyed that brotherhood.

'The Book was plucked out of the flames. Nothing remained

of all we might have done, the greatness that I thought we might achieve.'

The young man laughs. 'You speak as if you had a say in how the world unfolds.'

'You cite the Gospels. But Saint Mark says too that man has his role. "Prepare ye the way of the Lord; make straight his paths."' He thinks of Mentelin, setting Isaiah all those years ago: *Make straight in the wilderness the paths of our God.*

Trithemius blinks. 'Of course.' He nods. 'The Lord *does* act through us.'

'We're not just senseless tools.' The printer scowls. 'You must have read the teachings of Saint Hugh.' How lifted he had been, at this pup's age, to think that God resided in each particle of the created world – and thus in Peter, too.

'I have. Although . . .' The young man flails, and Peter senses how he calculates. He's thinking that he'd best not stop the printer now, before he's got the story safely down. 'It seems presumptuous, that's all,' he shrugs, 'to think that we complete His tasks.'

Complete – or start – or carry on: the master would have said that he'd been chosen from the instant he arrived in this harsh world.

'My point is simply this: that if he'd trusted us, it might have held.'

'That may be true. But – more than you perhaps, he trusted God.'

'Until you've heard it all, you cannot judge.'

'Then pray go on.'

Chapter 8

COVENANT

[49 of 65 quires]

January — April 1454

A day passed – two, then three. They waited for some repercussion. Then it had been a week, and still none came. Now, of course, Peter knows why. But at the time it struck him as a miracle, a proof, however halting and obscure, of God's design.

Their Bible was protected. Peter had believed, at least, that they'd inquire about the progress of that fake pontifical. Yet as the year turned and the silence held, he put aside his questions and his fears. He thought of all the marks the Jews put on their doors the night the deadly angels passed to slaughter the firstborn Egyptians. The sign protecting them was not as visible, but it was surely there. The Word of God willed its completion, after all.

Gutenberg himself, of course, was unrepentant. 'I will hear none of it,' he said to Peter when he coldly told him what the raid had cost. The master brushed away all talk of broken letters, missing reams of paper stock. He moved as if his garments shone, and none might touch them – as if the chain that bound him to the ordinary world had snapped. He stood, remote and folded in upon himself, and watched the presses crank. His chin was up, his body taut; for once he held his tongue. His mind was elsewhere, resurrected into glory: already he was planning the next book to come.

Peter watched him, torn between offence and a deep need he barely understood. The two of them were so alike in certain ways: both transported, burning with the energy of this new thing that only they could grasp. Both determined, and intent: for nearly four years they'd been hiding in plain sight. Even now they were untouchable, the young man marvelled – although young men will always see transcendence, not the calculation clear to older, wiser eyes.

The fasting time had come again: the world was waiting for Crusade. In the markets and the churches, people braced. They put by what little food they could; husbands showed their wives the counting books, the hidey-holes, the keys. The market scribes and private clerks to those of wealth bent to their parchments, scratching out the inventories of their clients' houses and their souls. Each citizen of Mainz was changed, inside that crumbling wall the city council made a last-ditch effort to repair. They were sinew, bone, and yet determined, fierce. They'd show the Lord that He had punished them in error. When work was done, the younger carpenters and masons honed their battle-axes and their swords and practised in the marshy fields along the Bleiche.

Fust too hauled out a breastplate that had been his father's, and his father's before that. The fit was snug, but not as snug as it would once have been; his air of bonhomie had melted with his excess weight. If once he had deferred – to the archbishop, or the council, or his partner, Gutenberg – now he was grim, his forehead permanently pleated. 'Such days as these I never hoped to see,' he'd say, and cross himself, yet at the same time he was strangely sanguine. He had delivered all his hopes, he said, into God's hands.

Which did not mean he could not use his own. At St Silvester's he had learned, on his return from Frankfurt, of the archbishop's raid. He went to Gutenberg without another word. He had his own key to the Humbrechthof; he'd rented that damned house with his own gold. He did not knock; he just appeared, like some fell warrior. That little escapade was a net loss, he said. Three reams would be repaid, five guilders per. His voice and face were devoid of expression. In Christian fairness he would credit any profit scraped from that disgusting screed.

The master looked in vain at Peter standing there. It was almost amusing, seeing how he turned to him, then looked away, lips working. 'Somebody had to dig us out.'

'*You* dug that pit,' said Fust. 'Not I.'

'Not you?' His partner with a black look swept the room, perceived that every ear was open and attuned. They cringed a bit, half turned away – and yet the need to know connected them, sharpened their hearing.

'If you don't pay—' The master dropped his voice so low that only those who stood the closest – Peter, Keffer, Hans – could hear. 'I have to scratch around.' His arms were spread, that same old parody of supplication; a sense of injury pinched at his mouth. *I hold this up; what do you do?* his cruciform and bitter body seemed to say. Fust merely snorted. A bolt of anger streaked across the master's face. 'Do not forget,' he hissed, 'you're not the only fountain in this town.'

Fust scowled and ordered them to box the sheets that he was due from the first volume. He'd hired the Austrian to do the painting. Peter nodded, keeping his own face averted from them both. Please God, just four more months, he prayed.

Grede too had changed: she saw portents, omens, in each bird, each bud, each rupture of the earth as it awakened into spring. She walked, head covered, on the Sabbath afternoons, when once she had preferred to stay at home beside the winter hearth or in her summer courtyard. The creatures of the earth would know before man did, she said. She swept her eyes to the horizon, watching for the wheeling flocks that meant that spring had come, and warring time, far eastward of the Rhine.

'When you are gone,' she said, and looked straight into Peter's eyes, 'every last one of you—' She shook her head, reproving; they walked across the boards that spanned the washing stream. He carried a large basket for the cattails and the pussy willows she had come to gather.

'What then?' he asked when she did not go on.

She took a seat on the bench, knocked from a log, that looked back towards the city. Behind them was a thick hedge and the sloping hillock of the Altmünster. She dropped her scarf and closed her eyes, as if to draw some strength from the weak sun, then opened them and stared across the roof tiles. 'Men never think,' she softly said, 'of all they leave behind.'

He pictured all the women then, the children in descending sizes clutching at their skirts. Imagined in a flash he tried to wipe out of his mind: the market square, a crush of arms and hair, pushed in a panic towards the steps of the cathedral; the screams and blood; the ripping cloth, the pawing, thrusting; glint of daggers and sharp lances.

'They wouldn't leave the city unprotected.' He tried to ascertain what she held hidden in her eyes. There were small creases at the corners now, like sparrow claws.

'Oh, no?' Her smile was bitter. 'There are few enough of you; if there is war, he'll have you all.'

Despite the Sunday prohibition there were youths across the

Bleiche, swinging arms like windmills, bulking up their muscles with huge hammers in their fists.

'But when they do' – her dark eyes narrowed – 'you'd better leave us, each of us, protected.'

He didn't understand. 'Whatever I can do.' He reached to pat her hand. Impatiently, she shook it off.

'What's wrong with men?' Grede looked back at the boys, their grunts and shouts, then at the stream, its bright green bank, its gentle and incessant murmur. 'What's wrong with you, why can't you feel your hearts?'

He knew then why she'd brought him to that spot. There was no smoke above the dyers' hut this time, no summer herbs nor bending grasses, dancing feet or laughter. But all around him he could feel the ghost of Anna.

'You are a member of the guild.' Her eyes bored into him. 'Yet you would still refuse her all the guild's protection.'

'I refuse her nothing. She refused me first.'

'And tried and tried to reach you – or do you deny that too?'

'It isn't your concern now – is it, Grede?'

'Will it be yours when you are dead?' She flushed in anger. 'You make us wait, then leave us, then refuse to do your duty when you're asked. For shame.' She pulled her shawl up to her chin, half turning from him.

'When we most need you,' she half whispered, 'none of you are there.'

He saw her once again, her bedclothes red with blood, her mourning weeds of black.

'And I should marry her, just so she has her widow's tithe and bread?' He almost laughed.

'How hard you are.' She looked at him as if she didn't know him. 'How hard you have become, inside that workshop.' She bit her lip, and shook her head. 'I almost think that I don't know you.'

He did not answer.

'Time was, when you wore all your feelings on your sleeve.' She looked at him with sorrow. 'You loved her, don't deny it. You love her still – you've just become too proud.'

Father Michael preached that day, as he preached every Sunday throughout Lent, of mankind's fall from grace. Of Adam's punishment for thinking he was not just greater than the creatures of the earth, but almost like to God. Peter heard, but did not heed the priest. *Imago Dei*, he said to himself: the Lord made mankind in His image. Someday there might be men who, with His grace and their own striving, could regain the divine spark that Adam through his greed had lost. How else were they to understand the meaning of this gift – this power given them to incarnate His Gospel?

As Easter neared, the Humbrechthof, released from fear, resounded to the music of the Psalms. By day they set those verses for the Bible, and at night he sketched a letter for the great new volume that the partners planned. A lectern psalter for the Benedictine order, said Gutenberg, lifting one sardonic eyebrow: why don't we see if we can make the colours print this time. Fust concurred, pleased at this turn, although he held the size of the edition to those abbeys of whose sales they could be certain. Peter worked beside the master once again, fashioning a new technique to print the red and blue initials, using interlocking metal *formes*. But he did not, for all of that, relax his guard. Gutenberg might have moved beyond the Bible, tossing forwards his inventive thought; Peter still had three quires from every setter to compose and send to press.

Nick Bechtermünze drew the setting of King David's songs of praise. He struggled, though, to keep the pages flowing. Peter lent a hand and picked up one of those three quires. The first full psalm he set was number thirty-nine: *With expectation*

I have waited for the Lord / And he was attentive to me. Inwardly, he smiled.

And then, as if to show just how attentive God might be, they made a beauty of those pages such as even Peter or his father never dreamed.

Each verse of David's psalms sings praise: thus the first letter of each line is large, and red or blue. They'd have to mimic this in type, leaving a gap for every one to be hand-lettered afterwards. Yet there were scores of gaps on every page, too many to fill up with wood. Hans stared a long while into space, scratching his bald pate. He started melting, tapping. The third day, with a tuck and turn, he hauled an answer from the coals. He had cast a plain square shaft the same size as a letter *m*, yet just a fraction shorter than their letters. When slipped between them it would make a gap, because it was too short to take the ink.

Peter proofed the trial page himself, to guarantee the gaps the metal squares made were sufficient. He drew three dozen rounded Lombards, carmine red and azure blue, then held the page up to show to Mentelin and Hans. They marvelled. Gutenberg was tickled, too – as much with Hans's ingenuity as with that startling beauty. The master cackled when he saw those spacing quads, and elbowed the old smith. 'Too bad you never had a twin. I could have used you for old Sibyl.' He stuck out his tongue and made a little taunting face at Peter. He'd made a hash of that whole prophecy, and they both knew it. He might have drafted several men, but he had likely set those lines himself – he was just proud and stubborn enough to attempt it. He was no better, though, at setting than at carving; as Hans had said, he couldn't carve to save his life.

Yet let the man who has not sinned cast the first stone.

As soon as he began to set those psalms, Peter saw that he'd miscalculated in the counting of the lines. The quire he set would come up half a column short; to his frustration, the next quire was already printed off and dried.

'Blind me,' he exclaimed, and slapped his type stick on his thigh.

Mentelin, his green eyes narrowed, leaned to see.

'Short a dozen.' Peter ground his teeth. 'Blind me, curse my eyes.'

The gold-scribe counted lines beneath his breath. 'Just stretch the whole thing out and short the page before. If God is with you, you can get them to align. No one will see.'

They sat there, pulling at their lips. 'In any case,' said Mentelin, and turned on him his easy smile: 'To err is human – to forgive, divine.'

'So I have heard.'

'And did you know,' his friend went on, his red head tilted, 'that in the Muslim creed they are prohibited from striving for perfection that might rival God's?' His eyes were calm, his freckled cheeks serene. 'Their artists therefore take the greatest care to put an error in each book or painting.'

'What error?' came the master's voice. He had an other-worldly tuning of his senses to the workshop's sounds. For all the din, he must have heard the way that Peter slapped his type stick down; he poked his beak into the room.

'The lines are short.' Sourly, Peter shrugged.

'Whose fault is that?' There was no trace in him of anything that might be called remorse; it was appalling.

'Mine,' was all his foreman said, and they locked eyes for just the briefest instant. The master made a face, but he retreated.

Peter watched his back. The man could never say as much – he'd never, ever, admit a mistake. Since Peter crossed him in the square, he'd barely spoken to him, except for things related to the work. Peter had dared to challenge him, to call him to account. And in response, the master cut him off; by this refusal he rebuked him. Admitting nothing, coiled into himself, hard as a chunk of iron ore. Eventually he'd let it go, as he had done a dozen times before. He'd act as if it never even happened. Never alluding afterwards to anything, as if the pain, the trust betrayed, did not exist.

To err was human, though.

Peter looked at Mentelin, all copper gentleness and mercy. How hard Peter had now become, his old friend Grede had said.

'And if the error is not by intent?' he asked. 'Instead an accident – of pride?' He saw himself, with horror, in the master's brittle, brutal mirror.

He too had coiled into himself – had been unwilling to admit his error.

Mentelin looked up and smiled. 'We all are sinners, Peter. All of us. Me and him and you included.'

He took the lettered sample, rolled it and tied it with a ribbon. How boastful now that psalm did seem: *With expectation I have waited for the Lord.* As if the Lord owed him or anyone a thing. He went out in the fields to find the early lilies of the valley as the ground began to thaw. The earth was there, resurgent, always underneath their feet, a greening present they unwrapped anew each spring. He gathered up the tender waxen bells with care. He walked for hours, mind churning, seeking the right words. At last the best that he could do was this: *My love, can you forgive me?*

He would have given anything to see her face when it arrived, to know if he would be allowed to hope. This was his punishment: submitting to the consequence of his own pride. He would not push her for an answer either. A day went by, another day; he could not eat or sleep. He set the letters in their lines; he threw them back; he set another page; he prayed.

On the third day he went to the marketplace, for it was market day. He was as rigid as a statue standing there beneath St Martin's eaves. A glimpse, he told himself: a glimpse is all, then I will know. Grede bent above the onions and the leeks; Anna was there behind her: fine small head, a basket at her elbow, swathed in a green shawl. He watched them speaking, Anna gravely, Grede embracing her with two swift pecks on either cheek. Anna nodded, walking briskly towards the chapel where he lurked.

He burned with shame. Would he leap out like some mad, costumed ghoul? Or simply shrink and, when she passed, slink back? He had no right to press her. Yet as she passed she must have sensed his presence; she turned her head, and looked. Her eyes burned fiercely, then her cheeks.

'Please,' he said, and stretched out his right hand.

Her own hand crept up to the clasp that held her cloak. 'I – wanted – to write back.' Her voice was a bare rasp.

'If we could only speak—' he said.

'Not here.' She glanced about.

'I know a place,' he said, and stepping from the column touched her elbow, prayed she'd follow as he swiftly left the square. He climbed the hill beyond the church of John the Baptist towards the stock market, into that bitter, pungent fug. Before the little-trafficked side lane that he knew, he turned around to watch her walk, her linen skirt hiked up above the straw and muck. 'No place to take a lady,' he said, looking for a place that they might sit.

'You needn't fear,' she said coolly, and followed him along the empty stalls. He found a wooden crate and turned it up into a stool. She did not take the hand he offered but stepped lightly, wrinkling her nose. The stench was choking: fur and sweat and urine and manure.

He cursed himself; the place was foul. 'You deserve far better,' he said, turning up a bucket, pulling it to where she sat. She shrugged. 'I've seen far worse.'

And then she waited, that small oval face, the deep, dark eyes made even deeper by the paleness of her skin, a bruising of fatigue in rings beneath them. Her cheekbones were more prominent; how she had suffered, Peter thought.

Their knees were almost touching.

'I wronged you. Terribly. I let my pride destroy it all.'

She did not move; her eyes roved over his whole face, as if to probe it for sincerity or hollowness.

'I never answered – it was all my fault. I was too – shattered, too disturbed by your rejection.'

'What I rejected was not you.' She held her hands clasped lightly in her lap. 'It was the thing you did, that seemed to me a blasphemy.' She pulled her lips in with her teeth, and looked away, and frowned. 'I would have told you, if you'd ever even let me.'

'It meant so much to me.' He shook his head. 'I could not bear that you refused.'

She gave a little laugh. 'Refused? Who did the refusing? Your father would not look me in the eye. Your master – well.' She shook her head, her nostrils flaring. 'He threatened me, if you recall. And you.' For the first time she looked, with vehemence, into his eyes. 'You – went away, you sucked the life out of the world, and tossed it down like rags.'

'I know.' He was a husk, unworthy of her love. He could not look at her; he kept his eyes upon her hands. 'I was a fool. An arrogant, obnoxious ass.' He shook his head and almost whispered it. 'I felt that I was touched by God.'

He raised his eyes at last and saw the way she looked at him, with pity and a certain tenderness. She reached one hand out, touched his cheek.

'As are we all.'

He felt a rush of feeling surge through his whole body: love, despair, a rawness without words. How light she was, how wise, the way she spoke and felt and moved so modest and so graceful. Unlike him – overweening, swollen thick with self-regard.

'You are too good for me,' he said, and felt his heart crack as he said it.

'If that were so, we would not be here face-to-face.' She glanced with meaning at the shit and muck and made a show of wrinkling her nose. 'You might at least have brought me scent,' she said, and in the tilting of her head, the fleeting smile that inked her lips, he knew he was forgiven.

'You shall have scent, and any other thing your heart desires.'

'I have but one desire,' she said, and leaned towards him, soft lips meeting his harsh mouth. He took her up into his arms, light as a lamb in May, the smell and touch of her a feast after the months of desert. He kissed her eyes, her nose, her cheeks, her neck, lifting and spinning her, his arms wrapped tightly all around her, crushing her to him with such fervency that he could feel her heartbeat thrumming like a bird's.

LETTERS

Chapter 1

SUNDAY BEFORE
JOHN THE BAPTIST

[58 of 65 quires]

23 June 1454

The afternoon of that midsummer's eve, Peter took his intended wife out walking past the waters of the Bleiche. Above them rose a chequerboard of yellow flax and tawny wheat, girded by the dark green ribbons of the hedgerows of the Altmünster. The bees were drinking greedily from blossoms rising up from the baked earth. Anna raised her eyes towards the convent. 'For a while I thought that I, too—,' she began to say, but Peter turned her face and kissed her quiet, murmuring, 'Then I'd have had to break the wall down.'

They clasped each other's hands and pushed on through the waving grass. The convent buildings were unscalable, he thought, a prison for those surplus daughters. All those Elder girls were penned there, spinning, sewing, baking, praying, giving confession to that toady Heilant – while every John the Baptist from this day on, the two of them would pick the mugwort, gaining strength for their life's journey.

The plants grew along a rock wall just below the cloister.

They gathered up the blossoms in her basket. Anna held one golden flower up. 'Luck.' She smiled. The blossom had four petals and not five. 'See, even nature can surprise us.'

'Only God is perfect.' Peter took it from her fingers. 'Mentelin says that Muslim craftsmen add an error into everything they make.' He gave a little laugh. 'We needn't fear that we have overreached. We've made as many errors with our type as any scribe.'

She put a hand up to his cheek. 'So it is not so different, then.'

He looked away across the waving, buzzing fields. 'I pray not. I always hoped that we might reach as great an artistry with this new craft as with the old.'

She laced her fingers into his and brought the blossom to her nose. 'I pray as well. That come what may, we never lose our hands, our touch – this closeness to the Lord's Creation.'

They left the fields by a small gate that opened on the lane below the cloister. From that high up, the river was a broad and lazy finger pointing north. 'Bingen, Koblenz, then Cologne,' he told her, gesturing towards the places they would go. 'And thence to Rotterdam and Amsterdam.' He traced the future's contours in the air.

'Is that a sermon on the mount I hear?' The faintly mocking voice was not a foot away behind the wall. Its owner's head poked up, sandy-haired and pink of cheek.

'That is your bailiwick, I think.'

On that slope, for once the scribe – confessor, *lektor*, spy – stood just at Peter's height and could look straight into his eyes. More was the pity, Peter thought, for eyes did mirror a man's soul, and Heilant's were like tarnish on a glass. Half a minute later he appeared along the lane, a little smirk on his broad face.

'So you *do* have a light you hide.' He winked and bowed, hands clasped before his ample waist, at Anna. 'The honour is all mine.'

'Petrus Heilant, Anna Pinzler,' Peter said. 'Confessor here, and once a fellow scribe.' He dwelt an instant on the 'once'. Heilant had tucked up his summer habit in his belt, exposing a white tunic. He had been resting, it would seem, among the apple trees in that extensive orchard.

Anna bent her head devoutly.

'What brings you up this high?' Heilant, hands laced, gave him a wry smile. He meant the word in every sense, undoubtedly. How quickly men put on the manners of their stations: he too, no less than Heilant.

'Saint Bildnis knew to choose the finest view,' he answered. 'One dear to every child of Mainz.'

'Indeed,' said Heilant.

'I don't imagine you'll enjoy it long though – will you?' Laconically he needled him. He had no doubt the monk had fingered them to his superiors. Yet he felt calm, almost relieved: the word was out, yet they had dodged the worst. 'There is a parish in your future, I am certain,' he told Heilant almost gaily.

'Perhaps.' Heilant looked strangely at him. 'Some of us must do as we are told.'

'I am no freer.'

'Oh, no?' Heilant cocked one eyebrow. 'You do quite well there, in your little workshop.'

Anna glanced between them, sensing all that was unsaid, and Peter squeezed her hand.

'I mind my business,' he said softly. The world would know at last. In six more weeks the truth of what they did would dazzle the whole Rhineland.

'Quite lucrative, that business.' Heilant's voice was odious.

Sharply Peter said, 'You've done enough. Leave it alone.'

'Unless' – the full lips lifted in a taunting smile – 'you're not apprised – have not been cut in on the latest?' The man was like a snake, coiled up and waiting on the sun-baked road. Peter shook his head and tasted bile; he tucked his love's hand in his arm and turned to go.

'I would have thought, since you know all, that you had heard about the Frankfurt order.' The scribe was smiling widely now, his eyes glittering with triumph.

'What order?' Anna asked, when Peter gripped her arm.

'A full indulgence from the pope. For the Crusade. He ordered some ten thousand. I'm surprised you haven't heard.'

'To fund an army,' Anna whispered. Heilant nodded; Peter felt her fear.

The stock phrase issued like a tapeworm from inside: 'He'll need an army, then, of scribes.' He kept his face impassive as he realized. Of course the Holy See would offer new *confessionalia*; it stood to reason they would use this means to raise the funds for the Crusade.

'Metal scribes, no doubt,' said Heilant with his leering, knowing smile.

'Who told you this?'

Heilant's chin rose almost infinitesimally. 'I hear much more than you imagine.'

Fust was in Calais to see what English merchants had for sale; no longer did he patronize Venetian thieves who trafficked with the Turk and sold the spoils in Bruges. He was at least two weeks away.

'So tell me straight.' Peter stood there, drained. 'Who Dietrich told to make them.'

Heilant laughed so suddenly and easily, they knew his mirth was real. And then he looked at Peter, wiping at the creases of his eyes – as if the printer were some village dunce, a sad thing only to be pitied. 'Come now,' he said. 'You know as well as I.'

He walked her home, and she released him, understanding, to retrace his steps back to the Cobblers' Lane. The shutters were unseeing eyes to either side, indifferent, sun-blistered. He turned into the Quintinstrasse, turned again into their cul-de-sac and fit the key into the lock and entered, crossed the court-yard and unlocked the workshop door.

Inside thin slats of light leaked in, casting bright stripes on the equipment. The presses loomed like crouching beasts, swathed in their thick protective cloths: how much they'd learned, not least about the dust – how even a small mote on the bed could throw the type from true.

He walked the passage from the door past the composing room, down the long drying hall, then back again towards his desk – the master's desk. The movement of the air he swept behind him set twelve hundred sheets to rustling on the lines. He stopped and tilted up his head and breathed the sweet yet acrid odour of the ink that scented all their nights and days.

After everything they had done together. *Please God, let this not be true.*

He'd hammered, and he'd carved, and mixed so many metals at the master's side. He'd etched his letters while the master etched those visions in his mind. Impossible, his foreman thought: he'd risked it once – but even Gutenberg would not be arrogant enough to risk it all once more.

Peter pushed one shutter open and sat and pulled the proof sheets towards him. Each one was lettered at the bottom corner with a faint brown scratch. He checked their order with the master book, and closed his eyes. How close they were. Last night he'd taken the completed quire of Acts of the Apostles to the storeroom: one hundred and eighty copies of each folded set, five sheets that made another twenty pages of this Book of Books.

He wondered as he sat there how they'd even had the heart to start. God knew they'd had no notion of the effort it would cost. Yet it was willed, and nearly done; he'd pledged his father they would have it finished by Autumn Fair. There were just four quires left to set and proof and print, eighty pages out of those twelve hundred and eighty-six – and then the forty extra copies of the first three quires, for it was only after those first few that Peter found the faster way of casting, and they decided to print more. Print more! How eager and fevered they had been! He drove the men now more like oxen, heads down, straining up the inclines. Day after day the ink balls hissed, the presses ground, their fingers flew from case to stick. They laboured as though sprinting towards some shining vision – driven towards that final page. Apocalypse. He felt a chill and looked back down.

The sheaf he held contained some pages from that final book. He felt his eyes sting, raised his head, looked blindly towards the metal pots, the huge composing stones. The great black letters of their Bible were too large for any small indulgence scrip. Could he have missed it? Could Gutenberg have cut a new type after all? There was no way he could have done it by himself: only one man beside Peter knew how to carve and cast. He tasted iron in his mouth. Hans.

He cast his mind back through the recent weeks. The old smith hadn't joked or horsed around the way he often did, divining with the drops of lead that gathered at the bottom of the water pans. Peter had simply thought that they were all worn to shreds. But now he asked himself if Hans instead had rolled the truth inside. For weeks he'd barely looked Peter in the eye. He tinkered late into the night; or else he loitered once his pages had been set, waiting silently for Keffer to wash up his press. Dear God, said Peter to himself again. *Let not this evil come between us.*

Could Gutenberg – could Hans – not see what they had done? They'd done it all together – one for all, and all for one. They were a crew, a brotherhood; he thought of Christ's apostles, gathered for their final meal, and Judas creeping from the room. He let the sheet fall back; he put his head into his palms. He ought to count the sacks of ore and sheets of vellum, but could not face it yet. Instead he groped and lifted up the glass, and laid it on one printed line.

There, wondrously enlarged, were his own letters. He bent to check the sharpness of each edge, the firmness of each angled line. He was, if nothing else, a scribe. He knew each contour as he knew the shape of his own wrist and fingertips. Slowly he scanned the two black columns. No letter could remain that grinding pressure had begun to splay. He searched for telltale signs: the fattened smear of battered letters, ladies turned to swollen-ankled hags. He struck out every sign he deemed unworthy of God's Word.

And if thine eye scandalize thee, said Saint Matthew, *pluck it out.*

He dropped his pen and raised the sheet up to the window to check the lines impressed on either side, laid back-to-back, entwined like lovers one atop another in the summer light. He rubbed his fingers lightly, felt the sweet, strong bite of deep-pressed type. And yes, Lord, he was proud.

'Perhaps the Book wills its own end,' Mentelin had told him, months ago. Peter bowed his head and crossed himself. *Lord, make it so.*

He stayed that night back at his father's house in his old upstairs room. He could not sleep among them as he did from time to time, twisting and turning as they snored. And even so he did not sleep; at four he stood and dressed. The air was warm before the sun had even peeked above the eastern hills. The summer heat was full upon them; he'd have to shift the work now to the night, as they had done the last two years. Silently he came into the workshop, well before the shop boys started stirring. He thought of other mornings long ago, when he had been the one to stoke the forge and sweep the floor. By five the crew would wake and clatter down the stairs.

Noiselessly he padded to the workbench by the great brick oven and sifted through the tools. Hans's chisels and small pack of awls were nowhere to be seen. The ores were as they ought to be, the paper too. They hadn't yet begun the casting or the printing then – if they had indeed cut a new small alphabet. In the night he'd tried to tell himself that this was only Heilant's bitter jibing. There was no proof that Dietrich had not turned, as always, to the scribes: Rosenberg, his vicar, could have ordered half the clerks in the archdiocese. There was a sound like drumbeats as the workers' feet began to pound the stairs. In the composing room, Peter took his apron from its hook and put on the cotton cap that held the hair out of his eyes. Wearily he bent his head to set his page, part of the letter from Saint James to the twelve tribes.

Hans grunted his hello and took his stick and started setting. Mentelin slid in between them and said cheerfully they'd better work at double time today. Peter stared at him, confused, and then remembered: it was the feast of John the Baptist; he'd given them all half a day. 'Right,' he said.

'Though by the looks of it you're better off in bed – alone,' his friend said, smiling. The three young setters grinned, and Peter forced a smile. Still, it warmed him that someone had noticed. Was this true friendship, then? Of that whole crew, the Strassburg scribe had always understood his calling and his burden. Sidelong, Peter stole a glance at Hans. His scarred brown head was bent, cheeks hollowed as he muttered every word; he did not look to right or left. Once, Peter thought with bitterness, they had been friends.

For three full hours they all sat silent, dropping letters in their sticks. The tower clock struck eight, and Peter read this line: '"Detract not one another, my brethren. He that detracteth

his brother, or he that judgeth his brother, detracteth the law.'"
His palms grew slick. He sat a moment, thinking, then abruptly
set his stick down. He stood and touched Hans's back. 'If I
might have a word.'

Hans blinked and stopped, and followed him out into
daylight.

'If there is something you're not saying' – Peter looked upon
his gnarled and weathered face – 'I think I have a right to know.'

Hans sighed and scratched his pate, looked everywhere but
into his eyes. 'I'm not to say.' Discomfort pinched his mouth.

Everything that had joined them seemed to drain away – just
like the grains in that old glass that Hans and Konrad used to
turn to time their idiotic games.

'It has no bearing on the book.' Hans licked his lips; his
mottled irises were ringed a milky blue. 'It wouldn't hurt or
hinder, Henne swore.'

The old smith's look was mournful as a hound. Peter did
not answer. *Let every man be swift to hear, but slow to speak and
slow to anger.* The words were sitting in his type stick. He turned
and walked back in.

All three presses were in motion: strong arms pumping,
platens crashing, sheets of paper rising, falling. The pressmen
sweated as they grunted, dancing in a fluid pattern as they
stepped away to let the beaters ink the *formes*. The pace had
punished all of them: Peter saw it in their cheeks and eyes.
Each one of them yearned for the Sabbath, not just to praise
the Lord. All twelve were broken in now, like leather straps.
They longed to put this book behind them – although he knew
the next one would be just as big, and harder still.

How far they'd come from those first shaky pulls on the bar.
Now even Neumeister had reached consistent speed. When all
was humming to the spheres, his crew cranked out twelve
hundred pages in a day. There stirred in him a feeling

of tremendous love and pride, knifed through with all the bitterness of this betrayal. They were a new, amazing brotherhood: a guild free of all rules. A priesthood, secret and disruptive as the early Christians. Though he was charged to lead them, Peter knew this was a lie. They led themselves – and therein lay the miracle. Each man there was the master of himself. Each had his skill, invented on the fly, his part to play in this great passion. The craftsmen in the shops of Mainz could only dream of working as such independent men.

Or so for months he'd thought. But now he understood the price. They stood alone, exposed, entirely at the mercy of the powers ranged above them. It wasn't just this book that Gutenberg and Hans betrayed, but their whole status as free, thinking men – this precious gift that in the working of the Bible they'd been granted.

The bastard kept him dangling until after noon. Every passing hour just reinforced the truth: Peter was the coachman, nothing more – his job to lash the team and scoop the droppings. He let the men go as he'd promised, sending the shop boys to stow the ink in crocks in the dark basement of his father's house. Each season brought its lesson, he thought, tensing at the slap of that sharp tread. The year before, they had not had that cooling thought.

'I hear the cat is out,' the master said without preamble. So Hans had met him on the stairs. He must have hoped his shamefaced smile conveyed sincerity.

'So it is true.'

'Damned nuisance. But it can't be helped.' He splayed those pity-me hands and shook his head.

'I guess you waited until your partner was away.'

A sharpness started in the master's face, spread down his neck, his arms, a molten thing that hardened as it cooled. 'You have no notion,' he said, 'of the things I have to juggle.'

Nor you, thought Peter acidly. 'I know full well how much is left to do.'

Gutenberg strode to the chart, which he had taken from the dining hall and put back near his desk. 'You think that you're the only one who checks?'

His fingers jabbed the columns – Peter's first, then Hans's. 'Two weeks, three at the most,' he growled. His fingers crooked above the other setters: 'Here too, except for this.' His finger hovered over Mentelin's, whose final quire lurched past the others like a hayrick dangling from a cliff. 'Another week for that.'

'Then three more weeks for the resetting,' said Peter grimly.

'Two presses will suffice.' The bastard didn't even turn to look him in the eye. 'I'll use Keffer's for the letter.'

'And hand the keys to Erlenbach.' What did he think? That Dietrich's minions would just trust him, leave him to it, without checking that the order went as planned? The thought of all those toadies in the workshop made him want to retch.

'Don't speak of what you do not know.'

Peter stared at him. Since Christmas he had lived in fear, expecting any moment that the soldiers would return. But now, with a sick twisting in his gut, he understood. The man had known what he was doing all along – had known since Erlenbach had let him go. He'd traded that indulgence for his freedom. And even so he hadn't had the decency to tell them – he'd simply let them writhe.

'I need Keffer's press to proof the psalter,' Peter said stiffly.

The master, irritated, shook his head. 'Proof it with soot.'

Only the Book, and all the love that he'd poured into it, restrained his rage. Peter felt the blood pound in his ears and face. That psalter type was his – a thing far finer than this cretin ever made with his own hands. The crowning piece of all he'd learned and done, by God, the measure of his mastery, his *Meisterstück*. He felt his fury flame, consume the love that he'd once felt and leave it in a smoking pile. To think he'd even toyed with showing him what he had tinkered at these recent weeks, the way he'd found to further their technique. He'd burned to take it to him, as he'd always done, the way a cat will drop its catch before its master's feet. A harder matrix, forged with a new alloy he had found, which he had thought might well work by itself in some device that cast one letter at a time. For Gutenberg was still the only one – save Hans – who had the wit to understand.

Instead the wilful Gensfleisch waved his hand. Dismissively he flapped it before reaching in a pocket of his apron.

'*This* is the proof,' he said, and thrust a paper towards Peter. 'The real proof – of all my press can do.'

Peter saw the letters – new ones, tiny, smoke proofs of that alphabet that Hans indeed had cut behind his back. Half the size of their black Gothic, a *bastarda*, truly.

'For chancelleries and city councils, letters and decrees.' The look upon the master's face could only be described as triumph. And in his eyes, thought Peter Schoeffer, the clearest and most naked greed.

'The matrices are struck. I need two men to cast and file.'

Peter looked into those wolflike eyes. 'So you don't care if we are finished by the fair.'

'War is coming.' Pompously, portentously, the master shrugged. 'The archbishop needs three thousand by next month. His will be done.'

Peter understood then Gutenberg's ambition, his design. He meant to use it as a cudgel, turn the press into a weapon made of metal – just like the cannon Mehmet II had wrested from the bowels of the earth.

Chapter 2

SPONHEIM ABBEY

February 1486

A letter of indulgence, of itself, is not a loathsome thing. Grede used to buy them, Anna too.

Speaking her name stops Peter for a moment. His lovely little wife. He lost her far too soon, along with their first child. His second wife, Christina, is the mother of his sons. And she too buys indulgences: she puts the shillings in the brass collection box, whenever functionaries of the church alight like crows at the four corners of the market square. She takes each printed form – on which the priest has filled in the blanks with her name and date – and folds it carefully away. All Christians hope to ease the burden of their sins, and pay such fines in counterpart for God's forgiveness.

'The problem was, he made the thing in secret, for the enemy,' says Peter now, returning to the abbot. 'There was no other way to see it but betrayal – not just of me, and of my father, but of the guilds who'd given cover to the workshop.'

The letter issued by the pope that year was of the highest kind: a plenary indulgence granting full remission of all sin. This was no normal letter of indulgence, good for ten days, sometimes thirty. It cleansed the sinner's soul in perpetuity:

there was no limit to it; heaven's gate stood open. It fetched the highest price and thus was a fat prize for all who had a hand in seeing to its distribution. Few argued with the underlying need, says Peter now: all knew it was a measure of the desperation of the Holy See to raise the funds for the Crusade.

'But naturally the guilds felt burned,' he tells the abbot. 'After the master's promises that Mainz – not the archbishop – would reap the benefit of this new press.'

Trithemius nods thoughtfully. 'What was the fee?'

'Two guilders per.'

A flutter parts the abbot's lips. 'Did many citizens of Mainz have that?'

'Precisely what my uncle asked.' One final fleecing of the poor, Jakob had called it. 'But still you must imagine,' Peter says, 'the terror that the people felt. God's wrath was kindled and their only hope was to deflect his ire. Repel the Turk! They heard it daily from the pulpits and the hawkers, saw the Elders buying left and right, and tried to do the same.'

The man the pope had charged with the collection in the German lands was one Paulinus Chappe. His territory stretched from Basel to Cologne. 'The archbishops of the Rhine, as you recall, refused more tithes to fund the church or, more specifically, the kaiser's coronation.' So the pope annulled the tithe, ordering instead this vast collect – which anyone who handled got a piece of, from Paulinus to archbishops and then bishops and the heads of the cathedral chapters and the monasteries charged with sending priests and monks to sell the letters in the villages and towns.

'And the producers, too, I guess.' The abbot cocks his head. 'The scribes who wrote them – or the printer?'

'Correct.'

The abbot looks long at him, thinking.

'Meanwhile things in Mainz had never been so bad. The

river trade was dead, except a little barter with our cloth and wine. The tradesmen barely fed themselves – and yet the church brought all that pressure down to bear. Two guilders – in a good year you might earn it in a month, but not then.' Peter understood now why the council had gone mad. 'They squeezed it out of those who least could pay – the whole while knowing less than half of it had any chance of reaching Rome.'

The abbot nods. ''Twas ever thus.'

'I think what rankles me the most,' says Peter softly, 'was how the clergy all exploited people's fear, yet never in their hearts believed in the Crusade.'

'It is a mystery.' The abbot nods. How thirty years can pass and the red tide of Islam lap, while the whole time the One True Church sits on its hands. 'So you will understand, perhaps, why I am . . . sceptical . . . that we can do much more than wait, and straighten our own house.' Trithemius lets out a sigh and cites Saint Mark:

Watch ye, therefore (for you know not when the lord of the house cometh, at even, or at midnight, or at the cock crowing or in the morning): Lest coming on a sudden he find you sleeping. And what I say to you I say to all: Watch.

'Now.' The abbot straightens and claps. The acolyte arrives with wood and wine. 'You say that Gutenberg had known of this indulgence months before.'

'He must have, and as early as the turning of the year.' Saying it aloud only enrages him anew. 'He must have made a deal with Dietrich when they hauled him off over that prophecy. That's why they let him go. He bought them off with what the diocese could skim from that indulgence.'

Trithemius is looking fixedly at Peter, round-eyed as an owl. Quietly he says, 'There is another explanation, though.' He tilts his head so slowly, with a look of such assessment, Peter half expects to see him turn his head around.

'You too have printed many letters of indulgence, I assume?'

'I have.'

'So you yourself are quite aware of the . . . accommodations . . . one must sometimes make with power.'

'That wasn't what he did.'

The abbot purses his pale lips. 'Who knows? If he were here . . . but he is not, and it is left to us to scrutinize his motives. He had his reasons, certainly.'

In irritation Peter shakes his head.

'Everyone put pressure on him,' says Trithemius. 'Especially your father.'

Peter hears the master's roar: *What will it take for you to grasp that there is no more gold?*

'Sometimes the step that looks wrong in our sight is part of something larger.' Trithemius nods to himself. 'As I learned here, three years ago. I did not choose this place – it chose me late one night when I was forced to find a shelter from a snowstorm.' He looks with meaning at the printer. 'The ways of the Most High are cloaked in mystery. Not everything is as it seems.'

'You think he had a . . . nobler reason, then?'

Trithemius is softer now, more the confessor than the judge. 'I only say our human sight is prone to error.'

To err is human, Peter thinks. He stands and goes to poke the fire. The coals are not as hot as those he banked to melt their metals. But even so his face feels warm. How many errors has he made along the way? He thinks of the mistakes in setting Genesis, of Mentelin's calm words that helped him see he'd wronged a girl. For thirty years he's stoked his pain and his resentment of the master, and for what? He mounds the glowing embers and then strikes them into flame, and for the first time feels a flicker of a doubt.

Chapter 3

MONDAY BEFORE THE TRANSLATION
OF SAINT BENEDICT

[61.5 of 65 quires]

8 July 1454

The leaders of the city council met *ex camera*, in the back room of Mompasilier. The better, Peter later thought, for Jakob to attack the battered tables with his fists and roar and goad the other council leaders into action. The chambers of the Rathaus were too crusted with the Elder wealth of years gone by: thick velour drapes and hammer vaulting, leaded glass that looked out on the Rhine. The back room of the guildhall smelled of woodsmoke and conspiracy and hate.

Molsberg was there, and Kraemer of the grocers' guild; the lawyer Humery had given up all hope of freeing Mainz from Dietrich's grip, and with that hope, his seat. While this was taking place, the world went on: the dyers dyed; the livestock lowed; the smiths sent up their sparks. Peter in his ignorance climbed to the ramparts in the early mornings, seeking strength to face the day. He had no notion of the movements in the mighty clockwork that whirred over Mainz, the back-and-forth of brute, uncaring forces. He only learned the hour had struck when one of Jakob's boys fetched him to Mompasilier.

He ought to know the council's action, Jakob told him, blue eyes bright. His uncle took a gulp and wiped his beard. The heavy seal on his finger glinted in the daylight, slicing through the dimness of the room. 'Enough's enough. We've waited long enough to cut this chain.' He made a chopping motion with his hand. 'We've sent the sheriffs off for Rosenberg to stop him promulgating this indulgence. Even now the thing is done.'

'What thing?' asked Peter.

'Our vicar general has to learn to share.' Jakob's smile was cruel. 'Let's see now who holds whom for ransom.'

The officers would seize Rosenberg as he was travelling on the archbishop's business, he said underneath his breath. A cell beneath the Rathaus was prepared.

'Good God.' It was insane. 'It's madness.'

'Madness, no. Lucidity, at last. Force is the only language Dietrich understands.'

'He'll go mad. It's an affront.' The protests piled up on his tongue. 'Not just to Dietrich but the pope. My God, it's treason.'

'Treason! Ha! It's freedom.' Jakob shoved the stein aside and pushed himself up onto his hands. 'What's a free city, otherwise?' He bent, a wild thing, pitched across the table. 'What's freedom, if not casting off the vassal's noose? To get up off our knees and cry enough! You shall not beggar us for all eternity.'

His face was strange, alight with bloodlust. Horrified, Peter felt himself recoil. 'You put us at his mercy, then. Each one of us in this whole city. God only knows what you'll draw down.'

'We've starving farmers plenty with their cudgels, working men with tools gone months without a job. A band enough of angry men, and every manner of sharp weapon.' Peter saw the youths with pikes and axes on the Bleiche.

'This is your plan then – to provoke a war?' His father was

still far away. The fastest horse and boat by now had barely reached him with the news of the indulgence. 'The walls are rotted, indefensible.' Anna's face flashed in his mind, and Grede's, the children's – the workshop, and their Bible. 'You know what happened outside Strassburg.' Six months before, Erlenbach had besieged a nearby fortress town to starve its people out in punishment for insufficient taxes. Strassburg's merchants, too, had been refused free transit through archdiocesan lands to sell their wares at Lenten Fair.

'For such an insolence in his cathedral city,' Peter hissed, 'he'll hit us even harder.'

'Meet force with force.' Jakob looked at him with scorn. 'You always were too soft. Use force, I say; then you can talk.' He spat into the sawdust on the floor. 'He ought to pay a portion of each cursed letter to the city. That's all we ask. We have a right; we're granting him the privilege of hawking his damned chits inside our walls.'

Peter did not even think of sharing this with Gutenberg. He'd learn it soon enough through his back channels. In Peter's mind the information snaked like a black thread from Dietrich's court into the waxy, intermediary ears of toadies in the Tiergarten, the Schreibhaus, friends from youth the master cultivated up at St Viktor's. In the event, it took less than a day. 'To hell with your damned council,' were the first words from the master's mouth at noontime the day after. 'Those cretins have seized Rosenberg.'

How Peter wanted, then and there, to laugh. Instead he donned a look of shock. 'What?' he said, but Gutenberg just growled, 'For once when goddamned Fust could be of use.' He thrust his lips out, twisting at his beard. 'I'll have to pry the bugger out myself, the devil take them.' He thrust an arm at Peter. 'You'll come, to keep them straight.' He did not even pause to let him shed his apron. 'Move, move!' he said, 'we might still save it if we're quick.'

Peter went as he was ordered. The days were past when he would let the man roll madly, muzzle blasting, out of sight. And yet the city council did not sit on this master's pleasure, much to his irritation. The Rathaus halls were empty, and the chambers; only Molsberg sat there in his office, leafing through some papers and – as Gutenberg swept in – a second man, a third, both seated, backs towards the burst-open door. His uncle, and another councillor, the master miller Heyt. Surprise, on Jakob's lean hard face, mutating swiftly into hate.

'Unhand the man,' the master said, advancing.

Molsberg, vast and bald, a pair of glasses on his nose, heaved up behind his desk. He wore the chain of the first *Bürgermeister*, a gleaming mass of gold upon his chest.

'You give no orders here.'

'This council has no right in law to interfere with matters of the archdiocese.'

'Nor do you represent the archbishop, as far as I'm aware.' The trader coolly looked at him through tiny squares of glass. 'What is your business here?' Although their clans were bound by marriage, there wasn't much love lost between them. Molsberg was a pragmatist, a calm, unhurried man, who though an Elder had no wish to quit the city and the woollen trade his ancestors had built.

Rapidly the master moved towards the desk. 'My business is to bring you back to reason.'

'Reason!' Jakob shot up from his chair. 'The nerve, to show your lying mug in here.'

It was as if the words, and he who spoke them, were mere vapour. Gutenberg did not break stride until he leaned and grasped the edge of Molsberg's desk.

'His Grace will bring his hammer on you, hard. It's folly, Reinhart, you must see. The damage still can be contained – if you'll unloose him.'

'Too late,' said Molsberg.

'You should have thought of that before you brought the vipers in the nest,' came Jakob's voice. He stood a bit behind and to the side, flashing like a blade – directing all his force towards this Elder who refused even to recognize his presence. 'Look at me!' he bellowed, and the master turned, just very slightly, with a curving of his lips, the faintest sneer.

'You took protection from us, let us shield you – and for what? Where is the counterpart, I say? Where is the payoff for a year of silence?' Jakob stepped towards him.

The sigh was great, theatrical; the master glanced at Molsberg and was tempted, Peter knew, to roll his eyes. 'The counterpart will come,' was all he said, 'when we are done.'

'And Mainz again is pumped and half the proceeds land in your own pocket.' Jakob, bright with fury, took another step, his body thin and hard and flexed. 'There will be something in it now, not later,' he said, his low voice thick with menace.

Molsberg was cleanly shaved, his chin the barest line of flesh above the lace that pinched his spreading neck. 'Indeed.' His voice was steady. 'Why should archbishops benefit, cathedral chapters, every grasping palm the whole way down, and Mainz should not?' He looked with meaning at his kinsman. 'We have our interest too. It stands to reason, as you say.'

'This is no way—' the master started. The council president put up his hand.

'There is no other way. He refuses to pay tax, yet we are squeezed and squeezed, each time a little more.' The Elder trader shrugged. His face was utterly impassive. 'He'll take it any way he can, but this time he – and you – have gone too far. We have to take a stand.'

'Then let me speak to Rosenberg, at least,' said Gutenberg. 'To try to – soften it, perhaps.'

Molsberg shook his head.

'Perhaps you'd like to join him,' Jakob said cuttingly. Gutenberg looked back, above him, through him, towards the goldsmith's nephew, standing silent at the door.

'As you wish.' His head swung back; his face was ugly, and his words. 'You choose to lie with thugs. That is your choice. The rest is on your head.'

For years afterwards, Peter wondered just how word of Gutenberg's appearance in that chamber got back to the archbishop. The city knew reprisal would be swift, but even so the reason Dietrich chose the course he took was never all that clear.

What had angered the archbishop most? The fact that he didn't even get a chance to promulgate his new indulgence, before those trumped-up labourers of Mainz had dragged it through the muck? Or fear those curs might get their mitts on his new secret toy – this printing press that now appeared a most efficient means of minting gold?

Whichever it had been, he did not hammer with blunt force – with excommunication, or with troops – as he had done four years before. He struck more surgically, and grabbed the things that had real value in his eyes: the master's press, still at the Hof zum Gutenberg – and then the master, too, drinking with his peers one evening at the Tiergarten.

How Gutenberg must have been furious – embarrassed too, to look up suddenly and see those soldiers, and then feel the rough cold metal of their gauntlets. Peter could not quite imagine it. He'd not have made a scene, not there: he would have stalked out, haughty, dark eyes glittering with rage. They'd taken him into the Little Court; once more, as if in a recurring nightmare, Peter learned this through a pounding at the workshop door.

Lorenz reached towards him, trembling and bewildered. Peter had to find the master, the old servant said. He had to find a way to make it right. The old press had been taken, piece by piece. Peter looked around him at his cranking presses and those sweating acolytes. Mentelin went past him, bearing a full tray before him like a chalice. Inside a week, the world had been turned upside down. Yet if he went, what was the chance that Peter too were seized, and all of this left undefended? The men were gathering by Mentelin and Hans; he heard them indistinctly muttering.

Only as it fell to pieces did he understand how much that brotherhood had sheltered and sustained him. The shop had been as much a cloister as the workshop of a guild. They had their rites, their prayers that shifted with the seasons. Freeze not, melt not, dry not: ink and metal, vellum and paper, bending to their wills. They had depended on each other, and for years the thing had held. Until first one, and then the next, had snapped the links that bound them. He thought of Thomas and his doubt, of Judas Iscariot. What brotherhood could hold, once faith and trust were lost?

Four weeks remained until Autumn Fair: the letters of Saint Paul, Saint James, Saint John, the blinding vision of Revelation. Hans had already started setting that last book. How fitting, thought their foreman bitterly. Yet Peter could not falter. He made a sign to Mentelin. As he came towards him, Peter thought of all those gentle souls whose lives depended more than ever on the men of Mainz, of little Tina, Henchin, Grede, and Anna. What words of comfort might she give him now?

'I have to go and see what's to be seen,' he said in a low voice. 'If I am taken, you must see it through.' He'd had a letter from his father, too; thank Heaven, Fust would soon be home.

'Don't go alone.' Mentelin gripped his forearm. 'Take muscle, if you must.'

'I can't just leave him there,' said Peter with the palest smile, 'though I am sorely tempted.'

Mentelin flashed a brief grin and went back towards his stool.

He'd have to go to Jakob and demand an escort. His uncle'd say, most likely, he should let the bugger rot. Two pawns, each rotting in his separate cell – how clever, Peter would be tempted to respond. Force – then impasse – this was your intent? It isn't anything to you, Jakob would sneer. *Ah, but.* If Mainz expected things to move, Gutenberg would have to talk to the archbishop. Someone would have to talk to the inventor and persuade him that there was no other way. And you know as well as I, Peter would have to tell his uncle: Johann Gensfleisch, known as Gutenberg, will never talk to you.

Even in broad daylight the deacon of St Martin's kept the torches burning at the Little Court. Pale ghostly flames hung from each column lining the long cloister. Dietrich von Erbach's representative in Mainz, Konrad von Greifenklau, could not receive the delegation, Peter and the pair of city wardens were informed. The porter eyed their hauberks and their belted swords.

'Wait here,' he said, and scuttled down the vaulted hallway. The marble arches rhymed its length like giant ribs, the ribs of a leviathan, inhaling all who entered there. The walls seemed to narrow as they vanished, glittering with a wealth so concentrated that the senses reeled. Colours burst from endless tapestries; oil paintings glimmered in their gilded frames. He'd always known the first spoils of the ships that docked in Mainz were theirs to take, but never had Peter seen them all displayed.

Father van Holzhausen would agree to hear their errand. The porter blocked the wardens' path. 'The weapons you must leave,' he said. 'You have no jurisdiction here.' Curtly Peter nodded, and the wardens, frowning, dropped their belts. Before they knocked he had instructed them to hug close to his heels if this transpired. He'd take no chances; seizure already had bred seizure, one rough deed engendering the next. The tension in the city was extreme.

They trooped to a reception room, where a thin figure rose from where it sat before the fire. An ancient priest, his bones just barely knit enough to bear the burden of his thick embroidered robes. So this was the 'Old Peacock', as they called him: resplendent in his crimson and yet wasted, bony hands like sticks that jutted from that costly habit. Past eighty, Peter guessed, so thin and hollow that even in the heat of summer he required a fire.

'God be with you,' came his reedy voice. He shuffled towards them, leaning on a cane. 'Urgent business, I am told.'

'I'm here to see Herr Gutenberg.'

'Ah.' Up went two stringy eyebrows. 'And you are?'

'Peter Schoeffer, his apprentice, Father.'

The Old Peacock looked him over, white eye-hairs bristling, loose lips quivering as he considered. 'I see.' His eyes darted towards the wardens. 'You wish to speak with him.'

'I do.'

'This is a house of God.' He raised one desiccated claw and waved it at them. 'Your men must wait. You'll be quite safe.'

'The times are tense,' said Peter.

The priest gave a grey smile. 'No more nor less than all the years before.' He nodded at the porter, then at Peter, and turned and started slowly back to his great chair.

The room in which they held the master was another level down, through limestone arches damp with ancient mould. As soon as they descended the steep stair, they heard a muffled sound, and saw two hands reach out and haul a face between the bars. 'I'll have you tarred,' the master snarled, before he recognized the man behind the guard.

'Thank God,' he said then, fingers tightening upon the iron grate set in the wooden door. They flew off at the rattle of the key. Gutenberg sprang back, the hinges groaning as the door swung slowly inwards. 'You took your time.'

His eyes blinked rapidly in the new light. His hair stood out in all directions, as if he'd passed the hours in yanking at it. There was a wooden platform and a bucket, nothing else in that dank cell.

'Knock when you're done,' the guard said as he shut the door. The master jerked, and Peter stepped inside. The darkness was a living blanket, muffling all hope.

'Are you all right?' He groped with his right hand along the stony wall. 'Leave light!' he called. A beam arrived, propped in a sconce out in the hall, to cast the bench in a faint glow.

'Calumny,' the master said in a hard, hollow tone. 'Calumny and criminality. I thought that you were here to get me out.' He sank onto the bench and pulled his cloak up to his nose.

'You're fed, you're not too cold?' The raw, cold comfortlessness of it was so shocking that Peter half forgot how they had fallen quite so low.

'Like any animal,' the master hissed, 'in Dietrich's little zoo.'

'I've come to see,' said Peter carefully, 'if there is anything you need.'

'I need to be released. If you're not up to that, then you can go.'

'I'm sure you know some leverage you might use. With the archbishop. Since manifestly, you're so close.' Peter did not try to hide his bitterness.

'The fault is with those jumped-up oafs.' Gutenberg thrust his face towards him. 'Your cocky uncle, and that turncoat.'

'You're blameless then, as always.'

Gutenberg said nothing, only tightened his thin lips.

'You put it all in jeopardy.' If Peter did not speak right then, he never would. 'The whole Book – and for what?'

At this the master's eyes snapped open. His head jerked like a doll's; he reached for Peter's sleeve. 'They didn't get it? Didn't find—'

'Only your press.'

The master sagged, his chin descending to his chest. 'Thanks be to God.'

No thanks to you, though, Peter told himself.

Gutenberg looked up. He tried to catch his foreman's eye. 'He thinks that I colluded with the council. I!' He gave a strangled laugh. 'Heard somehow I was talking to those asses, and decided I was part of the whole plot.'

'You did collude, though.' Peter said it quite deliberately. 'You did collude, against the Book, and us.'

'If you think that, you are a fool.'

'I must be. If you couldn't even find it in yourself to trust me.'

'Trust.' The master turned his face towards the wall. 'What good has trust been, ever?' He shook his head, his long hair clinging to his cheekbones. 'Only fools put trust in promises. I told you that before.'

'Not even your own foreman.' The pain was sharper than he'd thought.

'You are your father's son. Your loyalties are clear.'

Peter did not answer, only sat there listening to the dripping, the master's breath, the distant scrabbling of rats.

'I did what I had to do.' Gutenberg got to his feet. 'You might not like it, but—' He shrugged. 'I've come too far to let them get me now.' He reached and banged twice, hard, upon the wooden door.

The jailer turned the great brass key. Peter slipped out;

once again the fingers wound themselves around the bars. 'Just get it done,' the master hissed, and then the fingers disappeared.

They might have left him there. Peter's father certainly was of a mind to, when he rode back to Mainz. The snakes were in their baskets and defanged, was what he said – not only Rosenberg, but Gutenberg. The thing was in a kind of balance. But what a balance, Peter thought: a mix of elements both volatile and toxic, which the slightest added grain could well combust.

If nothing changed, the city would remain the focus of the archbishop's constant and unblinking eye. Peter did not like to think of what that eye might light upon and see.

He counted out the days that still remained. He counted the remaining pages, for they counted now in pages, not in quires. He watched as Hans and Keffer cast that new small type; when they had finished all their pages for the day, he let them set the pope's accursed letter of indulgence.

Three days had passed. He is your partner, Peter said to Fust; Fust spoke to Jakob; Jakob spoke to Molsberg; nothing moved.

'Where are his cursed books?' his father asked at last, as if examination of the ledger could relieve the impasse. 'He hasn't shown them, damn his soul.'

'Locked in his house, no doubt.'

His father's face was just as shuttered.

'It's not the point, though, is it?' Peter asked.

'Not to you, perhaps.' His father's look was distant.

'Gold. It's all the council cares about, and Gutenberg, and Dietrich.'

'Gutenberg the first.' Fust folded both his arms and stood there in the workshop in the heat of day, and brooded.

Peter sighed and rubbed his eyes. There was a way, he said

– the only way, at least, that he could see. Wearily he laid out the thin solution he had worried from his mind. What if another letter of indulgence could be found, another order, they could print? A second run of this one, or another, for some other diocese? So that the profits from this second letter – which he'd undertake to print himself – could be directly funnelled to the city council? 'If we can guarantee they'll get the bishop's cut, the council might relent, and release Rosenberg,' he said.

'Possibly,' said Fust.

'I can think of no alternative.'

'Then the archbishop gives up Gutenberg.' Fust gave him a queer smile. 'And you have saved us all.'

'The only thing that matters is the Bible.'

'And the psalter.' Fust looked down onto the desk where Gutenberg had left the latest proofs. 'And on and on the two of you will go,' his father said, shaking his head. His eyes were clear, all sentiment effaced. 'How did you plan to do it?'

'Father.'

'I should have known. But now I stand here – cut out, and exposed. Have you no notion of how much I owe?'

'How should I?'

Fust raised one eyebrow, answered mockingly: 'I'm sure that I don't know.'

A moment passed before he spoke again. 'You tell him he'll be freed as soon as I have seen his books.' There was an edge of something – satisfaction, vengeance – in his tone. 'I'll let you do another letter, yes – but only after he produces the damned ledger, as he pledged to months ago.'

'Two weeks,' said Peter, 'three at the most. And then the Bible's done.'

'The Bible, of all books,' his father answered, 'requires the truth.'

'When it is done, and sold—'

Alix Christie

Fust cut him off. 'We'll have to sell it two times over, just to climb out of this hole.'

Heinrich Brack was no longer the prior of St Jakob's monastery. Lubertus Ruthard was the abbot now, the prior Eberhard von Venlo. The former prior had no doubt these younger men, reformers all, would see the cloister through. Brack turned upon his visitor a small, contented smile. His final days now could be passed in prayer and meditation.

Indeed, said Peter, it was for prayer – and guidance – he had come.

They walked across the knoll to a small bench that had been set outside the wall, affording a fine eastward view across the Rhine. On a clear day, Brack said, he sometimes caught a glint of sunlight bouncing off St Bartholomew's spire some thirty miles away in Frankfurt. Quietly he set his body down; no longer did he jingle at each step with all the burdens of his office.

'In three weeks' time, God willing,' Peter said, 'Gutenberg will show our Bible there.'

'So it is done.' Brack traced a cross with his thin hand in the bright air.

Peter smiled. So Brack had known, and kept it to himself. 'Almost,' he said. 'If God is with us.'

'Have you some doubt?' Brack's eyes were flinty in their pouches.

'I never did before.' Peter turned his eyes across the water. 'It seemed so clear to me, the part we played. But now it all is clouded.'

The burden of so many months and years of lies and secrets felt unbearable, up there on that scoured knoll.

'It is a mighty thing for the renewal of our faith,' said Brack. 'That is enough, I think.'

'And yet did Jesus not say no discord should enter in his house?'

'"The life of man upon earth is a warfare."' Wistfully, Brack smiled.

'Father, I would give you my confession.'

The monk laid his right hand on Peter's head. And Peter spoke to him of all that had transpired: of subterfuge and pride and arrogance, and letters of indulgence that brought strife and not salvation. Brack's eyes were closed, his head bent forwards as he listened. In the silence afterwards he nodded, eyes still closed, communing with the Lord.

'My son' – he opened up his eyes – 'your sins are small. Johann Gensfleisch is a man who burns through earth and ore – and on occasion, more.'

There was a way, said Peter, they could end the feud, and save the council's and Archbishop Dietrich's face. He needed one more batch of letters, several thousand, at the very least. It felt to him like begging.

Brack reflected. 'I think that this can be arranged.'

Peter pressed his hand in thanks.

Ruefully, the former prior smiled. 'Thus, even in our own backyard do the eternal questions stand revealed.'

'Why God accepts duplicity, you mean?' Peter shook his head. 'You might as well ask why He allowed the Turk to destroy Constantinople.'

'Even Satan is a part of God's Creation – and thus a part of God.'

Then why did God not simply strike them down? he asked. Just wipe the whole world clean, as He had done before?

Their human view was partial, said the Benedictine. God alone could see the whole.

'He sees and blesses all that's base, as well as noble?' This Peter doubted. As long as he might live, he never would accept the master's treachery as part of the Lord's plan.

'He gives us gifts, out of His grace.' Brack's gaunt old face was luminous, and sage. 'And then He watches us, to see how we will use them.'

'To serve the Lord, you mean, or else our private gain.' Peter did not try to hide his bitterness.

Brack smiled, and placed a hand upon his forearm. 'We do not live upon this earth, my son, quite long enough to judge.'

His vision drifted over Mainz's rooftops and her spires, the remnants of the ancient camp beneath her vineyards and her orchards. 'The Romans, too, were geniuses at engineering. Inventors of such marvellous techniques. Yet they have left us nothing but some stones and rubble.'

Chapter 4

SPONHEIM ABBEY

March 1486

For a long time he thought he could prevent it. Peter would hold the two of them together as they strained apart, through his sheer strength, the force of his own will.

'The thought was unacceptable to me, that the workshop might be torn apart.'

Outside Sponheim Abbey winter has redoubled its assault, as if to punish the temerity of crocuses and hope. A freezing rain beats at the windows in which Peter sees reflected one old man, his hair gone pewter, and the back of one young Benedictine less than half his age. It strikes him that he's nearly the same age the master was, the year he died.

'This . . . altercation,' asks the abbot, 'happened the same year the pope declared Crusade?'

The printer shakes his head. 'The summer after. The princes and the clergy met incessantly for months, but could not come to terms.'

It was that letter of indulgence that destroyed the workshop, he has always felt. 'It might have ended differently, but for the Turk.'

Again the abbot gives a little smile. 'Yet as I've said, the book was done, as well as both of those *confessionalia*.'

'It wasn't the letters per se – but what they represented. Lies. Deceit. That was the fundamental breach.' Methodically, Peter sets out the counts of treason.

'First Gutenberg concealed too much. But more than that – he put the Book at risk. He was prepared, as well, to fleece my father and the guilds. Ends for him always justified the means, however roughshod he might run you over.'

'And you,' the abbot says, 'were caught between the hammer and the anvil.'

Mirthlessly, Peter laughs. 'The insane thing is that I still *hoped*. I had this wild belief that all would come out right, if we could only make it to the fair.' He shakes his head. 'We were so close! I thought if we could just hold on, the revenues would fill the holes – especially that gulf that since the prophecy had grown between them.' He shakes his head again and strokes his throat, a tenderness inside for his young self.

'I put my whole self on the line. I nearly killed myself, to make that second letter, carving every night those final weeks.' So cruelly had he pressed the crew and his own body that he hardly can recall that final burst. They were machines by then, churning blindly, truly.

'You didn't use Hans's type?' asks Trithemius, surprised.

'I didn't want to give him even that small satisfaction.' Peter looks the abbot in the eyes. Deceit will breed deceit; in those last months when he had felt betrayed, he'd kept his secrets, too. 'Besides, I had my reasons. Technical improvements I was working on, that I could use a smaller alphabet to test.'

The abbot waits, but Peter says no more. There is a kind of stiffness to the monk as he sits facing him, the printer thinks. He is polite, but something in his attitude suggests he is more critical inside. So be it: every chronicler must sift the stories he is told.

Trithemius will never see the shining city they had built, like

Augustine's, inside that workshop dug into the earth. He'll never know how it was both monastic cell and nave to that young man and all who laboured there. Peter wipes a hand across his face. He's had his fill of boats and wagons driving up this muddy forest track; he's tired of telling the whole sordid tale. It's painful still – the recognition is unwelcome. He'd thought that he'd forgiven them both long ago. But now he finds they're still inside his mind, both of those fathers, locked so blindly in their battle that they can't perceive the hellfire that they rain on those below.

How zealous – yet how fragile – he had been. He feels a twinge of pity for that stern young man, who offered his own self as the connecting wire – the thin grey bead of solder.

Chapter 5

FRIDAY AFTER THE TRANSLATION OF SAINT BENEDICT

[62 of 65 quires]

12 *July* 1454

Both hostages were freed, after some haggling over the cut that Mainz would get from every letter of indulgence printed for the Cologne diocese. The only one remotely pleased with this was Jakob. Gutenberg returned, his body clean, his bearing truculent; he thrust a packet under Peter's nose. 'Accounts, in black and white,' he said, and turned his back. No word of thanks, not even an acknowledgement; Peter should have known. The man could not be humbled. Just the reverse: his manner was abrupt, offended. How dare they question his veracity, was all his haughty look, his brisk resumption of command, conveyed.

He took a Bible sheet up off the press, found fault with it, asked querulously where the devil his own letter was. 'Set up for press,' came Hans's answer. Peter turned and made his escape. The packet in his hands was thick with wax, stamped front and back with that queer pilgrim's seal. As if he'd even think to spy its contents. The workshop's debts, thank God, were not his cross to bear. He had enough to carry with this second letter and those final quires.

Rapidly he walked down to the Brand and put his head in at the Haus zur Rosau. He heard his stepsister's keening from the moment Lothar opened the front door. The wails were coming from the kitchen door that gave out on the courtyard.

Tina's back was shaking from the sobs that racked her skinny frame. She didn't cease her frenzied wailing even when he sat down on the stoop beside her. 'There, there,' he said, and moved his palm in circles on her back. Grede must have left her there to blow the tempest out; no doubt she'd tried, and failed, to calm her. 'Tina, my big Tina girl,' he whispered. 'What's wrong? Give me your hands.'

She turned tear-thundered eyes on him and hiccupped, sniffed, resumed her keening at a lower and less frantic pitch. He lifted her limp hands and sandwiched them between his. 'Now, chickadee, tell me what's wrong.'

'Cassius,' she gulped, 'and Prinz. Father says—' She drew a ragged breath, and then came sobs.

'Father says what?'

'That they are to be sold. Oh, Peter!' she cried, turning and flinging both arms about his neck. 'Say you can stop him. He is mean and cruel to take my very favourites!'

He clucked and soothed and looked across the courtyard to the stables. 'Papa can't do everything. He must have a good reason.' The meaning of it bowed his shoulders, too.

He would not say to her that they were only horses. Only beasts – albeit Fust's most steady team. Two of the six that pulled his convoys and his wagons, and when home would whicker softly for their apples from the stalls. 'Perhaps we'll find a way to keep them, or to visit them, at least,' he said. She pulled away; she knew it was a lie.

In all these years not once had Fust been forced to sell a

horse. He'd leased them out, from time to time, when things were tight. The letter with the master's ledger dug at Peter's side. How bad was it, if Fust must sell the very assets he depended on to ply his trade? The interest on the loans that ran the workshop totalled one hundred guilders every year, Peter knew – part to the Jew, part to the Lombard.

Gently he disentangled Tina's arms and carried her inside. Grede came as he was laying her, a raglike bundle, on the couch. 'It's better now,' he said, and Grede put a cool hand on the child's brow. 'Sleep,' she whispered. The two of them stood watching for a moment, then went out. Grede draped the cloth she carried on the table. 'Won't you join us, just this once?' She gave him a wan smile. 'It's been so long.'

'It's true, then, that he's selling them?'

'Yes. Although it breaks his heart.'

'Things are that bad.'

She looked exhausted. 'The wagons are too light, the hay too dear.' She must have seen the way it shocked him. 'We'll find a way.' A rueful look came over her. 'It's not like I've not been this low before.' She turned and started laying out the plates. 'Just be a dear and fetch him from the Kaufhaus.'

On the Brand a group of travelling fiddlers had attracted a small crowd. Their music, though, was harsh and discordant to his ears. He slipped with some relief into the silence of the customs hall. Climbing each step, worn into hollows by the tread of countless feet, he was assailed by memories of all the evenings he'd been sent there as a boy. How often had he been dispatched by Fust's first wife, and then his second, on this very errand? How proudly he had come into the Kaufhaus those first months in Mainz: swelled up with pride, circumnavigating those great heaping piles, before ascending to the office and his task.

Fust was just locking up when he arrived. 'So you are back to playing herald.'

'Grede sent me, sir.' Peter smiled slightly, bowed.

His father looked at him for a long moment, as if he too measured the years behind.

'Before you go, you'll want to lock up this.' Peter pulled the letter from his waist and gave it over. Fust hefted it with his right hand. Without a word he turned the key again, and Peter followed him back in. When Fust had stowed it in his strongbox and locked up the cupboard with a second key, he turned to find his son entirely still and staring fixedly at him.

'What else?' Impatience edged his down-turned mouth.

Better now than later, Peter thought, when Fust had read the contents of that letter – though this was far from how he'd hoped this scene would go.

'I'd like to ask again for your permission, sir.' He held his cap before him, twisted in his hands. 'I still would marry Anna, with your blessing. If you can find it to accept this as my choice.'

'If I can find it,' Fust said quietly. He looked at Peter's cap, then back up at his face. 'My say-so hasn't counted much, these past few years.'

'I did your bidding.' He'd never satisfy him, ever. 'I stayed, as you requested, learned this trade. I think I've done my duty by your wishes.'

Fust took a long breath, and then he slowly let it out. They stood a pace apart, but in between them Peter sensed a packed and hard-edged distance, dense with disappointments.

'You left me long ago,' his foster father murmured. 'Your choices, as you call them, have been yours a good long while – more his, I think, than mine.'

'This isn't anything to do with him – but me, my life.'

Fust gave the lightest shrug. 'I have no power over you. You're nearly thirty, well past any hope of listening to guidance.'

'I've listened to you more than half my life.' Peter's chest was filling now, the heaviness between them seeping ineluctably inside. 'I listen to you still, and ask you to consider my own happiness.'

The large head dipped, and Peter saw the losses layered in those once-bright eyes. 'I wish you well – you know I've always only wished for you the best,' his father said.

'Then wish me this,' he softly answered. 'We've almost done what we set out to do – together. Let's finish it that way. Let me remain – not lost to you, but near, giving you books, and grandchildren to honour you, as long as I am able.'

Fust closed his eyes and sought; he prayed. His forehead creased as he stood waiting to receive, head bowed above the linen altar of the chest on which reposed his crucifix.

'Go then with God.' He opened up his eyes. 'May you and yours remain forever in His hands.' He held one hand out towards his son, a look unreadable upon his face – bittersweet in parting, yet softened by the bond that always would exist between them.

His hand hung half a heartbeat in the air until Peter clasped it.

'I always hoped and prayed to make you proud,' he said. 'And that will never change.'

A flicker lifted Fust's grey lips, and with a nod he shifted towards him and the two of them embraced.

What was this feeling that shot through him, prying open every vessel underneath his skin? That prickled at the lining of his chest, lifted the blood into his cheeks, the hairs upon his arms, as he stood with one hand lifted at that bright blue door? The gold of summer lighted the blue glaze, the same blue tint that once had stained her fingertips. He'd half forgotten he could feel this, had consigned it to a frozen depth. But now he knew, his fingers reaching for the knocker: this was joy.

Klaus Pinzler's shock was clear upon his narrow, bearded

face. His mouth worked for an instant as he looked upon the long-lost suitor on his doorstep. His eyes went to the bunch of daisies Peter had gone culling from the fields.

'I'm much delayed,' said Peter slowly, letting time expand, so that in this one drawn-out instant the whole year past might dissolve. 'I've been a fool,' he told the man. 'But I would hope to learn more patience in this house.'

Klaus wonderingly shook his head. Across his cheeks, a fleeting twitch. 'You are a lucky man.' His lips made a straight line. 'Luckier by far than I might have allowed.'

Anna, then, had spoken of him somehow. Her father stepped back and opened wide their house.

Peter should have made his declaration then – as Anna's mother came to join Klaus, drying off her hands and searching Peter's face, his Sunday clothes, with anxious eyes. But this to him would have been one more wrong he did their daughter. These were new times, he a new man. He could not ask her father until he showed her the respect that she was due: to choose herself, and to give freely her own hand.

'With your permission, I would speak to Anna,' Peter said. Klaus looked at his wife. Alone, he'd have refused, but Anna's mother nodded.

Above them, stepping lightly down her ladder, floating almost, Anna came: not retiring, but aglow, her dark hair flowing. Her parents disappeared behind the curtain to the kitchen. Peter held his arms out as she put her foot on the last step but two, and she released the rail and soared towards him. He smelled vanilla in her hair and musk; his lips brushed the soft down upon her cheek. Blood hammering, he set her down, hands lingering about her ribs, the dainty cage that held her heart. Her skirts were full as he went down upon his knees.

'Peter,' she said, reaching out her hand, but he would not be raised. He took it, pressed it to his lips. He looked up in those large and shining eyes and could not speak at first for the emotion.

'Get up,' she whispered, smiling, bending, dropping a light kiss on his head. The brush of her against him, breathing, the slight pressure of her breasts, fired him with desire. Firmly then he grasped her by the waist and held her out, away.

'If you will have me,' he said huskily, 'I would make you my beloved wife.'

She opened her red lips; her cheeks flared up. 'Yes,' she said. 'Oh, yes.' She smiled; her body shuddered, and the tears sprang in her eyes. She freed her hand to dash them, and then, turning, looked towards the alcove where her parents waited. 'Papa said yes?' she asked in a low whisper.

Peter stood and reclaimed both her hands. 'You had the right of first refusal.'

A look of sheer delight infused her face. She bit her lip, a girl again; a little laugh escaped. 'You never follow any rules.' She was still smiling, dark eyes bright.

'Just rules you give, from this day on.' He pressed her hands back to his lips. She beamed at him, and then, all seriousness again, she smoothed her skirts. 'I'll wait upstairs, then.'

He watched her float back up. Then he turned back to the old ways, formality and gravity, the manner in which such things were done. He sought and gained permission, posted banns. The fathers settled terms, modest though they were. Fourteen days later they all met again beneath the painter's roof to seal it with the handshake. The harvest was upon them; they'd have to wait at least until the grain was in. But in the eyes of Mainz their fates were joined, and so at last could be their bodies, after all this time.

It happened in a hayfield one late summer evening, when the sky was a deep teal, pricked by some early stars. The handles

of the pitchforks jutted from the stacks in a loose ring that Anna
fancied wove a charm around them. Her dress was sprigged
with flowers, but the flowers he most wanted were these two,
he said, and peeled the fabric from her shoulders. She lay against
the mound, and arched her back, eyes closed, as he caressed
her breasts with lips and hands. Her legs and skirts were wound
and crossed around his hips, and he could feel her strength,
her force, her youth and hunger, in the flexing as they kissed.
Gently Peter slipped his hand beneath her head and raised it,
looking for a moment into those clear dark eyes. 'I would not
hurt you for the world.' She laughed and pulled his face to
hers. 'No one can hurt us now,' she whispered, and he felt
himself expand and open, with a rush of blood, the power
flooding through his body and then hers. She cried out as he
entered her, but just as quickly threw her head back, opened
to him. Squeezed and rolled with him in pure abandon, like
the creatures that they were, alive, aroused, withholding nothing
underneath the open sky. They fit together like two interlocking
pieces, red and blue, then gilded, flecked about with stars: the
sense of freedom and surrender, when it came, was nothing he
had ever felt before. No one could touch them now; he fondled
her; he grazed his lips upon her throat, her belly. Anna darted
her light tongue across his cheeks, his closed and dreaming
eyes. She'd always be there, at his side. Her skin beneath her
clothes was just as white as the thin vellum she had finally
accepted as that other love of his – those metal letters with
which henceforth she would share his life.

Chapter 6

~~~

THURSDAY AFTER SAINT BERNARD
OF CLAIRVAUX

[65 of 65 quires]

22 August 1454

The final sprint was blind, their bodies pumping with rote motion. The last page to come off the press was from Ezekiel, the prophet. Gutenberg was there as the sun set, to watch all hundred and eighty copies of that page emerge that final night. All that was left now was the gathering of pages into books and printing off the guide to rubrication.

Already Peter sensed it all unwinding: Keffer and Ruppel printed the master's letter of indulgence; the Bechtermünzes and the extra boys had been let go, at least for several weeks. Peter and Mentelin prepared the guide that would be used to letter in the red *incipits* and *explicits*, lines of prologue, with instructions for their proper placement in the printed text. The psalter waited patiently: all efforts were directed towards the Bible, and Autumn Fair.

The night advanced, and then the run was halfway done. The master stood by Neumeister, joking with the men as each page was peeled off. Peter stood up suddenly. 'He never thinks of anybody but himself,' he said to Mentelin, who only nodded, eyes fixed on his lines.

'My father should be here,' he said to Gutenberg. Amazing, that a man could live for sixty years and still remain so ignorant. The master was all smiles; his breath was ripe. 'Indeed,' he said. 'A step or two ahead as always, Peter. I am in your debt.'

'I'll hold you to it,' he responded wryly. A boy flew through the darkness to fetch Fust, and then Lorenz arrived with Keffer, pushing one of Gutenberg's more precious private barrels. The wine was poured and shared around to all except the printers at the press. Fust came, rubbing the sleep out of his eyes, and when the last page settled on its pins, the master stopped the pressman with a hand. With a tilt of his grey head, he gestured towards his partner. Fust and Gutenberg put all four hands upon the bar.

'Heave-ho,' the master cried, and they both strained and with great effort dropped the platen.

'I never thought I'd see the day,' Fust murmured as the master peeled the page off, clearly stirred.

'Oh ye of little faith.' Gutenberg laughed.

He spun and took up glasses, handing them around. 'Well, men,' he said, and raised his high. 'We made it, thanks to you – and the protection of the Lord.' His eyes were burning just as bright as Peter'd ever seen them. He clanked his cup against each man's in turn and stood for a long moment before Fust. 'Let the Bohemians and Dutchmen eat our dust.'

'Amen,' Fust said. He was moved, and yet contained, it seemed to Peter.

The master turned to Peter. 'There's nothing like it on this earth.'

It was Mentelin who said they ought to raise a glass to Saint Bernard of Clairvaux, whose feast day had just passed. It was the order of Cistercians, after all, who had first harnessed God's Creation for man's use.

They raised their cups, and Peter wondered if he'd ever climb that mountain track to their great cloister above Eltville that the master had described some years before. The men were jabbering, the winecock flipping back and forth, and in that exultant clamour a strange and lonely feeling stole into his heart. He saw himself a solitary pilgrim, toiling all alone up the steep slope. To Gutenberg, they'd reached the summit: the dizzy height, the shocking newness of this Bible he had birthed. It was all his, the toil, the brilliance, and the long, exhausting haul. And everything that followed now for him would be a spreading, and a forking, from this monumental start.

Peter watched his flying hair, his twisted beard, the sparking in his gold-flecked eyes, and knew it was a moment Gutenberg could savour, and he should – though Peter felt a caving-in, surrounded by his fellows.

So much had come between the middle and the end. So little thought was spared for what might come thereafter. He watched his father nod farewell, slip out the door. His thoughts turned then to Anna, and to the psalter he had come to think of as his own, waiting patiently to be composed.

Hans was leaning on the wall with one knee up, foot braced behind him. He'd told them all that when the book was done, he'd pack his things and head back home to Strassburg. Though things were changed between them, Peter could not picture it – the workshop without Hans's gnomish, precise presence. He was a loyal servant, and old-fashioned, he supposed.

The smith looked straight across the room at him and raised his cup. Peter touched a finger to his cap in answer. Hans straightened, bellowed 'Oy!' The tumult stopped. He barked out, half embarrassed, 'A toast then too, to Peter. Fancy hands kept us on track.' The master added his hoarse voice to their loud cheers. 'I give you Peter Schoeffer, men – the greatest

printer who yet lives, save one!' There was a flash of warmth
between the master and his long-ago apprentice, just before the
roaring laughter.

Gutenberg had told him, not a week before, that he should
never spurn that bread-and-butter work, that there were many
ways to beat their ploughshares into swords. He revelled in the
war against the Turk, the master said: it was a matching of the
wits, the wages of the devil beaten back by their own tempered,
brilliant sword.

The master told them all that night that they'd have work
in Mainz so long as he had breath. No danger, Ruppel cracked,
of running out of that. Gutenberg just laughed. Not just such
mighty works, he went on, but books small and large, in Latin
and the common tongues, for princes and for paupers and the
church. 'That is' – he grinned – 'so long as they keep off my
back.' They had to hand him that: for all of Dietrich's power,
he had never learned about their secret scriptures.

The wine was put away; the folded sheets were hung to dry.
As they closed up, the master put one hand on Peter's back and
said, 'You choose your quires.'

It touched him, that he understood that need in him: to have
the darkest, crispest ink, the cleanest bite, to gather for his copy
the most perfect sheets that he could find.

'What about you?' the foreman asked. 'I can easily assemble
two.'

'Wait a while.' Detached, almost amused, the master lifted
one scraggly eyebrow. 'You never know what ballast you might
have to drop.'

Anna oversaw the painting of the quires by that odd Austrian
inside her father's workshop. As the painter finished every sheet
that Fust had set aside, she hung it carefully to dry, then marked
it and refolded it. In this way, she said, she moved now through

the scriptures as she pictured Peter doing all those months: verse by verse, chapter by chapter, book by book.

'I am amazed, I find,' she told him. Perhaps it was that fine illumination, married to his text, which helped her to accept it. His type was artificial, yes: but even so the words it made were still the same. Vain, to stand against it: printing would roll out and inundate the world regardless. 'But maybe there can still be care in it.' She looked intently at him. She prayed each day that they might keep some contact with the old and treasured ways.

They moved the rest of the copies Fust required up to the Kaufhaus on the day before the convoy left for Frankfurt. Two dozen had been earmarked for his buyers, who had taken the whole book illuminated, rubricated, and then bound.

Fust and Gutenberg were bent above the benches in the pressroom, mumbling like witches: this score, then fourscore more, also spoken for by long-since-spent deposits. In all, eighty copies still remained to offer at the fair. Each double set of books weighed nearly a stone: what beasts indeed, thought Peter, looking at each massive pile. Twelve hundred and eighty-six imprinted pages: from the doorway of the shop they looked like giant loaves.

A dozen paper copies went in Fust's cart, and then another eight of vellum. Hard as he tried, Peter couldn't read his father's mood. He had not shared his thoughts since he'd received the full accounting. Yet all would work out right; Peter felt it in his bones. They'd sell them all and right the ship somehow. The joy of finishing, and love, did buoy him. All was in place to carry on: Mentelin would stay in Mainz, to finish off the psalter type, while Peter went to Frankfurt with the partners.

The copies Peter had selected for his father were exceeding fine. Fust did not take the time to notice. He simply nodded when the cart was loaded, and asked if Peter could help put them into storage. He had arranged to have the barrels carted to the Kaufhaus treasure room on the first landing. Both keys were needed to unlock that space, one held by Kraemer of the grocers' guild, the other key by Jakob.

'A tidy fortune,' said his uncle as they tripped the tumblers in the proper order. Tightly Johann Fust said, 'Yes.'

Twelve paper, each at thirty guilders; eight vellum, each at ninety: eleven hundred guilders, in their raw, unpainted state: another hundred when they added in the painting and the binding.

'You ought to keep the lot,' his brother said, 'for all the likelihood you'll see a penny more.'

'Tsss,' hissed Fust. He glanced at Peter as if he didn't want his son to hear.

It pierced him to the quick. He felt a sickening, familiar pang – one he'd not felt for many years. Not since he'd first arrived in Mainz and entered Jakob's shop – an interloper, fatherless, untrusted. How dare they? Peter thought, his face tight. How dare Fust think that he could not be trusted? He ought to take his love and ride to Frankfurt – then keep riding, throw off this suffocating loyalty, once and for all.

Kraemer had slipped away; the brothers Fust stood stroking their two chins, one whiskered and one bare.

'We leave at first light,' his uncle said to Peter.

Peter looked at Fust. 'It sounds as if I'd be more welcome on the boat.'

Gutenberg had argued that the convoy, even with its large armed guard, was too unsafe. He planned to take the books upriver on the ship himself.

'Don't be absurd.' Fust made a sour face. 'I never said it was your fault.'

'It?'

'This mess,' said Jakob.

'Come,' his father said. 'Sit with us for a minute.'

They climbed up, then sat facing one another in the office until Fust leaned forwards. 'I need to know,' he said, 'which stand you'll man.'

'What are you driving at?'

'We need a close eye kept on the deposits.'

'You think he'd steal from you.' Disgusted, Peter shook his head.

Fust smoothed what wisps remained of his white hair. 'It isn't that I *think* it. I am certain.'

He opened his top drawer, pulled out a paper and unfolded it. Expression grave, eyes clamped on Peter's face, he pushed it over.

'Even if we sell the whole run out, there's hardly any profit after costs. Assuming that these costs are true, which doubtless they are not. It's plain to me he plans to pass these costs to me – then cut me out.'

Peter studied the two columns written in the master's hand. The income Gutenberg had listed at 7,000 guilders, of which 500 had come in – and been spent already – as deposits. The costs he'd listed at 5,000 guilders – which left net proceeds of some 1,500.

'We always knew the costs were huge,' he said.

'Can you not see it?' Fust retrieved the sheet. 'Even if we clear that measly profit, I get only half. I owe sixteen hundred on the loans alone, and even more in interest. He's pumped me, can't you see it?' He slumped, face bitter, staring at it. 'I bear the costs of his mismanagement, and all the risk. If I am even able to break even, it will be a bloody miracle.' His cheeks flamed as he cursed.

'I always said there was no margin.' Jakob was hunched over, frowning. 'If I were you, I'd pull the plug.'

It was a boot, a punch, in Peter's gut. 'You pull the plug, you throw away the psalter.'

His father stared at him, his lips compressed.

'It's true.' Peter stared at him. 'You have no faith. No patience, and no faith.' There was a rushing in his head, a roaring. 'The ink is barely dry – we haven't even sold the rest. It all can even out – if you but wait. You haven't even counted revenue from our own letter, or the psalter.'

'You heard him,' Fust said darkly, 'as did I. When he said not to worry, months ago: that I would get my money back.' His ears, his neck, were flushed. 'That's not the deal I signed, you damn well know it. I think he plans to pay me from this pittance, then use his share to pay the first loan back and cut me loose, and keep the workshop.'

'He'd have to cut me loose then, too.'

They looked at one another for a long, long moment.

'I wonder, though,' said Fust, eyes clouding, 'if that's entirely true.'

Peter stood. 'You either trust me, or you don't.'

'Believe me, I would like to.'

'What makes you think that I'd betray you?'

His father sighed. 'You cannot see the truth; he's got you blinded.'

'It's you who cannot see,' his son answered, reaching for the doorknob.

Fust harshly laughed. 'He doesn't give a damn about the book, you know. You just can't see the way he uses you.'

Peter turned the knob.

'Why do you think he made you foreman, anyway?' His father's words came lobbing as he turned. 'Not out of any great regard, of that I can assure you. He simply wanted to get hold of you – and then be shot of me.'

REVELATION

Chapter 1

TUESDAY BEFORE SAINT AUGUSTINE

27 August 1454

The journey started at the water's edge. Across the river Peter caught bright glints of buckles and clasps, a lifting veil of dust above the waiting convoy. The wares and horses had been shipped across the Rhine to Kastel in the days before. He stepped aboard the ferry taking Mainz's craftsmen to the farther shore. Fust and his brother were long since across, canvassing the train of wagons.

The guards that Frankfurt paid to see the foreign merchants safely in were local men: brown and muscled fellows scraped up from the Rhineland fields. Soon they would all be soldiers heading for the Bosphorus. But now, eyes flatly scanning the surrounding hills, they stood and waited, fingering their weapons. The convoy shifted, muzzles lifting above axles, creaking as the horses stamped in their impatience to be going. The only colour beyond brown of tarps and wagons was bright red. The flags of Frankfurt were tacked here and there to warn the highwaymen away: imperial, the city of the kings, a crown atop a white and outspread eagle. All across the Hessian plain, scores of caravans like this were even now converging on the fair of fairs, the greatest market in the world.

Peter swung up on a small hired mare. The brothers Fust themselves were high atop the leading wagon. Each carried tokens from their women and specific orders to fulfil. The shout went up just after seven; the whole line lurched and started moving. Gutenberg had gone ahead by water with the Bibles snug in barrels, lashed to others filled with Rhine wines and Mosels. In better years Johann Fust would have floated too, but river fares and tolls were doubled in the weeks before and after the Frankfurt fair – just one more small indignity that rubbed the well-worn place of his resentment.

The sounds of jangling and pounding hooves as they moved out eclipsed that nattering inside. Peter felt the power of the compact beast beneath him and breathed the summer smells of baking dirt and sweat. Alone with the blue sky above, the muddy Main a guideline to their right, he gave himself up to the open countryside. The fields to either side were dun or amber or entirely golden; smallholdings stitched their dark green edges to the horizon. He saw the highway winding like a string ahead, up hill, down dale, vanishing at length into the haze. He turned once in the saddle, looking back. The convoy inched like a great serpent as it wound and writhed. It still seemed a miracle to him that they had done it – that they had finished it. The Book of Books was made. The rest was beyond him now, beyond them all, and in God's hands. He felt his nervousness and fear subside. A feeling of tremendous peace descended. So much now lay ahead: a new day filled with triumph and his own new life, a great new book, with Anna at his side.

All through the blazing day they rode, stopping just to water horses and pay tolls. At Sindlingen the brother of the Count of Nassau took his cut; at Hoechst the minions of Archbishop Dietrich did the same. Passing the courts of law for the archbishopric, Peter felt a sudden spurt of joy. How lucky he had been to have escaped the life of an ecclesiastic scribe! What freedom he now had! He tasted it entirely, the sheer unfettered sweetness of the road.

A cheer went up among them when at last the spire of St Bartholomew's scratched its point onto the darkening horizon. The convoy had to stop and wait its turn to squeeze beneath a mighty gate whose torches glittered in the water of the moat below. Once through, the horses pranced and rolled their eyes at a great mass of penned and milling beasts off to the left, and then they were in the whirling din of Frankfurt. Strains of music could be heard, the hum of many thousand men and horses; every light in the city had been lit and threw its honeyed halo towards the green and purple sky. They passed through narrow streets lined by the steep stepped gables of the finer homes, and one by one the wagons split off to the quarters that the guilds had hired. The house the Fusts and the Mainz goldsmiths took for every fair stood just behind the Römerberg, the city's central square. Where Gutenberg was lodging no one knew.

The Frankfurters flung the whole city open twice a year: there were four hundred houses more or less within the inner wall, each packed to the rafters with guests and goods and traders from the farthest corners of the continent. Doubtless the master stayed among his peers, some Frankfurt Elders, Peter thought as they rode past the mouth of the great square. It hadn't even started, but already Autumn Fair seemed louder and much larger than the times he'd been there as a boy. He felt excitement seize him as they skirted that great plaza: ablaze with light and sweet with roasting smells, the fulcrum of it all, where kings were made and traders prayed for their salvation twice a year.

Gutenberg had set their stall along the Mainzgasse, the lane assigned to dealers in fine manuscripts. He'd put them in among their competition like sheep among the wolves, thought Peter the next morning when Lorenz led him there. The master had secured a good spot in the arches of a house that faced the street. Thus did Frankfurt's burghers turn their homes to storefronts: every ground floor now stood open to the passing throngs. The finest wares held pride of place up on the Römerberg: precious metals and armour and jewels and furs. The vast array of other goods fanned out to either side along the streets and alleys, spreading all the way down to the riverfront. Here, just before the wall that girded Frankfurt-on-the-Main, the buyers couldn't help but pass among the booksellers who offered codices and single leaves and scrolls. Among the scribes and monks were stalls that sold materials to the trade, hides and quills and pigments, oils and papers.

The morning air thrummed densely all around him: the groan of hinges, thunderclap of shutters, thud of mallets prying covers off casks. Peter spread their crimson cloth and reached into the barrel Lorenz rolled towards him. Just one full Bible would be shown, split in two volumes, freshly bound; beside this they would spread a few loose quires. Genesis, and Psalms, the Gospel according to John: which books could better sway a devout heart – and purse? Fust had required them to lock up the copies they had brought for sale at Jakob's stall beneath the Haus zum Römer. No thief could get within an arm's length of the gold- and silversmiths, thanks to the sheriffs that the Frankfurt council posted. The master had delivered a first batch of his new printed letters of indulgence for sale as well. They'd floated at his feet and doubtless raised his spirits the whole way from Mainz to Frankfurt.

The man himself came loping as the bell struck half past six, unexpectedly resplendent in the lane. 'No one has seen?' His eyes raked nearby vendors setting up their tables, and the rest behind them in the gloom. They hadn't had the leisure, Peter said.

'Excellent.' The master flashed his wolfish grin. 'Though you yourself look much the worse for wear.' He swiped off his cap and squeezed behind the stand. Peter took the velvet lump he thrust at him. Gutenberg wore the same – his only – suit, of dove grey with magenta slits.

'And you, I see' – Peter smiled – 'combed your hair.'

The master winked and smoothed the grizzled shock. 'My finest hour.' Suddenly it grew much brighter as the drays that blocked the light were banished from the lane. 'By God, we're here!' said Gutenberg, a sudden smile cracking his face before he shrugged off the cloak and rolled up his sleeves.

'You have no fear,' said Peter softly in his ear, 'of the archbishop?' His stomach once again was tight with nerves. Gutenberg bent and jogged the quires. 'I've paid my wages.' He threw a shrewd glance Peter's way. 'But all the same it pays to take precautions. I sent some pages to your cardinal' – he winked – 'through our old friend the prior.'

Peter looked at those squared shoulders and raised head – so regal and so proud. 'You what?' he whispered.

'Brack's cousin is Cusanus's man.' The master spoke so softly Peter had to crane to hear. Gutenberg rocked back and scoured the stand with his uncompromising eye. He turned those eyes on Peter, gold-flecked and shining. 'The local priests report to Dietrich, but' – his canines gleamed – 'a cardinal or two trump an archbishop.'

Peter sat back on the small, upended barrel. Incredible, the man was just incredible, he thought. He watched him wait; perhaps he prayed. The master's free hand crept up, plucking as it always did at lips and beard. He looked here at the end as if he too had stepped out of the Pentateuch, his foreman thought: erect and dignified, though battered by his trials. His eyebrows bristled like cockscombs and his cheeks were tanned and taut as vellum. The hair that had been dark when they first met had gone a shade of granite.

Johann Gutenberg stood half in shadow, his chest thrust out, and waited for the world to take some notice. The lane was filling now with friars seeking parchment, painters seeking oils and colours, scribes for pens and reeds, and then their targets: richer merchants down to eye the finished books from Basel or Louvain.

'Twelve hundred pages,' he sang out, 'on Turin rag, or finest vellum. The Book of Books, as fine as you will see, and for a fraction of the cost to have it copied.' He rubbed his hands with huge enjoyment as first one, then two, then half a dozen gathered and began to crane.

The looks were always just the same: perplexity, a frown, hands lifting up the hide, the paper sheet, palpation with a fingertip. The questions – startled – as they set it down. 'What manner of writing, then, is this?'

'Which instrument has punched this hide?'

'Who wrote these lines?'

The wonder turned to doubt, suspicion in their eyes. Yet Gutenberg appeared to never weary of responding. 'It is a new technique,' he'd say, 'of making letters.' *Imprimere*, or *impressum*, he began to add, when news of it appeared to spread. By ten o'clock there was a steady stream not just of traders but of clergy from across the empire, habits of all shades and kinds, and then the gawkers and the children and the fools, converging like a tide.

Their fellow dealers hardly noticed them at first, except to whisper and exchange brief looks. The sight of Gutenberg all decked for court and braying seemed to cause them more amusement than alarm. They had their hands full in the first few hours, when sharper buyers tended to swoop in. Lauber's Alsace workshop did brisk business in their knightly tales; another corner was reserved for routine clerking work, with a long, stolid queue. Peter didn't see the Brothers of the Common

Life, until one member of that scribal confraternity came to see what all the fuss was for. Peter watched him trace a finger over the tiny gullies only scribes would ever think to feel; he saw his eyes involuntarily go wide, then narrow; he knew exactly what the man must feel.

'The page is laid according to the golden section.' The words that Peter said were meant to reassure. The black quill in the man's cap dipped abruptly. 'The edge is like a razor,' he said, the feather wagging like a finger as he frowned and shook his head.

All morning Gutenberg had simply batted off their queries, saying, 'It's a gift from God, just like this earth – and who among you dares to ask Him how He made it?' The secret of the new technique was bound by oath, as ever – if anything, it should be held more secret now. Peter answered the man evasively: 'The lines line up remarkably, indeed.'

The scribe peered at him, troubled, and Peter saw a mirror of his own soul. How close he might have come himself to joining that great scribal brotherhood. He thought of Paris and the abbey, and the sacred calling to which he too once felt summoned. But for his father, and for Gutenberg, he would be standing now where this man stood.

A Spanish priest slipped in beside the monk and started fingering the quires. Once, then twice, he asked in his accented Latin what this miracle might be. Gutenberg smiled, saying, 'You use the word, not me!' He asked where the priest was from. Granada, said the priest, though now he served his cardinal in Rome. Gutenberg was merry as he glanced at Peter. 'By all means tell him of this miracle you've seen,' he said and briefly bowed. Before he could say more, a local priest had shouldered in, repugnance staining his broad cheeks.

'Miracle,' he sneered. 'Blasphemy, I think you mean.'

'There is no blasphemy in faithful copies of God's Word.'
Dismissively, the master turned.

'By devil's means? For only devilry could make this thing.'
The priest leaned, a black streak against the table.

A muttering began among the folk who pressed in from the
back, confusion moving from one face into the next; on others
Peter saw a growing fear.

'There is no feeling in it,' said the Brother of the Quill. 'No
spirit.'

'A godless simulacrum.' The priest's pale face was streaked
with red; his hands were lifted as if warding off some evil
seeping from the quires. 'Who granted you this dispensation?'

The master drew to his full height. 'Who granted it, you
ask?' His eyes swept through the crowd. 'The very Highest!'
His voice was booming as his arms rose up and grasped the air
and shook it as he doubtless wished to shake that priest's thick
neck. 'It has been granted by a God you cannot understand or
see, if you doubt this. Just look, if anyone among you has got
eyes – it is a miracle, a gift divine!' He dropped his hoary head
down within inches of the priest. 'Just look, instead of clutching
at your rosary!'

Peter stepped in before the master could make things worse.
'Each copy is the same – and freer than the scribe's from error.'
He put a little pressure in the hand he laid on Gutenberg's left
arm. 'The pope has called for this repeatedly, as you well know.'
He caught the Spaniard's eye. 'The meaning cannot slip from
text to text – and praise the Lord, the Word can spread the faster
in this way.' The Spanish priest looked back down at their Bible,
open-lipped; his soul quite palpably was stirred.

Gutenberg leaned his whole weight upon his hands. Steady,
Peter prayed: defend – do not offend. 'Blasphemy.' He let the
word out like a bitter trickle from his lips. 'The only blasphemy
consists in spurning what God in His wisdom has decreed.' He

reached and hefted up one volume of that massive and amazing book. 'See here! What God has given us, to share His Word across the world! A new technique, a miracle, that we in Mainz have birthed!'

He glanced at Peter. Then he winked. Peter had to turn away to hide his smile.

Gutenberg set down the Bible, flapped his arms to thin the crowd. 'Time's a-wasting,' he sang out. 'If you're not buying, get a move on. I have books to sell!' He flipped one volume open to Proverbs. 'Step up! Step up!' he cried, 'and touch the miracle from Mainz!'

A trader out of Kraków took him up at once. A paper copy, sir, to pledge to the Franciscans for his dear departed wife's eternal soul. And then another, from the Alpen lands. The master grinned and rubbed his hands. Peter took deposits, noting down each name and terms. 'You should have seen the man,' he would tell Anna later. Gutenberg had never been a trader, yet the whirl of all that selling did intoxicate him, plainly. His hair was wild again, rayed out in all directions. He took the sheets and rubbed them on the grey weave of his tunic, proving that the ink remained in place. He grinned and hooted, purred, cajoled. From time to time he turned and mopped his brow and squeezed Peter's arm. 'Blind me!' he said when they had sold off twenty in three hours. Elated, he embraced his foreman on both cheeks and then turned back, shouting hoarsely to the waiting crowd. He was a trickster and a showman, a performer, Peter thought: his gift lay just as much in coaxing coins from purses as in dreaming up his new machines. You never got the one without the other, he had always said.

At noontime Peter ventured from the bookstalls to see how Johann Fust was getting on. He let the human river carry him uphill, past the stink of fish and oil and resin into the bitter tang of hides and doggy mustiness of unspun wool. He rounded weighing scales just shy of the cathedral: bright slabs of brass slumped to the ground, chains lax; beside them lay great piles of hemp and flax. On the stairs of St Bartholomew's a priest stood sweating, swinging a small metal box. His other hand held Gutenberg's indulgences. 'Forgiveness from the pope, and blessings for the afterlife,' Peter heard him nasally intone. He laughed a little to himself and shook his head. They'd made it, despite everything, he thought.

He wedged his way into the dense throng on the square that moved in all directions like a shoal of salmon flinging their fat bodies upstream. Not since Paris had he seen such masses of humanity. Here were outlandish hats on traders out of Lodz and Prague, there the northern accents of the Hanseatic merchants, bartering their herring and their furs. The gentry in their velvets and their jewels moved in clots protected by their valets, colour high, eyes bright, fingering the leather harnesses and silks. The abbots and the masters of the sacred and the secular estates all bought their woollens and their metals and their raw materials here, and could be seen in their dark robes conferring. Peter passed a stand of arctic fox and sables and thought instantly of Anna. What choice! What vast arrays of sumptuous goods he might in these two weeks be tempted into buying! Emporium of wonders, fair of fairs, the greatest show and circus in the world! Entertainers drew their knots of gawkers, spitting fire and eating swords, and he had even heard that there were beasts from Asia held in cages by St Catherine's door.

Beneath the Römer's arches he found Jakob and his foreman in a vaulted space so glittering it hurt his eyes. All of Bohemia, it seemed, had set up shop with their glass beads; the colours bounced, refracting blindingly off gold and silver from the smiths of Mainz and elsewhere in the empire.

'How goes it?' he asked. Jakob only grunted. 'Too soon to say.' His uncle put his mouth to Peter's ear. 'Though I hear you have made a splash.'

Peter smiled. 'It's going well.'

'You'd better pray.'

Peter rolled his eyes and pulled his tunic open to reveal the coins wrapped tight against his waist. Though most goods sold on credit, they'd asked five guilders on deposit for each book. His uncle opened up the safe.

'What plans tonight?' asked Peter when the gold was stowed. He had a mind to see the whole of it, from gaming house to drinking ship, and not with Gutenberg or Fust.

'I dine with Frankfurt's council.' Jakob made a face. 'Though I've the clear impression I'm the meal.' He'd carried some five hundred guilders in a strongbox to fork over to the Frankfurt Elders who held Mainz's debt. His own guild hands were just as empty as the city treasury, meanwhile, owing to a shortage of raw ores. He gave his nephew his old hawklike stare. 'Go cheer Johann,' he said. 'You and Gensfleisch aren't the only ones with fortunes riding on this fair.'

Peter struck east across the square towards the house whose ground floor held the marketplace for cloth. From the Haus zum Lauberberg his father always said that he could look across to the pink gables of the Haus zum Römer and reflect that God indeed was most mysterious. If He were just, that house would still belong to Fusts, and not the Frankfurt council. He'd have been born there, if sixty years before his father's father had not sold it and moved down to Mainz. How low we've sunk, he'd joke, though he was halfway serious – and never more so than this year, at this uncertain Autumn Fair.

Just past the fountain Peter spied the Kraków furrier's back, and ran to catch him. Perhaps he'd like not just a book, he asked, but one decorated with fine painting and then bound?

The trader looked him up and down. 'Depends upon the price.'
He'd need to speak to Johann Fust, said Peter; he was heading
to the man just now. The trader's face relaxed. 'Ah, Fust,' he
said. 'That's fine, I know the man.'

His father was in conversation with a merchant out of Genoa
when they appeared. His face was grave, but cleared the instant
that he saw them.

'Waclaw!' he exclaimed and stood and heartily embraced the
Kraków trader. 'I think I owe you several belts of brandy.'

The Pole grinned broadly. 'Early as it is, I'll not say no. You're
looking trim,' the trader went on as the schnapps was poured.

'The sultan's work,' his father growled. 'The thieving Turks.'
They sat and drank and spoke of trade, and Peter listened. No
cloth or spice or pigments had come across the Middle Sea this
year for Fust to buy and trade against the cloth from England
and Brabant. He had been forced to sell off inventory, meagre
though it was.

His bolts of cloth indeed were few, as was his offering of
stones: some amber and some lapis out of Cornwall. Nor, Peter
realized, had he yet smelled that choking fug of spice – the
cloves and cinnamon and ginger – that had peppered his small
nose long years before. Throughout the cloth hall there was,
in fact, a marked lack of bustle. The streets were jammed and
other stalls were overflowing. Everything seemed rich and
pulsing, yet under it there was a hollowness. The traders from
the north were fine, but behind all the Flemish lace, the Russian
furs, the sardines and the cheeses and the hams, there was a
hole where all the products from the eastern flank of Europe
ought to be.

When the Pole had left, content to order an illuminated Bible,
Peter pulled out all the pledges they'd received. 'This ought to
help,' he said. 'You ought to come and see them sell.'

Fust licked a finger and riffled through the pile. Twenty, Peter said, at thirty guilders each – and even more once he had sought those buyers out and sold them the illuminations. Fust's nostrils flared. 'All paper,' he said shortly. 'None of vellum.'

'He says we'll have more luck with those among the princes.'

Fust snorted. 'If any of us have the funds to stay.'

The fair was over in two weeks, and two weeks after that the princes and archbishops and the dukes from all of Christendom were slated to arrive. They even said the kaiser might appear at Frankfurt's Reichstag, to bash those heads and get their armies pledged for the Crusade.

'It doesn't seem as if we have much choice,' Peter replied.

Fust looked at him as if he were a stranger. 'So now you're telling me my business.'

'Follow the purses,' Peter lightly said, the buoyant feeling of the morning bursting.

'He's followed them for sure. Collected his own payment for the letters while he's at it, I would warrant.' Fust shook his head and reached to grab a bolt of bright green silk. 'I'd be obliged if you could hold the stand while I conduct some business.'

'I only have an hour.'

'Before you spell your master, I suppose.' Fust's eyes were flat and hard. 'He has his business too, his interest to collect on all his bonds – while I go pawning to scrape up the interest on his debt.'

Chapter 2

SPONHEIM ABBEY

March 1486

Trithemius looks up and says, 'I saw it once. Your Bible.' He stands and scans his rows of books, one hand at his tired back. 'It would look well on any shelf.' A little wistfully, he smiles.

'I should have brought up mine to show you.' After the fair Peter had spent a few months rubricating his own copy, handing Anna the first page of every Bible book to embellish with her brush. It sits upon a lectern in his fine new house in Frankfurt, where he is in charge of that expanding market in new books.

'They all sold out, then?' asks the abbot. 'And the kaiser – did he get a copy too?'

'They went like wildfire. Buyers came that whole first week, who then told other buyers.' Peter sees the master frozen for eternity, a statue with one arm flung out, the other cradling that monumental Bible. 'It was amazing – though the Reichstag afterwards was even more a triumph.' Piccolomini, the kaiser's envoy who afterwards became Pope Pius II, came down in person to inspect their stand. *Miraculous*, he'd marvelled, holding up the pages of the Gospel according to John. 'He ordered quires to send to Wiener Neustadt, for the kaiser to inspect.'

'That must have tickled Gutenberg.'

'Oh, he was like a cow in clover.' Peter cannot help himself; he smiles. It *was* a triumph. A memory appears as if preserved in amber: the night he and the master were asked to dine at the archbishop's table. Gutenberg took his place among the clerks and envoys, secretaries, scribes; he was an old patrician, after all. The men bowed with great respect while he spoke knowledgeably of strategies and parleys and Crusade. Once or twice he looked intently over flaming candles at his old apprentice. *See?* his bright, amused expression seemed to say. Indeed Peter had seen, a thing that he more deeply than the others could perceive: the pleasure in the master's eyes, the acknowledgement so well deserved, so long desired.

'He was acclaimed, as you have always said,' Trithemius observes.

'They could not criticize it, not after the kaiser himself had seen the quires.' Peter never will forget the day he met the kaiser's envoy, an Italian prince with dark and velvet eyes. 'The whole first week of Autumn Fair, we rode so high.'

He sighs. Outside, the mist of early spring is sifting through the black boles of the trees.

'You made more Bibles afterwards, if I am right.' The abbot returns to his seat. 'Both you and he – though separately?'

The printer nods and looks up at the books that he has brought to Sponheim. No Bibles, but scholastic works, ecclesiastic law, appealing to an educated friar: Augustine, Aquinas, Clement V, and Boniface. They're handsome in their leather rows, but nothing like those first enormous volumes they made – their Bible and their psalter. The truth of it burns him inside.

Those were the best years of his life.

That fair, those heady days – his last untrammelled joy. Where did it go, that whirling ferment when they rocked the world with their own hands? The sheer creative power that they had?

He is an old man now, a businessman, a trader like the Fusts. The books he sells are mostly made by others; he packages them and sells them on. No volume he has ever printed has been as brilliant or sublime as those two books that he and Gutenberg made.

'You followed in his footsteps, anyway,' the abbot says.

Peter's eyes caress the deckled paper of the pages peeking out from every case. The ink on every one is just as glossy as the day he printed it, he thinks. It is as if his youth is held – forever fervent, charged – between two leather-covered boards.

'He would be proud of you, I think,' the abbot hazards.

Would he? Would he truly? Would Peter have allowed it, even if he had been? Loss and shame swirl suddenly, unstoppered after all this time.

'I'm not so sure.' Even now he cannot say with certainty: he never really grasped what drove the man. He knew him best – and still. The person who had stamped his life indelibly remained opaque and inaccessible somehow.

'You were His instruments,' the abbot says, in reassurance. 'As are we all.'

Peter looks into the young man's eyes. A mighty sword, the master called that Bible, swinging it above his head that autumn, thundering and braying. He was a force of nature, surely. How Gutenberg sent all those critics packing – the officious priests and thin-skinned guildsmen, even the archbishop. He refused to blink. That was the measure of the man, his mighty faith – in God, or in himself. It was his greatness, as the thing that they had done together too was truly great – stupendous. Yet Peter's bitterness, for all these years, has hid this truth from sight.

Trithemius is leaning towards him, fingers lightly brushing Peter's hand. 'You look quite tired,' he says. 'The chapel should be open, if you'd like to pray.'

Chapter 3

WEDNESDAY AFTER
THE NATIVITY OF
THE BLESSED VIRGIN

11 September 1454

The first week is the trading week, the second one of reckoning. The traders go from stall to stall with their fat ledgers, totting up their debts against their sales. When it goes right, no more than a few coins are passed, but a great deal of libation has changed hands. The whole thing ran on trust, Fust had explained to Peter years before. A man's word was his bond: any debts were carried over until the next fair, or the next.

The final night fell not too long before the feast day of Saint Matthew, the patron saint of those who keep accounts. By then the endless work and wine had left the buyers and the sellers hollow-cheeked and yearning for their homes. The master would remain in Frankfurt for the Reichstag in the hope of selling the remaining Bibles to the nobles. Fust ordered Peter to stay, too, to pocket the deposits and be sure his partner didn't cheat him. Peter only shook his head and balanced on the rope stretched between them, tighter now than it had ever been before. Thank God his fellows from the workshop had fetched up at last, halfway through the tumult and the revels. Keffer, Ruppel and young Götz, and even Mentelin, Lord bless them all. They'd meet that night aboard the drinking boat anchored beside St Leonard's Gate.

But first Fust required the three of them to meet and settle up. Peter and the master headed for the Haus zur Ecken, where the goldsmiths lodged, once all their barrels had been packed with the last quires. They took the long way through the Corn Market so Gutenberg could stop for some fresh clothes. He would dine well again that night among the retinue of the archbishop, where he had found a bed and laid his eiderdown.

Before they hit the Mainzer Hof they stopped, attracted by the lights and crowd. 'Let's have a look,' the master said, and they moved closer to the giant cages covered in dark tarps, from which came hisses and strange moans. A boy with a long stick was prodding something hidden by the tarp between the bars. The showman came in haste around and cuffed him, and the crowd booed and complained. 'Then pay your copper!' said the man, and Gutenberg stepped forwards.

'A gentleman, at last!' The circus master smiled. He waved them in and pocketed their coins and lifted up the tarp. The world went dim. 'This here's from the far Indies,' he whispered. Curled in a corner of the cage, his huge head resting on his paws, a giant cat opened one listless eye. His fur was golden, striped with black; his tail was thick as any rope used on the Rhine.

'What do they call it?' Peter asked, drawn by the beauty of the beast, imagining its speed. How had they laid their hands on such a thing?

'A tyger.'

'Stand back!' the man warned as the cat sprang up and showed its gleaming teeth. Its fur was soft and rich in appearance, yet worn in places. It seemed to Peter as it padded towards them that it looked right through him – did not see him, but the forest out of which it came, before it paced around the cage once more and dropped back like a sack. 'I've got an oliphant as well,' the fellow said, and led them wondering to the other cage. So huge a thing they'd never seen nor even dreamed of: as tall as the Mainz wall it seemed, and just as thick, all grey and knobbly, with a snake in place of a nose. It filled the space and pressed against the bars and looked like something ancient. 'They say the Turk used these to pull his cannon,' said the man, and Gutenberg gave a sharp laugh. 'No doubt,' he said, and reached to feel the thick, dry hide. The thing had tusks and tiny eyes and sloping shoulders Peter could imagine hitched to those vast tubes of iron. He'd thought that he would be amazed to see these rare, exotic creatures from the East, but felt instead an obscure sorrow.

'Some beasts, eh!' said the master as they moved away. 'Such things as no one's ever seen, in Frankfurt or in any other place, eh Peter?' He grinned and cracked his knuckles. 'We got the best of our old beast now too, lad, didn't we?' He slung his arm around his foreman's neck and squeezed him. Peter laughed out of the sheer delight of living at so marvellous a time. 'Indeed.' He smiled, and pictured that old humpbacked Bible Gutenberg had borrowed from St Christopher's two years before. The master dropped his arm, and they walked on.

His father was waiting for them in a large front room. Jakob was there too, curled in a chair, and Peter sensed the master's hackles rise.

'What's this?' said Gutenberg, but Fust just gestured that they both sit down.

'I asked you here to be quite clear in our accounts,' his father said, taking off his glasses.

'We've now sold fifty, plus the hundred you already sold.' The master shrugged his cloak off. He nicked his chin at Peter, as if he ought to reel off the new sales. But Jakob had the pledges in his safe – which Fust now brandished in a sheaf in his large hand.

'I know. But any way I count it, we do not come out ahead.'

Fust's eyes went back and forth between them, but Peter could read nothing in them.

'It's not enough.' His father was still speaking evenly. 'I will not throw good money after bad.'

'We'll pull it in,' the master snapped. 'Seven thousand at the very least, as we had reckoned.'

'While you charge five against that in your costs.' His father's lips curled. 'Leaving less than two thousand that we split – and I owe easily that much, on your account.' His face had hardened as he spoke.

'You act as if there is no more,' said Peter heatedly, 'when you know there will be more income from our own indulgence, and deposits on the psalter.' His father did not even twitch; he stood there stolid and unmoving. A rush of blood filled Peter's head. The man had made his mind up.

'Johann.' The master sprang to his feet and raised his hands. 'Let's not be rash. We haven't started to recoup what it will bring. The kaiser's coming – think of what that means!'

'You and your promises.' Fust's voice went low; his eyes were glittering. 'You promised everything and crept behind my back the whole time. The missal and the prophecy and the indulgence – and now the kaiser, by your leave! I do not trust a word out of your lips.'

'The book is done! It's selling! What more in God's name would you have me do?' Gutenberg looked stunned. He truly could not see why he should stand accused. And none of it did matter – all of it was dust and ash, thought Peter, trials that they'd surmounted in the wilderness they'd crossed.

They'd made it! They had reached the final page, the

Promised Land. The Revelation! – or else the Apocalypse. A band of metal cinched his chest. Peter stepped towards his father, his fists clenched. 'What do you mean? That you withdraw? That you can't wait, and have no faith in any of us, the whole workshop?' He saw his psalter type abandoned on the stone.

The master made a little sound, a kind of exhalation, which Fust took as another Elder sneer. He wheeled on Gutenberg. 'You've never been a partner in the true sense of the word. You ran your piece on your own terms, and hid the truth and your own follies. You must think me a fool, to accept all these years – and still more years ahead – you making hay while I am beggared.'

Fust's face went blank then as he turned his gaze on Peter. 'You even took my son,' he said. He shrugged, as if to show that he would not be wounded. 'It has occurred to me that this must be your purpose: to pay me off this pittance of a profit, then cut me out and carry on with Peter.'

Jakob stirred, and Peter saw that look of hatred and disdain – that poison that seeped out of Mainz to blight all life. 'How you can even think of such a thing,' Peter muttered.

'You wouldn't—' flew from Gutenberg.

'This partnership, as far as I'm concerned, is ended. I will instruct the court that you have used my funds to your own private profit. What's more—'

The master didn't even let him finish. 'Calumny!' he roared. 'Vile, underhanded slander!'

'The books don't lie.' His uncle rose, and Peter understood his role: both judge and witness to the slaughter. 'You skimmed it off, to fatten your own purse. Johann's too kind to call it what it is: pure simple theft, embezzlement.'

'Embezzlement!' The master hacked a laugh. 'Who is the thief here, stealing what he hasn't got the brains to grasp? This was no partnership – in this, at least, you're right.' He stabbed a finger towards Fust. 'What did you bring to it? Not wit nor toil but only lucre. A merchant's gold, and niggardly at that, while all the art and craft of it was mine alone.'

They stood face-to-face, chests heaving, spewing hate, and Peter's whole life shrank into the sliver of air between them.

Fust shrugged. 'You owe me interest on the first loan, too. Four hundred in total for these past four years.'

'You dare to lie and smear my name.' Gutenberg was feral then, his wild hair flying. 'When all along you only fed upon me like a vulture. This was no partnership, no true and equal meeting of the minds. This work was mine – from start to finish.' His maddened eyes fell then on Peter.

'Don't stand there – tell him! You know the truth. There was no interest due – he forced me into training you. And now you think' – he whirled back to face Fust – 'that you can simply pluck him up, and put him back to work to your advantage.'

Peter was a tool, a little clinking sack, that in their fury they just tossed between them.

'That's quite enough,' his father said.

The workshop, sacked. The presses, ores, the punches, men. The brotherhood, the priesthood they had been.

But Gutenberg was not done yet. He'd have the last word, always. 'Think on the Revelation, Johann,' he said bitingly. 'And all you merchants of the harlot in the time to come.'

'Good God!' said Jakob, springing to his feet.

'I spit upon your gold – it has no worth compared to all the wit that God has given me to rise above you grocers. Cast dust upon your head. I've come too far by my own hands against you fools who set yourselves against me.' Gutenberg snatched up his cloak. 'I did it all alone and owe you nothing, you who'd rip it from me, shame your soul. I need you not, I never needed you. I need no man.'

There was a rip then in the fabric of the world, and a faint ringing. Peter heard the door slam as the master left, leaving him – Gutenberg's apprentice, then his journeyman and foreman, finally his equal – staring mutely after him.

He'd done it all himself. He needed no man.

The work of letters and the tracery of ligature, the beauty of a well-proportioned line, were nothing to a man like that. He cared for nothing, no one, but his pride. A part of Gutenberg was cauterized inside. In that moment Peter understood that there would always be some moneyman to pump, new jobs to beg, new Elders, merchants, nobles, to connive. He stooped and picked up his own cloak.

Fust made a move towards him, but Peter stopped him with his hand. *Oh ye of little faith.* In Jakob's eyes he saw that smouldering resentment that turned everything it touched to rubble. He heard the harsh tongues of archangels as they poured their vials of poison from the sky: *For in one hour are such great riches come to nought.*

Chapter 4

~

SPONHEIM ABBEY

March 1486

Spring is coiled and waiting to arrive. There is a scoured feeling of expectancy in the dark earth underneath the abbot's windows. Peter gazes through the rippled glass. Memory is like this, with its lumps and thin spots and distortions, he thinks to himself. Trithemius waits patiently; for once he does not prod.

'It ended just like that?' eventually he asks.

'It takes some time to wind a business down,' says Peter, turning back. 'But yes, that's when it ended.'

Fust filed his lawsuit six months later, after Lenten Fair. Each partner had been ordered to appear and swear the truth of his accounts. 'But truth was never Gutenberg's strong suit.'

The reed keeps scratching, but the abbot makes no answer.

'My father claimed that he was owed two thousand with the interest, which was not exactly truthful either. The master couldn't pay – or wouldn't.'

He could have paid it if he wanted to, with the income from the Bible and indulgences, Peter still believes. 'But he did not contest it. He did not even turn up for the swearing. He simply walked away.'

Trithemius lifts his head and searches Peter's face. 'I see.'

'And so the shop was split. He went his way, and we went ours. Each got some type and some equipment.'

'Why didn't he contest it, do you think?'

'He knew who was to blame. I think he didn't want to show his books. But more than that, he knew my father had every reason to feel betrayed.'

'As you too have felt all these years,' the abbot says.

'Where there's no trust, there can be no partnership.'

'There was no trust on Fust's side, either.'

'That's true. He could not see – nor I – that we could keep on working on such terms.' A wave of sadness pushes at the printer's chest. 'Though it was hard for me, of course.'

He has gone on to build an empire. The master left two Bibles and some grammars and some letters of indulgence and the type for an encyclopedia. He died without a son to burnish his own name. Of course, right to the end he'd thought that Peter was the one who'd carry on his flame.

'Each of you followed your own conscience,' says the abbot gravely.

'You still defend him then.'

Trithemius puts down his pen. His face is thoughtful. 'You yourself know how it is to deal with power,' he says slowly. 'You've said yourself it takes a certain . . . flexibility to get things done.'

Peter nods. He knows the corridors of power, just as Gutenberg did once. A phrase floats up into his mind, a thing the master said before they'd even started on their Bible. *I know the ways of the Holy See, to my misfortune.*

'I just keep wondering,' the abbot says, 'why he felt he had to make that letter in such secrecy.'

'He made a deal to save his neck.'

'Or else he had been backed into a corner.' Trithemius pulls at his chin. 'Is it not possible he did it to keep Dietrich happy, and divert attention from the Book?'

'If that had been his thought, he could have told me.'

The abbot's face fills with compassion. 'He had a different code, most certainly, than you or I.'

'I only wish . . .' says Peter heavily, 'that the workshop could have been preserved.'

'It lasted for as long as it could last,' the abbot says. He gives a rueful little shrug. 'I'd say it was a miracle it even lasted for that long.'

'A miracle.' Peter closes his tired eyes. A miracle was what they made, not what they were. And yet. He opens them, surprised. 'It lasted for the time required.'

He and Trithemius lock eyes. They held together for the time it took, perhaps, to wreak that miracle – the time that God designed.

'Perhaps, like an apprenticeship, the term was fixed.' The abbot smiles.

'My wander years,' the printer says. Emotion fills his chest. He looks away towards the bright fresh world outside. 'He taught me what he knew,' he says, a feeling of tremendous love and sorrow rising through his body, leaving him at last. 'And then he let me go.'

The abbot nods. Neither speaks for several moments. 'You did not see him again?' he finally asks.

'Just once, the day we married.' Peter rolls the years back, conscious now that in the dross that he had buried there had been some glints of gold.

The surprise was not that Peter invited Gutenberg, but that the master came to join that wedding celebration. By then their common workshop was closed. The families and the craftsmen followed bride and groom in two long lines from Anna's house to St Quintin's, with Johann Gutenberg, flamboyant in a new green suit, alone right at the back. Fust had ordered tables set out on the Brand, and they had finished feasting and the music had begun when Gutenberg wandered over to salute them. 'Now, Peter,' he said thickly, for he'd had a few. 'Frau Schoeffer, bless your house.' He grinned and said a wife that comely might have weakened his own vow. And then he pulled a package out and handed it to Peter. 'This should by rights be yours.'

Carefully Peter opened it. 'I don't believe it,' he said to the master, who just laughed.

His gift was a new-bound edition of a book that never had existed – except in their extremity and need. Four sheets of printed canticles, bound with the songs of Moses and Isaiah written out in Peter's own fine hand: that old, fictitious present for a pope.

'A *unicat*,' the master said, 'so don't you lose it, now.'

Abbot Trithemius is smiling broadly. 'Unique indeed. As was the man.'

'I wish I'd had the wit right then to really thank him.'

'You never did?'

'Not in so many words.' Peter Schoeffer stands and reaches towards the bookshelves. He picks a volume out at random and opens it to the last page.

'Everything I print, I seal with this device,' he says. 'I think you'll see the meaning.'

His printer's signet is the knotted branch that he'd inherited from Fust, still bearing those two dangling shields. Except that he'd replaced the names with two Greek letters, chi and lambda, signifying Word of Christ. He'd placed three stars as well, to symbolize the Trinity – each book he prints thus harking back to that great Bible they had made together, and the Gospel according to John.

'In principio erat Verbum,' the abbot murmurs. *In the beginning was the Word.*

He moves swiftly to the lectern and dips his reed to capture one last note. Peter watches, but his mind has moved past that last meeting to a different day, the day that his apprenticeship had truly ended.

November, 1455: a bleak, cold morning. How long he waited, anxious and angry and filled with guilt, for the master to arrive. The witnesses for Gutenberg and Fust stood in a horseshoe in the great hall of the barefoot friars, across from their old workshop.

He did not come. Peter sees them all, suspended, waiting; still he did not come. He never did. His work was done. For an instant past and present merge inside his mind as Peter hears the scratching of the reed, inscribing all they'd done and been together in the hide.

Chapter 5

WEDNESDAY AFTER
THE NATIVITY OF
THE BLESSED VIRGIN

11 September 1454

The walk to Frankfurt's quayside was not long. Peter left the brothers Fust behind him in the goldsmiths' quarters, marching blindly into night. On the Römerberg rubbish piles were being burned. A bitter smoke rose heavenward, and Peter raised his cloak to shield his nose. His feet conveyed his body past the entry to the lane where they so briefly had rejoiced in their great triumph. The place was strewn with shavings from the casks that had been emptied. Through the small archway of St Leonard's Gate he saw the bobbing masts along the Main and quailed. He was not ready yet to face his fellows. He pushed the door and pulled aside the velvet drape and entered in the church instead.

The light was red from votive candles, and the stone walls blocked all sound. He genuflected and slipped into the front pew. Above him on all sides, stories from the Bible were written in the panes of glass. Before him to the right of the small altar stood a tall, carved Saint Sebastian, stung by arrows, slumped against his bonds. The pain that Peter felt was not like this. It was more a tearing at his heart, tied for so long to those two horses stepping steadily apart.

His eyes fell on the parish Bible chained to the oak pulpit. The book was fat; the hasp to which the chain was fixed was bright from years of rubbing. It would be anchored here until the iron rusted or the leather split. Had there been chains a thousand years before, when Benedict had heeded God's command to take His word and write it down? Peter didn't think so. He thought then of the finished copies of their Bible setting out on their own journeys. St Jakob's would receive one, old man Widder too; he'd seen the copy painted by the Austrian that Fust had taken to his mansion on the Brand. The trader planned to offer it to the Franciscans. Peter had fancied he might hear those barefoot friars reciting from that Book someday, their voices drifting out across the Cobblers' Lane into the Humbrechthof. That would not happen now; the workshop was destroyed. He bowed his head and prayed.

He pictured them, the hundred and eighty copies of their Bible, stowed in casks attached to boats – to convoys, caravans – spreading far beyond the Rhineland. It seemed to him they moved out ponderously, yet with great purpose, into the world. Like oliphants, he thought: great hidebound beasts out of the East, spreading across the land, bearing their thick and transcendental cargo.

Aboard the drinking vessel there were casks as well, bolted fore and aft, from which the Rhine wines flowed. He found the members of their workshop gathered at a table, Keffer with his bushy beard and Götz and Ruppel, then his dear friend Mentelin. 'Ahoy!' cried Keffer, 'here's our fearless leader!' They raised a toast to him. 'We did it, bloody hell!' Even the close-mouthed Ruppel grinned. Mentelin sloshed wine into his cup. 'To Hans and Konrad,' Peter said, and raised it. 'And all of you. Yours were the hands that mixed and carved and cast and made it happen.' They drummed their feet and bellowed. The hands that held those cups were blunt and hard and for a time held heaven in them, too. Like Anna's with her brush, his own clamped on his awl or quill. He wished then for his love and home. The roaring on the boat grew raucous, and beneath the cover of their songs he bent his head to Mentelin's. 'My father ended it,' he whispered. 'It's over – workshop, psalter, all of it.' The gold-scribe put his hand on Peter's shoulder. 'I guess it ran its course,' he said, and squeezed it. 'Gutenberg would try the Lord's own patience.'

By rights the master should have been there too, carousing with his workmen. There never was an Elder like him, who would roll his sleeves up, curse and joke and wrestle with the ores and metals right beside them. Damn him. When it most counted, he was gone. If he could just have been more honest, shown a little trust. But no.

'What will you do?' Mentelin asked low in Peter's ear.

He looked into those green eyes. 'I always prayed I would not have to choose.' He felt a shiver in his soul to have to walk on now alone.

The boat was bobbing with the motion of the river and the pounding of the drunks. Mentelin was nodding with a look of great concern when Peter felt a hand upon his back. He turned and saw the broad, inebriated face of Petrus Heilant. He had to laugh. 'I should have known I'd find you here,' he told the man. The scribe was always halfway in his sight, some kind of strange dark angel at his side. 'We've nothing to confess,' he drily said, 'though you are welcome to join in the celebration.'

Heilant looked beyond him towards the crew, his eyes unfocused, and began to speak in a slurred voice. 'Play now,' he seemed to say, and then 'repent'. Whatever else he said was swallowed in the din. Peter put a hand up to his ear, and Heilant tugged him by the elbow. Reluctantly the printer rose and followed him across the gangplank to a quieter place along the quay.

'A clever game you played,' his former schoolmate said. His cheeks were red, his breath was laboured; he had grown stout. 'All along I knew you were mixed up in this.' In his tone there was a note almost of reproach, as if some part of Heilant wished he'd been invited to share in that secret.

'I followed my own conscience,' Peter said.

'Still. This Bible that you peddle . . .' Heilant's eyes were inky dots, unreadable.

Peter did not answer. The skies were blazing with bright stars; the man before him was a clerk, a little man with great delusions of his power.

'I doubt His Grace will let it go for long.'

'He used it for his letters – and would have used it for his missal.'

'*His* letters and *his* missal. That's the point.'

'The Bible isn't his.' It wasn't any bishop's, any pope's – but God's. 'Dietrich will have no choice,' Peter continued calmly. 'When it is praised by cardinals and even by the kaiser, he will find he must embrace it.'

Then it was Heilant who fell mute, silenced by the truth of Gutenberg's manoeuvre.

Peter watched the human tide surge by, some to the drinking ships, others to the gaming houses and the brothels, those ordinary workers seeking out their momentary joy. There but for God's grace, he thought suddenly, go I.

'It cannot stay this way.' He rounded on the archbishop's clerk. 'You cannot hold the world – you cannot even hold the Bible now – in chains.'

The drink made Heilant's mocking smile more venomous, no doubt, than he intended. 'A moment's crisis, that is all.' He shrugged. 'You fail to see that all are lifted by the tide.'

'Your kind are lifted, but not mine.'

Heilant's face tightened. 'Providence decides.'

Peter smiled. 'The proof has already arrived.'

'You always did think that you had some private pact with God,' the clerk said with an ugly look.

Of course. How could he not? How could he – Peter Schoeffer, shepherd's son – have understood his own life otherwise? The world just opened, larger, ever larger, his life proceeding and unfurling year by year: from field to town, from classroom to academy to abbey, the walls of each succeeding room more open and expansive than the one that came before. Until at last he stood in this cathedral with his arms outstretched, holding this extraordinary book.

AFTERWORD

Peter Schoeffer went on to become the world's first major printer, producing nearly three hundred volumes through the firm of Fust & Schoeffer, including the 1457 Mainz Psalter, widely considered the most beautiful book ever printed. Upon Fust's death in 1466, Peter married his daughter, Christina, establishing a printing dynasty that spanned four generations. He invented the business of publishing and founded the event known today as the Frankfurt Book Fair, and died in 1503 at the ripe age of nearly eighty.

Johann Gensfleisch, known as Gutenberg, was immediately recognized as the inventor of printing with moveable type. Though he never signed a single printed book, the success of the *Biblia latina* led to another Bible commission from the bishop of Bamberg and to Gutenberg's appointment in 1465 to the court of the new archbishop of Mainz, Dietrich's successor. Until his death in 1468, aged about seventy, he is thought to have produced many papal bulls, calendars, and letters of indulgence in consortium with printers including Heinrich Keffer and Berthold Ruppel. His last work was a new type for a religious encyclopedia, the *Catholicon* of Balbus, which it is believed other printers brought to press after his death.

Johann Fust prospered as a merchant and publisher, selling the wares of Fust & Schoeffer across western Europe after his partnership with Gutenberg was dissolved in November 1455. While showing a printed Bible in Paris in 1463, he was hounded out by scribes who accused the firm of undercutting normal prices. On a later business trip, he contracted the plague and died in Paris in 1466, aged about sixty-five. Several years later, Peter Schoeffer and Konrad Henkis, Grede's second husband, donated a copy of the firm's *Letters of Jerome* to the abbey of Saint-Victor in Paris, which pledged to say a mass in perpetuity for Fust.

Jakob Fust was killed in battle in 1462, when Mainz's feuding factions descended definitively into civil war. As *Bürgermeister* (mayor) he had led the city council in a losing fight over Dietrich's successor as archbishop. The victor, Adolf of Nassau, swiftly turned the once-free city into a vassal of the archdiocese, stripping the guilds of power and the council of its sovereignty. Many, including the three men who made the first printed Bible, lost homes and businesses. Nassau's orders were eventually rescinded, and Gutenberg honoured as a member of his court, while Fust and Schoeffer re-established their press at the Haus zum Iseneck on the Brand.

Johannes Trithemius published accounts of his conversations with Peter Schoeffer in two chronicles, the *Chronicon Sponheimense* of circa 1500 and the *Annales Hirsaugienses* of circa 1514. His work *De Laude Scriptorum* (In Praise of Scribes) was printed in Mainz in 1494, presumably by Peter Schoeffer or his son Johann.

Pope Nicholas v died in March 1455, and with him any hope for Crusade against the Muslim Turks. No army was ever raised, despite the vehement exhortations of Enea Silvio Piccolomini, the former secretary to Kaiser Friedrich III, who was named Pope Pius II in 1458.

The fall of Mainz pushed journeymen who trained in those two rival workshops out as refugees into the wider world. The craft of printing spread like wildfire: within a decade, it was being plied by Johann Mentelin and Heinrich Eggestein in Strassburg, Heinrich Keffer in Bamberg and then Basel, the Bechtermünzes in Eltville – then Johann Neumeister, Berthold Ruppel, Albrecht Pfister, Konrad Sweynheym and others, the secret knowledge spreading from Germany to Italy and Switzerland and France. Printers set up shop in more than 250 cities between 1450 and 1500, a period known as the time of *incunabula* – the cradle years of printed books.

Forty-eight copies of the Gutenberg Bible still exist, complete or in part, out of the estimated 180 copies made. Some library collections generously cite the makers as 'Gutenberg – Schoeffer – Fust?' Most do not. The last time one was auctioned, in 1987, a buyer paid $5.4 million for the Old Testament alone.

ACKNOWLEDGEMENTS

This novel could not have been written without the help of experts whose scholarship and advice were crucial to my understanding of early printing. I am particularly indebted to Dr Lotte Hellinga, former deputy keeper of the British Library, and Paul Needham, director of the Scheide Library at Princeton University, for their unflagging patience with my queries. Dr Monika Estermann, editor of the Archive of the History of the Book (*Archiv für Geschichte des Buchwesens*) in Frankfurt shared invaluable insights, as did Dr Wolfgang Dobras, director of the Mainz city archive, and Dr Stephan Füssel, director of the Mainz Institute for Book Studies (*Mainzer Institut für Buchwissenschaft*) at the Johannes-Gutenberg University. Hearty thanks are also due to the staff of the Mainz *Wissenschaftliches Stadtbibliotek* and the librarians at the Gutenberg Museum in Mainz.

I have drawn on the painstaking research of eminent Gutenberg scholars over half a millennium, although the interpretation of the facts is my own. I relied heavily on Guy Bechtel's magisterial 1992 study, '*Gutenberg: Une Enquete*' and the art historical insights of Dr Eberhard König, among others. A bibliography of sources and images can be found at www.gutenbergsapprentice.com.

For most of my life, I have been inspired by formidable masters of the typographic arts. I was fortunate to apprentice as a letterpress printer under the foreman of the former Mackenzie & Harris hot type foundry in San Francisco, the late Lester Lloyd, and to the proprietors of the Yolla Bolly Press in Covelo, California, the late James Robertson and Carolyn Robertson. This book is dedicated to those master printers, who left an indelible impression on me and led me directly to Johann Gutenberg and Peter Schoeffer. Peggy Gotthold and Lawrence Van Velzer of Foolscap Press offered support at every step, along with hand-printed materials for special editions of the novel. Close readers Vonnie Madigan, Katherine Maxfield, and the North London Writers Group contributed enormously, and I have been blessed with exceptional editors in Terry Karten and Marion Donaldson and fantastic agents in Simon Trewin, Dorian Karchmar, and Annemarie Blumenhagen. My mother, sister, and brothers championed this book from the start, but it is my husband and children I owe the deepest thanks, for their love and forbearance during my long trek through the medieval world. *Vivat biblus*.

HISTORICAL NOTE

This is a work of fiction based on fact. Mainz was not only the birthplace of printing, but at the centre of events at a turbulent time in Europe. Gutenberg's press came into being at a turning point in the history of the Holy Roman Empire, which encompassed what has become Germany, Austria, the Netherlands, and parts of Italy, Poland, and the Balkans. The political strength of the Kaiser who ruled this fractious empire rested on the sacred authority granted by the Pope in Rome. Yet by 1450 the ruling class was under siege from both within and without: by increasingly strident calls for reform and the shocking loss of Constantinople, captured by Muslim Turks in May 1453. These crises had consequences that rippled through the Christian world, especially Mainz, whose archbishop was the empire's power broker. All of the public events described in the novel are accurate, to the best of my belief. The struggle for control of the city went on for decades; the movement against corruption in the Church was led by Benedictine monks, including Heinrich Brack at St Jakob's. A battle over a reform missal for the Bursfeld Congregation did take place, and suggests an answer to the puzzle of what Gutenberg may have tried to print before embarking on the Bible.

Nearly all of the named characters are based on real people who are thought to have learned printing in Mainz. Yet little can be said with certainty about the roles played by the three men most responsible. Historians have pieced together scraps, relying on a partial record of the lawsuit that ended the partnership of Gutenberg and Fust. The traditional view is that Fust deprived the inventor of his life's work by suing him for repayment just as the Bible was completed. More recent research has called this into question, and suggested that the collapse of the partnership was as likely due to Gutenberg's sharp business practice. Bibliographers increasingly agree that Fust and Schoeffer each played a major role in bringing the first book to print – Schoeffer as a gifted calligrapher and punch-cutter, and Fust as a venture capitalist with an aesthetic eye. And yet for centuries their part has been obscured by Gutenberg's long shadow. This novel is an attempt to sift the evidence anew and paint a fuller picture of this historic collaboration.

Much is now known about the actual production of the Gutenberg Bible, thanks to high-tech analysis of its paper, ink and types. The chronology of the novel is based on this new knowledge, which refines a production chart first proposed by a German bibliographer in 1923. I have freely introduced as journeymen in the documented workshop in the *Hof zum Humbrecht* men who later emerged as early printers. All of the Fust and Gutenberg family members did exist, with the exception of Anna Pinzler, a novelist's invention. For more on the technology of early printing and my assumptions, as well as images of books, places and people mentioned in the text, please visit www.gutenbergsapprentice.com.

The finished *Biblia latina* was publicly presented in October of 1454, in Frankfurt. The book and its 'miraculous' maker were described by the Kaiser's envoy, Enea Silvio Piccolomini, in a letter to a Spanish cardinal. Piccolomini may have seen it just after Frankfurt's legendary Autumn Fair, at a gathering of the empire's princes to debate Crusade against the Turks. The actual unveiling of the world's first printed book most likely occurred two weeks prior, among the manuscripts offered for sale along the *Mainzgasse*. Later renamed the *Buchgasse*, this lane was the original home of the Frankfurt Book Fair, and the birthplace of publishing.

Alix Christie, 2014

A Note on the Type

The display type of this book is Historical Fell Type, a digital revival of one of the oldest book faces cut in England. It was designed by Peter de Walpergen, a Dutch punch-cutter, in the late seventeenth century for John Fell, the bishop of Oxford, and was one of the founding typefaces of the Oxford University Press. The body type is a digital revival of Bembo, which itself was a modern revival of the humanist letter cut by Francesco Griffo for the Aldine Press in Venice around 1495.

An early wooden press depicted in Jaime Perez de Valencia:
Cantica Canticorum Salominis (Paris: 1507)

Image © liszt collection/Alamy

MEDIEVAL PRINTING GLOSSARY

Platen: The flat block or surface that puts pressure on the inked letters, transferring the ink from letters to paper. In wooden presses this hung from the press's top bar and was dropped by means of a lever.

Bed: The horizontal carriage of the upright printing press, in which the chase or tray containing the letters is securely placed.

Forme: A completed section of lines, usually a page, either tied or held by pressure in a frame that is placed in the bed of the press for printing.

Inkball: A stuffed leather ball set in a wooden handle. Used in pairs to spread the ink onto the letters. Said to have been made of poreless dog tongues and cured in urine.

Type case: A large wooden case divided into scores of compartments, one for each sort of letter to be set into lines.

Composing stick: Originally a wooden tray held in the hand and filled letter by letter by the compositor.

Punch: A tempered steel shaft on which each letter of a given font is carved.

Matrix: The mould, now usually copper, that is made when the punch is driven into it with a mallet. Other metals or even clay or sand may have served as matrices or moulds early on.

Hand-Caster: An ingenious hand-held device that clamps the matrix in its base, allowing a typefounder to pour molten metal in an upper hole to cast a letter.

Compositor: The person who sets the type.

Beater: The person who inks the forme.

Pressman: The person who operates the press.

Proof: Printed text, images, figures etc. used to check for errors and other issues prior to production printing. In the medieval era letters were coated with lampblack from a candle and checked; hence the term 'soot proof'.

Recto: The right side of a leaf, having an odd-numbered page or folio.

Verso: The left side of a leaf, having an even-numbered page or folio.

Quire: A folded gathering of printed sheets. Five sheets which when folded make twenty pages are called a quinternion.

A Q&A with Alix Christie

Q: The changes in society brought about by the invention of printing are fascinating to consider in the light of the way digital inventions are transforming the way we communicate in the twenty-first century. What do you think the most significant comparisons are? Can we learn from the past about how human beings adapt – or not! – to this kind of change?

I do believe we can learn from how our forebears dealt with changes that are similar to those we face. Human emotions and reactions don't evolve that quickly, even if how we conceive the world differs dramatically from age to age. People are amazed and sometimes frightened by new things whose consequences they can't foresee. It was only in writing the novel that I grasped the parallels between the technological revolution Gutenberg unleashed and our own. Both are changes in communications technology: in the case of printing, the spread of ideas enabled by the press transformed how people understood themselves and their place in the world. For the first time mankind was able to share ideas broadly, as well as preserve them, across all levels of society. This led to the scientific and industrial revolutions, political emancipation and democracy: profound changes from the medieval world. Most people think digital technology has a similar capacity to transform how human beings behave and interact. It's significant that both are the product of collaborations between people with different skills who are able to imagine something that hasn't existed before. That's why I call Gutenberg's workshop 'the world's first tech start-up'.

Q: Peter is initially one of those resistant to the way technology is bringing the era of hand-written texts to an end, yet he comes to see that technology can be used to produce great art. Are there other examples through history of a closer link between art and technology than is generally assumed?

I felt Peter incarnated a kind of ambivalence towards – and eventual acceptance of – new technology that many of us who love books feel today. But he's not just a craftsman, he's an artist, and art and technology have always been intertwined. One thinks of the great looms of the Gobelins Tapestry Manufacture, for example: the loom was in fact the first computer, as Ada Lovelace grasped. Technology is really just a fancy name for tools: sculptors in the Victorian era used the new technique of electrotyping to create gorgeous tomb effigies. Twentieth-century artists experimented with neon and light-emitting diodes and are now using sensors and microchips to create new kinds of responsive works. I love Hannah Arendt's definition of humans as 'homo faber' – man as maker. We make art, we make machines, and these two practices inform one another. What was important to me was that Peter realize that what counts is maintaining the same high standards in whichever form of art or craft we employ.

Q: Those involved in print creation during the fifteenth century faced an additional threat that modern inventors need not fear – the danger of offending the powerful forces of the Church. How might Peter and his colleagues have been punished had events taken a different turn? And what tensions did they share with modern innovators?

Innovators always upset the status quo. In contemporary terms, disruptive tech start-ups pose a threat to all kinds of institutions, from authoritarian regimes to companies and professional associations that benefit financially from the way things are. So I think the parallels are clear. By the mid-fifteenth century the Catholic Church was essentially a one-party state; local princes had to bow to Rome. In the book I had to imagine what the consequences might have been if the Archbishop's people had discovered the Bible workshop: seizure certainly, imprisonment, or being forced to use the press for the Church's own purposes. They were lucky I think in that initially nobody really grasped how much the press would erode the Church's power. This changed quickly: within thirty years the Church had instituted censorship, and by the time of Henry VIII, less than a century after the invention, people were being put to death for reading printed works not approved by the Pope.

Q: The novel puts Gutenberg and his workshop at the centre of the invention of printing, but others were developing printing techniques in parallel. Would mass printing eventually have emerged had Gutenberg been stopped, and how widely around Europe (and the world) was experimentation in the techniques occurring at the time when Gutenberg was active?

Printing from ceramic characters began in China 500 years earlier; metal type was invented somewhat later in Korea. There's no evidence, however, that news of this invention reached medieval Europe. Still there's little doubt that someone else would have invented printing there had Gutenberg not done so first: the conditions for its development were in *l'air du temps*. The existence of a goldsmith from Prague named Waldfoghel is documented in lawsuits from Avignon; he was training others in a new art of making 'alphabets of steel'. The Dutch were also experimenting with different techniques. Most of the technology required already existed: engraving and stamping metal letters onto bells or the spines of books; wood carving; precision metal casting. Paper had arrived in the fourteenth century from the east, making the production of even manuscript books much less expensive. Meanwhile there was a growing demand for books and learning. What was required was a creative mind to put these technologies together, with the brilliant addition of an adapted winepress and a new kind of ink.

Q: The Church establishment feared the power of printing and yet also wanted to take control of it and use it for its own purposes. Can you give us some insight into how church thinking evolved in line with a growing understanding of the power of printing?

At first the Church embraced printing as a gift from God and a *sancta ars*, a 'holy art'. The technology supported its aim of providing a standard interpretation of Scripture free from the errors that bedevilled hand-copied manuscripts. Mistakes could actually render spiritual texts such as letters of indulgence invalid. So spreading the Word better and faster was seen as a wonderful thing: as early as 1468, an Italian cardinal exclaimed 'God gave Christendom a gift which enables even the pauper to acquire books.' But within a few decades the press escaped ecclesiastic control, and people started printing whatever they liked, including 'heretical' texts that challenged Church doctrine. (Rome had long been trying to stamp out splinter groups that questioned its wealth and monopoly on Christian faith, such as the Hussites and the Waldensians.) The first move towards censorship was appropriately enough in the archdiocese of Mainz, where a new archbishop in 1485 decreed that all books printed must first pass the censor. By 1515, Pope Leo extended this to all of Christendom, saying that errors of interpretation were being spread, and they had to make sure 'no thorns get mixed in with the good seeds'. Two years later Martin Luther started the protest that became the Protestant Church; his 95 theses sold out as fast as they were printed and ultimately ran to dozens of editions.

Q: What percentage of the population of Europe would have been able to read a printed text at this time? Did the production of books on an unprecedented scale result quickly in a rise in literacy?

The fifteenth century was still largely feudal; it was mainly the nobility and clergy who had access to books. Printing did increase literacy, but it's important to see that it was also in part a response to a growing demand. There was a huge demand for learning among the rising middle class for several generations before Gutenberg; these were the merchants and artisans who manufactured and traded across the world and flocked for an education to newly founded urban universities. Labourers on farms and in cities were mostly illiterate; the 'texts' they read were stained glass and woodcut images. No one really knows the percentage of Europeans who could read and write in 1450, except that it was low. This changed, but not as rapidly as one might think. The glut of books at first served an already literate elite; by 1500 there were presses in 250 European cities. But as prices dropped general literacy rose, thanks largely to printing in local dialects. There was a vast production of everyday self-help and entertainment material that has largely vanished but was the real motor of increased literacy. These were almanacs and herbals, political pamphlets and blood-letting calendars, and then epics and romances for a mass market, just like today.

Q: Gutenberg was a fierce, driven and domineering character. Do you think that these characteristics are almost vital in the most successful entrepreneurs, whatever the era?

Throughout the novel Peter asks himself the very same question. It's one that can be answered both yes and no. Yes, because a real innovator has to be the kind of person who can withstand a great deal of failure and derision. One has to be incredibly focused on the goal, and not care what others think. This is true of protean innovators throughout history, in both science and the arts; I always think of Steve Jobs and Pablo Picasso as this kind of bloody-minded creator. There's little doubt from the records that Gutenberg was a sharp-tongued fellow who was quick to defend his interests: the Scottish book historian John Pettegree calls him 'a cranky German businessman', a description I love.

On the other hand, the lesson of technology collaborations today is that success requires that the inventor also be able to work with others who can execute the idea and bring it to market. This is what made this drama so poignant to me, the fact that the three of them did this incredible thing, and yet for reasons we will never really know, their fruitful partnership collapsed in recriminations.

Q: How did the idea for your novel originate?

My grandfather taught me to print when I was a teenager, and I've been a devotee of letterpress ever since. I own a wonderful old cast-iron Chandler & Price press that currently resides in San Francisco. Then one day I read a newspaper article that turned out to be the spark for this novel. Scholars at Princeton University in America had made a big splash in the book history world, reporting that Gutenberg's first types might not have been as advanced as people thought. I tucked that scrap away, and then I happened to move to Berlin, Germany, and started looking into the history of this incredible book, the Gutenberg Bible. What I discovered blew my mind – a whole new picture of this earth-shaking invention that hardly anyone knew about.

Q: Can you tell us a little about your writing life? For instance, did you plan the novel in detail before writing? Do you aim to write a set

*number of words every day? Do you have a special place where you like
to write, or can you write anywhere? Are there complex charts tracking
dates and settings? Do share some insights!*

For me writing this book was like a treasure hunt: I had to
discover and unravel the real story while I was trying to write
it as fiction. It was a kind of spiral, alternating between periods
of writing and periods of research; all told I wrote eight drafts.
I got quite excited as I dug deeper into the historical material
and did make a fabulously detailed little chart of which Biblical
chapter might have been printed when. I write mostly for a
chunk of four to five hours from morning to mid-afternoon.
Usually I get my best ideas while cycling to the lake where I
swim or in the water; then I dry off and get to a desk, either
at home or that oasis for officeless writers, the London Library.
I do write wherever I am – at friends' houses, on holiday, at
the weekend in cafés – because there's never enough time alone
with what I'm working on. Usually I write in my journal to
clear my mind before I turn to fiction. It's not the word count
that drives me so much as getting a draft of a particular scene
or section; I've always liked Hemingway's advice to stop while
you know what comes next, so the next morning you can take
off running.

*Q: Can you tell us about some of the novels that have inspired you as
a writer?*

In my experience most writers were mad readers as kids: I
certainly was. I read *The Lord of the Rings* eleven times, once in
French. I adored Narnia and read every single mystery featuring
Nancy Drew – an American girl detective – and Walter Farley's
The Black Stallion series. Looking back I think it was the immer-
sion in a complete world I most loved. As an adult I don't read
that much fantasy, but still like a world in a book. Dostoyevsky's

The Idiot was the first novel that set me on fire, followed by the Brontës and Austen; I'm a devotee of Eliot's *Middlemarch*, Flaubert's *Madame Bovary* and many great nineteenth-century novelists. Unsurprisingly I still gravitate towards ambitious books with exceptional language like Hilary Mantel's incredible historical novels (not just *Wolf Hall* but *A Place of Greater Safety*), Marilynne Robinson's *Housekeeping* and *Gilead*, W.G. Sebald's *The Emigrants* and most recently the Neapolitan novels of Elena Ferrante.